Measured Steps

The Claire Morrison Files

J.S. Warner

Dark Corridor Press

Published by Dark Corridor Press

An imprint of Warner House Press, USA

Copyright © 2026 by J.S. Warner

Text and Cover Design by Ablaze Media, www.ablaze.media, Arizona, USA

Visit: jswarnerauthor.com

Published 2026

Printed in the USA

Library of Congress Control Number: 2025927920

ISBN: 978-1-951890-74-2

10 9 8 7 6 5 4 3 2 1

For Mary and David,
and in loving memory of John,
my sister and brothers,
with love.

***

Special Thanks
To Janice: Thank you for reading this book in its
earliest form, and for your honest, thoughtful feedback.

The most beautiful people I've known
are those who have known trials,
have known struggles,
have known loss,
and have found their way
...out of the depths.

— Elisabeth Kübler-Ross

Contents

Chapter One

Chalk Outlines

The tic tac melted on Claire Morrison's tongue, masking the stale taste of cigarettes. Her fingers trembled slightly as she studied the crime scene photographs spread across her kitchen table, each image illuminated by the harsh overhead light of her Baltimore apartment at three in the morning.

She curled her hand into a fist, noting the tremor. Two years sober meant this wasn't withdrawal anymore, just caffeine, nicotine, and the gnawing anxiety that came with cases like this one. The victim's face stared up from the photos: Mathematics Professor Daniel Cromartie, found with chalk equations drawn around his body.

His eyes seemed to follow her as she paced her small living room, stepping over case files, and navigating around the meditation corner her therapist had suggested; a space that remained largely unused, save for the bronze Buddha watching her with indifference. The statue was one of the few mementos Claire had kept from her childhood; a gift from her mother shortly before she disappeared when Claire was nine.

Darwin, her orange tabby, watched from atop a bookcase with typical feline judgment. The cat's presence was a constant reminder of stability; she'd adopted him the day she got her two-year sobriety chip, a living marker of her new beginning.

Her phone vibrated against the wooden surface of her kitchen table, the sound loud in the pre-dawn quiet. Chief Matthews' name flashed on the screen.

"Dr. Morrison," she answered, already reaching for her coat.

"We've got another one," Matthews said, his voice carrying the weight of a long night getting longer. "Johns Hopkins Mathematics Department. Same signature."

Claire's stomach clenched. She popped another tic tac, a poor substitute for stronger solutions she'd once relied on. "Equations?"

"Everywhere. Like a beautiful mind had a breakdown all over our crime scene."

She caught her reflection in the kitchen window as she gathered her things: red hair escaping its messy bun, dark circles prominent under green eyes that had seen too much. At 5'2", she had her mother's compact frame along with her stubborn streak. The same eyes that had once stared back at her from countless bathroom mirrors as she'd promised herself "just one more drink." Her hand brushed against the sobriety chip in her pocket, a ritual before every case, a reminder of what she'd clawed back from the abyss.

"I'll be there in twenty," she said, already heading for the door.

Darwin meowed his protest, the sound following her down the three flights of stairs to the street. The warm August night hit her, carrying the mixed scents of the city: exhaust fumes, late-night takeout, and the perpetual dampness of the harbor.

Her car, a decade-old Honda that had seen her through the worst years of her addiction, started with a reluctant growl. As she drove through Baltimore's nighttime streets, Claire found herself passing landmarks of her former life, corner stores where she'd once purchased bottom-shelf vodka, bars where she'd sought oblivion in amber glasses. Finally, she passed the rehabilitation center where she'd begun the painful process of rebuilding her shattered life.

The center's sign glowed softly in the darkness: "Harborview Recovery: One Day at a Time." Claire slowed as she passed, a habit formed over the past two years. Sometimes, on her worst days, she still pulled into that parking lot just to sit, to remind herself of what waited if she ever stepped back across that threshold of "just one drink." Tonight, she drove past with only a glance, the familiar words echoing in her mind anyway: one day at a time.

The academic building loomed against the pre-dawn sky, a dark presence amid the quiet campus. Blue and red lights painted the scene in alternating waves, casting strange shadows across the building's facade through the misty Baltimore morning, the flashing emergency lights seeming to mirror the grimness of her task.

Officer Billy Thompson nodded in recognition as she approached. They'd worked together on several cases since Claire joined the department's forensic psychology unit. He'd been one of the few who hadn't treated her with suspicion when word of her past had inevitably spread through the department.

"Rough one, Doc," he said, his voice low as he handed her a coffee. Steam rose from the cup, dissipating into the cold air. "Second floor's been cleared for evidence collection, but the scene is in the courtyard."

She paused at the entrance, taking in the building's academic atmosphere. In her early days of sobriety, she'd found herself drawn to places like this, institutions of pure logic and reason, where everything could be proven or disproven with elegant certainty. Now she knew better. Human nature defied such neat categorization.

The building reminded her of the university where she'd earned her doctorate in psychology before her drinking had derailed her academic career. The same reverent silence, the same sense of accumulated knowledge pressing down from every surface. For a moment, she wondered what her life might have been if she'd stayed on that path, a professor, perhaps, writing papers on criminal psychology rather than confronting it firsthand at crime scenes. Perhaps she would have followed in her father's footsteps, become a renowned academic like Dr. Richard Morrison, whose textbooks on forensic psychology were required reading in doctoral programs across the country. The thought disappeared as quickly as it had come. There was no value in that kind of thinking; her sponsor had helped her understand that much.

The victim lay in the building's courtyard. The body was surrounded by equations drawn in classroom chalk; each formula precisely placed on the concrete. Claire pulled on latex gloves and crouched beside Detective Sara Martinez.

"Dr. Amanda Foster, thirty-eight, associate professor of applied mathematics," Martinez said, flipping through her notes. Her breath fogged in the cold morning air. "Security found her an hour ago during routine rounds."

Martinez was relatively new to Homicide, transferred over from Vice six months earlier. Her athletic build and ramrod-straight posture spoke of military background, while her dark amber eyes missed nothing at a crime scene. Honey-brown skin with a small scar beneath her right eye that Claire had never asked about, and black hair pulled back in a tight, professional bun. Her crisp pantsuits and immaculate appearance seemed at odds with the gritty nature of their work, but Claire had quickly learned to appreciate the woman's methodical approach and sharp eye for detail. Unlike some of the other detectives, Martinez never made her feel like the token "head doctor" brought in to perform parlor tricks at crime scenes.

Claire studied the scene with methodical precision, her eyes tracking every detail. The body was positioned with deliberate care, arms at exactly thirty degrees from the torso, legs perfectly parallel. Even in death, Dr. Foster was made part of the mathematical harmony surrounding her. The morning dew had begun to blur the chalk lines, creating halos around each equation.

"Notice the chalk residue on her hands," Claire pointed out, her voice steady despite the familiar flutter of anxiety in her chest. "The unsub made her hold the chalk. There are smudges on her fingertips, but the equations are too precise to be her work. The unsub wanted her to participate, even if only symbolically."

"Like a signature under duress?" Martinez asked, her dark eyes narrowing as she studied the victim's hands.

"More than that. It's about connection, forcing her to be part of the unsub's equation," Claire's mind flashed back to her time in recovery, the way her therapist had made her write her own name on her sobriety plan. *Ownership of the process*, Dr. Leland had called it. This was a perversion of that concept, not ownership, but forced complicity.

The equations spread outward like ripples from a stone dropped in still water, each formula connecting to the next in an elegant mathematical spider's web. The handwriting was precise, each symbol perfectly spaced and aligned. Claire photographed every cluster, noting how they formed concentric circles around the body. The flash cast brief shadows that made the equations seem to float above the concrete.

"The unsub took time," Claire said, switching to her phone's video function to capture the overall pattern. Her hands were steady now, focused on the task. "These aren't random. They're telling us something about the killer's thought process. Each symbol is placed with purpose."

"Yeah? What's that?" Martinez squinted at the nearest equation.

Claire's fingers itched for a cigarette. Instead, she pulled another tic tac from her pocket, aware of how the gesture mirrored her old habits with pills. The familiar ritual of popping it, the sweet texture against her tongue, all of it echoed past addictions. "These are decay functions. Terminal velocity calculations. But look at how they're arranged, they're progressive, telling a story. Each ring builds on the equations before it, leading to some final proof."

She walked the perimeter of the scene, continuing to photograph each equation cluster. Her mind cataloged the perfectionist tendency in the spacing, the obsessive attention to detail in each mathematical symbol. These weren't the actions of someone in a frenzy. This was methodical, planned, almost ritualistic. The precision reminded her of her own past obsessions, measuring drinks, timing doses, maintaining the delicate balance between function and oblivion.

As the crime scene techs worked, Claire stepped away to clear her head. The building's central heating hadn't fully activated yet, and her breath fogged in the air as she walked down a corridor lined with faculty offices. Nameplates on doors listed academic achievements like battle honors, Ph.D., FAAAS, Fields Medal Recipient. Behind one door, a phone rang unanswered, the sound oddly normal amid the abnormal circumstances that had brought her here.

The nearest 24-hour store was three blocks away. They sold vodka. Claire knew this because she knew where every store that sold alcohol was located, a survival mechanism from early sobriety that never quite faded. She could picture the bottles lined up behind the counter, their labels promising temporary escape. She pushed the thought away and returned to the scene, moving closer to examine the chalk marks on the concrete.

"Dr. Morrison?" A young patrol officer approached, holding an evidence bag. His uniform was still crisp, probably fresh out of the academy. "We found this by the east entrance."

Inside the bag was a piece of chalk, partially used. Claire examined it through the plastic, the white dust coating the inside of the bag like frost. "Standard classroom chalk but look at the ends, perfectly maintained angles. The unsub sharpens it, keeps it precise. Have we checked security footage for anyone carrying art supplies or drafting tools?"

The young officer shifted uncomfortably. "Are you okay? Your hands are shaking."

Claire tucked her hands into her pockets, feeling the reassuring weight of her sobriety chip. "I'm fine. Have CSU bag every piece of chalk in the building. We need to know which classroom this came from. And get me the pressure mapping on these equations, I want to know if it was pressed harder on any particular symbols."

She turned back to the body, noting how the victim's clothes were smoothed free of wrinkles, her hair arranged with the same mathematical precision as the equations. A strand of grey at her temple had been carefully aligned with the others. "The unsub is not just killing them," she said quietly. "But making them part of a proof."

The medical examiner, Dr. Patel, arrived as dawn began to lighten the sky. His movements were efficient, his dark face serious as he examined the body. Claire had worked with him long enough that they could communicate in professional shorthand.

"TOD?" she asked, crouching beside him.

"Between midnight and 2 AM, based on rigor," he replied, not looking up from his examination. "Cause appears to be asphyxiation, like Professor Cromartie. See the petechial hemorrhaging in the eyes?

And these faint bruises on the neck, consistent with manual strangulation. I'll know more after autopsy."

"Any defensive wounds? Signs of struggle?"

Dr. Patel carefully examined the victim's hands and arms. "Nothing obvious. No visible defensive injuries. She may have been subdued first; I'm seeing a possible injection site on the right side of the neck. I'll run a tox screen, but..."

"A paralytic was used," Claire finished his thought. "The unsub wanted her conscious but unable to fight back. Just like Cromartie."

"Your expertise, not mine," Dr. Patel said with a slight nod, "but that's consistent with what I'm seeing."

Claire stood, feeling the stiffness in her knees from crouching too long. The scene was being processed, photographs taken, evidence collected, measurements recorded. The rhythm of investigation was familiar, almost comforting in its predictability. Unlike addiction, which had been chaotic and destructive, this process was orderly, controlled, directed toward truth rather than oblivion.

As the body was finally removed, Claire noticed something caught in the victim's collar, a small white fragment. With tweezers, she carefully extracted it: a tiny shard of chalk, broken from the main piece. She bagged it separately, noting how it had been hidden within the fold of fabric, an overlooked detail in an otherwise meticulously arranged scene.

"Mistake or message?" Martinez asked, watching her work.

"Not sure yet" Claire replied. "But it's the first thing that wasn't in control completely."

By the time Claire left the scene, the sun had fully risen, casting long shadows across the campus. A few students were beginning to appear - the summer session was in its final weeks - their normal morning routines interrupted by police barricades and whispered speculation.

Back in her office at Baltimore PD, Claire spread the crime scene photos across her desk. The room still bore traces of its previous occupant, water stains on the ceiling that looked like copper sulfate crystals, a periodic table poster yellowed with age. She'd kept both when she took over the space two years ago, fresh out of rehab and determined to prove herself worthy of the second chance she'd been given.

The equations from Professor Cromartie's scene two weeks ago now lay side by side with Dr. Foster's. Claire's background in forensic psychology hadn't included advanced mathematics, but she recognized patterns. During her darkest drinking days, she'd been obsessed with patterns too, the precise timing between drinks needed to maintain a steady numbness, the careful calculation of how many bottles of vodka she could buy from different stores without arousing suspicion. These weren't just calculations; they were a narrative written in the language of certainty.

Her analytical mind traced the connections between the two crime scenes. Both victims were academics in related fields, Cromartie in pure mathematics, Foster in applied mathematics. Both had been found in symbolic locations, Cromartie in his office surrounded by chalk equations identical to those around Foster, who was found in the courtyard where knowledge was passed from one generation to the next. The killer was speaking through these choices, sending a message that went beyond the equations themselves.

She started a fresh page in her notebook, the familiar discipline of profiling bringing focus to her scattered thoughts. The unsub was highly intelligent, organized, methodical. The precision of the crime scenes suggested someone who planned extensively, who left nothing to chance. The mathematical theme pointed to someone with specialized knowledge, almost certainly connected to the academic world. The use of chalk was deliberate, symbolic, a traditional tool of teaching and learning, now repurposed for a darker lesson.

The lack of defensive wounds on either victim suggested someone who didn't fit the typical profile of a threat, someone the victims might have trusted enough to let their guard down. A colleague? A student? Someone who belonged in the academic spaces where the murders had occurred.

"Dr. Morrison."

The voice startled her from her thoughts. Chief Matthews stood in her doorway, his bulky frame filling the space. His face was grave, etched with the lines of two decades in Homicide. "How's it coming?"

"I'm working on the profile," she said, gesturing to her notes. "The unsub is definitely connected to the academic community. The equations aren't just random symbols, they're deliberately chosen, telling a story about inevitability and decay. There's also a strong ritualistic element to the staging. The precision, the positioning of the bodies, the mathematical patterns, it all points to someone with a compulsive need for order and control."

Matthews nodded, his gray eyes studying her with the same intensity he brought to crime scenes. "Any leads on specific suspects?"

"Not yet. I need to understand the equations better first. They're the key to the unsub's motive."

After Matthews left, Claire checked her watch. She needed to better understand these equations, and she knew just who could help her. Instead of making a phone call, she grabbed her coat and headed for the Johns Hopkins campus.

The mathematics department was housed in a different building from where Dr. Foster had been found. Claire flashed her badge at the reception desk and asked for Dr. James Wilson, head of the applied and pure mathematics department. She was led to Wilson's office, a space that perfectly encapsulated academic life; bookshelves overflowing with journals and textbooks, a whiteboard covered in equations, and a desk barely visible beneath stacks of papers. Dr. Wilson himself was a man in his sixties, with silver hair and wire-rimmed glasses that gave him the classic look of an absentminded professor. His eyes were red-rimmed, evidence of the grief that had struck his department twice now.

"Dr. Wilson? I'm Dr. Morrison from Baltimore PD. Thank you for seeing me," she said, extending her hand. "I'm very sorry about your colleagues."

Wilson shook her hand, his grip surprisingly firm despite his fragile appearance. "Anything I can do to help catch whoever did this. Please, sit down."

Claire took the offered chair and pulled out the photos of the equations from both crime scenes, spreading them on the only clear space on Wilson's desk. "I need your help understanding these. They were found at both crime scenes, and I believe they're the key to understanding the unsub's motives."

Wilson leaned forward, his professional curiosity momentarily overshadowing his grief as he studied the photos. Claire watched his eyes scan the equations, noting how his expression shifted from academic interest to growing concern.

"These are fascinating," he said finally, his voice both captivated and disturbed. "And deeply troubling. Whoever wrote these has a profound understanding of theoretical mathematics. They're all about inevitability, mathematical proofs showing how certain outcomes are predetermined based on initial conditions."

"Can you be more specific?"

"Look at the progression. The first ring establishes basic principles of entropy, the natural tendency of systems to decay. Then each subsequent ring builds on that, incorporating elements of chaos theory and statistical mechanics. But the notation... it's distinctive."

Claire leaned forward, her chair creaking in the quiet office. "How so?"

"It's classical, almost archaic. Modern mathematicians use different symbols, shorthand. This is like seeing Shakespeare's English in a text message. And see this recurring symbol? It's not standard notation at all. It's personal, like a signature. Someone's trying to make a point about mathematical elegance."

"Could a student have written these?"

"At this level? Only our most advanced doctoral candidates. But there's something else, these aren't just proofs about physical systems. They're philosophical. See how this section incorporates human variables? Whoever wrote this is trying to prove something about human nature itself."

Claire felt something click in her mind. Deterministic thinking, she recognized it from her own past, the way she used to justify her drinking. If everything was predetermined, why fight it? How many times had she used that logic to pour another drink, to surrender to the inevitable?

For a moment, she considered calling her father, Dr. Richard Morrison. Their relationship had been strained ever since he'd confronted her about her drinking five years ago, a painful intervention that had ended with her walking out of his life. They spoke occasionally now, strictly professional calls where she sought his expertise without revealing too much of her personal struggles. This case would interest him, with its intersection of mathematical brilliance and psychological deviance. But calling him would mean explaining the mathematical aspects that were beyond her training, admitting a gap in her knowledge.

"Send me everything you have on doctoral candidates from the last decade," she said to Dr. Wilson, her voice sharper than intended. "Especially anyone who's shown interest in applying mathematical principles to human behavior."

Dr. Wilson nodded, studying her with the same analytical gaze he'd directed at the equations. "You understand the unsub's thinking, don't you? I can see it in your eyes."

Claire stood, gathering the photos. "I understand patterns, Dr. Wilson. Especially destructive ones."

As she turned to leave, Wilson called after her. "These equations, they're not just academic exercises. They're a worldview. A dangerous one. Whoever wrote them believes that everything, even human choice, follows predetermined mathematical laws."

"I know," Claire said quietly. "That's what worries me."

The day stretched into evening as Claire pored over personnel files sent from the university. Grad students, faculty, visiting scholars, dozens of potential suspects who had the mathematical knowledge and access needed to commit these crimes. She cross-referenced them with police records, looking for red flags: complaints, restraining orders, incidents of escalating behavior. Most came back clean, the academic vetting process having already screened out obvious risks.

By six, her eyes burned from staring at the computer screen. She rubbed them, feeling the grit of exhaustion beneath her lids. The wall clock ticked loudly in the silence, reminding her that she'd been awake for almost twenty-four hours. A dangerous state. Tiredness lowered defenses, made the old cravings harder to resist. She needed rest, but her mind refused to let go of the case.

Martinez appeared in the doorway, carrying two cups of coffee. "Thought you could use this," she said, placing one on Claire's desk. "I added extra sugar; you look like you need it."

"Thanks," Claire took a grateful sip, the sweetness momentarily overwhelming the bitterness. "Any updates from the crime scene team?"

Martinez settled into the chair across from her desk. "Preliminary DNA results show only the victim's profile; our unsub was careful. The chalk fragment you found is being analyzed, but initial reports confirm it's standard classroom chalk, available in any supply closet on campus. And here's something interesting. Security footage shows a custodial worker entering the building at 11:30 PM, but there's no record of scheduled maintenance for last night."

"Did you get a clear image?"

"Not really. Baseball cap pulled low, standard uniform. The unsub knew where the cameras were, kept their face turned away," Martinez sipped her coffee. "We're checking employment records now, but my money says we find a stolen or fake ID was used to access the building."

"They're organized, plan ahead," Claire nodded, the profile taking sharper form in her mind. "But this is personal for them. The mathematical signature proves that. The unsub isn't just killing; they're making a statement."

As Martinez left, Claire turned back to her computer, pulling up the faculty and student directory for the mathematics department. She scanned faces, looking for something. Intensity, obsession, the subtle markers of someone living on the border between brilliance and delusion. Her training had taught her to look for these signs, but her own experience with addiction had given her a deeper understanding of how easily that line could be crossed.

Three names caught her attention: a postdoc whose research had been rejected, a visiting professor with a history of academic disputes, and William Harrison, a doctoral candidate whose funding had recently been cut. Claire made notes on each, creating a preliminary ranking based on motive and opportunity.

She pulled up Harrison's file first. Something about the academic photo drew her attention. Thin, with intense eyes and perfect posture, dark hair precisely parted. The thesis title made her pause: "Deterministic Patterns in Complex Systems: Proving the Inevitability of Decay."

"Interesting," she murmured, digging deeper into the academic record. Notes from Harrison's faculty advisor expressed concern about "increasingly rigid thought patterns" and "difficulty accepting criticism." Six months ago, Harrison's research funding had been terminated following a heated disagreement with Professor Cromartie about the validity of the mathematical approach.

Claire felt the first spark of recognition. Cromartie had been their first victim.

She quickly cross-referenced Foster's committee assignments, her pulse quickening when she found it: Foster had served on the review board that ultimately voted to terminate Harrison's funding. Both victims were directly connected to Harrison's academic downfall.

"Martinez," she called out, but the detective had already left for the evening. Claire checked the time. Nearly 8 PM. She pulled up Harrison's complete academic history, noting the pattern of brilliance coupled with increasing isolation. Recent evaluations showed work becoming more focused on deterministic theories with each passing semester. Other professors also noted "brilliant but rigid thinking" and "difficulty accepting criticism." Classic warning signs of someone whose worldview was narrowing, hardening into unshakable certainty.

Claire drove home with Harrison's file, her mind already working through the implications. The academic papers showed a brilliant mind, but one increasingly fixated on determinism and mathematical inevitability. Recent work had focused on applying decay functions to human systems, essentially arguing that all human behaviors, all social structures, followed predictable patterns of deterioration.

Back in her apartment, Claire spread Harrison's academic history across her kitchen table. Darwin watched from his perch atop the bookcase, his orange fur catching the harsh kitchen light. The cat's presence was grounding, a reminder of the stability she'd built in sobriety.

She understood the appeal of Harrison's thinking. During her worst days, she'd convinced herself that her addiction was inevitable. Genetic predisposition, childhood trauma, job stress. All variables in an equation that could only produce one outcome. Recovery had taught her the flaw in that logic: human will, the variable that couldn't be quantified or predicted.

At 2 AM, she stood smoking on her fire escape. Baltimore hummed below, a city that never quite slept. Distant sirens wailed, carrying stories she'd rather not imagine.

That's when it clicked.

Claire stubbed out her cigarette and rushed back to her laptop. The blue light of the screen cast shadows across her face as she pulled up Harrison's academic calendar alongside the murder dates. The timing wasn't random. It followed the mathematical progression outlined in his thesis chapters. Each death occurred at intervals that corresponded to specific proofs about decay and inevitability.

"Son of a bitch," she whispered, her fingers flying across the keyboard. Harrison wasn't just killing people who'd wronged him. He was following a predetermined schedule, each murder timed according to his mathematical theories. And if her calculations were correct, the next death was scheduled for tomorrow night.

She reached for her phone, calling Martinez despite the hour.

"Dr. Morrison?" Martinez answered, voice thick with sleep but alert. "What's wrong?"

"I found our killer. William Harrison, doctoral candidate whose funding was cut by both victims. His thesis is basically a mathematical justification for murder, arguing that decay and death are inevitable, predetermined by initial conditions." Claire's words came in a rush, fueled by caffeine and adrenaline. "But here's the critical part. He's not killing randomly. The murders follow a timeline based on his mathematical proofs. Each death is scheduled according to specific intervals in his thesis progression."

"At 2 AM? You're sure about this?" Martinez replied, but Claire could hear her already moving, the rustle of bedsheets, the click of a lamp.

"Both victims were on the committee that cut his funding. The mathematical signature matches his thesis work exactly. And Martinez, if I'm right about the timing pattern, he's planning to kill again tomorrow night. We need a search warrant for his apartment and we need to find him before he completes his 'proof.'"

"What's the evidence?"

"The mathematical notation Dr. Wilson mentioned, it's identical to Harrison's thesis style. Classical notation, archaic symbols, the same philosophical approach about deterministic decay. Plus, both victims had direct connections to ending his academic career. This isn't just revenge, it's a systematic proof using human lives as variables."

"I'll call the judge. Meet you at the precinct in thirty."

By dawn, they had the warrant. Harrison's apartment, a spartan efficiency in a building popular with graduate students, yielded the evidence they needed. Chalk identical to that found at both crime scenes. Drafting tools for precise mathematical notation. A wall covered in equations matching those at the murder scenes. And most damning, a list of names, each with a date beside it. Cromartie and Foster had checkmarks by their names. Three more names remained unchecked, each with future dates noted.

"You're right," Martinez said, photographing the list. "Next one's scheduled for tomorrow night."

"Dr. James Wilson, the department chair," Claire said, recognizing the name. "He was the head of the committee that cut Harrison's funding."

They moved quickly after that, arrest warrant issued, officers dispatched to Harrison's known locations. But Harrison wasn't at the usual campus haunts. The university was searched, security increased around potential victims. Harrison had vanished, a variable they couldn't account for in their equations of justice.

Claire returned to her office, running on coffee and determination. She spread the evidence photos across her desk, looking for anything they might have missed. Harrison's apartment had been impeccably organized, everything in its place. Books arranged by height and subject, clothes folded with military precision, dishes stacked according to size. The only chaotic element had been the wall of equations, a sprawling, interconnected web of mathematical symbols that covered an entire wall. Not random, she realized, but a system she hadn't yet decoded.

"He's not running," she said to Martinez when the detective returned from canvassing Harrison's neighborhood. "This was always part of the plan. The timing, the sequence, it's all predetermined in his mind."

"Where would he go?" Martinez asked, frustration evident in her voice. "We've checked everywhere Harrison is known to frequent."

Claire studied the photograph of Harrison's equation wall, noting how certain symbols were circled, connected by lines to others.

"Harrison is not just killing people who hurt his career. He's proving a theorem. Each murder is a step in a mathematical proof about inevitability."

Her eyes caught a pattern in the equations, a recurring reference to a specific location. Not an address, but coordinates expressed through mathematical symbols. She grabbed her phone, calling Dr. Wilson again.

"These equations on Harrison's wall, they're referencing a specific place on campus, aren't they?"

There was a pause as Wilson studied the image she'd sent. "Yes, these could be interpreted as coordinates. Using the university's central point as the origin... this would be the old library. The 24-hour study area in the mathematics annex."

"That's where Harrison will be," Claire said, already reaching for her coat.

Claire, Martinez, and two patrol officers approached the university library as dusk settled over the campus. The building was quieter than usual; most students having been evacuated after Harrison was identified as a threat. The 24-hour study area occupied the library's oldest section.

"Stay back," Claire instructed the officers. "Harrison's not violent by nature, these killings are intellectual, not emotional. If he feels cornered or that the 'proof' is threatened, that could change."

The study area was empty except for one figure surrounded by chalk dust and papers. The space smelled of old books and filtered air, with rows of dark wooden tables stretching into shadow. Green-shaded reading lamps cast pools of light that seemed to float in the darkness. Claire approached slowly, Detective Martinez and two officers hanging back by the entrance. Her heart pounded, but her mind was clear, clearer than it had been during her drinking days when she'd mistaken the burn of vodka for courage, when she'd believed that enough alcohol could make any situation manageable.

"Mr. Harrison?" she called softly, her voice barely disturbing the library's hushed atmosphere. "I'm Dr. Morrison from Baltimore PD."

He looked up, chalk still poised against a blackboard covered in equations. Harrison's eyes were clear, focused, with the same intensity she'd seen in the photo.

"You understand, don't you?" Harrison asked, gesturing at the equations. Chalk dust floated, catching the light like stars. "It's all inevitable. Every death, every decay. I just proved it. The mathematics don't lie."

Claire felt Martinez and the officers tense behind her, but she raised her hand slightly, a signal to wait. This wasn't a situation for drawn weapons and shouted commands. Harrison wasn't a typical violent offender driven by rage. The actions were governed by a warped intellectual framework, a mathematical certainty that justified murder as simply another variable in a complex equation.

"The equations are beautiful," Claire said, taking a careful step forward. The wooden floor creaked beneath her feet; the sound amplified in the quiet library. "You've spent years developing them, refining them. Proving your theory."

Harrison nodded, a flicker of something like pleasure crossing his face. "No one else could see it. They dismissed it as abstract, unprovable. But I knew, the patterns are undeniable once you identify the correct variables."

Claire glanced at the blackboard behind them. The equations stretched across its surface, written in the same precise hand as those at the crime scenes. Concentric circles of mathematical symbols, each building on the last, leading to what Harrison saw as an inescapable conclusion.

"Tell me about the pattern," she said, taking another step. "Help me understand what they couldn't see."

Her training had taught her to establish rapport, to find common ground with the subject. But it was her experience with addiction that guided her now, the knowledge of how a brilliant mind could construct elaborate justifications for destructive behavior, how logic could be twisted to serve the darkest impulses.

Harrison turned back to the blackboard; the chalk hand raised. "It starts with basic entropy, the fundamental tendency of all systems toward disorder. But I discovered something deeper." The chalk traced a series of symbols. "Human systems follow the same mathematics as physical ones. Decay isn't just likely, it's predetermined. From the moment of creation, everything moves toward dissolution at a calculable rate."

Claire's hand slipped into her pocket, finding her sobriety chip. The familiar metal was warm against her fingers, grounding her. She thought about her first day in recovery, how impossible two years had seemed then. How each day had felt like fighting against mathematical certainty. The urge to drink had seemed as inevitable as gravity.

"What about intervention?" she asked, her voice steady despite the trembling in her hands. The fluorescent lights hummed overhead, a sound like distant bees. "External forces acting on the system?"

Harrison shook his head, frustrated. "Temporary deviations. The larger pattern always reasserts itself. Death, decay, they're written into the equations from the start." He gestured at the formulas with the chalk. "Cromartie and Foster couldn't see it. They called it pessimistic, unscientific. They took my funding because they were afraid of the implications."

"So, you proved it with their deaths," Claire said, not a question but a statement of understanding. "Made them variables in your equation."

"They were always variables," Harrison replied, voice frighteningly calm. "I just demonstrated what the mathematics had already determined. Their deaths were inevitable from the moment they denied the truth of my work."

Claire took another step closer. She was within arm's reach now, could see the chalk dust on Harrison's fingers, the dark circles beneath his eyes. The graduate student had been working for hours, perhaps days, perfecting the mathematical proof. The obsessive focus was familiar to her, that single-minded pursuit that excluded all other considerations, all human connections.

"I used to believe in inevitability too," she said, her voice steady despite the trembling in her hands. "Used it to justify a lot of things I did to myself. But patterns can be broken, Harrison. Choice exists. I prove that every morning when I wake up and choose not to drink."

Her hands shook as she reached for a tic tac, the movement deliberate, letting Harrison see her vulnerability. Harrison watched the movement, recognized something in it. Their eyes tracked her trembling fingers. "You've fought patterns yourself."

"Every day. And I can help you fight this one. Your equations aren't wrong, entropy is real, decay happens. But they're incomplete. They don't account for human will, for the variables that can't be quantified. For the choice to change, to grow, to heal."

Harrison's face suddenly contorted with frustration. "No! You don't understand. The proof is almost complete. I just need more time, more variables." The chalk scraped frantically across the blackboard, creating new symbols, new connections. "Two deaths aren't enough. The sample size is too small. I need more data points, more victims to establish the pattern beyond statistical doubt."

The chalk in Harrison's hand snapped under pressure, and he stared at the broken piece with horror. Claire saw her opening, the momentary fracture in his certainty. She continued, drawing on every therapy session, every recovery meeting she'd attended. Every morning she'd woken up and chosen to face the day sober.

"Determinism is seductive. Makes us feel like we're not responsible for our actions. But you chose the classical notation. You chose your victims. Those weren't inevitable, they were choices. Just like I'm choosing now to stand here, unarmed, talking to you."

Harrison's face showed the first crack in his mathematical certainty, a flicker of doubt, of recognition. Claire pressed forward, sensing the shift. "The most complex systems can't be reduced to simple equations. That's why quantum physics still baffles us, at some level, indeterminacy is built into the universe itself. Your brilliance led you to see patterns others missed, but even the most elegant mathematics can't capture the full complexity of human choice."

"No, no, no!" Harrison's voice rose in panic. "You're wrong! I just need to refine the equations. I just need more work, more proof!" His hands shook as he grabbed a fresh piece of chalk. "If I can just complete this next section, you'll see it. Everyone will see it."

Tears streaked down Harrison's face. "The proofs... they're perfect. The math doesn't lie."

"No, it doesn't. But it can be incomplete. Like a theorem missing its human variables," she took a careful step forward. "Let me help you add those variables back in."

The chalk fell to the floor, the sound echoing in the empty library. As Martinez moved in with handcuffs, Claire saw her own reflection in the library window, red hair wild, green eyes intense. For once, she didn't look away.

She stayed with Harrison as he was being processed, watching as his mathematical certainty crumbled into human grief and regret. The confession came in terms of variables and constants, in references to chaos theory and quantum uncertainty. The brilliance that had made Harrison capable of such precise, calculated violence now turned inward, analyzing his own actions with the same cold clarity.

"I thought I was proving something profound," Harrison told her in the interrogation room, voice hollow. "But I was just finding an elegant justification for my own brokenness."

Claire nodded, understanding all too well. "That's what addiction taught me; how easy it is to build beautiful logical structures around our darkest impulses. To make self-destruction seem inevitable."

Harrison looked up, his eyes seeking something in hers. "How did you break the pattern?"

"One day at a time," she said. "By accepting that the math is never complete, that there are always variables we can't account for. By choosing, again and again, to believe that the next moment isn't predetermined by all the moments that came before it."

Later, writing her report in her office, Claire added one final note about patterns and choices. She'd declined Martinez's invitation to celebrate closing the case, crowds and bars still held too many dangers, even after two years. The old patterns still called to her, like equations waiting to be solved.

Instead, she found herself adding one more equation to her report, the statistical probability of maintaining sobriety, a number she'd memorized during her darkest days. But unlike Harrison's equations, she knew this pattern could be broken. Had to be broken, one day at a time.

As she finished typing, her phone rang. Dr. Leland, her therapist, checking in after hearing about the case on the local news. "You did good work today," the older woman said, her voice carrying the calm wisdom that had helped guide Claire through recovery. "How are you holding up?"

"I'm okay," Claire said, surprised to find it was true. "The case... it hit close to home. All that mathematical certainty about inevitable outcomes. It reminded me of how I used to think."

"And how do you think now?"

Claire glanced at her reflection in the darkened window, at the woman who had fought her way back from addiction one uncertain day at a time. "That the most beautiful equation in the world can't capture the complexity of a single human choice. That decay isn't the only pattern in the universe."

"That's good," Dr. Leland said, the smile evident in her voice. "That's growth. Will I see you at your regular session tomorrow?"

"I'll be there." Claire ended the call and turned back to her report, adding one final sentence: "The suspect's mathematical worldview, while elegant and internally consistent, failed to account for the most unpredictable variable in any human system, the capacity for choice."

Claire found herself scrolling to a name in her contacts: Dad. Dr. Richard Morrison's number had sat unused for months, their last conversation a brief, stilted exchange about a journal article he'd published. She hesitated, then pressed the call button.

He answered on the third ring, his voice carrying the same authoritative tone that had intimidated generations of psychology students. "Claire? Is everything all right? It's late."

"I'm fine, Dad. I just closed a case," she paused, uncertain how to bridge the distance between them. "A mathematician who thought he could prove that human behavior follows deterministic patterns. That decay and death are inevitable."

"Ah," he said, and she could picture him leaning back in his leather office chair, glasses perched on his forehead. "The old determinism versus free will debate. Always fascinating when it manifests in criminal behavior."

"I thought of you," she admitted. "Some of the ideas reminded me of your early work on pattern recognition in serial offenders."

There was a pause, charged with unspoken history. "I'd be interested to read your case notes, if you're willing to share them."

It wasn't quite an olive branch, but it was something. "I'll send them over tomorrow," she said, then added, "I'm still sober, Dad. Two years now."

"I know," he said softly. "Your mother would be proud." The mention of her mother hung between them like a shared grief. "You're doing good work, Claire."

"Thanks, Dad." The words felt inadequate for the moment, but they were a start. "I'll call again soon."

The sun rose over Baltimore as Claire finished her report. She stood at her office window, watching the city wake up. Morning light caught the edge of her sobriety chip, now resting on her desk beside the last tic tacs from her pocket. The new day painted the world in shades of possibility.

She gathered her things to head home. Her hands were steady as she picked up the chip, leaving the tic tacs behind. Some patterns were meant to be broken, and others, like the mathematical precision of sunrise, like the daily choice to begin again, were worth keeping.

In her pocket, the sobriety chip pressed against her leg, a constant reminder that not all patterns were destiny. Sometimes the most complex equation was simply the choice to begin again, one uncertain variable at a time.

Chapter Two

Perfect Mirror

D r. Claire Morrison examined the small package on her desk with suspicion. No postmark, hand delivered, with her name printed in precise block letters. The last time she'd received an unmarked delivery; it had contained case files from a stalker who'd later confessed to three murders. This package triggered the same instinctive wariness.

"Another mystery delivery?" Detective Sara Martinez asked, approaching Claire's desk with two coffee cups in hand. She placed one before Claire, the gesture of camaraderie that had been developing between them over the past six months of working together.

"Something unexpected, at least," Claire replied, turning the package over. "No sender information, no security checkpoint stamp."

Claire had developed a deep respect for Martinez's methodical mind and unwavering focus during their collaboration on the Harrison case four months ago. The detective's cool demeanor and sharp intellect complemented Claire's more intuitive approach, creating an effective partnership that Chief Matthews had been quick to formalize on subsequent cases.

As she carefully opened the package, first scanning it for any powder residues or suspicious contents, Martinez sipped her coffee and watched with professional curiosity. Inside was a glossy department store gift box, white with a silver ribbon.

"Doesn't look threatening," Martinez observed, though her posture remained alert.

Claire removed the lid to reveal a small ornate hand mirror, silver-backed with an art deco design of intertwining flowers. It was beautiful but sent an immediate chill through her. She turned it over carefully, looking for any markings or messages, but found only a small manufacturer's stamp indicating it was vintage, circa 1930s.

"Secret admirer?" Martinez suggested, though her tone remained professional rather than teasing.

"I doubt it," Claire replied, setting the mirror aside. "I'm more inclined to think it's related to something I've consulted on."

She turned to her computer to check her calendar. "I've been asked to review three case files this week. One domestic violence, one arson pattern, and one possible serial exhibitionist. Nothing that screams 'symbolic mirror gift' to me."

"Log it anyway," Martinez advised, straightening her immaculate pantsuit as she prepared to leave. "Anonymous gifts to law enforcement are rarely innocent coincidences."

Claire nodded, already reaching for an evidence bag. As she slipped the mirror inside, she spent the next hour reviewing files from her other pending consultations, trying to focus on the domestic violence case that had been flagged for psychological evaluation. But her attention kept drifting to the bagged mirror in her desk drawer. She pulled it out twice, studying it through the clear evidence bag, searching for any detail she might have missed. When that proved futile, she turned to her computer and ran searches on similar vintage mirrors, learning more about 1930s art deco designs than she'd ever expected to need. Darwin appeared and disappeared from her office three times, each visit accompanied by his expectant meow for attention she was too distracted to provide. She was deep into reading about the symbolism of mirrors in criminal psychology when her phone rang with Chief Matthews' distinctive tone.

"Morrison," she answered, cradling the phone against her shoulder as she labeled the evidence bag.

"We've got a situation in a penthouse apartment in Harbor East," Matthews said. "Body positioned in front of a vanity mirror. Multiple other mirrors placed around the scene. Detective Martinez is headed there now. I want you on this one."

"On my way," Claire replied, her gaze falling on the bagged mirror. Sometimes coincidences weren't coincidences at all.

She tucked the evidence bag into her desk drawer and locked it, grabbing her coat and the half-finished coffee. At the door, she glanced back at Darwin, who'd somehow appeared on her filing cabinet, his orange fur stark against the gray metal.

"Don't go anywhere," she told the cat, who slow-blinked in response, a promise she knew he wouldn't keep. Somehow Darwin always managed to find his way around the building, adopting various officers as temporary caretakers when Claire was in the field.

The Harbor East penthouse occupied the top floor of one of Baltimore's newest luxury buildings, all glass and steel against the harbor skyline. Claire showed her credentials to the uniform at the door, noting the careful atmosphere of controlled chaos that marked a well-managed crime scene.

Martinez stood in the main living area, her dark hair pulled back in its usual precise bun, her posture straight as she made notes. She nodded as Claire approached.

"Victim is Sandra Wells, forty-two, nonprofit executive," Martinez said, falling in step beside Claire as they moved through the apartment. "Husband found her this morning after returning from a business trip. Her body is in the master bath, positioned in front of a vanity mirror. Multiple other mirrors have been arranged around her. ME's still examining the scene."

The master bathroom was a study in luxury, marble and glass, chrome fixtures gleaming under the crime scene lights. But it was the tableau at its center that commanded attention. Sandra Wells sat in a decorative chair before a large vanity mirror, her body positioned with unnatural precision. Her wrists were bound to the armrests with silk scarves, ankles secured to the chair legs. What caught Claire's immediate attention, however, was the semicircle of smaller mirrors arranged around the chair, each angled to show the victim a different aspect of herself.

Claire approached carefully, noting the paths cleared by crime scene technicians. "How long has she been dead?"

"ME estimates between eight and midnight last night," Martinez replied, keeping her voice low. "Husband was in Chicago, alibied by hotel security footage and his key card usage. He arrived at BWI at 6:35 this morning, taxi dropped him here at 7:22, he discovered the body and called 911 at 7:26."

Claire pulled latex gloves from her pocket, focusing on the victim. Sandra Wells had been dressed in an expensive silk blouse and tailored slacks; her hair arranged in a sophisticated updo. But it was her makeup that drew Claire's attention, flawlessly applied eyeshadow and lipstick, too perfect for someone who'd been dead for hours.

"The unsub did her makeup postmortem," Claire observed, leaning closer without disturbing the scene. "Look at the precision of the application. This wasn't rushed."

"Like dressing a mannequin," Martinez agreed, her eyes cataloging every detail.

Claire circled the chair slowly, studying each mirror's angle. Her own reflection fragmented and multiplied as she moved, a dozen versions of herself in her black blazer, dark circles under her green eyes despite the concealer she'd applied that morning. Two years and four months sober, and she still carried the physical markers of her past excesses, though Dr. Leland assured her that would fade with time.

She popped a tic tac, the subtle minty taste grounding her as she fought the familiar anxiety that rose at crime scenes like this one.

"The positioning is deliberate," she said, gesturing to the arrangement. "Each mirror shows a different angle, forces a different perspective. The unsub wanted her to see every part of herself."

"But she was dead when they did this," Martinez pointed out, her brow furrowing.

"Yes, which suggests this isn't about the victim's perception, but about the unsub's need to create a specific scene, to communicate something through this arrangement." Claire gestured to the largest mirror. "This is the main event. The others are supporting players, creating a visual echo chamber."

"Staging takes time and confidence," Martinez said, surveying the elaborate setup. "This isn't a first-timers work."

"No," Claire agreed, studying the victim's makeup more closely. "But there's something almost reverential about this. The care taken with her appearance, the precise arrangement. This isn't about humiliation or degradation. It's about transformation. Making her into an idealized version of herself."

Dr. Patel, the medical examiner, approached from where he'd been examining evidence near the shower. "Initial observations suggest manual strangulation as the cause of death. No signs of sexual assault. She was killed elsewhere and placed here postmortem."

"Meaning the unsub had to transport her," Martinez noted. "That's risky in a building with security and cameras."

"Check for service entrances, delivery access," Claire suggested. "And the victim's movements yesterday. Where was she last seen alive?"

They left the crime scene technicians and moved to the living room, where Sandra Wells' husband sat slumped on a leather sofa. James Wells was in his mid-forties, his business suit rumpled from travel and stress, his face ashen with shock.

"Mr. Wells," Martinez began gently, "we need to ask you some questions. I know this is difficult."

He nodded, his movements mechanical. "Anything to help. I just... I don't understand. Who would do this to Sandra?"

"That's what we're going to find out," Claire assured him, taking a seat across from him. "Can you tell us about your wife's routine? What she might have been doing yesterday?"

"It was a normal workday for her. She's, she was, the executive director of the Baltimore Community Foundation. She texted me around six to say she was headed to dinner with Andrea, her deputy director. They were finalizing a grant proposal." His voice broke. "That was the last time I heard from her."

"And the mirrors," Claire said carefully. "Were they already in your home?"

Wells looked confused. "The vanity was Sandra's, but those other mirrors. I've never seen them before."

Claire nodded, making a note. "One more question, Mr. Wells. Did your wife use any specific photo editing apps or filters for her social media?"

He blinked at the apparent non sequitur. "Yes, actually. She was always trying new ones. Said the right filter could make all the difference in how people perceived her progress."

"Progress?"

"Sandra lost nearly a hundred pounds over the past year," he explained, a flicker of pride momentarily displacing his grief. "She documented her journey on social media. Before and after photos, workout routines, healthy meals."

"Do you remember the names of any specific apps she used?" Claire pressed gently.

"There was one she paid for, a premium subscription. Perfect s omething... Perfect Lens, I think. She liked it because it had body transformation filters specifically designed for weight loss journeys."

Claire and Martinez exchanged a glance, the connection to the mirror imagery becoming clearer.

As they left the penthouse, Martinez pulled out her phone to check incoming messages from the team canvassing the building. "Security footage shows our victim entering the building alone at 8:42 PM. No sign of her leaving. At 9:15, an individual wearing a housekeeping uniform, entered through the service entrance. The face is obscured by a cap, but the build is consistent with someone who could have overpowered our victim."

"So, our unsub posed as housekeeping staff," Claire mused. "Smart. Invisible in a luxury building, access to master keys, knowledge of which units are temporarily vacant."

"We're checking employment records now, but my guess is we'll find our unsub used a stolen or forged ID."

Back at her apartment that night, Claire sat cross-legged on her small balcony, crime scene photos spread around her. Darwin watched through the sliding glass door, too pampered to brave the November chill. The Baltimore skyline glittered beyond her fire escape, the harbor lights reflecting on the water.

She lit a cigarette, letting the smoke curl around her face as she studied the carefully arranged mirrors. Each one positioned to capture a specific angle, to create a complete visual catalog of the subject. The makeup carefully applied to highlight certain features while minimizing others. The expensive clothing that wasn't the victim's own.

Her phone rang. Martinez.

"Got something interesting from the husband's follow-up interview," the detective said. "Sandra Wells had recently lost nearly a hundred pounds, as we know. What we didn't know is that she'd been increasingly dissatisfied with the results. According to the husband, she kept saying she 'didn't recognize herself anymore.' She'd doubled her therapy sessions in the past two months."

"Weight loss that dramatic can cause body dysmorphia," Claire said, the psychological angle immediately clear. "The mind can't keep up with the physical changes. Who was her therapist?"

"Dr. James Warner, specializes in body image issues. He's expecting us tomorrow at ten."

After hanging up, Claire opened her laptop and logged into the Baltimore PD database, searching for cases involving mirrors or elaborate postmortem arrangements. Nothing in their jurisdiction matched the specific pattern, but she flagged two cases from neighboring counties involving posed bodies for follow-up.

She then switched to Sandra Wells' social media accounts, using the login information the husband had provided. The transformation was thoroughly documented, hundreds of posts tracking weight loss progress, new clothes, new hairstyles. The early posts had a genuine quality, simple photos with minimal editing. As time progressed, the production value increased, sophisticated lighting, careful poses, professional-looking editing. The captions changed too, from simple updates about pounds lost to philosophical musings about identity and perception.

The final post, three days before her death, was a mirror selfie. The caption read: "Sometimes I catch my reflection and wonder who's really looking back."

Claire rubbed her eyes, realizing she'd been squinting at the screen too long. Darwin had given up his door vigil and was curled atop her bookcase, one eye still tracking her movements. She envied his simple relationship with mirrors; they were just another surface to ignore unless there might be another cat inside.

Her own reflection in the sliding glass door caught her attention. The glass created a darker, ghostly version of herself, edges softened by the night behind it. Sometimes she still expected to see her old self staring back; eyes glossy with false confidence, cheeks flushed with vodka warmth. She'd avoided mirrors during her drinking days, the disconnect between her self-image and the reality too painful to confront.

She wondered if that's how Sandra Wells had felt, constantly searching her reflection for traces of who she used to be, never quite reconciling the before and after.

Dr. Warner's office was in a converted Victorian in one of Baltimore's more upscale neighborhoods. The waiting room was deliberately calming, soft colors, plush furniture, gentle classical music playing just above the threshold of hearing. Claire and Martinez arrived precisely at ten, both studying the room with professional interest.

"No mirrors," Claire noted quietly to Martinez. "Unusual for a therapist's office, especially one specializing in body image."

Martinez nodded, her dark eyes taking in the deliberate absence. "Interesting choice."

Dr. Warner emerged from his inner office, a man in his early sixties with a balding head and thick glasses. "Detective, Dr. Morrison, please come in."

The therapist's office continued the soothing aesthetic, bookshelves filled with psychiatric texts, comfortable chairs arranged around a small table rather than the traditional couch setup. Still no mirrors, Claire noted, not even the small decorative kind that often adorned professional spaces.

"Thank you for seeing us," Claire began once they were seated. "We're investigating the death of Sandra Wells, and we understand she was a patient of yours."

Warner's professional demeanor flickered briefly. "Yes, such a tragedy. I'm still processing it myself. Sandra was making significant progress with her issues."

"Which were?" Martinez prompted, notebook ready.

"I can't discuss specific details of her treatment due to confidentiality, even after death," Warner said carefully. "But I can tell you that Sandra was struggling with body dysmorphia following her significant weight loss. It's quite common. People expect their psychological self-image to realign with their physical changes, but it's rarely that simple."

Claire nodded. "Did she ever mention feeling watched or followed? Any concerns about a specific person?"

"No, nothing like that. Her issues were internal, not paranoia about external threats." Warner hesitated, removing his glasses and polishing them with a handkerchief. "There was something, though. In our last session, she mentioned seeing her reflection in a store window and not recognizing herself at all. She said it felt like looking at a stranger. I was concerned enough to increase our sessions to twice weekly, but our next appointment never happened."

"Do you have other patients with similar issues?" Claire asked. "Others who've undergone significant physical transformations and struggle with the psychological aftermath?"

Warner's eyes narrowed slightly as he replaced his glasses. "Several. Body image issues are my specialty. Why do you ask?"

"We're establishing patterns," Claire said smoothly. "One more question, did Sandra use any specific photo editing apps? Something called Perfect Lens, perhaps?"

"She mentioned using filters for her social media posts, yes. It was part of what we were working on, the disconnect between her curated online image and how she actually saw herself." Warner glanced at his watch. "I'm sorry, but I have a patient arriving soon."

Outside in the parking lot, Martinez raised an eyebrow. "You think the killer might be targeting Warner's patients specifically? That would lead directly back to Warner himself."

"Not necessarily," Claire countered. "Warner likely isn't the only therapist in Baltimore specializing in body image issues. But it gives us another angle to explore. If there are more victims, they might share similar psychological profiles rather than obvious external connections."

"You think there will be more," Martinez said. It wasn't a question.

"Unless we catch the unsub quickly, yes. The level of planning, the specificity of the staging, this isn't someone who's going to stop at one. The mirrors, the makeup, the positioning, it's a ritual, not a one-time event."

Back at the precinct, Claire added the new information to her case board, connecting Sandra Wells' therapy, her weight loss journey, and the mirror-focused crime scene. She placed the photo of the anonymous mirror she'd received that morning in the upper corner, not yet sure how or if it connected, but unwilling to ignore the timing.

Chief Matthews stopped by her desk, his large frame filling the doorway. "Where are we on the Wells case?"

Claire outlined their findings so far, emphasizing the deliberate, ritualistic nature of the crime scene. "The unsub spent considerable time with the victim postmortem, applying makeup, arranging mirrors, positioning the body. This level of care suggests a deep psychological investment in the scene itself, not just the act of killing."

"Meaning?"

"Meaning the unsub is likely to strike again, creating another elaborate scene. The mirrors are a crucial element, forcing the victim to see themselves from multiple angles, even in death. It's about perception, about forcing a specific kind of self-reflection."

Matthews rubbed his chin, the gesture he made when processing troubling information. "I don't like the sound of that. What's our timeline?"

"Impossible to say with only one data point," Claire admitted. "But given the level of planning involved, I'd expect the unsub to be meticulous about timing as well. They'll need time to select the next victim, prepare the scene, gather the necessary props."

"So, we've got some breathing room," Matthews concluded.

"Possibly," Claire said. "But I wouldn't count on much."

Her prediction proved grimly accurate. Two days later, a second body was discovered in a converted warehouse loft in Fells Point. Same setup: multiple mirrors, postmortem makeup, carefully chosen outfit. But this time the victim was male, Thomas Reid, thirty-four, a personal trainer.

Claire arrived to find Martinez already processing the scene, her efficient movements betraying none of the frustration Claire knew she must be feeling.

"The unsub's evolving," Claire said after her initial examination. "The first scene was about forcing self-reflection. This is about transformation." She pointed to the mirrors. "They're arranged differently. Sandra's were about seeing every angle at once. These create infinite reflections, endless copies stretching into nothing."

"Both victims had undergone major physical changes," Martinez noted, consulting her notes. "Sandra with weight loss, Thomas with bodybuilding. His Instagram was full of progress pics, before and after transformations."

"It's not about the changes themselves," Claire said, more certain with each detail she cataloged. "It's about the gap between reality and perception. Both victims documented their transformations publicly but struggled privately." She turned to Martinez. "We need to find anyone else in the area who's been publicly showcasing major physical transformations. The killer is choosing victims who exemplify this disconnect."

The loft was minimalist, all concrete and exposed pipes, the perfect backdrop for Thomas Reid's carefully curated social media presence. His phone had been placed in his hand, positioned so the screen reflected in the largest mirror. On screen was his own Instagram profile, open to a before and after photo from three years earlier. Skinny to muscled, insecure to confident, at least on the surface.

"Check his medicine cabinet," Claire instructed one of the crime scene techs. "Look for antidepressants, anti-anxiety meds, anything indicating psychological struggles."

The tech returned with an amber prescription bottle. "Escitalopram, 20mg. Prescribed by Dr. Karl Bennet."

"That's our connection," Claire said, turning to Martinez. "Not Warner specifically, but the psychiatric community specializing in body image. Check if Bennet and Warner know each other, any professional overlap."

As they continued processing the scene, Claire noted the precise arrangement of the mirrors. Unlike the semicircle in Sandra Wells' bathroom, these were positioned to create endless recursive reflections, the victim's image repeating infinitely in diminishing perspective.

"The staging is more sophisticated," she observed. "Our unsub is refining their technique, becoming more confident."

The victim's roommate, Alex Garrison, arrived as they were finishing their preliminary investigation. Another personal trainer, his muscular frame seemed at odds with his obvious emotional distress.

"Thomas was obsessed with perfection," he told Claire during their interview in the building's lobby. "Not just with his body, but with how others perceived him. He'd take a hundred photos to get one for Instagram, spend hours editing it. And he was never satisfied."

"Did he talk about why?" Claire asked gently. "What drove that need for perfection?"

Alex shrugged. "He grew up skinny, got bullied a lot. When he started transforming himself, getting stronger, he said it was like becoming a different person. But sometimes I'd catch him looking in the mirror with this weird expression, like he was looking at a stranger."

"Did he use any specific photo editing apps?" Martinez asked. "Something called Perfect Lens, maybe?"

Alex nodded. "Yeah, all the time. Said it was the best for muscle definition, showing off his gains without looking obviously edited. Cost like twenty bucks a month for the premium filters, but he said it was worth it."

Claire and Martinez exchanged a glance. The connection was growing stronger.

"One more question," Claire said. "Did Thomas ever mention feeling like someone was watching him? Any unusual fans or followers online who showed too much interest?"

"There was one person," Alex said slowly. "About a month ago, Thomas mentioned someone who kept commenting on his transformation posts, asking specific questions about his psychological state, how it felt to become someone new. Thomas blocked them eventually, said the questions were getting too personal, almost invasive."

"Do you remember the username?" Martinez leaned forward.

"Something about mirrors... MirroredTruth or ReflectedSoul, something like that." Alex said. "Thomas said he thought the person might be a psychologist or something because the questions were so clinical."

Back at the precinct, Claire spread photos from both crime scenes across the conference room table. The similarities were unmistakable once you knew what to look for, both scenes staged with the victims positioned to confront their reflections, both with makeup applied to highlight the physical characteristics they'd worked so hard to transform, both found with their social media profiles open to before and after photos.

"We need to search platforms for these usernames," Claire told the tech analyst assigned to their case. "MirroredTruth, ReflectedSoul or anything similar. Focus on accounts that interact with transformation posts, weight loss journeys, bodybuilding progress."

That night, Claire couldn't sleep. She sat on her balcony until 1 AM, chain smoking and watching the occasional car crawl through the streets below. Darwin had given up trying to coax her inside and was sleeping under her desk.

She thought about her own transformation, the photos she refused to keep from before sobriety. She'd been good at hiding it near the end, functioning alcoholics usually were, but mirrors had been her tell. She'd stopped being able to look at herself while she poured drinks, had covered the bathroom mirror with a towel during her worst binges. Even now, she usually got ready in the morning with just the medicine cabinet mirror, avoiding the full-length one on her closet door.

The anonymous mirror she'd received still troubled her. Its timing, just hours before the discovery of Sandra Wells' body, couldn't be coincidence. But if it was connected to the killer, why send it to her specifically? Was it a taunt? A clue? A warning?

She returned to her laptop, digging deeper into both victims' online presences. There was something she was missing, some connection beyond the surface similarities. She pulled up Thomas Reid's Instagram, reading through comments on his transformation posts. Most were supportive, generic encouragement or questions about his workout routine. A few came from profiles specializing in fitness. But one username caught her attention, appearing repeatedly on posts showcasing particularly dramatic changes: TruthfulReflection.

The comments were superficially positive but contained odd undertones, questions about whether Thomas ever felt disconnected from his reflection, whether his new body felt like a costume he was wearing. Claire checked the account's other activity and found similar comments on dozens of transformation accounts, including Sandra Wells'.

The break came at 4 AM, when she was cross-referencing social media posts from both victims. She found it in the metadata; both had used the same photo editing app to prepare their transformation photos. Not just the same app, but the same premium filter package, purchased within days of each other three months ago. It wasn't much, but it was a thread.

She called Martinez, disregarding the hour. "I found a connection. Check out an account called TruthfulReflection. Comments on both victims' transformation posts, and probably others. The language is revealing, questioning the authenticity of physical transformation, suggesting it's a form of deception."

Martinez's voice was gravelly with sleep but alert. "I'll get the tech team on it first thing. You should try to get some rest, Claire. You sound wired."

"I'm fine," she lied, popping another tic tac. "Just following the thread."

"The thread will still be there after a few hours of sleep. You know how you get when you don't rest." Martinez's tone was gentle but firm. "We need you sharp."

Claire knew she was right. After six months working together, Martinez had learned to recognize when Claire was pushing herself too hard, falling into old patterns that had once led to the bottle. The detective had become not just a colleague but a friend, one of the few people who understood Claire's drive without judging the demons that fueled it.

"Fine," Claire conceded. "But call me the second you get anything on that account."

She managed three restless hours of sleep before her phone buzzed. Darwin, perched on her chest, meowed in protest as she fumbled for the device.

"Morrison," she answered, voice still thick with sleep.

"We've got a hit on the TruthfulReflection account," Martinez said. "IP address traces back to a Michael Smith, former lead developer for a photo editing app company called Aperture Dynamics. Guess what their most popular product is?"

"Perfect Lens," Claire said, already rolling out of bed. "Where is he now?"

"That's the problem. Address on file is an apartment Smith moved out of three months ago. Current location unknown. But I've got more. Smith wrote a blog post six months ago about the ethics of photo manipulation, criticized their own work in creating filters that 'distort reality and corrupt authentic self-perception.' A month later, he was fired after a dispute with management."

"Send me everything you've got on him," Claire said, hunting for clean clothes. "I'll meet you at the station in thirty."

The app company cooperated quickly once they understood the stakes. Claire and Martinez spent the next day running down everyone in the Baltimore area who'd purchased that specific filter package in the last three months. By midnight, they had a promising lead: David Foster, 45, professional photographer specializing in "transformation photography," before and after shots for weight loss clients, fitness competitions, and plastic surgery practices.

"Look at his website," Claire told Martinez, turning her laptop to show her. "Every shot is about reflection and mirrors. Foster calls it 'capturing the moment of self-recognition.'" She clicked through the portfolio. "These aren't just before and after photos. They're studies in dysphoria, the disconnect between perception and reality."

They brought Foster in for questioning, but Claire knew before he opened his mouth that he wasn't their killer. His relationship with mirrors was professional, aesthetic. He didn't understand their power as instruments of torture.

"I know Michael Smith," Foster confirmed when they showed him the photo. "He consulted on a project I did last year, a series on physical transformation and identity. Brilliant person, but intense. Kept talking about how we were complicit in cultural delusion, helping people hide from themselves."

"When did you last have contact with Smith?" Martinez asked.

"About two months ago. Mike reached out about collaborating on what was called 'a project about authentic reflection.' Wanted to use my studio space. I turned him down, something about his energy felt off. He had changed since I worked with him before, become almost fanatical about these ideas."

"Do you know where Smith's working now? Any other photographers or studios he might have connections with?"

Foster thought for a moment. "There's an old photography studio in Fell's Point that closed down last year. Echo Paradigm, I think it was called. Mike mentioned it once; said it was a shame to see all that equipment gathering dust. If he was looking for space with proper lighting setups and backdrops, that might be worth checking."

The third scene appeared before they could find another lead. This time in a department store after hours by the cleaning crew; the victim posed in a three-way mirror in the closed fitting room. Claire stood in the doorway, fighting a wave of nausea as she cataloged the scene.

"Jessica Michaels, 29," Martinez said, reading from her notes. "She was a plastic surgery consultant. Had multiple procedures herself."

Claire stepped closer. This victim wore a hospital gown instead of expensive clothes. The makeup was different too, designed to highlight recent scars, not conceal them. The mirrors were arranged to create an infinite loop of reflections, each showing a slightly different version of Jessica.

"The unsub's dropping the pretense," Claire said, her voice hoarse. She cleared her throat, tried again. "The first scene was about forcing self-reflection. The second was about the impossibility of transformation. This…" She gestured to the endless reflections. "This is about the futility of trying to fix what's on the outside."

She moved closer, noting the precise positioning of each mirror. The largest one had a message written in lipstick across the top: "No filter can fix what's broken inside." The handwriting was precise, the letters perfectly spaced.

"They're getting bolder," Claire said, popping a tic tac. "More explicit in the messaging. The unsub wants to be understood now, not just feared."

She felt a flutter of anxiety in her chest, the tight knot that formed whenever a case started getting under her skin. Over two years ago, she would have reached for a drink, something to numb the edges.

"I need everything we can find on Jessica Michaels," she told Martinez. "Social media, medical history if we can get it, and especially any connection to the companies or Michael Smith."

After the techs finished processing the scene, Claire examined the lipstick message more closely. The shade was expensive, she recognized it as a brand she couldn't afford on her government salary. The application was steady, no shaking or hesitation, suggesting confidence and practice.

"The mirrors," she said suddenly. "They're different at each scene, but they all feel curated, chosen specifically."

Martinez looked up from her notes. "What are you thinking?"

"We need to trace these mirrors, find out where they came from. Not just the antique dealers, but storage facilities, estate sales, anywhere someone could acquire multiple vintage mirrors."

Back at the precinct, with three murder boards now filled with crime scene photos and victim information, Chief Matthews called Claire and Martinez into his office.

"The press is starting to connect these cases," he said. "We've managed to keep the details of the mirror arrangements quiet, but they've got the basics, three victims in two weeks, all with some connection to physical transformation."

"We're closing in," Claire assured him. "Michael Smith is our primary suspect. Former app developer who created filters for Perfect Lens, then had some kind of ethical crisis about their effect on users' self-perception. We've traced recent activity to an abandoned photography studio in Fell's Point."

"Then get a warrant and check it out," Matthews ordered. "I want this wrapped up before we have a full-blown panic about a serial killer targeting people with body image issues. Half the city would qualify as potential victims."

The abandoned photography studio, Echo Paradigm, occupied the ground floor of a converted warehouse. The windows had been covered with black paper from the inside, and a chain secured the front door; Claire noticed signs of recent activity, the lock appeared well-maintained, and there was a clear path through the accumulated dust and debris near the side entrance.

"SWAT's on standby," Martinez said as they approached, her hand resting on her holstered weapon. "Warrant covers the entire premises. They're ready if we need them."

The side door opened with surprising ease, suggesting recent use despite the building's abandoned appearance. Inside, they found a fully equipped photography studio, with multiple backdrop setups, lighting equipment, and most disturbingly, a collection of antique mirrors similar to those found at the previous crime scenes.

"This is it," Claire said, examining the workspace without touching anything. "Look at the setup, perfect for staging the scenes and documenting them."

On a desk in the corner, they found a laptop connected to a high-end digital camera. Martinez, wearing gloves, carefully opened it to find a password screen.

"We'll need tech for this," she said, already reaching for her phone.

Claire moved deeper into the studio, her attention drawn to a large curtained area at the back. Pulling the heavy fabric aside, she revealed what could only be described as a work in progress, a circle of mirrors arranged around an empty chair, positioned under professional lighting.

"He's planning another one," she called to Martinez. "The setup's already in place."

As they waited for the tech team to arrive and process the scene, Claire examined the mirrors more closely. Each was different, some antique, some modern, some distorting, some crystal clear. Together they created a complete visual catalog of whatever would be placed in that central chair, capturing every possible angle and perspective.

"It's a fishbowl," she said softly. "No privacy, nowhere to hide from your own reflection."

The tech team arrived and began processing the scene, focusing first on the laptop, which proved to be encrypted but not beyond their capabilities. Within an hour, they had access, revealing folders of photographs that confirmed their worst fears.

"He documented everything," the tech specialist reported, turning the screen so Claire and Martinez could see. "Each murder, meticulously photographed from preparation to final scene. And there are more folders, labeled with dates and names we don't recognize yet."

"Previous victims?" Martinez suggested.

"Or future ones," Claire said grimly. "Check those names against our database and social media. Look for transformation narratives, weight loss journeys, plastic surgery, bodybuilding, anything that aligns with our victims' profiles."

The search yielded immediate results. Three additional names in Smith's folders corresponded to local residents who maintained active social media accounts showcasing body transformations, a woman who'd lost significant weight after bariatric surgery, a man documenting his transition, and a former athlete recovering from a career-ending injury.

"We need protective details on all three immediately," Martinez ordered, already on the phone with dispatch. "And an APB and BOLO on Michael Smith."

While the tech team continued processing the digital evidence, Claire examined a corkboard mounted on the wall behind the desk. It was covered with photographs of people, some she recognized as the victims, others unfamiliar, alongside handwritten notes analyzing their "authenticity scores" and "reflection integrity." Smith had been creating a rating system, evaluating people based on how closely their public image matched what he perceived as their true selves.

"Listen to this," Claire called to Martinez, pointing to a journal open on the desk. "'Subject 3 represents the ultimate deception, surgically altering her appearance while counseling others about body acceptance. Her reflection must be forced into alignment with her true nature.' He's justifying the murders as some kind of moral correction."

"Classic grandiose delusion," Martinez agreed, joining her at the desk. "He sees himself as revealing truth, not committing murder."

"The staging is the point," Claire added, pieces falling into place. "The killing is just the means to create his tableaux. He needs them dead to manipulate them completely, to position them exactly as he envisions."

Their examination was interrupted by a call from one of the officers stationed at a potential victim's home. "Detective, we've got a situation at the Parker residence. The subject didn't answer when we knocked. After repeated attempts, we entered to find signs of a struggle. She's gone, and there's blood on the floor."

Martinez cursed under her breath. "Emma Parker, the bariatric surgery patient. How long ago?"

"Can't say for sure. We were checking in on fifteen-minute intervals. Last confirmed visual was approximately forty minutes ago."

Claire was already heading for the door. "He moved faster than we anticipated. The preparations we found weren't for a future scene; they're for tonight. He already has her."

"But where would he take her?" Martinez asked, falling into step beside her. "Not back here, he has to know we've found this place."

Claire stopped suddenly, her mind racing through the evidence they'd collected. "The mirrors at each scene were different, chosen specifically for the location and victim. What if each location is significant too?"

"The department store fitting room," Martinez recalled. "Jessica Michaels was a plastic surgery consultant who helped clients choose their 'new look'."

Claire nodded. "And Thomas Reid was found in his loft, where he took most of his transformation photos. Sandra Wells was positioned in her own bathroom, where she'd have seen her changing reflection daily." She pulled out her phone, quickly searching for information on Emma Parker. "Parker works as a nutritional counselor at Mercy Hospital. She'd have access to..."

"The diet center," Martinez finished, already dialing for backup.

The hospital was eerily quiet as they approached through the staff entrance, following the directions of a security guard who'd confirmed seeing someone matching Smith's description entering with a cleaning cart thirty minutes earlier. The diet and nutrition center occupied a section of the third floor that housed outpatient services, most of which were closed for the evening.

"No alarms triggered," the security supervisor reported as they gathered in the monitoring room. "But we have limited coverage in the nutrition center itself, privacy concerns for patients."

Claire studied the floor plan. "Is there a room with mirrors? Anywhere patients might evaluate their physical progress?"

"There's a body composition room," the supervisor confirmed. "It has a full-length three-way mirror setup for patients to track their visual progress alongside the medical measurements."

"That's where he'll be," Claire said with certainty. "He'll want her to see every angle of herself as he creates his scene."

SWAT assembled quickly, with Claire and Martinez hanging back as they prepared to enter. The team leader outlined the approach, two entry points, simultaneous breach, minimum force necessary to secure the hostage.

"Our suspect may be armed, but is primarily motivated by a desire to complete his ritual," Claire advised. "Interrupting that process will be deeply disturbing to him, potentially triggering violence. The priority has to be securing the victim before he can harm her."

The breach went precisely as planned, the team entering through both doors of the body composition room simultaneously. Inside, they found exactly what Claire had feared, Emma Parker strapped to a chair in front of the three-way mirror, her face streaked with tears but alive. Michael Smith stood behind her, a syringe in his hand, his expression one of frustrated rage at the interruption.

"You don't understand what you're stopping," he shouted as officers secured him. "She needs to see her true self! They all do! The filters, the angles, the lighting tricks, it's all deception!"

As medical personnel attended to Parker, who had been drugged but not seriously injured, Claire approached Smith cautiously. The man was thin to the point of gauntness, with hollow cheeks and dark circles under eyes that burned with zealous conviction. He didn't look like a killer; he looked like someone consumed by a mission.

"The mirror you sent me," Claire said, standing just out of reach as officers prepared to transport him. "Why? Were you warning me? Taunting me?"

Smith regarded her with an eerie calm that contrasted with his earlier outburst. "I recognized something in you, Dr. Morrison. You understand reflection. You've looked into the darkness of the glass and seen your true self looking back. Not many people have that courage."

A chill ran down Claire's spine at the personal recognition. "How do you know who I am?"

"I do my research, Doctor. Your recovery journey is documented in academic circles. 'Substance use disorder as a response to cognitive dissonance in high-functioning professionals', that was the journal article, wasn't it? Your father's analysis of your case, published without your name but with enough details for those who know how to look."

Claire felt the blood drain from her face. Her father had published a case study, anonymized but recognizable to anyone who knew their connection, during the first year of her sobriety. It had been the final breach that had severed their relationship until the tentative reconnection following the Harrison case.

"That still doesn't explain the mirror," she pressed, fighting to maintain her professional demeanor.

"A gift from one truth-seeker to another," Smith replied, his voice taking on an almost gentle quality. "Some people spend their lives avoiding their reflection, curating false images, hiding from what the mirror shows them. You chose to face yours. I respect that."

As officers led Smith away, Claire stood motionless, disturbed by his words and the implication that he saw a kindred spirit in her. Martinez appeared at her side, her steady presence a welcome anchor.

"You okay?" the detective asked quietly.

"Fine," Claire lied, not meeting her eyes. "Let's finish processing the scene."

Back at the precinct, as Smith was processed and formally charged with three counts of murder, kidnapping, and one count of attempted murder, Claire retreated to her office. The case was essentially closed, the evidence overwhelming, no real question of Smith's guilt. Yet something still nagged at her, some loose thread she couldn't quite identify.

She spread the crime scene photos across her desk one more time, studying each scene, each mirror arrangement. There was a progression in the scenes, a building narrative from Sandra Wells to Thomas Reid to Jessica Michaels, each more elaborate, each message more explicit. And now Emma Parker, who would have been the fourth chapter in Smith's twisted story.

"A gift from one truth-seeker to another," she murmured, recalling Smith's words about the mirror he'd sent her. She removed it from her desk drawer where she'd kept it secured as evidence, turning it over in her hands. It was beautiful, vintage, the silver tarnished in ways that couldn't be faked. A genuine antique, not a reproduction.

Something about it tickled her memory. She'd seen this pattern before, the art deco floral design around the edges. Claire opened her laptop and searched through the crime scene photos until she found what she was looking for, a similar mirror, with the same design elements, that had been part of the arrangement around Sandra Wells.

"They're a set," she realized. "He sent me one from the same collection he used in his first murder."

This new connection disturbed her deeply. If the mirror had been part of a matched set, it meant Smith hadn't just sent her any mirror as a symbolic gesture, he'd specifically connected her to his first victim, to the beginning of his "truth-revealing" mission.

Her desk phone rang, interrupting her thoughts. It was Dr. Patel from the medical examiner's office.

"Dr. Morrison, I thought you should know, we've completed the preliminary toxicology on all three victims. The same compound was used in each case, a paralytic followed by a lethal injection. But there's something unusual about the timing. The paralytic was administered several hours before death, keeping the victims conscious but immobile while the killer... worked on them."

Claire felt sick. "He wanted them aware. Conscious for the make-up, the positioning, the mirrors. They saw everything he was doing to them."

"I'm afraid so," Patel confirmed. "From a forensic perspective, it's unusually cruel. The victims would have been fully aware, unable to move or speak, but experiencing everything."

After hanging up, Claire sat in silence, absorbing this new information. The cruelty wasn't just in the killing, it was in forcing the victims to witness their own transformation into Smith's idealized vision of their "true selves." The mirrors weren't just for aesthetic effect or symbolic meaning; they were instruments of torture, forcing the victims to watch their own helplessness.

Martinez appeared in her doorway, two coffee cups in hand. "Thought you could use this," she said, placing one on Claire's desk.

"Smith's been processed. He's talking freely, seems almost eager to explain his 'work' to anyone who'll listen."

Claire accepted the coffee gratefully. "Did he mention the mirrors being a matched set?"

"No, but he did say something about having more 'subjects' identified. We're going through his notes now, contacting anyone who might have been on his list." Martinez studied Claire's face with the perceptive gaze that had become familiar over their months working together. "You sure you're okay? Smith seemed to know a lot about you."

"He read an academic case study my father published," Claire explained, not meeting Martinez's eyes. "Anonymous, but identifiable to someone who knew what to look for."

Martinez's expression hardened. "Your father published details about your recovery without your consent?"

"It's complicated," Claire said, not wanting to open that particular wound. "Standard practice in medical literature, names removed, identifying details changed. Just not enough for someone determined to connect the dots."

"Still sounds like a violation to me," Martinez observed, her loyalty evident. "Especially from family."

Claire changed the subject. "Patel called. The victims were conscious during the staging. They saw everything Smith was doing to them, unable to move or speak."

"Jesus," Martinez breathed. "That's a special kind of sadism."

"Not sadism in the traditional sense," Claire corrected. "Smith doesn't derive pleasure from their suffering, it's incidental to his mission. He wants them to see their 'true selves,' and in his mind, that requires them to be conscious. The suffering is a byproduct, not the goal."

"Does that distinction matter to the victims?" Martinez asked, her practical nature cutting through the psychological theory.

Claire considered this. "No. The result is the same. But understanding his motivation helps us anticipate what he might do next."

"There is no next. He's in custody, case closed," Martinez reminded her. "We got him."

"Yes," Claire agreed, though the nagging sense of something unfinished remained. "We did."

That evening, Claire found herself once again on her small balcony, watching the city lights shimmer across the harbor. Darwin had abandoned his usual protest at the cold and joined her, curled in her lap seeking warmth. The case was solved, the killer apprehended, three future victims saved from Smith's "truth-revealing" mission. By any measure, it was a success.

Yet Smith's words continued to echo in her mind. "You've looked into the darkness of the glass and seen your true self looking back."

Had she? During the worst days of her drinking, she'd avoided mirrors entirely, unable to face the disconnection between how she saw herself and what the mirror showed. The eyes looking back at her had belonged to a stranger, someone hollowed out by addiction, someone she refused to recognize. It was only in recovery that she'd begun to reconcile those fractured reflections, to see herself clearly in all her complexity.

Her phone rang, interrupting her thoughts. Dr. Leland, her therapist.

"I heard about the case," Leland said. "The mirrors, the psychological manipulation. Are you processing it all right?"

Claire smiled slightly at the directness. Leland never pretended their relationship was anything other than what it was, a professional therapeutic connection, not a friendship, but one built on genuine care.

"I'm fine," she said automatically, then caught herself. "Actually, I'm disturbed by how much the killer seemed to know about me. How he claimed to see a parallel between us."

"That's common with this type of perpetrator," Leland reminded her. "They project their own distorted worldview onto others, seeking validation by claiming connection with people they perceive as similar."

"I know that intellectually," Claire acknowledged. "But emotionally, it got under my skin. The idea that he sent me that mirror because he saw me as someone who'd understand his mission..."

"Does it bother you because you're afraid there might be some truth to it?" Leland asked gently. "That somewhere in his distorted perception, he recognized something genuine about your own journey with self-reflection?"

Claire was silent for a moment, considering. "Maybe. During my drinking days, I created an elaborate false image for the world, competent, controlled, functional. The mirror didn't lie, but I refused to see what it showed me. There's a parallel there, I suppose, to what Smith was trying to expose in his victims."

"The difference being consent and agency," Leland pointed out. "You chose to confront your reflection. His victims had that choice taken from them. That distinction matters tremendously."

"Yes," Claire agreed, feeling the knot in her chest loosen slightly. "It does."

After ending the call, she sat with Darwin a while longer, watching his steady breathing, the simple contentment of a creature unburdened by complex self-reflection. There was wisdom in that simplicity, she thought. The ability to be fully present in one's own skin without the constant evaluation and re-evaluation that plagued human consciousness.

The next morning, she arrived at the precinct to find Martinez already at her desk, a case file open before her.

"There's been a development," the detective said, looking up as Claire approached. "Remember how we thought all the mirrors were antiques, collected over time by Smith?"

"Yes, part of his deliberate aesthetic."

"Well, it turns out the mirrors in the Sandra Wells scene were purchased from an estate sale three weeks ago. Paid for with a credit card belonging to Lindsay Crawford, not Michael Smith."

Claire frowned. "Who's Lindsay Crawford?"

"That's what I've been trying to figure out. No obvious connection to Smith that I can find. She's 31, works as a graphic designer for a marketing firm downtown. No criminal record, no apparent interest in photography or mirrors or any of Smith's obsessions."

"We need to talk to her," Claire said, the loose thread she'd been sensing now beginning to unravel. "What about the mirrors from the other scenes?"

"Tech is tracking the purchases now. But here's where it gets really interesting, the mirror Smith sent you? It was purchased at the same estate sale as the ones used in the Wells scene, but it was a separate transaction, different credit card. This one belonging to a David Kline, another person with no obvious connection to Smith."

Claire's mind raced, connecting dots. "Smith wasn't working alone. He had accomplices, people helping him acquire materials, possibly helping with the scenes themselves."

"That's what I'm thinking," Martinez agreed. "The question is, how many?"

The investigation shifted focus, expanding to identify Smith's potential network. Lindsay Crawford was brought in for questioning, initially denying any connection to the murders. But when confronted with the credit card evidence, she broke down, admitting she'd met Smith through an online forum dedicated to "authentic perception" and "visual truth."

"Mike helped me see how filtered everything has become," she explained, tears streaming down her face. "How we're all living behind screens and edits and careful angles. He was trying to show people the truth, that's all."

"By murdering them?" Martinez asked incredulously.

"They were already dead inside," Crawford insisted, her voice taking on the same zealous quality they'd heard from Smith. "Walking around with fabricated exteriors, deceiving everyone, even themselves. He was just making their outsides match their insides."

Claire studied Crawford carefully, noting the genuine belief in her eyes. "How many of you are there? People helping Michael with his mission?"

Crawford hesitated, then lifted her chin defiantly. "We call ourselves the True Reflection Collective. There are seven of us in Baltimore. But we're everywhere, in every city where people hide behind filters and surgeries and fake transformations."

Claire and Martinez exchanged glances. If Smith had indeed created a network of like-minded individuals, the case was far from closed.

"We need names," Martinez said firmly. "Everyone in this 'collective.'"

"I can't," Crawford replied, her defiance crumbling into fear. "They'll know I betrayed the mission. Mike was just the first phase. There's so much more to come."

The revelation of a larger conspiracy sent the investigation into high gear. Search warrants were obtained for Crawford's apartment and electronic devices. The "True Reflection Collective" turned out to be real, with members communicating through encrypted messaging and private forums. Smith was indeed their ideological leader, but the group had developed its own momentum.

"It's like a cult," Claire explained to Chief Matthews as they reviewed the evidence. "Smith tapped into people's discomfort with our increasingly filtered reality. He offered them a mission, a purpose, to expose what they see as society's epidemic of self-deception."

"And this mission involves murdering people who use filters on their selfies?" Matthews asked incredulously.

"It's more specific than that," Claire clarified. "They target individuals who publicly document physical transformations while privately struggling with the psychological aftermath. People whose external changes haven't resolved their internal issues. In their warped worldview, these individuals represent the ultimate deception."

The investigation expanded, with officers tracking down each member of the Baltimore collective. Three were arrested while preparing what appeared to be another murder scene, complete with mirrors and makeup kits. The others went underground, their digital footprints vanishing as word of the arrests spread.

A week after Smith's capture, as the larger case against the collective took shape, Claire found herself once again examining the mirror that had started it all. Forensics had cleared it as evidence, allowing her to reclaim it. She turned it over in her hands, studying her own reflection in the slightly tarnished surface.

The face that looked back at her was tired but clear-eyed. Her recovery had erased the puffiness, the bloodshot eyes, the slight tremor that had once been her constant companions. She wasn't entirely comfortable with her reflection yet, might never be, but she no longer feared what the mirror showed her.

Martinez appeared in her office doorway. "Judge granted the warrants for the servers hosting the collective's forums. We should have access by tomorrow."

Claire nodded, setting the mirror aside. "Good. We need to understand how far this network extends, whether there are cells in other cities."

Martinez stepped into the office, closing the door behind her. "Are you keeping that?" she asked, gesturing to the mirror.

"I'm not sure," Claire admitted. "Part of me wants to get rid of it, given its connection to the case. But another part feels like that would be... I don't know, avoiding something important."

"The mirror isn't the problem," Martinez observed, perching on the edge of Claire's desk. "It's just an object. The meaning we attach to it, that's what matters."

Claire smiled slightly. "That's very philosophical for a homicide detective."

"I contain multitudes," Martinez replied with a rare smile. "Besides, working with a forensic psychologist rubs off on you eventually."

Their conversation was interrupted by a call from the tech team. Another member of the collective had been identified, this one working at the company that developed the Perfect Lens app. The investigation continued to expand, revealing a network more extensive than they'd initially imagined.

As Claire gathered her things to join Martinez at the new suspect's workplace, she glanced once more at the mirror on her desk. Smith had been right about one thing, she had learned to face her reflection honestly. But unlike his victims, she'd made that choice herself, undertaken that journey willingly.

The distinction, as Dr. Leland had reminded her, mattered tremendously. It was the difference between growth and violation, between healing and harm. Between a perfect mirror that showed truth and a distorted one that showed only what the viewer wanted to see.

She locked the mirror in her desk drawer before leaving. Whatever power it held, whatever message Smith had intended by sending it, she wouldn't let it dictate her perception of herself or the case. Some reflections were worth facing; others were simply distortions best left behind.

As she joined Martinez in the precinct lobby, Claire felt the familiar weight of her sobriety chip in her pocket, a more meaningful talisman than any mirror could ever be. It represented not just who she had been or who she was now, but the choice she made every day to see herself clearly, without filters or deception.

"Ready?" Martinez asked, holding the door.

"Ready," Claire confirmed, stepping out into the crisp November afternoon.

Chapter Three

Skin Deep

Claire Morrison gazed down at the corpse lying on the steel table beneath the morgue's fluorescent lights. The victim, Jason Cooley, 35, lay perfectly composed, arms at his sides, expression peaceful. At first glance, there was nothing unusual, another overdose in a city that had seen too many. But Claire knew better. Her trained eye caught what others might miss: a slight discoloration at the edges of the elaborate tattoo that covered the man's chest.

"This wasn't here before," she said, leaning closer to examine the intricate design. A stylized scale of justice dominated the artwork, surrounded by an ornate pattern of thorns and roses. Each element was rendered with exceptional skill, the lines clean and precise, the shading subtle and dimensional.

Detective Sara Martinez nodded as she consulted her notes. "According to his girlfriend, Mr. Cooley had a small tattoo of a star on his chest. Nothing like this."

Claire studied Martinez's face. The small scar beneath her right eye she'd never asked about, the military-straight posture that spoke of a disciplined background. After working together on the Harrison case and then the mirror killers, they'd developed a rapport that made their collaboration increasingly effective.

Dr. Patel, the medical examiner, pointed to the skin around the tattoo. "The ink was applied post-mortem, within six to eight hours after death. No inflammation response, no bleeding into the tissue. Whoever did this knew what they were doing. The technique is flawless."

Claire pulled a packet of tic tacs from her pocket, popping one into her mouth. The mint flavor didn't help clear the antiseptic smell of the morgue from her senses. Two years and 5 months sober, and she'd traded one oral fixation for another, less destructive one.

"The artwork is telling us something," she said, pulling out her phone to take detailed photographs. "These aren't random images. The scales of justice, the thorns... there's symbolism here. A message."

"Cause of death?" Martinez asked, turning to Dr. Patel.

"Fentanyl overdose, but an excessive amount; much more than a typical street dose. And there's no visible injection site anywhere on the body, which is unusual. I've examined him thoroughly, and there's no puncture mark, no bruising, nothing to indicate how the drug entered his system. So, most probably through his skin or ingested."

Claire circled the table, studying the tattoo from different angles. The design was beautiful in a macabre way, the kind of work that would cost thousands from a top artist. Whoever had created it had significant skill and artistic vision. But more than that, they understood the power of symbolism, the language of visual metaphor.

"We need to check if there have been other cases like this," she said, her mind already assembling the profile. "The level of detail, the quality of the work, this isn't a first-time effort. And the post-mortem timing suggests this is about transforming the victim, making a statement about them."

Martinez nodded. "I'll have the team run a search for similar cases, see if anything matches the M.O. What's your initial read on the unsub?"

Claire stepped back from the table, letting her mind process what she'd observed. "We're looking for someone with extensive knowledge of tattooing, obviously. But also, someone who believes they're delivering justice or making a statement. The scales on the chest tell us that much. This isn't random. The unsub chose this victim specifically and created a design that speaks to some perceived wrong or failing."

"Avenging angel complex?" Martinez suggested, her brow furrowing.

"Possibly. Or a morality enforcer. Someone who believes they're exposing the truth about their victims." Claire's phone buzzed with a text from Chief Matthews: Another body with a tattoo. 1650 Park Avenue.

Claire held up her phone to show Martinez. "Looks like we've got a pattern."

The crime scene was a tidy apartment in an upscale neighborhood, the kind of place that spoke of careful curation rather than actual living. The victim, Elizabeth Markham, 42, lay on her bed, positioned as if asleep. Like Cooley, she had been given a post-mortem tattoo, this one covering her left forearm and extending onto her palm.

"Peacock feathers," Claire observed, crouching to study the intricate design. "And look at these small symbols hidden within the pattern."

Martinez leaned in. "They look like tiny eyes."

"Eyes that see everything," Claire murmured. "Our unsub is making a statement about witnessing. Dr. Patel, preliminary COD?"

"Similar to Mr. Cooley. Overdose with no visible means of administration. I'll know more after the autopsy."

Claire stood, her knees protesting after too long in a crouched position. She was only 34, but some days her body reminded her of every late night, every stress-filled case, every year she'd spent poisoning herself with alcohol before getting sober. Her body kept score, as Dr. Leland often reminded her.

"The unsub sees themselves as exposing truth," she said, piecing together the emerging profile. "The tattoos are revelations, not desecrations. In the unsub's mind, they're creating art that reveals something essential about each victim."

"How are they choosing the victims?" Matthews asked from the doorway. He'd arrived minutes earlier, his bulky frame making the spacious bedroom feel suddenly cramped. "Any connection between Cooley and Markham?"

Claire shook her head. "Nothing obvious. Mr. Cooley was a paralegal at a corporate law firm, lived in Fells Point. Ms. Markham was a marketing executive for a cosmetics company, lived here in Mount Vernon. Different social circles, different life patterns."

"But the unsub connected them somehow," Martinez added. "These aren't random targets."

Claire's phone buzzed again. A text from the tech analyst at the precinct: Found a similar case from six weeks ago. Victim Theodore Walsh, 39. Post-mortem tattoos of broken chains on his legs.

She showed the message to Martinez and Matthews. "We've got a serial killer."

"Three victims that we know of," Matthews said grimly. "I want a task force on this. Morrison, you'll take point on the profile. Martinez, coordinate with the tech team to find any other connections between these victims. I want to know everything, where they shopped, who cut their hair, which coffee shops they frequented. Someone saw these people and marked them for death."

When sleep proved elusive that night, Claire found herself at Rusty's Diner, her occasional late-night haunt and unofficial office during the midnight hours. The vinyl booth in the corner had become her refuge on nights like these, when case details swarmed her mind like angry hornets.

"Well, look who's back," Betty said, coffeepot already poised over a fresh mug. "It's been a few months since I've seen you. Regular?" The waitress's gray-streaked hair was pulled back in a practical ponytail, her eyes kind but knowing. From Claire's previous late-night visits, they'd developed a quiet understanding.

"Please," Claire nodded, spreading crime scene photos across the table. Betty was one of the few civilians who didn't flinch at such sights, having seen just about everything in her thirty years working Baltimore's night shift.

"Rough one?" Betty asked, placing a slice of apple pie next to the coffee. "On the house. You look like you could use the sugar."

"Thanks, Betty." Claire managed a smile. "Yeah, this one's getting under my skin."

"Well, I'll leave you to it. Holler if you need a refill." Betty retreated, creating the perfect balance of availability and privacy that made Rusty's ideal for Claire's midnight ruminations.

Claire studied the three victims' photos, searching for connections. Three elaborate tattoos, each telling a different story. The scales of justice for Cooley, the watchful peacock feathers for Markham, and broken chains for Walsh. What was the unsub trying to say?

She popped another tic tac, eyes burning from fatigue. The diner's quiet hum of late-night activity faded to background noise as she lost herself in the details.

Later that morning at the precinct, Claire spread crime scene photos across the conference room table. Darwin, her orange tabby, somehow materialized on the chair beside her, having escaped from her office again. The cat had developed an uncanny ability to find her no matter where she went in the building, a talent that both amused and unnerved her colleagues.

"Your FBI is here again," Martinez said, dropping a stack of files on the table. She'd seen "Furry Bureau of Investigation" in a meme somewhere and thought it was too perfect not to use for Darwin, especially after the cat had proven adept at finding crucial evidence by knocking it off desks.

"He knows when I'm onto something," Claire replied, absently stroking Darwin's orange fur. The physical contact helped ground her, kept her from falling too deeply into the dark minds she studied. "Did the tech team find any connections between the victims?"

"Nothing obvious yet. Different gyms, grocery stores, and social circles." Martinez pulled up a chair. "But they're digging deeper. Financial records, phone logs, social media activity. If there's a connection, we'll find it."

Claire nodded, turning her attention back to the photos. "These tattoos were chosen specifically for each victim. The unsub knows something about them, something they believe deserves exposure." She tapped the image of Cooley's chest. "Scales of justice for a paralegal, maybe suggesting corruption or imbalance in his work? Markham gets watching eyes, perhaps the unsub felt she was hiding something behind a carefully maintained appearance?"

"And Walsh? The broken chains?"

Claire studied the photo of the first victim's legs. "Freedom from something? Or someone breaking free of his influence? We need to know more about who these people were, not just on paper but in reality."

"I'll talk to their friends, families, coworkers," Martinez offered. "See if there are any skeletons these victims might have been hiding."

"Good. And I want to consult with tattoo artists in the area. The level of skill displayed here is exceptional. This isn't amateur work. We're looking for someone with significant training and experience." Claire gathered the photos. "I'm going to map these designs, see if there's any pattern when we look at all three together."

That night, Claire spread the case files across her apartment floor, Darwin watching from his perch on the bookshelf. The victims' lives laid out in paper and photographs seemed disconnected on the surface, different jobs, neighborhoods, and social circles. But the unsub had seen something that linked them, some pattern invisible to everyone else.

She moved to her meditation corner, a small space with a cushion and the bronze Buddha statue. The corner remained largely unused except by Darwin, who seemed to find the cushion an ideal napping spot.

She pinned photocopies of the tattoo designs to her wall, stepping back to study them collectively. Each was beautiful in its own way, the artistry undeniable. There was something familiar about the style, something she couldn't quite place. The use of light and shadow, the flowing lines that somehow seemed to move even in static images. She'd seen work like this before, but where?

Her phone rang, Martinez's name flashing on the screen.

"I think I found something," the detective said. "All three victims attended the same gallery opening eight months ago. 'Transformation' at the Lockwood Gallery in Station North. It featured body modification as art, tattoos, scarification, the works."

Claire's pulse quickened. "Who was the featured artist?"

"Several, but the headliner was someone named Ashe Blackwood. Known for 'revelatory body art' according to the gallery blurb. Get this, before becoming a tattoo artist, he studied anatomy and worked as a mortuary assistant."

"He knows how to work with dead bodies," Claire said, the profile coming into sharper focus. "Send me everything you have on Blackwood. We need to find out if our victims had any direct contact with him."

After hanging up, Claire went to her laptop, searching for Ashe Blackwood's work. The images that appeared made her catch her breath. The style was unmistakable, the same flowing lines, the same masterful use of light and shadow, the same hidden symbols embedded within larger designs. And the artist's statement on the website seemed almost prophetic considering their investigation:

"The skin is our first deception. What I create is truth made visible; the inner reality exposed for all to see. My art doesn't change the subject; it reveals what was always there."

Claire texted Martinez: Blackwood's our primary suspect. The tattoos on our victims match his artistic signature. We need surveillance on him ASAP.

She was about to close her laptop when a notification popped up, an email from Dr. Leland, her therapist. Their regular session was tomorrow, and Leland was checking if Claire wanted to reschedule given the new case. Claire hesitated, her finger hovering over the keyboard.

Well into her recovery, and she still struggled with the idea that self-care wasn't selfishness. Her instinct was to cancel, to throw herself completely into the case. But she'd learned the hard way that her sobriety depended on maintaining certain boundaries, certain rituals of health.

I'll be there; she typed back. Could use the perspective.

The next morning, Claire and Martinez briefed Matthews on their findings. The chief listened intently; his gray eyes sharp under heavy brows as they laid out the evidence connecting Blackwood to the gallery event attended by all three victims.

"It's not enough for a warrant," he said finally. "Gallery openings have dozens, sometimes hundreds of attendees. We need something more concrete connecting Blackwood to these specific victims."

"We're working on that," Martinez assured him. "The tech team is going through social media posts from the event, looking for any direct interactions between Blackwood and our victims. And we've got surveillance on Blackwood's studio and residence."

"What's your assessment of his psychological state?" Matthews asked, turning to Claire.

She popped a tic tac, gathering her thoughts. "Based on his public persona and artistic statements, Blackwood presents as someone who believes he's revealing truth through art. The tattoos on our victims aren't random; they're personalized indictments. Blackwood sees himself as exposing something hidden about each victim, some sin or failing he believes deserves to be brought to light."

"A morality killer," Matthews nodded. "But why the elaborate tattoos? Why not just kill them?"

"Because the message is as important as the act," Claire explained. "Blackwood wants these deaths to be understood as judgments, not just murders. The tattoos are both sentence and explanation."

"Do we think he's done?" Martinez asked the question they'd all been considering.

Claire shook her head. "No. The pattern is escalating. Six weeks between the first and second victims, only three weeks between the second and third. The compulsion is growing stronger. And there's something else, I think these tattoos are part of a larger design."

She spread the photos on Matthews' desk. "Look at the placement. Walsh's broken chains run across his legs. Cooley's scales cover his chest. Markham's peacock feathers extend down her left arm. If you mapped them onto a single body, they'd create a connected design."

"Jesus," Matthews muttered. "How many more pieces in this sick puzzle?"

"I don't know yet," Claire admitted. "But we need to know before he completes it."

Her session with Dr. Leland that afternoon provided a brief respite from the intensity of the case. Leland's office was the same as always, warm lighting, comfortable chairs, the subtle scent of lavender in the air. The familiarity helped ease the tension that had been building between Claire's shoulder blades all day.

"You seem preoccupied," Leland observed. At sixty-two, she carried herself with the quiet confidence of someone who had seen humanity at its worst and best and remained unshaken by either.

"New case," Claire said, settling into her usual chair. "Someone is killing people and giving them elaborate tattoos post-mortem."

"And it's affecting you more than usual," Leland noted. Not a question.

Claire nodded, finding the smooth surface of her sobriety chip in her pocket. "The tattoos are beautiful, in a disturbing way. Art created in the aftermath of violence. It's making me think about transformation, about how we change our bodies to reflect something inside us."

"Or to hide something," Leland suggested.

"Yes." Claire's mind flashed to her own small tattoo, a simple Celtic knot on her wrist, gotten during her first year of sobriety. A reminder of interconnection, of the way everything in life tied together. "The killer seems to believe they're exposing truth about their victims. But it's their truth, their perception."

"Much like your last case with the mirrors," Leland observed. "Another killer imposing their view of reality onto victims."

Claire hadn't made the connection consciously, but Leland was right. Michael Smith and his cult had forced victims to confront reflections stripped of filters and deception. Blackwood was inscribing his judgment directly onto victims' skin. Both were about exposure, about stripping away what the killers saw as falsehood.

"There's something almost intimate about it," Claire admitted. "The killer spends hours with the victims after death, creating something permanent on their skin. It's violation, but it's also..."

"Art," Leland finished for her. "And that's what disturbs you. The blurred line between creation and destruction."

Claire nodded, grateful as always for Leland's ability to articulate what she couldn't quite grasp herself. "The killer believes they're revealing something true about these people. But truth is subjective, isn't it? What gives anyone the right to permanently mark another person with their version of reality?"

"A question worth exploring," Leland agreed. "Especially for someone who studies human behavior for a living. We all impose our interpretations on others to some degree. The difference is in whether we recognize the limitations of our perception."

By the time Claire left Leland's office, the sun was setting, casting shadows across the city. She checked her phone to find several missed calls from Martinez, followed by a text: We found the connection. All three victims left negative reviews for Blackwood's work online. Anonymous accounts, but we traced the IP addresses.

Claire called her immediately. "They rejected Blackwood's art, and now Blackwood is imposing it on them in death," she said when Martinez answered. "Have we located him?"

"Not yet. Blackwood's studio is empty, and he hasn't been home in days according to neighbors. But we found something else, a storage unit rented under his name. We're getting a warrant now."

"I'll meet you there," Claire said, already heading for her car.

"It's at a storage facility on Eastern Avenue. I'll text you the exact address," Martinez said. "Should have the warrant within the hour."

The storage facility was in an industrial area near the harbor, rows of identical metal units stretching into the darkness. Martinez was waiting by her unmarked car, along with two uniformed officers. The warrant had come through minutes earlier.

"Unit 237," Martinez said, leading the way. "Manager says Blackwood pays in cash, comes at irregular hours. No one's seen him in the past week."

The padlock on the unit yielded to bolt cutters, the metal door rolling upward with a protesting screech. Claire flicked on her flashlight, illuminating what lay inside.

The space had been converted into a makeshift studio. A tattoo chair dominated the center, surgical lights positioned above it. Along one wall ran a workbench with professional tattoo equipment, inks in dozens of colors, and detailed sketches pinned above. But it was the opposite wall that seized Claire's attention.

A life-sized human outline had been drawn there, divided into sections. Three of these sections contained detailed renderings of the tattoos found on his victims, the scales of justice, the peacock feathers, the broken chains, each in exactly the position where they'd been inked onto the bodies. But there were other sections too, still blank, waiting to be filled.

"There are seven sections total," Claire said, counting the designated areas. "We've found three victims. Blackwood is planning four more."

"Or already has them," Martinez said grimly, gesturing to a small refrigerator in the corner. "Forensics needs to process that. Could be storing inks, could be…"

"Trophies," Claire finished, the familiar knot of dread tightening in her stomach. "We need to find out who these other targets are before Blackwood gets to them."

Forensics arrived, the small storage unit quickly becoming crowded with personnel photographing and cataloging evidence. Claire focused on the wall design, taking pictures of the complete outline with her phone. There was something familiar about the pose, the way the figure's arms were positioned, one raised as if in benediction, the other extended outward.

"It's based on the Vitruvian Man," she realized, referring to Leonardo da Vinci's famous drawing of human proportions. "The perfect human form according to classical ideals. Blackwood is creating his own version of anatomical perfection, but with moral judgments instead of measurements."

Martinez joined her at the wall. "So, each tattoo represents some kind of sin or failing?"

"Yes, but specific to each victim. The scales for Cooley suggest injustice or corruption. The watchful eyes for Markham imply deception or vanity. The broken chains for Walsh might indicate some form of bondage or control."

"But why these people specifically? Leaving bad reviews seems like a thin motive for murder."

Claire studied the detailed sketches pinned above the workbench. "I don't think it was just the reviews. Look at these notes." She pointed to handwritten comments beside each sketch. "Cooley's says 'falsely balanced.' Markham's says 'watches others but never sees herself.'

Walsh's says 'claims freedom while binding others.' These are personal judgments, not just professional grievances."

"So, Blackwood had more significant interactions with these victims than just online reviews," Martinez concluded. "We need to dig deeper into their connections."

The refrigerator, when opened, contained only specialized inks that required cooling, not trophies as they'd feared. But on the inside of the door, secured with tape, was a memory card.

Back at the precinct, the tech team accessed the card's contents: detailed dossiers on all three victims, plus four more individuals. Photos, daily routines, personal information, and in each file, a section labeled "Revelation" that described the tattoo design chosen for them and the symbolic meaning behind it.

"We have our next targets," Matthews said, studying the information displayed on the conference room screen. "Gabriel Mercier, financial advisor. Mary Doyle, social media influencer. Robert Kit, university professor. And Sarah Werner, addiction counselor."

Claire felt a chill at the last name. "A counselor? Does it say where she works?"

Matthews checked the file. "Harborview Recovery Center."

The same rehabilitation center where Claire had gotten sober. She kept her expression neutral, but her hand found her sobriety chip in her pocket.

"We need protection details on all four immediately," Matthews ordered. "And I want every available officer looking for Blackwood. Current photo has been distributed to patrol. He can't have gone far, that storage unit was recently used."

Claire studied the "Revelation" notes for the remaining targets. Mercier was to receive a tattoo of a wolf in sheep's clothing. Doyle's design featured a mask with streaming tears. Kit's showed books with empty pages. And Werner, the counselor, a garden of withered plants, what Blackwood described as "the false healer whose care kills what she claims to nurture."

The personal nature of that last judgment made Claire's stomach tighten. Had Blackwood been a patient at Harborview? Or known someone who had? The connection felt too close, personal.

"I'll take the lead on interviewing Werner," she told Matthews. "I'm familiar with Harborview from previous cases." The slight deception came easily; only Martinez knew the full details of Claire's history with the recovery center.

Matthews nodded. "Good. Martinez, you check on Mercier and Kit. I'll have Officer Jenkins talk to Doyle. Let's move fast."

Sarah Werner was a petite woman in her mid-forties with prematurely white hair put in a practical bob. She didn't seem particularly surprised when Claire and an officer arrived at her office at Harborview, the familiar building bringing back complicated memories for Claire.

"I suppose this was inevitable," Werner said after Claire explained the situation. "Ashe Blackwood. I wondered if he'd ever come back into my life."

Claire blinked. "You know him?"

"I was Ashe's counselor five years ago," Werner confirmed. "He came here for opioid addiction following a motorcycle accident. The injuries ended his career as a traditional artist, he was a painter before the accident damaged the fine motor skills in his dominant hand."

"So, he turned to tattooing," Claire said, the pieces falling into place. "Using his non-dominant hand."

Werner nodded. "It was part of his recovery plan, finding a new artistic outlet. And he was talented. But there were always concerning aspects to Ashe's world view. Ashe believed in absolute truths, in black and white. He couldn't accept the gray areas we all live in."

"What happened? Why did he leave treatment?"

"We had a disagreement about the nature of recovery. Ashe believed that people who relapsed were moral failures, not just individuals struggling with a complex disease. When another patient who he had befriended relapsed and subsequently died of an overdose, he couldn't bring himself to blame his friend. Instead, he blamed me. Said my 'permissive approach' had killed his friend. He needed someone else to be the villain."

Claire tried to keep her expression neutral, but something must have shown in her face because Werner studied her with sudden recognition.

"You were a patient here too," she said quietly. "I don't remember you, so it must have been after I moved to the outpatient program."

"Nearly two and a half years ago," Claire confirmed, seeing no point in denial. "Dr. Leland was my counselor here."

"Ah, Elaine," Werner nodded with recognition. "She was excellent, one of our best before she moved to private practice. But you see now why Ashe might have targeted me. He believes I failed his friend, that I'm a fraud presenting myself as a healer while actually enabling destruction."

"We'll have an officer with you at all times until we locate Blackwood," Claire assured her. "But we need to understand more about his thinking, his patterns. Is there anywhere special he might go, anywhere significant from his time here?"

Werner considered the question. "There was a place Ashe would go to sketch between sessions. The botanical gardens in Druid Hill Park. He said it was the only place in the city where he could see both growth and decay in perfect balance."

After ensuring that Werner had police protection, Claire called Martinez to share what she'd learned. The detective had already interviewed Gabriel Mercier and was on her way to Robert Kit's university office.

"Both Mercier and Kit had professional interactions with Blackwood," Martinez reported. "Mercier was Blackwood's financial advisor during an insurance settlement after his accident. Apparently, Blackwood accused him of mismanaging the funds, claimed he was 'a predator posing as a protector', hence the wolf in sheep's clothing design. I'm still trying to connect with Doyle, but from her social media, it looks like she did a promotional post for Blackwood's studio about a year ago, then never delivered the agreed-upon follow-ups."

"And Kit?"

"Professor of art history who rejected Blackwood's work for inclusion in a textbook on modern body modification art. Called it 'derivative and lacking in genuine insight' in his rejection letter."

"So, all the victims either rejected, betrayed, or failed Blackwood in some way," Claire summarized. "From his perspective, they're all guilty of some form of deception or hypocrisy."

"Looks that way. How'd it go with Werner?"

Claire filled her in on the connection to Harborview, careful to maintain her professional tone. "I'm heading to Druid Hill Park now. The botanical gardens were significant to Blackwood during his recovery. It's a long shot, but worth checking."

"Want backup?"

Claire hesitated. The smarter move would be to wait for Martinez, but something told her time was running short. "No, I'll just do a preliminary check. I've got patrol officers on standby if I find anything. You focus on securing Kit and connecting with Doyle."

The botanical gardens were quiet in the late afternoon, most visitors having left as closing time approached. Claire showed her badge to the attendant, who confirmed that someone matching Blackwood's description had been a regular visitor, often staying until closing.

"He's usually in the desert garden," the young woman offered. "Says he likes how the succulents survive in harsh conditions. Weirdo."

Claire ignored the comment, thanked her, and headed toward the glass-enclosed space housing desert plants from around the world. The air inside was warm and dry. Tall cacti stretched toward the glass ceiling, while smaller succulents created a tapestry of shapes and textures at eye level.

The space appeared empty at first glance, but as Claire moved deeper into the garden, she spotted a figure seated on a bench partially hidden by a large agave plant. Ashe Blackwood was sketching, his pen moving across the paper with fluid precision despite using what Claire now recognized was his non-dominant hand.

Blackwood didn't look up as Claire approached, though he must have heard her footsteps. "I wondered who they'd send," he said, his voice surprisingly soft. "A detective? A SWAT team? But they sent you instead. Interesting choice."

Claire kept her distance, positioning herself where she could see Blackwood's hands. "I'm Dr. Claire Morrison, forensic psychologist with Baltimore PD. I'd like to talk with you about your artwork, Mr. Blackwood."

Blackwood looked up, his face angular and striking, with high cheekbones and intense dark eyes. A geometric tattoo extended from behind his right ear down his neck, disappearing beneath his collar. "My artwork. Which pieces specifically, Dr. Morrison? The commissions I've done for living clients. Or my revelatory series on the morally deceased?"

"I'm particularly interested in the work you've been creating at your storage unit studio," Claire said evenly. "The composite design you're building across multiple subjects."

A flicker of something, surprise perhaps, or admiration, crossed Blackwood's face. "You found my blueprint. I'm impressed. Most people don't see the connections, the larger pattern. They focus on the individual pieces without understanding they're part of a greater truth."

"The Vitruvian Man reimagined as a moral diagram," Claire said, taking a careful step closer. "With each victim bearing the mark of their specific failing."

"Not victims, Dr. Morrison. Canvases. Each was empty in life, presenting false fronts to the world. I simply revealed their true natures in death." Blackwood set aside his sketchbook, and Claire noted he had no visible weapons. "But you understand this, don't you? The concept of authentic revelation."

"What makes you say that?"

"I recognize the signs of someone who's rebuilt themselves. The careful way you hold yourself, the watchfulness in your eyes. You've seen your own reflection clearly and made changes. That takes courage."

Claire kept her expression neutral, though internally she was reassessing the threat level. Blackwood was observant, intuitive. Dangerous qualities in someone who'd already killed three people. "Is that why you chose these specific individuals? Because you felt they lacked that courage?"

"I chose them because they were liars," Blackwood said, his voice hardening slightly. "Cooley claimed to serve justice while helping corporations escape it. Markham built a career selling false images to vulnerable women. Walsh preached freedom while controlling everyone around him. Each presented a false front while hiding rot beneath."

"And the others? Mercier, Doyle, Kit, and Werner? What are their sins?"

"So, you know about them too." Blackwood nodded appreciatively. "Each betrayed truth in their own way. Mercier is a predator disguised as a financial advisor. Doyle sells her followers products she doesn't use herself. Kit rejects authentic art while promoting derivative work by his academic friends. And Werner…" He paused, a flash of real pain crossing his face. "Werner let my friend die while claiming to help him."

"Jamie Carson," Claire said, recalling the name from Werner's file. "He relapsed after six months of sobriety."

Blackwood's eyes widened slightly. "You've done your research."

"Addiction is complicated, Mr. Blackwood. Relapse doesn't mean the treatment failed or that the counselor was negligent."

"You speak from experience," Blackwood observed. "You've been there yourself, haven't you? The careful way you choose your words. The empathy in your voice when you mention relapse. You're in recovery too."

Claire didn't confirm or deny, instead taking another step closer. "Jamie's death was tragic. But what you're doing won't bring him justice or peace."

"This isn't about peace," Blackwood said, standing. He was taller than Claire had expected, well over six feet. "It's about truth. Something permanent in a world of lies and impermanence. Every day, people change their stories, their faces, their realities with filters and editing and careful curation. But what I create can't be erased or altered. It becomes part of them forever."

"Even though they're dead and can't see it," Claire pointed out. "Who is the message really for?"

"For anyone who knew them. For everyone who was deceived by them." Blackwood took a step toward her. "For a world that values appearance over substance."

Claire was calculating the distance to the exit, estimating her chances of subduing someone with Blackwood's height advantage, when the artist made a sudden move, not toward her, but toward his bag on the bench. Her hand went to her weapon.

"You're wondering if I'm armed," he said, a trace of amusement in his voice. "I'm not. That's not how this works. I don't take subjects by force. The drug is in their system long before they know they've been chosen."

"How?" Claire kept her hand near her weapon.

"Various methods. Contaminated pharmaceuticals for those who take daily medications. Doctored drinks for the social ones, synthetic patches." Blackwood held out the sketchbook. "You should see the complete design before they take me away. You're the only one who's understood it so far."

Claire took the sketchbook from his hands. "But we found evidence at your storage unit," she said, flipping through the pages. "And this? This is evidence too. Your entire plan, documented in detail…"

Blackwood's serene expression shattered, his face contorting with rage. "No! You don't understand what you've done!" He lunged forward, only to be restrained by the approaching officers. "The work must be completed! The truth must be revealed! They deserve their markings!"

"The only thing being revealed today is your delusion," Claire said firmly, stepping back as the officers secured him. "Your so-called truth is your own perception."

As officers took Blackwood into custody, reading him his rights, he continued to struggle against their grip. "This isn't over! The pattern demands completion!" he shouted, his earlier composure completely abandoned.

Claire was already on her phone. "Martinez, we need medical teams at Mercier, Kit, and Werner's locations immediately. Blackwood administered drugs this morning. They'll be experiencing effects soon."

"Already on it," Martinez replied, the sound of sirens audible in the background. "We got your emergency signal. Medical teams dispatched to all three locations. Matthews is coordinating from the station."

Claire watched as Blackwood was led away, still shouting about his unfinished work, his mask of calm completely shattered. Even in defeat, the intensity of his conviction was evident, the dangerous certainty that had driven him to kill three people and attempt to kill four more, his absolute belief that his perception was truth, his judgment righteous.

By nightfall, all three potential victims had been stabilized. All three were found unconscious when medical teams arrived. All three were immediately given NARCAN.

"Werner later told the medical staff she recognized what was happening: the drowsiness, the slow breathing," Martinez told Claire as they sat in the hospital waiting room. "Her training kicked in, but the synthetic stuff works fast. She was reaching for her phone when she lost consciousness."

Claire nodded, relieved but still troubled. "And Doyle? Any sign of her?"

"Found her at a retreat in Virginia. She's safe, being brought back to Baltimore. Looks like her deceptive social media posting habits accidentally saved her life."

An hour later, back at the precinct, Matthews joined them, carrying coffee cups that Claire knew contained the office's notoriously terrible brew. "Blackwood's not talking, but the evidence from the storage unit is damning. The memory card contained detailed files on all seven targets, plus photos documenting the first three murders. Ashe was meticulous about recording everything."

"For the final reveal," Claire said, accepting the coffee despite her misgivings. "Blackwood saw this as an art installation as much as a series of murders. The documentation was essential to the project."

"Well, the project's over now," Matthews said grimly. "Three counts of first-degree murder, kidnapping, and three attempted murders. Blackwood won't see freedom again."

"What about the pattern?" Martinez asked. "The complete design Blackwood was creating. Do we release that to the public?"

Matthews shook his head. "Absolutely not. The last thing we need is copycats or fame for Blackwood's 'work.' As far as the press is concerned, this was a straightforward case of targeted homicide. No mention of the composite design."

Claire understood the reasoning but felt a nagging discomfort at the decision. Blackwood's work, horrific as it was, revealed something important about human nature, our capacity to impose our judgments on others, to see our perspective as absolute truth. Leaving that insight buried seemed like a missed opportunity for understanding.

But that wasn't her call to make. She finished her coffee, wincing at its bitterness. "Matthews always forgets to add sugar," she murmured to Martinez. "I'll have the full psychological profile on your desk tomorrow morning," she told Matthews. "But the core of it is already clear. Blackwood suffered a traumatic loss, both physical function after his accident and then his friend Jamie and found meaning in a rigid moral framework. The tattoo art became a way to impose order on a world he experienced as chaotic and deceptive."

Matthews nodded. "Good work, both of you. Go home, get some rest."

Claire's apartment was dark when she arrived, but Darwin appeared immediately, winding around her ankles with his usual mix of indignation at her absence and pleasure at her return. She fed him, then stood for a long moment looking at the case notes she'd spread across her living room floor before leaving that morning. The photos of the tattoos stared back at her, beautiful despite their macabre context.

Claire moved to her small balcony, lighting a cigarette as she looked out over the city. Baltimore's lights glittered in the darkness, each one representing lives she would never know, stories she could never fully understand. The humility of that recognition felt important, a counterbalance to Blackwood's terrifying certainty.

Darwin joined her on the balcony, settling by her feet in a rare show of outdoor bravery. Claire finished her cigarette, stubbing it out in the small ashtray she kept hidden behind a flowerpot. In the morning, she would complete her report, detail the psychological factors that had transformed Ashe Blackwood from a talented artist into a killer. She would put her professional assessment on record, tie the case up with the neat bow of clinical language.

But tonight, she let herself sit with the uncomfortable truth the case had revealed. How thin the line was between someone like her and someone like Blackwood. A few wrong turns, a few bad breaks, and anyone might start believing their pain justified everything.

She thought of the tattoo on her own wrist, the Celtic knot she'd chosen to mark her first year of sobriety. A symbol of interconnection, of continuity, of the way all things tied together. Her own small rebellion against the isolation of addiction, her permanent reminder that healing happened in community, not in judgment.

She considered calling her father to discuss the case. Her relationship with Dr. Richard Morrison had warmed slightly since the Harrison case six months ago, when she'd finally sent him her case notes as a tentative olive branch. They'd spoken twice since then, brief but less strained conversations. The patterns in Blackwood's work would fascinate him, perhaps enough to inspire another call. But that would wait until tomorrow.

Tomorrow would be soon enough for conclusions. Tonight was for questions, for the humility of uncertainty, for the recognition that truth was rarely simple and never complete. As Darwin purred by her feet, Claire looked up at the night sky, barely visible through Baltimore's light pollution, and allowed herself to rest in the questions.

Chapter Four

Baltimore Winter

The first snowflake caught Claire Morrison by surprise, a tiny crystalline messenger of the storm to come. She watched it land on her windshield, perfect and delicate, before the wiper blade swept it away. More followed in quick succession as the gray Baltimore sky opened, releasing what the meteorologists had been warning about all week: the worst blizzard to hit the city in decades.

Claire cranked the heat in her decade-old Honda, the engine protesting with a raspy growl. The digital display on her dashboard read 2:17 PM, but the darkening sky made it feel much later. The crime scene she'd just left, a body discovered in Patterson Park, partially covered by the season's first dusting of snow, had taken longer than expected. Now she faced the prospect of beating the storm home, a race she was already losing.

Her phone buzzed. Detective Sara Martinez's name flashed on the screen.

"Tell me you found something," Claire answered, keeping her eyes on the increasingly treacherous road.

"Victim's been ID'd," Martinez replied, the familiar background noise of the precinct evident in her voice. "James Wilson, 42, high school chemistry teacher. Divorced, lives alone, no priors. And here's where it gets interesting: his ex-wife has a restraining order against him, claims he became obsessed with her after the divorce, sending letters, showing up at her workplace."

Claire pulled to a stop at a red light, watching snowflakes gather on her windshield faster than her wipers could clear them. "So, we're thinking the ex-wife might have reached her breaking point?"

"That's the obvious angle, but there's a twist. Ex-wife is in the Bahamas, has been for a week. Perfect alibi."

"Unless she hired someone," Claire mused, pulling forward as the light changed. "What about defensive wounds?"

"None that we could see, but Dr. Patel might find something during the autopsy. Though with the delay from this storm, they're not starting until tomorrow at the earliest." Martinez paused. "Where are you now?"

"Trying to make it home before the worst hits. The roads are getting bad already."

"Chief's ordering everyone who's not essential to go home. They're predicting eighteen to twenty-four inches by morning, with winds gusting to fifty miles per hour. You might want to hunker down wherever you can."

Claire glanced at her gas gauge, hovering just above a quarter tank. Not ideal for sitting in traffic that was already beginning to snarl around her. "I'm going to try for my apartment. I'll call you if I get stuck."

After ending the call, Claire edged her car forward in the thickening snow. The radio warned of road closures beginning in the next hour, and the traffic report described gridlock forming on every major artery out of the city.

Her phone rang again, this time with a number she didn't immediately recognize. She answered on speaker.

"Dr. Morrison? It's Jenna from Johns Hopkins. I'm calling about your father."

Claire's grip tightened on the steering wheel. "Is he all right?"

"Oh, he's fine physically, but we're implementing emergency protocols due to the storm. The university is closing, and we're trying to arrange transportation for faculty members who might have difficulty getting home. Dr. Morrison has refused our shuttle service and insists on driving himself, but given the conditions…"

Claire closed her eyes briefly, trying to control her frustration. Her father's stubbornness was legendary within the psychology department. At seventy, Dr. Richard Morrison still insisted on teaching a part-time course load since his semi-retirement, refused teaching assistants, and maintained regular office hours. The idea of him attempting to navigate Baltimore's treacherous hills in a snowstorm made her stomach clench.

"Where is he now?"

"Still in his office in the Behavioral Sciences Building. He says he has papers to grade before heading home."

Claire checked the car's navigation system. Johns Hopkins was a fifteen-minute detour from her route home in good weather. In these conditions, who knew? But the alternative was letting her father drive his rear-wheel-drive sedan through increasingly hazardous conditions.

"Tell him I'm coming to get him," she said, already signaling to change lanes. "And if he tries to leave before I arrive, please… I don't know, hide his keys."

"I'll do my best, Dr. Morrison, but you know your father."

"Indeed, I do," Claire muttered after ending the call.

The history between Claire and her father was complicated at best. Dr. Richard Morrison was a legend in the field of forensic psychology, his textbooks required reading in every doctoral program in the country. When Claire had followed him into the field, the expectations had been crushing. Their relationship, strained since her mother's unexplained disappearance when Claire was nine, had frayed further during her later struggles with alcoholism. Now they maintained a careful professional distance, occasionally consulting on cases, their personal relationship reduced to stilted holiday dinners and brief phone calls about academic publications.

The Harrison case was six months ago. She'd finally sent him her case notes after as a tentative olive branch. They'd spoken more frequently since then, their conversations becoming marginally less strained. The mirror killer case and Blackwood would have fascinated him, though she hadn't consulted him officially on them.

Claire reached for the small packet of tic tacs in her pocket; the mints had become her constant companion, helping to ground her in moments of stress. She popped one in her mouth as she navigated the increasingly dangerous roads.

Traffic slowed to a crawl as she neared the university campus. Looking at the line of cars ahead of her, Claire made a split-second decision and turned onto a side street. If she cut through the residential areas, she might make better time.

The narrow streets of the neighborhoods adjacent to the university were less congested but more treacherous. Twice her car slid on unseen ice patches beneath the fresh snow. By the time she reached the university gates, the windshield wipers were struggling to keep up with the heavy snowfall.

The campus was nearly deserted, the buildings taking on a haunted quality under the swirling snow. Claire parked as close as she could to the Behavioral Sciences Building and trudged through already ankle-deep snow to the entrance.

The building's lobby was dark except for emergency lighting, the usual bustle of academic life absent. The security guard looked up from a paperback as she entered, stomping snow from her boots.

"The university's closed, ma'am."

Claire showed her Baltimore PD credentials. "I'm here to pick up my father, Dr. Richard Morrison. Behavioral Sciences, fifth floor."

The guard nodded in recognition. "Dr. Morrison, yes, he's still up there. One of the last holdouts. Elevators are shut down for safety, I'm afraid. You'll have to take the stairs."

The stairwell was lit only by battery-powered emergency lights that cast shadows as Claire climbed. Her footsteps echoed in the empty space, five flights feeling like fifty after her long day. Her mind drifted back to the body in Patterson Park, the strange positioning, the lack of defensive wounds. Something about the scene nagged at her, but she couldn't quite place what.

The fifth-floor corridor was dark except for light spilling from under one door at the far end. Claire didn't need to read the nameplate to know it was her father's office. As she approached, she could hear the scratching of a pen on paper, the familiar sound of her childhood when her father would grade papers late into the night, a soundtrack to her early years.

She knocked; the sound unnaturally loud in the deserted hallway.

"Office hours are canceled due to the weather emergency," her father's voice called out, irritation evident even through the closed door. "Please consult the syllabus and email any urgent questions."

Claire opened the door without waiting for an invitation. "I'm not one of your students, Dad."

Richard Morrison looked up from his desk, pen still poised over a stack of papers. At seventy, he remained an imposing figure, tall and straight-backed, with a full head of silver hair and the same piercing green eyes Claire saw in the mirror each morning. Wire-rimmed glasses perched on his aquiline nose, and his tweed jacket hung precisely on the back of his chair.

"Claire," he said, surprise and something unidentifiable flashing across his face. "What are you doing here?"

"Saving you from yourself, apparently." She gestured toward the window, where snow swirled visibly even in the gathering darkness. "The university's closed. They called me because you refused the shuttle."

Her father checked the time, his eyes moving to the ungraded papers. "I promised my students these would be ready tomorrow."

"Dad, classes will be cancelled. I guarantee it." Claire kept her voice gentle but insistent. "I've already come out of my way in this weather. Let's not wait until we're stuck here."

Richard studied his daughter for a long moment. Despite their difficult relationship, he'd always respected her directness, a trait she'd inherited from him. Finally, he sighed and began gathering his papers into his briefcase.

"I suppose it would be irresponsible to further delay you in these conditions," he conceded, reaching for his coat on the rack behind the door.

Claire waited as he organized his desk, turning off his desk lamp, locking filing cabinets. The routines of academia, unchanged in the decades since she'd visited this office as a child, hiding under this same desk while her father finished lectures.

"How did you know I was still here?" he asked as he shrugged into his heavy wool overcoat.

"The university called me. Apparently, you're on some list of stubborn faculty members who need babysitting during emergencies."

A hint of a smile crossed her father's face. "Jenna from the dean's office, I presume. She's been trying to get me to fully retire for years."

"Smart woman," Claire said, leading the way back to the stairwell. "It's going to be slow going. I hope you don't have any urgent dinner plans."

"Just my usual exhilarating evening with Proust and a bowl of soup," her father replied. Claire couldn't tell if he was joking. Their interactions rarely included humor.

The stairwell descent was slower than the climb up had been, her father setting a deliberate pace that betrayed his age despite his otherwise vigorous appearance. As they reached the ground floor, Claire's phone buzzed again.

"Martinez," she said, reading the text message. "They found something at the crime scene I was at earlier. She sent photos. I'll have a look when we're somewhere safer."

Her father raised an eyebrow. "A case? Anything interesting?"

"Body found in Patterson Park this morning. Relatively straightforward at first glance, but something felt off about the scene." She hesitated, then added, "The positioning was unusual. Arms perfectly aligned at his sides, legs straight, like he'd been placed rather than having fallen."

Richard nodded, professional interest displacing his typical reserve. "Postmortem manipulation often indicates a personal connection. The killer reordering chaos into something that satisfies their emotional need for control."

The security guard looked up as they exited the stairwell, relief evident on his face. "Dr. Morrison, good to see you're finally leaving.

Weather service just upgraded the warning. They're saying this could be a once-in-a-generation storm."

"Thank you, George. Be careful getting home yourself," Richard replied with the easy courtesy he extended to everyone except, it sometimes seemed to Claire, his own daughter.

Outside, the snow had intensified, now falling in thick, heavy curtains that reduced visibility to just a few yards. The wind had picked up as well, driving the snow horizontally at times. Claire led the way to her car, now covered with several inches. She brushed off the windshield with her sleeve, unlocked the doors, and they both hurried inside.

The car started grudgingly, the heater blowing cold air that gradually warmed as Claire navigated the deserted campus streets. Beyond the gates, the city was transforming into a winter landscape, familiar landmarks rendered strange and new under their blanket of white. Cars moved at a crawl, hazard lights blinking like fireflies in the swirling snow.

"My apartment is closest," Claire said, squinting to make out the street signs. "We can wait out the worst of the storm there."

Her father shifted uncomfortably in the passenger seat. "I wouldn't want to impose. If you could drop me at home, I'll be fine."

Claire turned to him, incredulous. "Your house is on the other side of the city. It would take hours in this traffic, if we make it at all. This isn't the time for polite distance, Dad."

The words hung in the car between them, laden with more meaning than their immediate context. Richard said nothing, turning his attention to the window and the transformed city beyond.

By the time they reached Claire's neighborhood, the conditions had deteriorated further. Abandoned cars lined the streets, their owners having given up and continued on foot. Claire maneuvered as close as she could to her building before admitting defeat.

"We'll have to walk the last block," she said, turning off the engine. "Stay close. The wind is disorienting."

They pushed through snow that now reached mid-calf, the wind cutting through their coats like icy blades. Claire led the way, occasionally reaching back to steady her father when he faltered in the drifts. By the time they reached her building's entrance, they were both covered in snow, cheeks stinging from the cold.

The lobby was mercifully warm, though the lights flickered as they waited for the elevator. A handwritten sign taped to the wall warned residents about potential power outages.

"Third floor," Claire said as they stepped into the elevator, suddenly aware that her father had never visited her apartment. Their interactions were always on neutral ground, restaurants, his campus office, occasionally the precinct when he consulted on a case. Her home was her sanctuary, the one place untouched by their complicated relationship.

As she unlocked her door, Darwin began meowing loudly at the unexpected guest. The orange tabby regarded Richard suspiciously from his perch atop the bookcase.

"That's Darwin," Claire explained, shedding her snow-covered coat and boots. "He's not great with strangers."

"A fitting name for a creature who seems to be studying me for signs of weakness," her father remarked, carefully removing his wet outerwear.

Claire's apartment was small but comfortable, more lived-in than her previous residences. Bookshelves lined the living room walls, filled with an eclectic mix of psychology texts, crime fiction, and philosophy. A small meditation cushion sat beneath the window, and nearby, a collection of plants that showed signs of recent care. The kitchen was open to the living area, a small island separating the spaces. Case files were stacked neatly on the table, evidence of work brought home.

"Make yourself comfortable," Claire said, heading to the kitchen. "I'll make some coffee. We might lose power before this is over, so I'd like to get something hot into us while we can."

Richard moved cautiously through the space, studying the books on her shelves, the framed degrees on the wall (including one from his own university, though he'd had no hand in her admission), the photographs on the side table. He paused at one: Claire as a child, sitting with a woman whose face was partially obscured by shadow.

"I don't have this one," he said, his voice uncharacteristically soft.

Claire glanced over from the kitchen. "Mom's sister gave it to me a few years ago. She found it going through old albums."

Richard nodded, replacing the photo exactly where it had been. "Your aunt Elizabeth. She has your mother's laugh."

The coffee maker gurgled as Claire filled two mugs. Outside, the storm raged, snow accumulating on the windowsills, the wind howling around the building's corners. The lights flickered again, longer this time, before stabilizing.

"I have emergency supplies," Claire said, handing her father a steaming mug. "Flashlights, batteries, extra blankets. If the power goes out, it will get cold, but we'll manage."

Richard accepted the coffee with a nod of thanks. "You've always been prepared."

An awkward silence fell between them, filled only by the sounds of the storm and Darwin's occasional curious meow. Claire's phone buzzed, breaking the tension. The screen showed a notification from Martinez, a case update and several attached files.

"May I?" she asked, gesturing to the phone.

Richard waved a hand. "Please. Don't let me interrupt your work."

Claire opened the files, enlarging the photos Martinez had sent. They showed a close-up of the victim's clothing, a small stain that had initially been missed among the bloodier evidence of violence. A second photo showed the same stain under different lighting, revealing a distinct shape.

"That's interesting," she murmured, zooming in further.

"May I?" her father asked, professional curiosity evident in his voice.

Claire hesitated only briefly before handing him the phone. Richard studied the images, his expression shifting from casual interest to focused analysis.

"That's a botanical emblem of some kind," he said, enlarging the image further. "Deliberately placed, not accidental transfer."

Claire moved to look over his shoulder, their professional rapport momentarily superseding personal distance. "The positioning, the arrangement of the body, now this... there's intentionality here."

Richard handed back the phone. "This reminds me of a case in Buffalo, about fifteen years ago. The Gardener, they called him. He left botanical symbols on his victims, placed them in similar formal poses."

"I remember reading about that," Claire said, sending a quick text to Martinez asking her to check for similar cases. "He was caught after the third murder, wasn't he?"

"Yes, a botany professor from the local university. He's still in prison, as far as I know."

The lights flickered again and then went out completely, plunging the apartment into sudden darkness. Outside, the howl of the wind seemed to intensify in the silence left by the absent hum of electronics.

"Stay here," Claire said, carefully making her way to the kitchen drawer where she kept emergency supplies. The beam of her flashlight cut through the darkness as she found candles and matches.

Soon, a warm glow filled the apartment as she placed candles on the coffee table, kitchen counter, and bathroom. The effect was almost peaceful, the storm's fury rendered distant by the warm light and enforced isolation.

"I heard the emergency broadcast predict power outages lasting up to three days in some areas," Richard said, accepting a second flashlight from his daughter. "It seems we may be in for an extended visit."

Claire searched her father's face in the candlelight, looking for signs of disapproval or discomfort. Instead, she found only calm acceptance and perhaps a hint of something unexpected, relief?

"I have plenty of food, at least," she said, moving to check the contents of her refrigerator before the cold air escaped. "And the building has good insulation. We won't freeze."

Richard nodded, then gestured to the case files on her dining table. "Perhaps you could tell me more about your current investigation. Professional consultation only, of course."

Claire considered this unexpected opening. Their interactions were usually limited to formal consultation requests, paperwork filed, and meetings scheduled through proper channels. This impromptu collaboration felt different, personal in a way they rarely allowed themselves to be.

"All right," she agreed, retrieving the file on James Wilson. "But fair exchange. You tell me more about this Buffalo case that seems similar."

For the next hour, as the storm transformed Baltimore into an unrecognizable landscape of white, they worked. Claire spreading crime scene photos across her dining table, Richard examining them, and offering insights that came from decades of experience. The candles burned lower, casting long shadows that danced across the walls as they discussed victimology, profiling indicators, potential motivation.

"The placement of the body suggests respect rather than anger," Richard noted, studying a photo of the crime scene. "Combined with this botanical symbol, I'm convinced we're looking at a ritualistic element. Something meaningful to the killer beyond mere concealment of evidence."

Claire nodded, jotting notes in the margins of her file. "Martinez is checking for similar cases, but with the storm, we might not hear back until tomorrow at the earliest. The Buffalo connection is interesting. Could it be a copycat?"

"Possible, though the original case didn't receive much national attention. It was before social media amplified these stories." Richard paused, looking at her notes. "Your handwriting hasn't changed since you were a child. Still slants the same way."

The personal observation caught Claire off guard. "I didn't think you'd notice something like that."

Richard's expression softened briefly before returning to its usual reserve. "I notice more than you might think, Claire."

The moment hung between them, fragile as the candlelight. Then Darwin jumped onto the table, scattering photos and breaking the tension. Claire scooped him up before he could walk through the crime scene documentation.

"He's usually better behaved," she said, setting the cat on a nearby chair. "Though he has developed a disturbing interest in crime scene photos."

"Perhaps he's learning from his owner," Richard remarked with the barest hint of a smile.

Claire's thoughts drifted to Martinez, wondering how her colleague was faring in the storm. They'd developed a solid working relationship over the past year. Martinez was one of the few people at the department who seemed to understand Claire's drive and the demons that fueled it. She made a mental note to check in once they had more reliable cell service.

Claire realized with a start how little she knew about her parents' early life together. Her mother had disappeared when Claire was nine, and in the aftermath, her father had rarely spoken of their time together. What she knew came mostly from her aunt's stories and a handful of photographs.

"Is there anything new in the investigation of Mom's disappearance?" she asked suddenly, the question escaping before she could consider its wisdom. The power outage, the storm's isolation, the unusual intimacy of working together on a case, all of it had created a space where such questions felt possible.

Richard looked startled, then thoughtful. He set down the crime scene photo he'd been examining, removing his glasses to clean them methodically with his handkerchief, a gesture Claire recognized as his way of buying time to compose his thoughts.

"No," he said finally, replacing his glasses. "The police still consider it an open case, but there have been no new leads in years."

The candlelight caught the green of his eyes, so like her own, and Claire saw something there she'd rarely witnessed: vulnerability.

"After she disappeared," he continued, his voice steady through clear effort, "I didn't know how to be both father and mother to you. The academic world made sense to me, logic, analysis, structured inquiry. I failed you there, I know."

The admission hung in the silence between them. Outside, the wind howled, driving snow against the windows with a sound like sand on glass. Darwin had curled up on the chair, watching them with half-closed eyes.

Claire found herself without words, the practiced responses of their usual careful interactions inadequate for this sudden shift. Before she could formulate a reply, her phone buzzed with an incoming text, the screen illuminating briefly in the dimness.

"It's Martinez," she said, grateful for the interruption. "They've found a match to our case. Similar botanical emblem found on a victim in Frederick County last month. They didn't connect it until now because it was a different jurisdiction."

Richard leaned forward, professional focus returning. "Does she have details?"

"Limited. The Frederick victim was also positioned carefully, male, similar age to our victim. They're sending the full file once they get it, but with the storm..." Claire trailed off, glancing at the window where snow continued to accumulate. "We're not going anywhere soon."

"Two cases makes a pattern," Richard noted. "If this is a serial killer beginning a sequence, the storm may disrupt their timeline. Weather affects predatory behavior, forces adaptation."

Claire nodded, sending a quick acknowledgment to Martinez before setting her phone down. "The power outage affects us the same way. We need to adapt."

The double meaning wasn't lost on either of them. This forced proximity, the unexpected candor about the past, these were adaptations neither had planned for.

"Are you hungry?" Claire asked, standing.

Richard followed her to the kitchen, his tall frame casting long shadows in the candlelight. "Can I help?"

Together they assembled a meal from the contents of Claire's refrigerator and pantry, cheese, crackers, cold cuts, and a bottle of sparkling water. They ate by candlelight, the storm providing a strange soundtrack to their improvised dinner.

"You have a good eye for detail," Richard said as they cleared the plates. "Your analysis of the crime scene photos showed insights I wouldn't have immediately seen."

Coming from her father, whose standards were exacting, this was high praise indeed. Claire felt an unexpected warmth at the words, a reflexive pleasure she'd spent years trying to outgrow.

"I learned from the best," she replied, then added, "Your textbook is still required reading in forensic psychology programs across the country."

Richard waved away the compliment. "Outdated in places now. The field has evolved considerably since I wrote the original text."

"But the fundamentals you established still hold. Your work on predatory typologies revolutionized how we profile certain types of offenders."

"Perhaps," he acknowledged. "Though I've been considering a substantive revision for the next edition. There are nuances to predatory behavior that weren't fully explored in earlier versions."

The conversation shifted to professional ground, a space where they both felt secure. They discussed recent developments in forensic psychology, cases that had challenged established profiling methods, areas where the field needed further research. As they talked, the candles burned lower, the apartment grew cooler, and outside, the storm continued its assault on the city.

"The Buffalo case I mentioned," Richard said, bringing the conversation back to their earlier discussion. "It had elements that were never made public. The botanical symbols were only part of the signature. Each victim also had a specific quote placed with them, written on fine stationery. Quotes about rebirth, renewal."

"A transformation fantasy," Claire suggested. "The killer believed he was helping his victims achieve some kind of metamorphosis."

Richard nodded. "Precisely. The botanical symbols were specific to each victim, plants that represented aspects of their personality the killer found worthy of 'transformation.' It was a highly personalized form of delusion."

"If our killer is following a similar pattern, the emblem on Wilson might tell us something about why he was chosen." Claire reached for her phone, scrolling to the close-up Martinez had sent. "We need a botanist to identify this."

"I have a colleague in the Biology Department who might help, assuming she has power and internet access during the storm."

Claire looked up, hearing the exhaustion in her father's voice despite his effort to hide it. The day had been long for both, and the emotional terrain they'd navigated was unfamiliar and taxing.

"We should get some rest," she said, gathering their notes. "The case will still be here in the morning, and we're not going anywhere until the storm passes."

The practical matter of sleeping arrangements presented itself. Claire's apartment had only one bedroom, and while her couch was comfortable enough for sitting, it was too short for her father's tall frame to sleep on.

"You can take the bed," she offered. "I'll make up the couch for myself."

Richard shook his head. "I wouldn't think of displacing you from your own bed. The couch will be fine."

"Dad, you're six-foot-two. The couch is barely five feet long. It's not practical."

They stared at each other in the candlelight, the simple logistical problem becoming another battlefield in their complicated relationship. Finally, Richard sighed.

"We're both adults capable of compromise. Your bed is presumably large enough that we can share it without discomfort, maintaining appropriate distance. It's the logical solution."

Claire almost laughed at the formal, academic way he approached the problem. "All right. The logical solution it is."

She found him sleepwear, a Baltimore PD sweatshirt and sweatpants that would be too short but were the best option available and showed him to the bathroom. While he changed, she arranged extra blankets on the bed, anticipating the apartment would grow colder as the night progressed.

When Richard emerged from the bathroom, the oversized sweatshirt and too-short pants gave him an unexpectedly vulnerable appearance. His silver hair was slightly mussed, his feet bare, his usual formal demeanor impossible to maintain in such attire. To Claire, he suddenly looked older, more human, than the academic legend she'd grown up with.

"Your turn," he said, gesturing to the bathroom.

Claire changed quickly into flannel pajamas, brushed her teeth in the dim candlelight, and returned to find her father standing awkwardly by the bed, clearly uncertain about the protocol of this unprecedented situation.

"Left or right side?" she asked, trying to normalize the strange circumstance.

"Left, if it's all the same to you," he replied. "Force of habit."

They settled into the bed with careful distance between them, both lying rigid on their backs, staring at the ceiling where shadows danced in the candlelight. Darwin appeared from wherever he'd been hiding and jumped onto the foot of the bed, curling up in a spot that was technically between them but slightly closer to her father.

"Traitor," she whispered to the cat, who merely blinked at her before closing his eyes.

The wind rattled the windows, and occasionally the building creaked as it withstood the storm's onslaught. In the strange, forced intimacy of the moment, Claire found herself thinking of childhood nights during thunderstorms, when she'd been allowed to sleep in her parents' room, nestled between them in a cocoon of safety before her mother vanished from their lives.

"Dad," she said softly, not turning her head. "Do you ever wonder if Mom might still be out there somewhere?"

The question hung in the darkness. For so long that Claire thought he might have fallen asleep or chosen to ignore it.

"No," he finally answered, his voice quiet but clear. "I don't believe she would have left us willingly, Claire. Whatever happened... I don't think she's still alive."

Claire absorbed this, thinking of her father's solitary life, his house filled with books and research but little else. She'd always assumed his academic focus had been a choice, a prioritization of career over personal life. It hadn't occurred to her that it might have been the result of a grief so profound it precluded other attachments.

"It wasn't your fault," Richard continued, each word measured. "My inability to connect with you emotionally after your mother disappeared. That was my failure, not yours. I want you to know that."

Claire felt her throat tighten with unexpected emotion. "I think we both did the best we could under the circumstances."

A long silence followed, broken only by the sounds of the storm and Darwin's gentle purring at their feet. When Richard spoke again, his voice had a different quality, reflective and distant.

"You remind me of her, you know. Not just physically. It's your determination, your ability to connect with people. I've watched you work with victims, with colleagues. You have her gift for understanding others."

Claire turned her head on the pillow, studying her father's profile in the dim light. "I always thought I took after you. The analytical mind, the attention to detail."

"You got the best of both of us, I think." A pause, then, "I'm proud of the work you're doing, Claire. I should have told you that more often."

The words she'd waited decades to hear, delivered matter-of-factly in a power outage during a blizzard. Claire found herself smiling at the absurdity of it, at how perfectly it encapsulated their relationship.

"Thank you," she said simply. "That means a lot to me."

They fell silent again, but it was a different silence now, less strained, more companionable. The candle on the nightstand burned lower, its light softening as the flame consumed the last of the wax. Outside, the storm began to lose some of its ferocity, the wind's howl diminishing to a persistent moan.

"We should sleep," Richard said, stifling a yawn. "Tomorrow will bring its own challenges."

"Goodnight, Dad."

"Goodnight, Claire."

The morning light filtering through snow-covered windows woke Claire. For a moment, she was disoriented by the unfamiliar weight on the bed beside her, until memory returned, the storm, the power outage, the unprecedented night spent sharing her bed with her father.

Richard was still asleep, his breathing deep and regular, his silver hair tousled against the pillow. Darwin had migrated during the night and now lay curled against Richard's side, a surprising development given the cat's usual wariness with strangers.

Claire slipped out of bed quietly, shivering as her feet hit the cold floor. The apartment was chilly but not unbearable, the building's insulation doing its job despite the lack of heat. Outside, the storm had passed, leaving behind a transformed landscape. Baltimore lay buried under at least eighteen inches of snow, the morning sun creating a blinding brilliance across the untouched white surface.

Her phone, which she'd put on low-power mode to conserve battery, showed several messages from Martinez. The Frederick County case file had come through, along with news of a third potential victim with similar botanical markings discovered in Washington County two months earlier. A pattern was emerging, one that suggested a killer moving systematically through Maryland counties.

Claire put on water to boil on her gas stove, grateful that at least this utility remained functional. As she spooned instant coffee into mugs, her father appeared in the kitchen doorway, Darwin winding around his ankles like an old friend.

"Good morning," he said, hair combed but still wearing the too-small sweatpants. "I see we survived the night."

"More than survived," Claire replied, gesturing to Darwin. "You've made a conquest. He usually hides from visitors for at least three days."

Richard bent to scratch the cat behind the ears, receiving a purr of approval in return. "Animals have always liked me. It's people I have more trouble with."

The self-awareness in the comment surprised Claire. She handed him a steaming mug of coffee, which he accepted with a nod of thanks.

"Martinez sent more information," she said, showing him her phone. "A third case with similar markings. All three victims are men in their forties, all educators of some kind. The Washington victim was a high school science teacher, Frederick taught at a community college, and our victim was a high school chemistry teacher."

"Chemistry, science... subjects related to transformation," Richard noted, arranging the photos in a timeline. "The killer is selecting victims who represent change or transformation in some way. The poisonous plants underline this, substances that can heal or kill depending on dosage and application."

The gas stove provided enough heat to make coffee and heat soup from Claire's pantry for lunch, but the apartment continued to cool as the day progressed. They worked in coats and gloves, their breath occasionally visible in the chill.

By early afternoon, Claire's phone battery was running low, and she had to make decisions about its use. "I need to check in with Martinez, let her know what we've found. According to the city emergency alerts, they're estimating power restoration could take anywhere from twenty-four to seventy-two hours, depending on the area."

"Your insights about the botanical signatures might help them identify potential future victims," Richard agreed. "The sooner they have that information, the better."

Claire called Martinez; the connection scratchy but functional. "We've got a working theory," she explained, outlining what she and her father had pieced together from the case files. "The killer is targeting educators in scientific fields, probably moving eastward through Maryland counties. Each victim is marked with a different poisonous plant that has traditional medicinal uses, it's a transformation motif."

"That fits with what we're learning," Martinez replied, her voice occasionally breaking up. "Background checks show all three victims recently underwent major life changes. Wilson was recently divorced, the Frederick victim had just recovered from cancer treatment, and the Washington County teacher had lost significant weight after bariatric surgery. Transformation, like you said."

"The killer is selecting victims who are already in transition," Claire confirmed, excitement building as the pieces connected. "Have you been able to identify the specific plant emblem on Wilson?"

"Lab confirms it's belladonna. Also known as deadly nightshade."

"Beautiful but deadly," Richard commented from where he sat close enough to hear. "Used medicinally to dilate pupils, women in the Renaissance used it to appear more attractive, hence the name 'beautiful lady.' Another duality."

Claire relayed this to Martinez, then asked, "Any luck identifying potential suspects?"

"We're cross-referencing botanists, herbalists, and alternative medicine practitioners in the region with connections to these counties. The list is long, and with the storm, verification is slow. Many officers can't even make it to the precinct."

"Focus on anyone with academic connections, particularly those who might have been rejected or removed from scientific institutions," Claire suggested. "This killer has a scholarly approach, almost didactic in how they're presenting their victims."

After ending the call, Claire turned to find her father looking at her with an expression she couldn't quite read.

"What?" she asked, suddenly self-conscious.

"You're very good at this," Richard said simply. "Better than I was at your age."

The compliment, delivered without qualification or comparison, was so unexpected that Claire didn't know how to respond. She busied herself with making notes in the case file, but the warm glow of professional recognition lingered.

Outside, the city began the slow process of digging out. Through the window, Claire could see neighbors emerging to clear sidewalks, children building snow forts in drifts that reached their waists, the occasional emergency vehicle navigating streets barely passable despite their efforts.

"It will be days before things return to normal," Richard observed, standing beside her at the window. "The city's infrastructure isn't built for this kind of weather event."

"We're not going anywhere soon," Claire agreed. The reality of their continued forced proximity settled over them, not unwelcome after the unexpected ease of their collaboration.

"I could teach you a card game your mother and I used to play," Richard offered unexpectedly. "To pass the time until we hear more from Detective Martinez."

Claire looked at him in surprise. "I'd like that."

Richard produced a deck of cards from his briefcase, "I always carry them for long faculty meetings," and taught her the game, a variation of rummy with complex scoring. As they played by candlelight, the apartment growing darker as the winter afternoon waned, Richard shared more memories than he had in years.

"Your mother was brilliant at this game," he said, studying his cards. "She could calculate odds faster than anyone I knew."

Claire tried to reconcile this information with her limited memories. Her mother's disappearance had left so many questions unanswered, an open wound that had never fully healed. "I wish I had more memories of her," she admitted. "Most of what I know comes from photographs."

Richard set down his cards, his expression softening in the candlelight. "She loved you more than anything, Claire. That much I know with absolute certainty."

The conversation might have continued in this vein if Claire's phone hadn't buzzed with an incoming text. Martinez again, with an update that shifted their attention back to the case.

"They've identified a potential suspect," Claire read. "Dr. Eleanor Wright, former professor of botanical medicine at the University of Maryland. Lost her position after advocating unorthodox treatments involving potentially toxic plants. Has connections to all three counties where bodies were found."

She showed the text to her father, who frowned in concentration. "The name sounds familiar. She may have applied for a visiting position at Hopkins a few years ago. There was some controversy, though I don't recall the details."

Claire texted back, asking for Wright's current location and any additional information. The response came quickly: "Last known address is in White Marsh. Officers attempting to locate but roads still largely impassable. Will update when we have more."

"White Marsh is in Baltimore County," Richard noted. "If she's following her pattern eastward, that puts her in position for her next target."

"But who?" Claire wondered aloud. "And has the storm disrupted her timeline, or is it facilitating it somehow?"

They returned to the case files, looking for any additional connections between the victims that might help identify a potential target in Baltimore County. As they worked, the apartment grew colder, the batteries in their flashlights began to dim, and outside, darkness fell once more.

"We should conserve the remaining candles and batteries," Claire said, closing the file reluctantly. "And we need to eat something substantial."

They prepared a simple meal of pasta with canned sauce on the gas stove, eating at the dining table. The domesticity of the scene struck Claire as surreal, her father in borrowed clothes, sharing a meal in her apartment, discussing a case as equals rather than as mentor and student.

"I've been meaning to ask," Richard said as they finished eating. "The meditation cushion and the Buddha, is that a new interest?"

Claire followed his gaze to the small cushion positioned beneath her apartment's only decent window. "It was my therapist's suggestion, actually. Dr. Leland thought I should create a space dedicated to stillness."

She waited for the judgment; the subtle indication that seeking psychological help was a failure in some way. Instead, Richard surprised her again.

"A sound recommendation. The mind needs quiet to process trauma. I should have suggested something similar years ago, but I was too caught up in traditional cognitive approaches."

Before Claire could respond to this unexpected validation, a sharp knock at the door startled them both. They exchanged puzzled glances, who would be visiting in these conditions?

Claire approached the door cautiously, flashlight in hand. "Who is it?"

"Baltimore Police Department, ma'am," came the reply. "Welfare checks during the emergency. Is everyone all right in there?"

Something about the voice triggered Claire's professional instincts. It was too precise, too rehearsed. She glanced back at her father, who had clearly noticed the same thing. He moved silently to retrieve her service weapon from where she kept it secured.

"Could I see some identification through the peephole?" Claire called, stalling for time.

There was a pause, then the sound of something being placed against the peephole, a badge, but Claire couldn't make out the details in the dim light. Her instincts screamed danger.

"Officer, I'm Detective Claire Morrison with the Baltimore PD," she said, injecting authority into her voice. "What's your badge number and precinct?"

The silence that followed confirmed her suspicion. Then, unexpectedly, a woman's voice replied, all pretenses gone. "Dr. Morrison. I've been waiting to meet you. I think we have a mutual interest in transformation."

Claire's blood ran cold. She glanced at her father, who had positioned himself out of sight of the door. He nodded, understanding the situation instantly.

"Dr. Wright?" Claire asked, keeping her voice steady. "Eleanor Wright?"

"You know who I am," the woman sounded pleased. "That saves time. May I come in? It's quite cold in the hallway."

"I think we can talk just fine like this," Claire replied, her mind racing. Her phone was in the living room, out of reach. Even if she could get to it, reception had been spotty at best.

"Your father is with you, isn't he?" Wright continued, her voice eerily calm. "Dr. Richard Morrison, the great analyst of destructive patterns. I applied to study under him once, did you know? He rejected my application. Said my research methods were 'ethically que stionable.'"

Richard's expression hardened, recognition dawning. "Eleanor Wright," he whispered. "Proposed research on plant alkaloids as behavior modifiers. Wanted to test on subjects without informed consent."

Claire nodded, understanding the connection. "Dr. Wright," she called through the door, "whatever grievance you have with my father, we can discuss it properly. Let me call my colleagues, arrange a meeting."

"There's no need, Doctor," Wright replied. "You've seen my work. You understand what I'm doing, don't you? Each subject represents a stage in the transformation process. From crude material to refined essence. Your father's rejection delayed my work, but it made it stronger in the end. More precise."

As Wright spoke, Claire saw a thin stream of liquid beginning to seep under her door, clear, with a distinctive, sharp odor that made her eyes water even from several feet away.

"Gas!" she mouthed to her father, pointing at the liquid. Whatever it was, it was volatile, evaporating rapidly into the air of her apartment.

Richard moved quickly, grabbing the dish towels from the kitchen and stuffing them along the bottom of the door to slow the entry of the substance. Claire headed for the windows, intending to open one for ventilation, but stopped short when she saw movement on the fire escape outside. A shadowy figure was visible through the snow-covered glass, waiting.

"She's not alone," Claire whispered, backing away from the window. "There's someone on the fire escape."

The realization hit them simultaneously: they were trapped. The chemical smell was growing stronger, and Claire felt her eyes burning, her throat beginning to constrict. Through the door, Wright's voice continued, taking on an almost lecturing tone.

"The botanical symbolism is key to understanding the process. Each plant represents a stage in the journey from ordinary to transcendent. Foxglove for rhythm, belladonna for vision, hemlock for transition. Your father would be monkshood, wisdom before departure. And you, Dr. Morrison, would be lily of the valley, return to purity."

"She's using plant-derived toxins," Richard said, his voice dropping to ensure Wright couldn't hear. "The liquid under the door, it could be a distillation of something like water hemlock, causing respiratory paralysis."

Claire's training kicked in. They needed to neutralize the threat, secure their position, and call for backup. All while dealing with an unknown toxin already entering their system.

"Bathroom," she whispered, pointing toward the small room at the back of the apartment. "We can seal the door."

They moved quickly, grabbing Claire's phone and service weapon on the way. Once inside the bathroom, they sealed the crack under the door with towels soaked in water from the sink, then turned on the shower, hoping the steam would help dilute whatever was in the air.

"Wright isn't working alone," Claire said, trying to control her increasingly labored breathing. "The figure on the fire escape, she has at least one accomplice."

"Former student, perhaps," Richard suggested, his own breathing ragged. "She taught at the university level for years before her dismissal."

Claire attempted to call Martinez, but there was no signal in the bathroom. Text messages weren't going through either. They were effectively cut off from help.

"We need to neutralize the toxin," Richard said, his analytical mind still working despite their dire situation. "Most plant alkaloids can be counteracted with activated charcoal, which absorbs the poison before it's fully metabolized."

Claire scanned her bathroom cabinets desperately. "I don't have activated charcoal, but..." Her eyes landed on the bottle of makeup remover on her sink. "Charcoal face mask. Would that work?"

Richard examined the bottle. "It contains activated charcoal, yes. Not ideal, but better than nothing. Mix it with water, as much as we can manage to swallow."

They prepared the makeshift antidote, the absurdity of using a beauty product as emergency medical treatment not lost on either of them. Outside the bathroom, they could hear movement in the apartment, Wright or her accomplice had gained entry.

"Morrison!" Wright's voice called, closer now. "You're only delaying the inevitable. The transformation requires submission to the process."

Claire checked her weapon, the weight of it reassuring in her hand. "She'll come through that door eventually," she whispered to her father. "When she does, I'll be ready."

Richard nodded, then suddenly clutched at his chest, his breathing becoming more labored. "Claire," he gasped.

Alarm shot through Claire as she watched her father struggle for breath. The makeshift charcoal mixture hadn't been enough to counteract whatever they'd been exposed to. She helped him sit on the floor, her mind racing for solutions.

"Dad, stay with me," she urged, "Focus on slow, deep breaths."

Outside the bathroom door, Wright's voice continued, taking on an almost sing-song quality. "The great Dr. Morrison, reduced to hiding in a bathroom. How disappointing."

Claire's anger flared, providing clarity through the increasing fog of the toxin's effects. Wright wasn't just a killer; she was a narcissist who craved acknowledgment of her "work." Perhaps that could be used against her.

"Your methodology is flawed," Claire called back, her voice stronger than she felt. "The botanical symbols are inconsistently applied. The Washington County victim's hemlock placement was imprecise, suggesting a lack of understanding of its historical significance."

A pause, then Wright's voice, sharper now. "You're wrong. Each application was meticulously planned. The placement corresponds to ancient medicinal practices for each plant."

"Then why belladonna for Wilson?" Claire pressed, watching her father's breathing ease slightly as the distraction bought them time. "If you were following historical usage, foxglove would have been more appropriate for a chemistry teacher, given its relationship to modern heart medications."

Wright's response was immediate and defensive. "Wilson represented the dilated perception stage, the expansion of vision before true understanding. Belladonna was the only choice!"

As Wright continued to justify her "work," Claire noticed something crucial: the chemical smell was dissipating. Whatever had been pumped under the door was volatile enough to evaporate quickly or be neutralized by the steam from the shower. Her father's color was improving slightly as well, his breathing becoming less labored.

More importantly, Wright's voice was getting closer to the bathroom door, her need to defend her methodology apparently overriding caution. Claire positioned herself by the door, weapon ready, her father now able to stand behind her.

"Your entire premise is fundamentally flawed," Richard called out, his voice stronger than Claire had expected. "You've misinterpreted the basic pharmacological principles of these plants. No wonder your academic work was rejected."

The insult hit its mark. There was a sound of frustrated rage from just outside the bathroom door, then the handle turned violently. As the door began to open, Claire was ready. She kicked it hard, sending it crashing back into whoever stood on the other side.

There was a cry of pain and surprise. Claire pushed the door open fully to find Wright sprawled on the hallway floor, a mask covering the lower half of her face and a small canister in her hand, the source of the chemical agent. Without hesitation, Claire secured the woman's wrists, removing the canister and kicking it away.

"Eleanor Wright, you're under arrest for the murders of James Wilson and others," Claire recited, her training taking over despite the lingering effects of the toxin. "You have the right to remain silent..."

As she secured Wright, Richard emerged from the bathroom, moving with surprising agility to check the rest of the apartment. "The fire escape!" he called.

Claire looked up in time to see a figure rushing toward her from the living room, Wright's accomplice, a young man with wild eyes and a similar mask covering his face. Before she could react, Richard tackled him with unexpected strength, sending them both crashing into the kitchen island.

The struggle was brief but violent. Despite his age, Richard moved with the precision of someone who understood human biomechanics, using leverage rather than strength to subdue the younger man. By the time Claire had Wright securely restrained, her father had the accomplice pinned, a knee between his shoulder blades.

"Not bad for a seventy-year-old academic," Richard remarked, slightly breathless but with a hint of satisfaction in his voice.

Claire couldn't help but smile despite the gravity of the situation. "There's always another chapter in the textbook, isn't there?"

Outside, miraculously, sirens could be heard approaching through the snow-muffled streets. Martinez had apparently grown concerned by their lack of response and dispatched officers to check on them. The timing couldn't have been better.

Within the hour, Wright and her accomplice, identified as Jason Mercer, her former graduate student, were in custody. The apartment had been ventilated, and medics had arrived to examine them and administer proper treatment for the toxin they'd been exposed to. The preliminary analysis suggested a compound derived from water hemlock, just as Richard had suspected, intended to immobilize rather than kill immediately. Wright had wanted them conscious for her "transformation" process.

As dawn broke on the second day after the blizzard, power was restored to Claire's neighborhood with a hum and flicker. The sudden brightness seemed almost intrusive after so many hours by candle-light. Claire and Richard sat at her dining table drinking real coffee from a working machine, both still processing the events of the past forty-eight hours.

"Martinez says Wright is already confessing," Claire reported, scrolling through texts on her recharged phone. "Apparently, she sees herself as some kind of botanical pioneer, using her victims to prove theories about plant-based transformative substances."

"A brilliant mind, tragically misaligned," Richard observed. "Her early work in botanical medicine showed promise before she became fixated on these metamorphosis delusions."

"She targeted you specifically," Claire noted. "You were meant to be her next victim, monkshood for wisdom."

Richard nodded soberly. "The rejection of her research proposal affected her more deeply than I realized. A reminder that our academic decisions can have profound consequences beyond the classroom."

They fell into a companionable silence, the trauma of their near-death experience creating a bond that decades of careful distance had not been able to forge. Eventually, Richard cleared his throat, looking slightly uncomfortable.

"I should probably head home now that the roads are being cleared," he said, gesturing to the MDOT traffic updates on Claire's phone. "I've imposed on your hospitality long enough."

Claire studied her father's face, seeing past the formal exterior to the vulnerability beneath. The past two days had revealed more about him than the previous twenty-five years, his grief for her mother, his regrets about their relationship, his quiet pride in her work. To return to their usual distant dynamic seemed suddenly impossible.

"Maybe we could look through some old cases together," she said instead of acknowledging his statement. "Your experience with the Buffalo Gardener case was invaluable here. And... I'd like to hear more about your theories on the disappearance of Mom. Maybe over dinner next week?"

The surprise and cautious hope in her father's eyes answered the question before he spoke. "I'd like that very much, Claire."

As Richard gathered his things, preparing to depart now that the emergency had passed, Claire found herself reflecting on the unexpected gift of the Baltimore winter storm: not just the case solved or the lives saved, but the tentative bridge being built across decades of misunderstanding and unspoken grief.

Darwin, who had hidden during the confrontation with Wright, emerged from his hiding place to wind around Richard's ankles once more. The cat's usual wariness had been replaced by apparent affection, as if he recognized something in her father that Claire herself was only beginning to see.

"I'll drive you home," she offered. "The roads still won't be great."

Richard nodded, then hesitated before adding, "Perhaps we could talk about looking into your mother's case. I've... I've been reviewing some old evidence. There might be connections we missed before."

Claire felt a flutter of something between hope and trepidation. "You never wanted to discuss it before."

"Perhaps it's time," Richard said quietly. "Some mysteries shouldn't remain unsolved forever."

Like relationships, Claire thought but didn't say. Instead, she simply smiled and reached for her coat, ready to step out into the transformed landscape of Baltimore after the storm, where familiar streets had been made new again beneath the blanket of snow, and paths long closed might now be cleared for passage.

Chapter Five

Adverse Reactions

Claire Morrison focused on the patient chart, her expression growing concerned as she analyzed the clinical notes. Something didn't add up. As a forensic psychologist for the Baltimore Police Department, she wasn't typically called in for medical mysteries. But her friend Dr. Eleanor Larson at Baltimore General, requested her expertise.

"I need someone who sees patterns," Dr. Larson had told her over the phone that morning. "Someone who understands behavior in ways most people don't. Claire, these patients don't make sense medically. I think something else is happening here."

Now sitting in Dr. Larson's office, Claire could see why her friend had been concerned. Over the past six weeks, sixteen patients had presented with similar signs and symptoms: episodic confusion, visual disturbances, heart palpitations, and extreme anxiety. The pattern was too consistent to be coincidental yet too varied in patient demographics to suggest a common medical cause.

"What do the toxicology reports show?" Claire asked.

Dr. Larson shook her head. "Nothing conclusive. Some showed trace amounts of benzodiazepines, but nothing that explains the full range of signs. And the strangest part is that most resolve within twenty-four hours of admission."

Claire reached for her tic tacs in her pocket. Three years sober. It was a major accomplishment, yet Claire still felt vulnerable. "Have you looked for behavioral patterns? Any common staff among the affected patients?"

"That's actually why I called you," Dr. Larson said, switching to another chart on her desktop. "I started tracking which nurses, techs, and doctors interacted with these patients. There's significant overlap, but nothing conclusive. The hospital administration is calling it mass hysteria, but I've seen hysteria. This isn't it."

Claire agreed. Mass hysteria typically spreads through visual contact and psychological suggestion. These cases occurred in different wings of the hospital with patients who never interacted. Some were emergency admissions; others were scheduled surgeries. The only common factor was the hospital itself.

"I'd like to bring Detective Martinez in on this," Claire said, already reaching for her phone. "If there's something happening here beyond medical causes, we need to investigate properly."

Dr. Larson hesitated. "Claire, the hospital board is already concerned about negative publicity. Chief of Medicine Matthews…"

"Is related to my Chief Matthews, I know," Claire said. Dr. Robert Matthews was the younger brother of Police Chief William Matthews. "But if patients are being harmed, we need to investigate, regardless of publicity concerns."

An hour later, Detective Sara Martinez entered Dr. Larson's office. Her crisp pantsuit and perfect posture stood in stark contrast to Claire's more rumpled appearance after hours of reviewing files. The small scar beneath her right eye seemed more pronounced in the fluorescent lighting as she frowned in concentration.

"Dr. Morrison," Martinez greeted her with a professional nod before turning to Dr. Larson. "I understand you have concerns about patient safety."

Claire appreciated Martinez's ability to cut to the heart of the matter. Since working together on several cases, and most recently through the blizzard case with Claire's father, she'd developed a deep respect for the detective's sharp mind and unwavering focus. Their partnership had evolved into a solid professional relationship and budding friendship.

"Sixteen cases with nearly identical signs and symptoms," Claire explained, handing Martinez the summary she'd compiled. "No clear medical cause, signs that resolve too quickly for most toxins, and no obvious pattern to who's being affected."

Martinez reviewed the information.

"Have you considered deliberate poisoning?" she asked, looking up from the files.

Dr. Larson's face paled. "I didn't want to jump to conclusions, but yes, it's crossed my mind. That's why I called Claire. If someone is doing this intentionally, we need to identify them before more patients are affected."

"We'll need complete access to hospital records, security footage, and staff schedules," Martinez said, already making notes. "And this investigation needs to be discreet. If someone is targeting patients, we don't want to alert them."

Claire nodded. "And we should notify Chief Matthews. Given his brother's position here, he should be informed from the beginning."

Martinez's expression tightened almost imperceptibly. "Agreed. Though it may complicate matters politically."

Claire understood Martinez's concern. Chief Matthews was a good cop but highly attuned to political considerations. With his brother as Chief of Medicine, the potential for conflict of interest was significant. But proceeding without his knowledge would create bigger problems.

"I'll call him," Claire offered, stepping into the hallway with her phone.

Chief Matthews answered on the third ring. "Morrison, please tell me you're calling with good news about the Waterfront case."

"Actually, sir, I'm at Baltimore General. We may have a situation involving patient safety that requires investigation. Detective Martinez is with me."

A lengthy silence followed. "My brother's hospital?"

"Yes, sir. Dr. Larson has identified sixteen patients with unexplained signs and symptoms that may indicate deliberate harm."

Another pause. "I'm assuming you have actual evidence and not just speculation?"

"The pattern is concerning enough to warrant preliminary investigation," Claire replied carefully. "We'd like your authorization to proceed officially, given the sensitive nature of the location."

Matthews sighed audibly. "Fine. Investigate, but quietly. I want a daily report, and nothing goes public without my direct approval. Clear?"

"Crystal, sir."

When Claire returned to the office, Martinez and Dr. Larson were reviewing security protocols for the hospital's medication system.

"We have authorization," Claire informed them. "With conditions. We keep it quiet, report directly to Matthews, and nothing goes public without his approval."

Martinez nodded, unsurprised. "We should start by interviewing the affected patients who are still hospitalized. How many are currently admitted?"

"Three," Dr. Larson answered, pulling up their records on her computer. "Mrs. Kathleen Jenkins in orthopedics, recovering from right hip replacement. She experienced manifestations yesterday afternoon. Martin Cooper in cardiology for monitoring after a minor heart attack three days ago, indications began this morning. And Sophia Reyes, a nineteen-year-old admitted through the ER last night with appendicitis. Her signs and symptoms started about four hours after her surgery."

Claire studied the hospital floor plan displayed on Dr. Larson's wall. "Different wings, different medical teams, different reasons for admission. The only commonality is this hospital."

"And the timing," Martinez noted, reviewing the cases. "Most manifestation onsets occur between four and twelve hours after admission, regardless of the time of day."

"That could suggest administration of something during the admission process," Claire mused. "Or someone who has access to patients during that window."

Dr. Larson looked troubled. "That could be dozens of staff members. Nurses, techs, food service workers, janitorial staff, not to mention doctors and specialists."

"Then we start with the patients," Martinez decided. "See if they noticed anything unusual before their symptoms began. Dr. Larson, we'll need temporary credentials to move through the hospital without raising questions."

"I'll arrange it immediately," Dr. Larson promised, reaching for her phone. "And Claire, I've scheduled a consultation with an external clinical psychologist, Dr. Booker, allegedly about a patient with trauma-related symptoms. She can provide psychological insights without drawing attention."

Claire nodded in approval. Dr. Booker's expertise in trauma and behavioral psychology would be valuable.

By late afternoon, Claire and Martinez had interview credentials and were making their way to the orthopedic wing to speak with their first patient. The hospital corridors bustled with activity. Claire observed it all with a profiler's eye, looking for patterns, anomalies, anything that might explain what was happening to these patients.

Kathleen Jenkins was a seventy-two-year-old retired schoolteacher with a keen mind and observant eyes. Her room was filled with get-well cards, and she greeted them with surprising energy for someone recovering from major surgery.

"More doctors?" she asked as they entered. "I've already told three different people about the weird episode yesterday."

"Actually, Mrs. Jenkins, we're conducting a patient experience survey," Claire explained, using their cover story. "We'd like to hear about your entire hospital stay, including any unusual experiences."

Martinez pulled out a notepad, assuming the role of assistant. "Just speak freely about your time here, from admission onward."

Mrs. Jenkins proved to be an excellent observer. She described her pre-surgical procedures, the staff who had attended her, and her post-operative care in detail.

"Everything was fine until yesterday afternoon," she recalled. "I'd had lunch, chicken that was terribly overcooked by the way, and my afternoon medications. Then my daughter visited around two o'clock. After she left, I started feeling strange. The room seemed to shimmer, like looking through water. My heart was racing, and I couldn't seem to think clearly. I pressed the call button, and the next thing I remember clearly is waking up with doctors all around me."

"Do you remember who gave you your afternoon medications?" Martinez asked casually.

"A nurse I hadn't seen before. Young man, very polite. Had a little pin on his scrubs, a butterfly, I think. Seemed new, checked my wristband twice."

Claire and Martinez exchanged glances. A new face administering medication just before symptoms appeared was potentially significant.

"And before that," Claire continued, "was there anyone else who interacted with you that wasn't part of your regular care team?"

Mrs. Jenkins considered this. "Well, there was a woman from nutritional services who came to discuss my dietary preferences. And someone from housekeeping cleaned the bathroom. Oh, and a respiratory therapist stopped by briefly, though I'm not sure why. I don't have breathing problems."

Claire made note of each of these interactions. They repeated this process with the other two patients, and distinctive patterns emerged. Each patient reported interactions with staff members who seemed out of place or whose purpose wasn't entirely clear. Martin Cooper mentioned a respiratory assessment despite having no pulmonary issues. Sophia Reyes recalled a nursing student who had drawn blood samples, even though her chart showed no ordered blood work during that time.

"We need to verify if these staff members were legitimate," Martinez said as they left Sophia's room. "The respiratory therapist, the nursing student, the nutritional services worker. We need to confirm they were supposed to be with these patients."

"And we need hospital-wide security footage," Claire added. "If someone is impersonating staff or accessing patients inappropriately, we should be able to identify them on camera."

They reconvened in Dr. Larson's office, where Dr. Booker had joined them. The psychologist's calm presence was a welcome addition to their growing investigation team.

"From a psychological perspective," Dr. Booker offered after hearing their findings, "these cases don't fit the pattern of mass hysteria or psychosomatic illness. The manifestations are too consistent, and there's no evidence of a triggering event or shared anxiety source. Moreover, the symptoms include signs that would be difficult to produce psychologically."

"So, we're definitely looking at something being administered to these patients," Claire concluded. "Something that produces confusion, visual disturbances, anxiety, and cardiac symptoms, but metabolizes quickly enough to be nearly gone by the time toxicology screens are run."

Dr. Larson nodded grimly. "There are several compounds that could produce those effects. Certain anticholinergics, hallucinogens, or a combination of medications might cause similar reactions."

"The question is why," Martinez said, tapping her pen against her notebook. "Random poisoning? Testing some kind of substance? Or is there a specific motive targeting these patients?"

Claire had been wondering the same thing. "Let's look at patient demographics. Any patterns in who's being affected?"

They cross-referenced their files online using Dr. Larson's desktop. The affected patients ranged in age from nineteen to eighty-four. They were diverse in gender, race, and socioeconomic background. Their medical conditions varied widely.

"No obvious targeting criteria," Martinez observed. "Which suggests either random selection or some factor we haven't identified yet."

"Maybe it's not about the patients at all," Claire suggested. "Maybe it's about the hospital itself. Creating incidents that force additional testing, extended stays, or procedural reviews."

"That would mean someone inside the system," Dr. Larson said, troubled by the implication. "Someone who understands hospital protocols and knows how to manipulate them."

"Which brings us back to staff," Martinez concluded. "We need that security footage and verification on these suspicious interactions."

Dr. Larson made a call to security, using her authority as department head to request footage covering the timeframes when patients reported unusual staff encounters. While they waited, Claire reviewed the medication logs for each affected patient, looking for irregularities.

"Here's something," she said after twenty minutes of analysis. "Twelve of the sixteen affected patients received some form of pain medication within two hours before manifestation onset. Different medications, but all administered around the same time relative to when signs appeared."

Martinez looked up. "That could be our delivery mechanism. Pain medications are expected to cause some side effects. A patient might attribute initial symptoms to their regular medication."

"We should check the medication supply chain," Dr. Booker suggested. "If someone is tampering with pain medications, they must have access to the pharmacy or medication storage areas."

Dr. Larson shook her head. "Our medication system is highly secured. Narcotics and controlled substances require double verification and biometric access. It would be extremely difficult to tamper with them."

"Unless someone has the proper access," Martinez pointed out. "Someone in the pharmacy, or with high-level clearance."

The security footage arrived, delivered by a technician who clearly wondered why a department head needed hours of hospital surveillance video. They spent the next several hours reviewing footage, focusing on the timeframes when patients reported interactions with suspicious staff members.

"There," Claire said, pointing to a figure on the screen. A man in respiratory therapy scrubs was entering Martin Cooper's room at precisely the time the patient had mentioned. "Can we get a clearer image of his face?"

Martinez manipulated the controls, zooming in and enhancing the image as much as the system allowed. The man wore a standard ID badge, but kept his head angled away from cameras.

"He's deliberately avoiding showing his face," Martinez noted. "That's not normal behavior for legitimate staff."

They found similar instances for other patients, staff members whose body language indicated awareness of the cameras, who moved with purpose but kept their identities obscured. In one striking case, a woman entered Sophia Reyes's room without any interaction with the nurses' station, spent exactly three minutes inside, then exited and took a service elevator to another floor.

"We need to identify these people," Martinez said. "Dr. Larson, can you check if these individuals match actual hospital employees?"

Dr. Larson was already on her computer, pulling up staff records. "I'll need clear images of their badges; even partial numbers could help us identify them."

By midnight, they had identified several suspicious individuals on the security footage. Some appeared to be legitimate staff working outside their assigned areas. Others couldn't be matched to any current hospital employees, suggesting either outdated records or imposters.

"We should notify Chief Matthews," Claire said, checking her watch. "This is looking more deliberate with each piece of evidence we uncover."

Martinez nodded in agreement. "And we need to establish surveillance on medication storage areas and patient rooms. If someone is targeting patients, they'll likely continue the pattern."

Claire called Chief Matthews, despite the late hour. He answered with the gruffness of someone woken from sleep.

"This better be important, Morrison."

"We have evidence suggesting deliberate targeting of patients, sir. Several unidentified individuals accessing patient rooms, symptoms consistent with administration of unknown substances, and a potential pattern involving pain medications."

Matthews was silent for a moment. "Are you telling me someone is poisoning patients at my brother's hospital?"

"We don't have definitive proof yet," Claire answered carefully. "But the evidence strongly suggests intentional harm."

"Christ." Matthews exhaled heavily. "My brother's going to have a conniption. How many people know about this investigation?"

"Just our team, sir. Dr. Larson, Dr. Booker, Detective Martinez, and myself."

"Keep it that way for now. I'll talk to Robert in the morning, privately. In the meantime, set up whatever surveillance you need, a few plainclothes, but keep it discreet. I don't want this turning into a media circus before we have concrete evidence."

After ending the call, Claire turned to Martinez. "We have authorization for surveillance. Matthews will speak with his brother tomorrow."

"That conversation should be interesting," Martinez remarked dryly. "In the meantime, we need to focus on protecting current patients and identifying our suspects."

They developed a surveillance plan with Dr. Larson, strategically placing plainclothes officers in key areas of the hospital. By 2 AM, their preliminary measures were in place, and they agreed to reconvene in the morning.

Claire crashed at her apartment for a few hours, greeted by Darwin's meow for being neglected all day. She fed him, showered, and collapsed into bed; her mind still working on the puzzle of the hospital mystery even as exhaustion claimed her.

Morning came too quickly. Claire arrived at the hospital by 7 AM, fortified by strong coffee. She found Martinez in Dr. Larson's office, reviewing overnight surveillance reports.

"Anything?" Claire asked, setting down her coffee.

"Nothing conclusive," Martinez replied. "One medication storage area was accessed at 4:12 AM using valid credentials, but the employee claims she wasn't on shift. We're verifying her statement now."

"Could be credential theft," Claire suggested. "Or someone pressuring staff to share access."

Dr. Larson entered, looking harried. "The Matthews brothers are having a closed-door meeting. From what I could gather, it's getting heated."

Claire grimaced. "Political considerations meeting public safety concerns. Never a pleasant conversation."

"In the meantime," Martinez said, "we should interview the pharmacy staff. If medications are the delivery mechanism, someone in pharmacy might have noticed irregularities or unauthorized access."

The hospital pharmacy was a secure, high-tech operation on the second floor. The head pharmacist, Dr. Reglan, met them in his office, clearly uncomfortable with their presence.

"Dr. Larson explained the situation," he said, adjusting his glasses nervously. "I've reviewed our logs and security protocols. There have been no unauthorized access events in our systems."

"What about authorized access that might seem unusual?" Claire asked. "Staff accessing medications at odd hours or for patients outside their care areas?"

Dr. Reglan hesitated. "Well, there have been some workflow changes recently. With our new electronic medication verification system, pharmacists and techs sometimes process orders in batches rather than individually. It's made tracking specific personnel to specific medications more complicated."

"When did this system change occur?" Martinez asked sharply.

"About two months ago. Part of a hospital-wide efficiency initiative."

Claire and Martinez exchanged glances. The timing aligned perfectly with the onset of the mysterious patient symptoms.

"We'd like to see the records for this new system," Martinez requested. "Particularly any unusual patterns in access or distribution."

Dr. Reglan brought up the records on his computer, and they spent the next hour identifying potential anomalies. Several stood out: medication orders processed outside normal workflow patterns, pain medications prepared but documented at unusual times, and most significantly, a recurring employee ID accessing the system during off-hours.

"Who does this ID belong to?" Claire asked, pointing to the recurring number.

Dr. Reglan frowned. "That's strange. It's registered to Dr. Marcus Olsen, but he's only part-time in our outpatient clinic. He shouldn't have this level of system access."

"We need to speak with Dr. Olsen immediately," Martinez said. "Is he in the hospital today?"

"Let me check the schedule." Dr. Reglan typed quickly. "Yes, he's scheduled in the outpatient clinic from 10 AM to 2 PM today."

As they left the pharmacy, Claire's phone buzzed with a message from Chief Matthews: "Meeting concluded. Brother cooperating. Proceed with investigation, but QUIETLY. Hospital board involved now. Keep me updated hourly."

"The politics are intensifying," Claire told Martinez, showing her the message. "We need to move quickly before this gets any more complicated."

They decided to split up. Martinez would continue reviewing security footage with a focus on Dr. Olsen's movements, while Claire would interview more of the affected patients who had been discharged but might be willing to speak about their experiences.

Claire spent the morning calling former patients, carefully framing her questions as part of a quality improvement initiative. Most reported similar experiences: unusual staff interactions, unexpected procedures or assessments, and then the onset of symptoms that resolved within a day.

One detail caught her attention. Three patients mentioned receiving "special pain management protocol" as part of a study they'd supposedly agreed to during admission. When Claire checked with Dr. Larson, no such study existed at Baltimore General.

By noon, she had rejoined Martinez in their makeshift command center. The detective had discovered something significant.

"Dr. Olsen appears on security footage entering the hospital outside his scheduled hours at least twelve times in the past month," Martinez reported. "Always using the service entrance, always during shift changes when staffing is in transition."

"And look at this," Claire added, sharing her notes from the patient interviews. "Three patients were told they were part of a pain management study that doesn't exist. They all remember signing something during the admission confusion, but none received copies of what they signed."

Dr. Booker, who had joined them again, looked troubled. "That suggests premeditation and deliberate deception. Not opportunistic harm, but a planned approach."

A knock at the door interrupted them. Dr. Robert Matthews, Chief of Medicine and the police chief's brother, entered without waiting for a response. Unlike his older brother's bulldog build, Robert Matthews was lean and academic in appearance but shared the same penetrating gaze.

"Detective, Dr. Morrison," he acknowledged them tensely. "My brother has informed me of your investigation. I want to be clear that patient safety is my highest priority, but I'm concerned about your methods and the potential impact on hospital operations."

"We understand your concerns, Dr. Matthews," Claire replied diplomatically. "We're conducting this investigation as discreetly as possible."

"Be that as it may," he continued, "the hospital board is extremely concerned. If word gets out that patients are being deliberately harmed in our facility, the damage would be catastrophic. Not to mention the liability issues."

"With respect, sir," Martinez said, her voice professionally neutral but with underlying steel, "our priority is preventing further harm and identifying those responsible. Hospital reputation is secondary to patient safety."

Dr. Matthews's expression tightened. "Of course, patient safety comes first, Detective. I'm simply asking for appropriate caution and discretion. What have you found so far?"

Claire and Martinez shared a condensed version of their findings, omitting specific names until they had more concrete evidence. Dr. Matthews listened with growing concern.

"This is deeply troubling," he admitted when they finished. "If someone is using our systems to harm patients, they must be stopped immediately. But I insist on being kept informed of every development. No arrests or public actions without consulting me first."

After he left, Martinez shook her head. "Political complications are mounting. We need to move faster."

"Agreed. Dr. Olsen will be in the outpatient clinic until 2 PM. We should observe him first, then approach him for questioning."

They positioned themselves in the outpatient clinic waiting area, posing as a patient and companion. Dr. Olsen turned out to be a man in his early forties, with an efficient manner and a practiced bedside charm that seemed to put patients at ease. Nothing in his demeanor suggested someone who might be harming patients.

"He seems completely normal," Claire observed quietly. "But the evidence points strongly in his direction."

"Normal appearance is often the best disguise," Martinez replied. "Wait until his last appointment, then we'll approach him."

At 1:45 PM, Dr. Olsen finished with his final patient of the day. As he returned to his office to gather his things, Claire and Martinez intercepted him.

"Dr. Olsen?" Martinez showed her badge discreetly. "Detective Martinez, Baltimore PD. This is Dr. Morrison. We'd like to ask you a few questions."

Olsen's expression remained pleasant, but Claire noticed an almost imperceptible tightening around his eyes. "Of course, Detective. Is there a problem?"

"We're investigating some unusual incidents at the hospital," Claire explained. "Your name has come up in connection with system access outside your normal working hours."

"There must be some mistake," he replied smoothly. "I only access hospital systems during my scheduled clinic times."

"Then perhaps you can explain why your credentials have been used to access the medication management system at 4 AM multiple times this month?" Martinez asked.

Olsen's composure slipped slightly. "I sometimes review patient files from home. The system might show access even if I'm not physically present."

"The system shows physical badge swipes, Doctor," Claire countered. "Not remote access."

Olsen glanced at his watch. "I'd like to be helpful, but I have another appointment to get to. Perhaps we could continue this conversation later? With hospital legal present?"

"We can continue at the station if you prefer," Martinez said, her tone hardening slightly. "This is a serious investigation involving patient safety."

Something changed in his expression, a calculation, a decision made. "Actually, I just remembered I need to check something in the pharmacy before I leave. Would you mind waiting here? I'll be right back."

Before they could respond, he turned and walked quickly down the hallway. Martinez immediately moved to follow him.

"He's running," she said tersely. "Call for backup."

Claire alerted the officers stationed throughout the hospital while following Martinez. Dr. Olsen had a head start and clearly knew the hospital layout well. He disappeared around a corner, and by the time they reached the intersection, he was nowhere in sight.

"He could have gone anywhere," Claire said, frustrated. "Service elevator, stairwell, patient rooms. There are too many options."

Martinez assessed the situation quickly. "He'll head for an exit. Alert security to watch all exits and have them check the security feeds. I'll take the nearest stairwell. You check the service elevator."

Claire raced to the service elevator, finding it already in motion, descending from their floor. She took the adjacent stairs, hurrying down while updating their backup on her phone. By the time she reached the ground floor, alarms were sounding throughout the hospital, a code that indicated security alert without causing patient panic.

Her phone buzzed with a message from Martinez: "Basement level. Supply area."

Claire redirected to the basement, navigating the corridors of the hospital's lower level. The area housed maintenance facilities, storage rooms, and the supply chain operation that kept the hospital functioning. It was also largely deserted during midday, most staff being occupied with patient care on the upper floors.

She found Martinez outside a door marked "Medical Research Supply" with two security officers already in position.

"He's in there," Martinez said quietly. "Security saw him on camera entering with his badge. No other exits from the room."

"Do we know what's in there?" Claire asked.

"Research chemicals, experimental medications, equipment for clinical trials," one of the security officers supplied. "Highly restricted access."

"Which Dr. Olsen apparently has," Martinez noted. "We need to approach carefully. If he's been exposing patients to unknown substances, he may have access to dangerous materials."

They positioned themselves strategically, with security officers covering the only exit. Martinez took the lead, her hand near her weapon as she called out.

"Dr. Olsen, this is Detective Martinez. We need you to come out with your hands visible. The room is covered."

Silence greeted them. Martinez tried again.

"Dr. Olsen, cooperation now will help your situation. Come out slowly."

The door opened fractionally, and Olsen's voice came through the gap. "I want immunity. Full immunity and witness protection."

Claire and Martinez exchanged glances.

"Immunity from what, exactly?" Martinez asked.

"I'm not the one in charge," Olsen said, his voice tight with stress. "I'm just following orders. If they find out I've been caught, they'll kill me."

"Who will kill you, Doctor?" Claire asked, stepping closer. "Who are you working with?"

"I can't say. Not until I have guaranteed protection."

Martinez kept her voice steady. "We can discuss protection options, but you need to come out now and explain."

After a tense moment, Olsen opened the door fully. He appeared disheveled, his professional demeanor completely abandoned. In his hand, he clutched a flash drive.

"Everything's on here," he said, holding it out. "The whole operation. But you have to promise they won't find me."

Martinez took the flash drive while security officers secured Dr. Olsen. "Who are 'they,' Doctor? You need to give us something concrete."

Olsen looked around, as though expecting to be observed. "Pharmaceutical research. Off the books. Testing compounds without FDA approval or patient consent. I was recruited three years ago, told it was advancing medicine, helping patients who had run out of options. By the time I realized what was really happening, I was in too deep."

Claire studied his face, reading the genuine fear in his expression. "You're saying the hospital is involved in illegal pharmaceutical testing?"

"Not the hospital officially," the doctor clarified. "A group within it. They identify suitable test subjects, administer experimental compounds, and document the effects. The signs and symptoms are temporary by design, they don't want to raise too many alarms. Just enough data to refine their formulations."

"Names," Martinez demanded. "We need names."

Dr. Olsen shook his head. "It's all on the drive. But they're powerful people. Connected. The operation goes beyond this hospital."

As they escorted him upstairs to a secure room, Claire received a call from Chief Matthews.

"Morrison, what the hell is happening? Hospital security just informed me there's a situation in progress."

"We've apprehended a suspect, sir. Dr. Marcus Olsen. He claims to be part of a larger operation involving illegal pharmaceutical testing on unwitting patients. We have what appears to be evidence on a flash drive."

Matthews was silent for a moment. "Bring it directly to me. No one else sees that drive until I've reviewed it. And keep Dr. Olsen isolated, no contact with anyone."

The gravity in Matthews's voice concerned Claire. "Sir, is there something you're not telling us?"

"Just do as I say, Morrison. This could be bigger than you realize."

Within an hour, Olsen was secured in an interview room at the police station, and Claire and Martinez were in Matthews's office, watching him review the contents of the flash drive. His expression darkened with each passing minute.

"This is a catastrophic mess," he finally said, rubbing his face wearily. "According to these documents, a research group called Norvis Biotech has been using Baltimore General and two other hospitals as testing grounds for experimental psychoactive compounds. They're bypassing clinical trials by administering micro-doses to patients and documenting the effects."

"Who's behind it?" Martinez asked.

Matthews looked distinctly uncomfortable. "That's where it gets complicated. The leadership includes several prominent physicians, researchers, and my brother."

The revelation landed like a physical blow. Claire felt her breath catch. "Dr. Robert Matthews is involved?"

"According to these files, he's not just involved, he's coordinating the Baltimore operation." Matthews looked physically ill. "I've known Robert to be ambitious, but this crosses every ethical and legal line imaginable."

"We need to bring him in for questioning," Martinez said firmly. "Regardless of his position or relationship to you."

Matthews nodded, his professional duty clearly winning over family loyalty. "I'll handle it personally. But this must be managed carefully.

The implications for the hospital, for patient trust in the healthcare system, this could have devastating consequences beyond the immediate legal issues."

"There's something else," Claire said, having continued reviewing the files while they spoke. "According to Dr. Olsen's notes, the testing has been escalating. They've been increasing dosages, trying more potent compounds. The most recent formulation is significantly stronger than previous versions. If they're continuing the testing pattern, more patients could be at serious risk."

Matthews stood, decision made. "Martinez, assemble a team. We move now, before anyone else is harmed or evidence is destroyed. Morrison, coordinate with Dr. Larson to identify any current patients who might be at risk based on the patterns we've seen."

As they prepared to leave, Matthews stopped them with a final thought. "Whatever happens next, remember that patient welfare comes first. Politics, reputations, even family, none of that matters compared to protecting people under their care."

The next hours unfolded in a carefully orchestrated operation. While Martinez led a team to secure key areas of the hospital and detain suspected participants in the scheme, Claire worked with Dr. Larson and Dr. Booker to identify and monitor potentially vulnerable patients.

By evening, seven hospital employees had been taken into custody, including two pharmacists, a nurse manager, and a research coordinator. Dr. Robert Matthews was notably absent from his office, having apparently left shortly after their earlier conversation with him.

"He's running," Chief Matthews said, when informed of his brother's disappearance. "Put out an alert but keep it internal for now. I want him found before this hits the news."

Claire coordinated with Dr. Larson on patient protection measures. As they finished implementing safeguards for current patients, Dr. Booker joined them, her expression troubled."

"I've been thinking about the psychological aspects of this case," she said. "Specifically, what would motivate established medical professionals to engage in such clearly unethical behavior."

"Money is the obvious answer," Dr. Larson suggested. "Pharmaceutical development is worth billions."

"Yes, but these are already successful people," Booker countered. "Dr. Robert Matthews, for instance, has a distinguished career, significant wealth, professional respect. Why risk everything?"

Claire considered this. "Sometimes it's not about what you have, but what you believe you deserve. Dr. Matthews may have felt entitled to more recognition, influence, and legacy than traditional channels offered him."

"A common trait in certain personality types," Booker agreed. "The belief that normal rules don't apply because one's work is too important to be constrained by conventional ethics or regulations."

Their conversation was interrupted by Martinez's arrival. "We found something in Dr. Matthews's private office," she reported. "A hidden safe containing research journals documenting experiments going back five years. This didn't start with the new medication system, it's been ongoing much longer than we thought."

"Any indication of where he might have gone?" Claire asked.

"Nothing concrete, but there are references to a research facility in northern Maryland. We're getting a warrant now."

Chief Matthews joined them, his face etched with the strain of the day's revelations. "The hospital board has been informed of the situation. They're cooperating fully with our investigation and implementing emergency protocols to ensure patient safety."

"And your brother?" Claire asked carefully.

Matthews's expression hardened. "My brother betrayed his oath, his patients, and his profession. When we find him, he'll face the full consequences of his actions." He turned to Martinez. "As soon as that warrant comes through, I want that research facility searched top to bottom. If he's there, or if there's any evidence of ongoing experimentation, I want it shut down immediately."

The warrant came through by midnight. Claire joined Martinez and an FBI tactical team as they approached the research facility located in a secluded wooded area outside Baltimore. The building appeared innocuous, a modern, single-story structure that could have housed any legitimate medical research operation. Only the excessive security measures and lack of clear signage suggested something more secretive.

"Standard approach," the tactical team leader instructed. "Secure the perimeter, then move in. We don't know who or what is inside, so exercise extreme caution."

Claire and Martinez waited in a command vehicle while the initial entry took place. Within minutes, radio confirmation came through that the building was occupied with minimal resistance encountered.

"Clear to enter, Detective," the team leader reported.

They found a fully equipped research laboratory with state-of-the-art equipment. Several researchers had been detained, looking both frightened and resigned. Of Dr. Robert Matthews, however, there was no sign.

"He was here earlier today," one of the researchers admitted during preliminary questioning. "Left in a hurry about 30 minutes ago. Said something about contingency plans."

Martinez organized a search of the facility while Claire examined the research documentation. What she found disturbed her deeply, detailed records of experiments conducted on unwitting patients, cat-aloged effects, chemical formulations, and projected market valuations for the compounds being developed.

"This goes beyond anything we imagined," Claire told Martinez, indicating the extensive documentation. "They've been testing multiple compounds on hundreds of patients across three hospitals. The manifestations we investigated were just the most recent formulation."

Martinez's expression darkened as she examined a financial spreadsheet. "And incredibly profitable, according to these projections. They were bypassing years of clinical trials and regulatory approvals, reducing development costs by millions while accelerating time to market."

"By using vulnerable patients as unwitting test subjects," Claire added.

Her phone rang, Chief Matthews calling for an update.

"We've secured the facility," she reported. "Multiple staff in custody, extensive evidence of illegal experimentation, but no sign of your brother. According to staff, he left 30 minutes before we arrived with mention of contingency plans."

Matthews sounded exhausted. "We're tracking his vehicle and credit cards. Nothing yet, which suggests he was prepared for this possibility."

"The evidence here is damning, sir," Claire continued. "Documentation of testing on patients without consent, detailed formulations, financial projections. This operation was sophisticated and has been running for years."

"Preserve everything," Matthews instructed. "By the book. I want this case airtight when it goes to prosecution."

As they continued processing the scene, Dr. Booker arrived, having been called in to help assess the psychological aspects of the operation.

"This is disturbing on multiple levels," she observed, reviewing the research protocols. "Not just the obvious ethical violations, but the calculated nature of the deception. They designed systems specifically to bypass patient consent protections while maintaining plausible deniability."

Claire noticed Martinez examining a wall of photographs, the research team at various social functions, professional achievements, celebratory moments. Dr. Robert Matthews featured prominently in many images, often central to the group, clearly the leader.

"He built a culture around this," Martinez observed. "Created a bubble where ethical boundaries blurred. These aren't just criminals, they're people who convinced themselves they were pioneers, that the normal rules didn't apply because their work was too important."

"A common rationalization," Dr. Booker noted. "The end justifies the means. Particularly seductive in medical research, where one can always claim to be ultimately helping future patients."

A tactical officer approached with a laptop. "Detective, you should see this. We found it in what appears to be Dr. Matthews's office here. It was still logged in."

The screen displayed an open email, apparently interrupted mid-composition. It was addressed to multiple recipients with the subject line "Contingency Protocol Alpha."

"He was warning the others," Martinez realized, scanning the partial message. "There are references to offshore accounts, document destruction protocols, and alternate research locations."

"Which means there could be more facilities like this," Claire said grimly.

Martinez immediately contacted Chief Matthews with this new information. While she coordinated with him, Claire and Dr. Booker continued examining the research documentation.

"There's something else here," Claire said, indicating a section labeled "Secondary Effects Analysis." "They weren't just documenting the immediate symptoms we've been investigating. They were tracking long-term neurological impact through disguised follow-up appointments."

Dr. Booker reviewed the data. "If these observations are accurate, some of these compounds could cause subtle but significant long-term effects. Memory issues, mood disturbances, cognitive changes that might not be immediately apparent but could develop over months."

"We need to identify every patient who may have been exposed," Claire decided. "Not just the recent cases we've been investigating, but potentially hundreds more over the past five years."

By dawn, they had established a clearer picture of the operation's scope. Norvis Biotech was a shell company created to commercialize the compounds being developed through the illegal testing. Investors included several pharmaceutical executives, venture capitalists specializing in medical technology, and even two hospital board members from institutions involved in the testing program.

Chief Matthews arrived personally as morning broke, looking haggard. "Still no sign of Robert," he reported. "But we've frozen the accounts we know about and alerted border patrol and transportation hubs."

"Sir," Claire said hesitantly, "given the documented long-term effects of some of these compounds, we need to implement a patient notification and monitoring protocol immediately. The hospital will need to contact potentially affected individuals."

Matthews nodded grimly. "Already in progress. Dr. Larson is coordinating with hospital administration and the ethics committee. They're developing a protocol for patient notification that balances full disclosure with avoiding unnecessary panic."

"The media will get hold of this soon," Martinez pointed out. "We should prepare a statement."

"The department's public affairs team is working on it," Matthews confirmed. "Complete transparency about the investigation without compromising patient privacy or the case against those involved."

As they continued processing the facility, Claire's phone buzzed with a message from Dr. Larson: "Urgent. Need you at the hospital. Another patient presenting with symptoms. Different manifestation."

Claire showed Matthews and Martinez the message. "I need to go."

"Go," Matthews authorized. "Martinez and I will continue here. Keep us updated."

Claire arrived at Baltimore General thirty minutes later to find Dr. Larson waiting anxiously in the emergency department.

"Female patient, 42, admitted for routine gallbladder surgery yesterday," Dr. Larson explained as they hurried through the corridors. "Started experiencing symptoms two hours ago, but they're different from our previous cases. More severe neurological effects, signs of potential seizure activity."

"One of the new formulations mentioned in the research documents?" Claire suggested.

"Not sure. But here's what's concerning, she received her pre-surgical medications before we implemented our security protocols. If someone administered something then, it's been in her system for over 24 hours, much longer than previous cases."

The patient, Sandra Moore, lay in a treatment room, medical staff monitoring her closely. Her eyes were open but unfocused, her movements jerky and uncoordinated. A neurology specialist was performing an assessment as they entered.

"Status?" Dr. Larson asked.

"Progressive neurological symptoms," the neurologist reported. "Started with visual disturbances and confusion, now showing signs of seizure activity. Toxicology results pending, but preliminary blood work shows unusual markers."

Claire studied the patient, then pulled Dr. Larson aside. "I saw something in the research documents about an 'accelerated neurological response protocol.' They were testing compounds with more pronounced effects, specifically targeting the central nervous system."

"Which means they're still active," Dr. Larson concluded. "Even with the lab raided and key personnel detained, someone is continuing the testing."

"Or this was administered before we uncovered the operation," Claire suggested. "The research mentioned staggered release formulations, compounds designed to remain dormant in the system before becoming active."

"That would explain the delayed onset," Dr. Larson agreed. "But it doesn't help us treat her now. Without knowing exactly what she was given, we're limited to symptomatic management."

Claire called Martinez to update her while Dr. Larson consulted with the neurology team. When she finished her call, Dr. Booker had arrived, having followed her from the research facility.

"I've been reviewing additional files," Dr. Booker informed her. "There's reference to an antidote compound developed for emergencies, something they could administer if the effects became too severe during testing."

"Would it be at the research facility?" Claire asked urgently.

"Possibly, or..." Dr. Booker hesitated. "The files mentioned a secure storage location within each participating hospital. Emergency protocols in case of adverse reactions that couldn't be explained away."

Claire immediately contacted Martinez, who promised to search for the antidote compound at the research facility. Meanwhile, Claire and Dr. Larson began investigating potential storage locations within the hospital itself.

"It would need to be secure but accessible to authorized personnel," Claire reasoned. "Somewhere not subject to regular inventory or oversight."

"The research wing," Dr. Larson suggested. "We have several locked facilities for clinical trials."

They hurried to the research wing, finding it unusually quiet. Most staff had been reassigned during the investigation.

"Dr. Matthews had a private laboratory here," Dr. Larson recalled, leading them down a corridor. "Ostensibly for special projects related to his administrative responsibilities."

The laboratory was locked, but Dr. Larson had administrative override credentials. Inside, they found a standard research space, equipment, computers, storage units. Nothing immediately suspicious.

"It has to be here somewhere," Claire insisted, beginning a search. "Check for hidden compartments, false panels, anything unusual."

Dr. Booker examined a bookshelf filled with medical texts and research journals. "In psychology, we often discuss how people hide significant items in plain sight, surrounded by the mundane," she observed, pulling books forward to check behind them.

Claire noticed a refrigeration unit in the corner, its digital display with temperature control. Unlike the other equipment, which showed signs of regular use, this unit appeared untouched, its exterior immaculate.

"This doesn't fit," she said, examining the unit more closely. It required a biometric scan for access, unusual security for standard laboratory equipment.

"We can override it with emergency protocols," Dr. Larson said, already accessing a wall-mounted security panel. "All research equipment has emergency access provisions for safety purposes."

After a tense minute of security protocols, the refrigeration unit unlocked with a soft click. Inside, they found dozens of carefully labeled vials arranged in precise rows. Each bore an alphanumeric code rather than a conventional medical label.

"This is it," Dr. Larson breathed, carefully examining the contents. "These match the formulation descriptions from the research documentation."

"But which one is the antidote?" Claire wondered, the urgency of the patient's condition weighing on her.

Dr. Booker had been reviewing additional files on her tablet. "According to these records, the emergency counteragent should be labeled with an 'X' prefix, followed by the specific formulation number."

They searched through the vials until Dr. Larson identified one labeled "X-49-NK" that matched the description.

"This should be it," she said, carefully removing the vial. "But administering an unknown compound without testing..."

"The patient's condition is deteriorating," Claire reminded her. "And we have documentation of this compound's purpose, if not its exact formulation."

Dr. Larson made the difficult decision. "I'll consult with the neurology team. If they agree her condition warrants emergency intervention, we'll proceed with appropriate caution."

While Dr. Larson rushed the potential antidote to the medical team, Claire and Dr. Booker continued examining the hidden pharmacy. Claire photographed everything for evidence before securing the unit.

"We should have the entire research wing searched," she told the security team that had arrived. "There may be other hidden storage locations."

Her phone rang, Martinez with an update from the research facility. "We found documentation about the antidote compounds," the detective reported. "Sending it to your phone now. And something else, we've located Dr. Matthews."

Claire felt a surge of alertness. "Where?"

"Attempting to board a private plane at a small airfield outside Annapolis. Local police have him in custody now. Chief Matthews is on his way there."

Within the hour, Claire received confirmation that the antidote compound had been administered to Sandra Moore, with neurology closely monitoring her response. Initial signs were promising; her symptoms had stabilized and showed early signs of improvement.

By evening, a preliminary search of the hospital's research wing had uncovered two additional hidden storage locations containing experimental compounds. Patient identification efforts were ongoing, with a team of medical ethicists developing protocols for notification and follow-up care.

Claire joined Martinez at the police station, where Dr. Robert Matthews sat in an interview room. Chief Matthews observed from behind the one-way glass, his expression unreadable as he watched his brother.

"I'll lead the interview," Martinez decided. "You observe, see if anything in his statements contradicts what we've found in the research documentation."

Claire nodded. Martinez entered the interview room with professional detachment, setting a recorder on the table between them.

Dr. Robert Matthews looked remarkably composed for someone whose world had just collapsed. He sat straight-backed in his chair, his resemblance to his brother particularly striking in the harsh lighting of the interview room.

"Dr. Matthews," Martinez began, "you've been advised of your rights and declined counsel for this preliminary discussion. Is that correct?"

"It is," he replied, his voice steady. "Though I expect I'll need representation soon enough."

"Let's start with the basics. Norvis Biotech, your organization?"

"My creation, yes. Though with significant investment from others who shared my vision."

"And what vision was that?" Martinez asked, keeping her tone neutral despite the evidence of harm they'd uncovered.

Dr. Matthews leaned forward slightly. "Accelerating medical innovation. The current system of pharmaceutical development is broken, Detective. It takes an average of ten years and billions of dollars to bring a new medication to market. Patients die waiting for treatments trapped in regulatory limbo."

"So, you decided to use patients as unwitting test subjects?" Martinez's professional facade cracked slightly, revealing her disgust.

"We used minimal doses with temporary effects," Matthews replied defensively. "The risk to any individual patient was calculated to be extremely low, while the potential benefit to millions of future patients was enormous."

"Except you escalated those doses over time," Claire interjected from her observation position, speaking through the room's communication system. "Your latest formulations caused seizure-like activity and potentially permanent neurological changes."

Matthews appeared briefly surprised by Claire's disembodied voice, then composed himself. "Complications arise in any research program. We had protocols for managing adverse events."

"By hiding antidotes in secret compartments throughout the hospital?" Martinez challenged. "That doesn't sound like responsible medical research."

"Contingency planning," Matthews countered. "And clearly necessary, given recent events."

The interview continued for two hours, with Matthews alternating between scientific justification for his actions and careful evasion of questions about specific patients or compound methods. He admitted to orchestrating the operation but attempted to frame it as revolutionary medical research rather than criminal activity.

Afterward, Claire joined Chief Matthews in his office, where he sat reviewing the interview transcript with a tumbler of untouched bourbon on his desk.

"He still believes he was justified," Matthews said, looking up as Claire entered. "My own brother, violating the most fundamental principles of medical ethics, and he speaks of it like he was some kind of visionary."

"The rationalization isn't uncommon in these cases," Claire offered gently. "The greater good becoming an excuse for unconscionable actions."

Matthews nodded tiredly. "The district attorney is preparing charges. Multiple counts of assault, malpractice, fraud, conspiracy, the list goes on. He'll likely spend the rest of his life in prison."

"And the others involved?"

"We've identified twenty-three conspirators so far, across three hospitals and the research facility. Most are cooperating in exchange for consideration during sentencing." Matthews finally took a sip of his bourbon. "But the damage to patient trust, that may never be fully repaired."

Over the following weeks, the full scope of the operation became clearer. Nearly four hundred patients had potentially been exposed to experimental compounds over the five-year period. A comprehensive medical monitoring program was established, with affected patients offered free neurological screening and ongoing care.

The hospital board, itself under investigation due to two members' involvement, appointed an interim leadership team and invited independent oversight of all research activities. Dr. Larson was asked to lead the patient safety task force to reshape the hospital's protocols and restore trust.

Sandra Moore, the patient whose severe reaction had led them to the antidote, recovered fully.

One month after the investigation began, Claire sat in Dr. Leland's office for her regular therapy session. The weight of the case had taken its toll, bringing back memories of her own vulnerability during her struggles with addiction.

"I keep thinking about the patients," Claire admitted, "People at their most vulnerable, trusting the system to care for them, and instead being used as test subjects without their knowledge."

Dr. Leland nodded in understanding. "The violation of that trust resonates with your own experiences."

"During my drinking, I made my own choices, however destructive they were," Claire reflected. "These patients didn't even get that choice. Their choice was completely removed."

"Which is why your work to uncover this was so important," Dr. Leland pointed out. "You restored that choice, that right to informed decision-making about their own bodies."

Claire considered this perspective. "I suppose that's true. And now they at least have information and support moving forward."

"How are things with Chief Matthews?" Dr. Leland asked, shifting the conversation slightly.

"Complicated. He's doing his job impeccably, no special treatment for his brother, complete transparency with the investigation. But personally? He's devastated. Not just by his brother's crimes, but by how completely he misread someone he thought he knew."

"Another form of trust violation," Dr. Leland observed. "One that hits close to home."

After her session, Claire met Martinez at Rusty's Diner. The detective looked as tired as Claire felt, the case having demanded everything from both of them. Since working together, they'd developed a partnership that had evolved into a genuine friendship.

"The DA says it's one of the strongest cases she's ever seen," Martinez reported, stirring her coffee absently. "Between the physical evidence, financial records, and cooperating witnesses, there's no way for Robert Matthews or the others to escape significant consequences."

"Good," Claire said. "Though I imagine Chief Matthews has mixed feelings about that."

"He's a professional above all else," Martinez replied. "But yes, I've seen the toll it's taking. He's requested a week's leave once the initial phase of the investigation concludes."

They sat in companionable silence for a moment, both processing the events of the past month.

"You know what still bothers me?" Claire said finally. "How they justified it to themselves. How they convinced themselves that using patients without consent was somehow noble rather than predatory."

"The human capacity for self-justification is remarkable," Martinez agreed. "Each small ethical compromise making the next one easier, until you've crossed lines you once thought unimaginable."

"Dr. Booker says it's why ethical guidelines exist in the first place, because we can't always trust our own moral compass, especially when ambition or noble-sounding goals enter the equation."

Martinez nodded thoughtfully. "In Vice, we saw similar patterns with officers who crossed lines. Always for the 'right reasons' at first, to catch a dangerous criminal, to protect an informant. Then the exceptions became the rule."

"The patterns of behavior," Claire murmured, remembering other cases where similar psychological mechanisms had been at work. "We're all vulnerable to them, I suppose."

"Which is why we need each other," Martinez concluded. "Other perspectives to challenge our reasoning when it starts to go astray."

After dinner, Claire returned to her apartment where Darwin greeted her with his usual mix of indignation at being left alone and pleasure at her return. As she settled on her small balcony with a cup of coffee, watching the city lights, she reflected on the case and its implications.

The vulnerabilities of patients in a hospital setting had struck her deeply. Her own experiences with vulnerability, during her addiction, during the recovery process that was now three years, had given her a particular sensitivity to situations where choice and agency were compromised.

Her phone buzzed with a text from her father. Since the blizzard case had brought them closer, they'd been communicating more regularly, rebuilding their relationship.

"Saw the news about Baltimore General. Impressive work. Call when you can."

The message was brief but represented significant progress in their relationship. Six months ago, he would have commented only on the professional aspects, never acknowledging her personal contribution. Now, there was recognition, however understated.

Claire smiled slightly. Trust, once broken, was difficult to rebuild. But not impossible. The patients affected by Dr. Matthews's actions would face similar challenges, learning to trust medical professionals again, healing not just physically but emotionally from the violation they'd experienced.

Some wounds would heal quickly; others would take time. But what mattered was the process, the commitment to moving forward with greater awareness and stronger protections in place.

She typed a response to her father: "Thanks. Will call tomorrow. Dinner next week?" Then she set aside her phone and watched as the lights of Baltimore glimmered below, a city of strangers connected by invisible threads of trust and vulnerability, each navigating their own complex journey toward healing.

Chapter Six

Martinez

The harbor lights reflected across the black water as Detective Sara Martinez stood at the edge of the pier. Her silhouette remained perfectly still despite the crisp November wind that swept across Baltimore's waterfront. Only the occasional plume of breath confirmed she was more than a statue.

Claire Morrison approached, the hollow sound of her footsteps on the wooden planks. It was nearly midnight, an unusual time for the message she'd received: West Harbor Pier. Come alone. Important.

Three years and three months sober, and Claire still felt the pull of old habits during moments of stress. Her hand found the familiar packet of tic tacs in her pocket.

"Sara?" Claire called, stopping a few feet away.

Martinez turned, her skin pale in the moonlight, making the small scar beneath her right eye more pronounced than usual. In over a year of working together on Baltimore PD's most complex cases, most recently the hospital conspiracy that had exposed corruption at the highest levels, Claire had never seen the detective without her armor of professional detachment. Martinez always maintained crisp pantsuits, perfect posture, and hair tight in a bun.

Tonight was different. Martinez wore jeans and a black leather jacket, her hair loose around her shoulders. But it was her eyes that caught Claire's attention, the usual sharpness replaced by something Claire had never witnessed before: uncertainty.

"Thank you for coming," Martinez said. "I apologize for the hour and location."

"What's going on?" Claire asked, pulling her coat tighter against the cold.

Martinez didn't answer immediately. Instead, she reached into her pocket and removed something small that caught the faint light; a carved jade pendant in the shape of a serpent coiled around itself.

"Have you ever had a ghost from your past return?" Martinez asked, her voice quiet as she stared at the pendant in her palm. "Someone you were certain was dead?"

Claire studied her colleague carefully. "What's happened?"

"Four years ago, I wasn't with the Baltimore PD." Martinez's finger unconsciously traced the scar beneath her eye, an action Claire had never seen her do before.

"I was part of a joint task force operation in Myanmar. My partner was killed. Our asset was captured. I barely made it out alive."

Over a year of late-night case discussions, shared coffee at crime scenes, and Claire had never suspected Martinez carried such a profound secret.

Sara held up the pendant. "This was left at my apartment door this morning. With a message in Burmese that said, 'The serpent still lives.'"

"Serpent?" Claire asked.

"Our asset's codename." Martinez's eyes met Claire's directly. "A woman I've believed dead for four years. A woman whose capture and presumed execution I blamed myself for."

Claire glanced at the scar beneath Martinez's eye. "The scar..."

"From the ambush that killed my partner." Martinez's voice hardened with pain. "Captain Brooke Carter. We were extracting our asset, a high-level source inside Myanmar military intelligence, when everything went wrong."

Martinez's hand closed around the carved pendant. "For four years, I've carried this scar as a reminder of my failure. Of what happens when you miss the signs, when you trust the wrong people."

"And now someone's suggesting your asset is alive," Claire concluded. "After all this time."

"Yes." Martinez turned back toward the water, her profile sharp against the distant lights. "I'm flying to Bangkok tomorrow. From there, I'll make my way to the Myanmar-Thailand border region."

"Is that wise? If this is connected to what happened four years ago..."

"Then it's likely a trap," Martinez finished. "I know. But if there's even a chance that my asset, Thiri Myat Noe, is alive, that what I've believed for four years is wrong..." Her voice trailed off.

Claire studied her colleague's face, seeing the person beneath, someone carrying a burden, someone whose controlled exterior had been constructed to contain grief and doubt.

"Why tell me this?" Claire asked. "Why here, now?"

Martinez turned to face her. "Because I need someone I can trust. Someone who'll know where I've gone and why, in case I don't return."

The statement hung between them, weighted with all it revealed about Martinez's isolation and the careful walls she'd built around herself.

"I've secured information in my apartment," Martinez continued, offering Claire a key. "This opens a lockbox inside my safe. Here is the combination to the safe." She handed Claire a piece of paper. "Inside the lockbox is everything you'll need if something goes wrong."

Claire accepted the key, feeling its weight in her palm, not just metal, but the responsibility it represented. "When do you leave?"

"My flight departs in seven hours." Martinez's gaze returned to the harbor, where a distant cargo ship moved silently through the darkness. "I told Chief Matthews I have a family emergency. If anyone asks, that's all you know."

Claire nodded. "And if you don't come back after a certain time?"

"If you don't hear from me within 72 hours," Martinez replied, "then you'll be the only one who knows where to look for answers."

As they stood in silence, watching the harbor lights shimmer on the water, Claire realized she was seeing a side of Martinez that few, if any, had been allowed to witness; a glimpse beneath the professional facade to the person shaped by loss and unanswered questions, marked by a scar that carried more meaning than Claire had ever suspected.

For the next 72 hours, Claire waited, tracking the passage of time with growing anxiety. She checked her phone obsessively for any message, any sign that Martinez had arrived safely. She found herself staring at the key Martinez had given her, turning it over in her palm, contemplating what it might unlock beyond just a physical box.

On the first day, she managed to track down everything she could about Myanmar without raising suspicions, learning about its political climate, the border regions, and the complex history that might have drawn Martinez there years ago. At night, she researched military and intelligence operations in the region, wondering what kind of mission could leave such an indelible mark on someone as composed as Martinez.

By the second day, her colleagues had noticed her distraction.

"Hey, Morrison, you with us?" Detective Johnson called during their morning meeting, bringing her attention back to the homicide case they were discussing.

"Sorry," she mumbled, tucking her phone away after checking it for the twentieth time that morning.

Later, at her desk, Detective Johnson stopped by. "You're worried about Martinez," he stated rather than asked, his voice low enough that others wouldn't hear.

Claire looked up, surprised. "What makes you say that?"

"You check your phone every five minutes. You've been researching Southeast Asia. And Martinez takes off suddenly for a 'family emergency' when everyone knows she has never mentioned having family." Johnson leaned against her desk. "Something's up."

Claire hesitated, weighing Martinez's request for discretion against the potential need for allies. "If I needed help with something sensitive, off the books... could I count on you?"

Johnson studied her for a moment before nodding once, definitively. "Martinez is good people. If she's in trouble, I'm in."

When the 72-hour deadline passed without word from Martinez, Claire knew it was time to act. She headed to the detective's apartment.

Using the key and combination Martinez had provided, Claire opened the safe and retrieved the lockbox within. Unlike Claire's chaos of case files and half-dead plants, Martinez's space revealed the same disciplined precision she brought to crime scenes, clean lines, muted colors, everything in its place.

The lockbox contained a manila envelope, a notebook, and a burner phone. Inside the envelope, Claire found photographs showing a younger Martinez in civilian clothes that couldn't disguise her military bearing, standing beside a tall blonde woman with an easy smile. They were in front of a temple, ornate spires rising behind them, red dust coating their boots.

"Captain Carter," Claire murmured, recognizing the name Martinez had mentioned. The warmth in Martinez's eyes in the photograph was something Claire had never witnessed, a lightness, an openness that had disappeared.

The notebook contained Martinez's observations from four years earlier, detailed notes about their asset, their mission, and concerns about security. The final entries showed growing concerns about information leaks and changed protocols.

Claire continued reading, finding an entry from a few days before the ambush that transformed Martinez's life.

Brooke found something. Won't tell me what yet, says she needs to verify first. Whatever it is has her rattled. She's changed our extraction protocols, insisting on a new route and earlier timeline. Says we can't trust the usual channels. I've never seen her this concerned.

The final entry, dated the day of the ambush:

Brooke showed me the photos. If she's right, this goes higher than any of us imagined. The extraction point has been changed again. Thiri Myat Noe will meet us at the eastern temple gate. God help us if she is right about who's betrayed us.

Claire closed the notebook, the weight of what she'd read settling over her. Martinez hadn't just lost a colleague; she'd lost someone who might have uncovered a significant betrayal within their own ranks. The scar beneath her eye wasn't just from a mission gone wrong, it was from a mission that was sabotaged.

She picked up the burner phone, turning it over in her hands. Making the call would irrevocably involve her in whatever Martinez had stepped back into. But not making it might leave Martinez without critical support if things had indeed gone wrong.

Decision made, she dialed the single number programmed into the phone. It rang three times before a male voice answered, speaking English with a British accent.

"Yes?"

"The serpent needs a charmer," Claire said, following Martinez's instructions.

A pause, then: "The Victor building. Rooftop. Thirty minutes. Come alone."

The line went dead before she could respond. Claire checked her watch, 5:17 AM. The Victor building was downtown, a twenty-minute drive.

Claire gathered the notebook and the burner phone, putting them in her bag, and locked Martinez's apartment while departing. As she drove through the streets of Baltimore, her mind raced with questions about what Martinez might be facing halfway around the world.

The Victor building's rooftop was accessible through a service elevator that required a key, but Claire found the door propped open. The roof itself was largely empty except for ventilation equipment and a small seating area likely used by employees on breaks. A solitary figure stood near the edge, looking out over the city.

"Dr. Morrison," the man said without turning. He was tall and lean, dressed in a dark suit that suggested government service. When he finally turned to face her, Claire noted his features, mid-fifties, silver at his temples, the weathered look of someone who had spent significant time in harsh conditions.

"How do you know my name?" Claire asked, tensing slightly.

The man looked at her with a small, calculated smile. "Detective Martinez's contingency protocols. When you called the number and used the activation phrase, it identified you as her trusted contact. We've been monitoring for that call since she missed her scheduled check-in 12 hours ago. Standard procedure for operations of this nature."

"And your name?" Claire asked.

"David Keller, station chief, Southeast Asia desk."

"You know where she is?" Claire asked, keeping a careful distance.

"Yes. And she's in trouble." He gestured toward the seating area. "Please, we haven't much time."

Claire remained standing. "How do I know I can trust you?"

"You don't. But Detective Martinez gave you the activation phrase, which means she trusts me. Or at least, she trusted me four years ago." He removed a photograph from his pocket and handed it to her.

It showed a younger version of the man standing before her, alongside Martinez and Captain Carter, all in gear against a tropical backdrop. "I was their handler for the Myanmar operation."

Claire studied the photo, then the man. "Why are we meeting like this? Why not go through official channels?"

"Because official channels are what got Captain Carter killed." Keller's voice hardened. "And what nearly killed Martinez and our asset."

"What do you know about her current situation?"

"She arrived in Bangkok on schedule, made contact with my associate at the border, and crossed into Myanmar yesterday morning." Keller's expression grew grave. "She was traveling to the Temple of Three Hills in Yangon for the meeting when she was intercepted by hostile forces. She's now being held at a remote compound in the border region between Myanmar and Thailand."

Claire felt her stomach tighten with concern. "The message she received, about the serpent still living, was it legitimate?"

"That's the question, isn't it?" Keller moved to the edge of the roof again, looking out at the city as if the answers might be found in its lights. "Four years ago, our operation was betrayed from within. Captain Carter discovered evidence suggesting involvement from someone high in the intelligence community. Before she could report her findings, she was killed."

"And Martinez blamed herself," Claire continued.

"Yes. The scar she carries..." Keller touched his own face beneath his right eye. "It came from the ambush. A bullet fragment. She believes it's a mark of her failure to protect her team. Her partner."

"But you think differently," Claire prompted.

"I think it's a reminder of betrayal." Keller turned back to face her. "And I think whoever was responsible has spent four years believing all loose ends were tied up. Until now."

"If Thiri Myat Noe is alive..."

"Then she has information that someone desperately wants to keep buried." Keller checked his watch. "I've arranged extraction for Martinez, but I need your help."

"What can I possibly do from here?"

"The evidence Captain Carter gathered before her death, Martinez believes it may be here in Baltimore. Something secured that only she would know how to access." Keller's intensity grew. "Did she leave anything with you? Any indication of where such information might be stored?"

Claire thought about the notebook and the photographs. "Nothing specific. She told me about the operation, showed me some photographs, but..."

"The photographs." Keller interrupted. "May I see them?"

"I don't have them. They're in her apartment."

Keller's disappointment was visible. "We need to access them. Immediately. Whatever Captain Carter discovered may be the key to understanding who betrayed them and why, information that could be critical to extracting Martinez safely."

Claire considered her options. Martinez had trusted her with knowledge of the contents of her safe, with the contingency plan if something went wrong. But she hadn't explicitly authorized sharing access to her apartment with anyone else, even someone claiming to be a former handler.

"I need to verify your identity first," she said, buying time to think. "Let me call..."

"There's no time for that," Keller cut her off. "And there's no one you can call who could verify my involvement in an operation that officially never happened. Martinez is in danger right now."

The urgency in his voice seemed genuine, but something didn't feel right. Martinez's notebook had mentioned concerns about betrayal from within their own ranks, about not trusting usual channels. And Keller had appeared with suspicious convenience just as the 72-hour window closed.

"The Myanmar operation," Claire said carefully. "What was its codename?"

Keller's expression didn't change. "That's classified."

"Martinez told me. If you were her handler, you'd know it."

A flash of something, annoyance, perhaps, crossed Keller's face before his composed expression returned. "Operation Jade Wind. Now, Dr. Morrison, we're wasting precious time. The photographs..."

"Martinez never mentioned a codename to me," Claire said quietly, taking a step back. "I was bluffing."

Keller's demeanor transformed instantly. The concerned former handler vanished, replaced by cold calculation. "A shame. I'd hoped we could handle this professionally."

He reached inside his jacket, but Claire was already moving; she knocked his arm aside as he withdrew a syringe, sending it skittering across the rooftop. Keller recovered quickly, his movements revealing combat training.

"Who are you really?" Claire demanded, maintaining distance between them. "What do you want with Martinez?"

"To finish what began four years ago," Keller replied, his accent slipping slightly. "Some loose ends refuse to stay tied."

He advanced swiftly, but Claire had strategically positioned herself near the roof access door. She seized the syringe and opened the door, then activated the fire alarm she had observed earlier. The sudden blaring sound diverted Keller's attention, allowing Claire to pass through the door and secure it by jamming the handle.

She ran down the stairs, pulling out her phone to call for backup. But who? If Keller was telling the truth about infiltration at high levels, she couldn't risk official channels. Instead, she called Detective Johnson.

"Johnson?" he answered, confusion evident in his voice at the late-night call.

"I need your help. Martinez is in trouble," Claire said urgently.

By the time she reached her car, Claire had made two more calls, one to an IT specialist Martinez had worked with in the past who might be able to trace the burner phone's origins, and another to Dr. Patel, the medical examiner who had occasionally aided them in sensitive cases.

Whatever shadow operation had claimed Captain Carter's life four years ago had now reached out for Martinez.

Claire returned to her apartment, still shaken from the encounter with the fake Keller. She locked and secured her door, then spread the materials from Martinez's safe across her desk. For the next several hours, she meticulously documented everything, creating a timeline of events from four years ago and connecting them to Martinez's current situation.

The IT specialist called late that evening with information about the burner phone. It had been purchased through a shell company with connections to private military contractors operating in Southeast Asia. The web of connections was growing clearer, but Claire still lacked critical information about who might be behind both the original betrayal and the current threat to Martinez.

"This goes deeper than we thought," the specialist had warned. "These contractors have connections to high-level government officials. Be careful who you trust with this information."

"I'm only trusting people Martinez would trust," Claire assured him before ending the call.

She stared at the wall above her desk, now covered with photographs, notes, and strings connecting related elements. The face of Captain Brooke Carter stared back at her from multiple images, a woman whose discovery of corruption had cost her life. Claire studied the photographs of Martinez and Carter together, noting the easy camaraderie between them, so different from the rigid professionalism Martinez now projected.

"What did you find that got you killed, Captain?" Claire whispered to the photograph. "And how does it connect to Martinez now?"

She unpacked more materials from the lockbox, finding sealed envelopes with names she didn't recognize, contingency plans Martinez had prepared but never activated.

Over the next day, Claire worked with Johnson to establish surveillance on Martinez's apartment, anticipating that whoever had sent the fake Keller might send someone else to search for the evidence. They set up a rotation, with Johnson taking the first watch while Claire continued analyzing the materials from the safe.

"They'll come looking eventually," Johnson had said when they set up the surveillance. "People like this don't give up easily."

"When they do, we'll be waiting," Claire replied, checking her weapon before handing him a secure radio. "No phones for communication. We can't risk being monitored."

By early evening on the second day after the rooftop encounter, the wall above Claire's desk was covered with photographs and notes, a mirror of the crime scene walls she created for her cases, but this time focused on Sara.

Johnson called over the radio from his surveillance position outside Martinez's building.

"Dr. Morrison, someone accessed the apartment before we set up surveillance. Motion sensors show entry and movement yesterday evening."

"Are they still inside?" Claire asked.

"Unknown. Building security says the apartment door was found slightly ajar this morning during routine checks. Whoever it was might still be there."

She grabbed her coat and the files she'd compiled before hurrying out. The drive to Martinez's building took fifteen minutes, during which Johnson provided updates on building security.

Claire parked a block away, meeting him at the service entrance they'd identified during their security assessment of the building.

"Security found the door unsecured this morning," Johnson reported. "Could be our intruder got spooked and left, or they're waiting inside."

"Let's go," Claire said, drawing her weapon.

They took the service elevator, approaching Martinez's apartment from the rear stairwell. Johnson positioned himself to cover the main entrance while Claire moved toward the partially open door, using the mirror technique she'd learned to peer inside without exposing herself.

A woman was searching the living room, checking behind picture frames and examining the books on Martinez's shelves. Her back was to the entrance, allowing Claire a moment to observe her. She had a medium build with dark hair.

Claire stepped into the doorway, weapon raised. "Baltimore Police. Don't move."

The woman froze, then slowly raised her hands. "Dr. Claire Morrison, I presume," she said, her Burmese accent fluent but evident.

Claire was momentarily surprised at the woman's recognition but kept her weapon steady. "How do you know who I am?"

"I've been watching you since Sara left for Myanmar. You're her contingency plan."

"Turn around slowly," Claire commanded, keeping the weapon steady.

The woman complied, revealing a face marked by experience. A long scar ran from her left temple across her cheek, and her right arm moved with the slight stiffness of an old injury. But it was her eyes that caught Claire's attention, dark, intelligent, and hauntingly familiar from the photograph Martinez had shown her.

"Thiri Myat Noe," she said, recognizing the woman.

"Yes." The woman lowered her hands slightly. "And I need your help to save Sara before it's too late."

Detective Johnson appeared at the doorway, his weapon also trained on the woman. "Dr. Morrison?"

"It's all right," Claire said, though she didn't lower her weapon. "This is the asset Martinez went to find. The one who's supposedly dead."

"Not dead," Thiri Myat Noe corrected. "But forced into deep cover for four years. Until now."

Claire gestured toward the living room. "Explain. Quickly."

Thiri Myat Noe moved carefully to the sofa, keeping her hands visible. From her pocket, she removed a carved jade pendant in the shape of a serpent coiled around itself, identical to the one Martinez had received.

"Four years ago, Captain Carter discovered something that got her killed, evidence of a joint operation between corrupt elements in your intelligence community and mine, trafficking weapons and intelligence. When she was eliminated, I was forced to disappear." She placed the pendant on the coffee table. "I've spent years gathering evidence against those responsible. Last month, I finally had enough to act."

"So, you contacted Martinez," Claire concluded.

"Indirectly. I had a courier leave the pendant and message at her door. I couldn't risk direct contact until I was certain it was safe." Her finger traced the edge of the pendant. "But I underestimated how closely they still watched her. They intercepted her en route to the meeting point."

Claire felt her stomach tighten. "Is she alive?"

"For now. They're holding her at a remote compound in the border region between Myanmar and Thailand. They believe she knows where Captain Carter hid the original evidence."

"And do you know where it is?" Johnson asked, his weapon still trained on the woman.

"I know that Captain Carter created a system for storing critical information," Thiri Myat Noe said, then hesitated. "But I need Sara's personal items to decode the location."

She reached into an inside pocket of her jacket, movements slow and deliberate to avoid alarming them. She withdrew a folded piece of paper that had yellowed with age.

"Captain Carter left this with one of our mutual contacts before the ambush. She said if anything happened to her, it should reach Sara. But the contact was killed two weeks later, and the paper didn't reach me until recently."

Claire took the paper, keeping her weapon ready. It contained a series of numbers and a simple drawing of what appeared to be a compass rose.

"Does this mean anything to you?" she asked Johnson, who had extensive military experience.

He studied it briefly. "Looks like coordinates, possibly with an encryption key. The drawing could indicate a dead drop location."

"Captain Carter had a system," Thiri Myat Noe explained. "Before any high-risk operation, she would secure critical information in multiple locations. She called it her insurance policy."

"Standard procedure for some intelligence operations," Johnson confirmed.

Claire studied the drawing more carefully. "I think I know where to look," she said. "But first, we need to establish your legitimacy beyond that pendant."

Thiri Myat Noe nodded calmly. "Ask me anything about Sara or Captain Carter that only someone who worked with them would know."

"The scar beneath Martinez's eye," Claire began. "How did she get it?"

"I wasn't there when it happened," Thiri Myat Noe said honestly. "But from what my contacts reported, it was during the ambush at the eastern temple gate. An explosion, debris from the blast. Captain Carter was killed trying to protect Sara during the extraction."

Claire noticed the difference, this wasn't the intimate firsthand knowledge someone present would have, but intelligence gathered afterward. It felt more authentic.

"One more question," Claire said. "What did Martinez always carry with her during your operation together? Something personal."

Thiri Myat Noe's expression softened slightly. "A silver compass. My handler mentioned it in his reports, said it was a gift from her grandfather. She would check it whenever she was nervous about a mission."

Claire lowered her weapon slightly. The details were consistent but came from external observation, not intimate knowledge.

"Johnson, what do you think?"

"Her details are consistent with intelligence gathered about covert operations, and she's honest about what she does and doesn't know firsthand. I'm inclined to believe her."

Claire made her decision. "All right. I think I know where Captain Carter's evidence might be hidden."

Claire examined the decorative compass mounted on Martinez's bookshelf. Unlike the other precisely arranged items in the apartment, this one was set at a slight angle that had initially seemed like an oversight in an otherwise perfectly ordered space.

"It's not decorative," Claire realized, carefully removing it from the wall. The back had a hidden compartment that slid open when pressure was applied to specific points, revealing a small microSD card.

"Captain Carter's insurance policy," Thiri Myat Noe breathed. "Now we need to get this to my contacts and formulate an extraction plan for Sara."

"We'll need a secure location to work from," Claire said, slipping the SD card into her pocket. "Somewhere off the grid."

"I have a safe house prepared. From there, we can make the necessary arrangements."

As they prepared to leave, Claire noticed Thiri Myat Noe's gaze lingering on a photograph of Martinez that sat on a side table, one of the few personal touches in the otherwise spartan apartment. In it, Martinez stood beside Chief Matthews at a department commendation ceremony, her posture military-straight, her expression professionally composed, the small scar beneath her eye visible even from a distance.

"She carries that mark as a reminder of failure," Thiri Myat Noe said quietly. "But it was never her fault. The mission was betrayed before it began."

"She needs to hear that from you," Claire replied. "We're going to make sure she gets the chance."

The trip to the safe house was deliberate and cautious. They changed vehicles twice, first at a designated spot where one of Thiri Myat Noe's contacts had left a nondescript sedan, then again at an underground parking garage where Johnson's personal vehicle was parked. Claire watched for any signs of surveillance.

The safe house was above a closed Vietnamese restaurant in a quieter section of Baltimore. The space was sparsely furnished but clearly prepared: communications equipment had been set up and weapons secured in a cabinet.

"My contacts arranged this," Thiri Myat Noe explained as she locked the door behind them. "It's been maintained for emergency situations. No paper trail, no digital footprint."

Johnson moved immediately to check the perimeter. Claire watched as Thiri Myat Noe activated the communications equipment.

"You've been planning this for some time," she observed.

"Years," Thiri Myat Noe confirmed without looking up. "Waiting for the right moment, gathering evidence, establishing a network of people I could trust." She connected the SD card to a secure laptop. "Sara doesn't know I survived that day. I let her carry that burden because exposing the truth too soon would have meant death for both of us."

"And now?" Claire asked.

"Now we have enough evidence to move against those responsible." Thiri Myat Noe's voice was calm but determined. "Financial records, operational details, names. Captain Carter died trying to bring this to light. It's time to finish what she started."

Over the next twenty-four hours, they worked tirelessly to coordinate Martinez's rescue. The evidence from the card was authenticated and transmitted to specific individuals Thiri Myat Noe had identified as trustworthy within the intelligence community and Justice Department. A response team was assembled, drawing from legitimate elements within the CIA who had been investigating the rogue operation for years.

Claire studied the satellite imagery of the compound where Martinez was being held, a remote facility nestled in the densely forested mountains along the Myanmar-Thailand border. The extraction plan was methodical, leveraging Thiri Myat Noe's contacts in the region and the sudden cooperation of officials who had seen the evidence against their corrupt colleagues.

The mission planning was intricate, with multiple contingencies for various scenarios. Johnson's military expertise proved invaluable as they mapped approach routes and identified potential extraction points. Throughout the preparations, Claire found herself drawn to the photographs of Martinez from four years earlier, seeing the person behind the professional facade she'd known, a younger woman with an open expression so different from the carefully controlled detective she'd come to respect.

"She was different then," Thiri Myat Noe observed, noticing Claire's interest in the photographs. "From what my contacts reported, before the ambush, she was more open, less guarded."

"What was she like?" Claire asked, genuinely curious.

"According to the reports I received, passionate about the work. Driven. My handler mentioned she had a lightness that disappeared after the mission." Thiri Myat Noe's expression softened. "The scar changed her, not just physically."

"I've only known her as she is now," Claire said, studying the photographs. "Controlled. Precise. Keeping everyone at a distance."

"A survival mechanism," Johnson offered from where he was checking equipment. "Common after trauma. You build walls, maintain control of everything you possibly can because you lost control of something that mattered."

Both women looked at him, and he shrugged. "Two tours in Afghanistan. I've seen it before. Hell, I've lived it."

Claire turned back to Thiri Myat Noe. "If we get her back, when we get her back, she'll need to reconcile these two versions of herself. The person she was and the person she became."

"Yes," Thiri Myat Noe agreed quietly. "And she'll need to understand that some burdens aren't hers to carry alone."

"Extraction team is in position," the communications specialist announced approximately 48 hours after they had arrived at the safe house. "Operation commencing."

Claire watched the secure video feed, heart pounding as the team moved swiftly through the compound, neutralizing guards. The search seemed to take forever, but finally came the words she'd been waiting for:

"Target acquired. Extraction proceeding."

Relief flooded through Claire that Martinez had been found alive.

Three days later, Claire stood in a private room at Walter Reed, where Martinez had been transferred after initial treatment overseas. The detective sat upright in the hospital bed, her usual composed demeanor somewhat diminished by hospital scrubs. A fresh bandage covered her right temple, but Claire's eyes were drawn to the familiar scar beneath Martinez's eye, the mark that had started this whole journey.

"Dr. Morrison," Martinez greeted her, voice steady despite her ordeal. "I understand I have you to thank for the extraction."

"I had help," Claire replied, taking the seat beside the bed. "Someone who's been waiting four years to see you."

Martinez's eyes widened slightly, the first genuine surprise Claire had ever seen register on her face. "She's really alive?"

"Yes. And she'll be here soon. The debriefing team needs to finish first." Claire studied her colleague. "How are you? Really?"

Martinez's hand moved unconsciously to the scar beneath her eye, a gesture Claire now understood carried years of complicated history. "Processing. Four years believing one truth, only to discover another."

"The burden you carried, believing your actions led to their deaths, it wasn't yours to bear," Claire said.

"No," Martinez acknowledged. "But it shaped me all the same." Her professional composure slipped further, revealing a vulnerability Claire had glimpsed only once before, that night at the pier. "When they captured me, when I realized it was a trap, my first thought was that history was repeating itself. That I'd failed again."

"But you didn't fail," came a voice from the doorway. "Not then. Not now."

Thiri Myat Noe stood there, weariness evident in her eyes. The scar was visible in the hospital lighting, but her eyes held the same intensity Claire had seen in the photographs Martinez had kept.

Martinez went still, her composure faltering completely as she stared at the woman she'd believed dead for four years.

"Thiri," she whispered, her name almost a question.

Thiri Myat Noe moved into the room, stopping at the foot of the bed. "I'm sorry, Sara. For letting you believe I was dead."

Martinez's eyes never left her face, as if trying to reconcile the ghost from her past with the woman standing before her. "I saw the reports. Your body..."

"A substitute. Someone killed in a border skirmish the day before. The right build, features unidentifiable." Thiri Myat Noe's voice carried the weight of her years in hiding. "By the time I learned you had survived, the people responsible had already buried the truth so deep that coming forward would have meant death for us both."

Claire watched as Martinez processed the information, the detective's analytical mind visibly reconstructing the narrative she'd lived with for all these years.

"Brooke," Martinez said finally. "What she found..."

"Evidence of an operation that went beyond weapons trafficking," Thiri Myat Noe confirmed, moving closer. "Senior officials in both our governments, private contractors, intelligence operatives, all working together to profit from instability in the region. She discovered financial records, operational details, names that went all the way to Washington and Naypyidaw."

"And they killed her for it." Martinez's voice hardened with old grief transformed into fresh anger.

"Yes. She knew the risk she was taking. From what I learned later, her last instructions before the ambush were about where to hide the evidence if something happened to her." Thiri Myat Noe gestured toward the door, where Detective Johnson waited with a secure briefcase. "Evidence that has now been delivered to people who will use it properly."

Claire sensed the two needed space for a conversation four years delayed, but before she could excuse herself, Martinez spoke.

"Claire." The use of her first name stopped Claire in her tracks. "Stay. Please." A pause, then: "You're part of this now."

Claire nodded, resuming her seat as Johnson brought in the briefcase, setting it on the bedside table before leaving. Inside was the hard drive Thiri Myat Noe had compiled over four years in hiding.

"Captain Carter's instructions reached me through a network of contacts," Thiri Myat Noe explained. "She suspected someone on your team had been compromised. The instructions were to ensure the evidence reached the right people if anything happened to her."

"And what I believed was your body being recovered..." Martinez began.

"Was staged to ensure everyone believed that I died in the ambush. It gave me the cover I needed to disappear, to continue gathering evidence." Thiri Myat Noe's expression softened. "I never intended for you to carry the burden of believing you had failed us."

Martinez's finger traced the scar beneath her eye. "This came from the ambush. Shrapnel from the first explosion. It's been a reminder of what happened. Of what I lost."

"And now?" Claire asked quietly.

Martinez looked up, meeting first Claire's eyes, then Thiri Myat Noe's. "Now it's something different. A reminder that the truth finds its way to the surface eventually."

Thiri Myat Noe took a step closer, her hand hesitantly reaching toward Martinez before pulling back. "I watched your career from afar when I could safely do so. I saw how you transformed your grief into purpose, how meticulously you built your new life. But I also saw the weight you carried in the way you moved, the way you held yourself."

"You could have contacted me," Martinez said, a rare note of emotion breaking through her controlled tone.

"Not without endangering us both," Thiri Myat Noe replied.

A knock at the door interrupted their conversation. A man in a nondescript suit entered, the kind of bureaucratic presence that suggested government service without specifying which agency.

"Detective Martinez, Ms. Thiri Myat Noe," he acknowledged with a nod. "Dr. Morrison. I'm Daniel Weber, Deputy Director of Operations." The agency went unmentioned, but his authority was clear. "I wanted to personally inform you that the information you provided has resulted in multiple arrests across three countries. The operation Captain Carter uncovered has been dismantled."

"And the people responsible for her death?" Martinez asked, the professional detachment returning to her voice.

"Being dealt with through appropriate channels." Weber's carefully neutral expression suggested some things would remain classified. "Your official debriefing will continue tomorrow, but I wanted to convey our appreciation for your service. All of you."

After Weber left, the room fell silent as they absorbed the implications of his visit, official acknowledgment of an operation that had technically never existed, recognition of sacrifices made, and burdens carried in silence for years.

"What happens now?" Claire asked finally.

Thiri Myat Noe looked to Martinez. "That depends. My cover identity is compromised. I'll need to establish a new life somewhere."

"And I have questions that will take more than one conversation to answer," Martinez replied. "Questions about what you've been doing these years. About how you survived."

"And I owe you those answers," Thiri Myat Noe said, finally taking the seat on the other side of the bed. "All of them."

Claire recognized the beginning of a new chapter forming between them, one that would require time to develop. "I should go. Let you both talk."

This time, Martinez didn't stop her. Instead, she nodded, gratitude visible in her expression. "Thank you, Claire. For helping when you didn't have to."

"That's what colleagues do," Claire replied with a small smile. "Or maybe, friends."

As she left the hospital room, Claire glanced back to see Martinez and Thiri Myat Noe deep in conversation, the detective's hand no longer touching the scar beneath her eye but instead holding Thiri's hand.

A month later, Claire sat across from Martinez at Rusty's. The worn vinyl booths and wooden tables had witnessed decades of Baltimore's stories, and now it would be part of this one too.

Betty approached their table with coffee and a knowing smile. "The usual for both of you ladies?"

"Thanks, Betty," Claire replied with a nod.

"Good to see you back, Detective," Betty said to Martinez, refilling her cup. "Missed seeing you in here these past few weeks."

"Good to be back," Martinez replied, with a warmth in her voice that Claire had rarely heard before.

After Betty moved away, Claire studied Martinez across the table. The detective had returned to duty the previous week, her physical recovery complete although the psychological adjustments continued.

The crisp pantsuit and professional demeanor had returned, but subtle changes were evident to those who knew where to look.

"How's the readjustment going?" Claire asked, stirring her coffee.

"Officially, I was never gone," Martinez replied with a smile. "Family emergency, remember? Though Chief Matthews has his suspicions."

"And unofficially?"

Martinez's finger briefly touched the scar beneath her eye, a gesture Claire now recognized carried different meaning than before. "Adjusting. Learning to reconcile the narrative I lived with for years with what actually happened."

"And Thiri Myat Noe?"

"Relocated under a new identity. Consulting for certain agencies on Southeast Asian security matters." Martinez's expression remained neutral, but her eyes softened slightly. "We talk regularly now. There's a lot of history to process. Years of separate lives to learn about."

Claire nodded, understanding that some wounds required time to heal, some connections needed space to redevelop. "The scar," she said, gesturing toward Martinez's face. "You touch it differently now."

Martinez seemed surprised by the observation, her finger moving unconsciously to the mark beneath her eye. "Do I?"

"Before, it seemed like a reminder of pain, of failure. Now it's more... reflective."

"Perceptive as always, Claire." Martinez's eyes met Claire's directly. "For four years, it was a mark of what I'd lost, what I'd failed to prevent. Now..."

"Now?"

"It's a reminder that the truth doesn't stay buried forever. That sometimes our absolute certainties turn out to be incomplete." Her voice softened. "And that colleagues can become unexpected allies when we need them most."

Claire recognized the sentiment for what it was, the closest Martinez would come to admitting their relationship had evolved beyond professional boundaries, had become something approaching friendship.

"That works both ways, Sara," she replied with a small smile.

Betty returned to refill their cups, commenting with a wink, "You two actually taking a break for once? Usually, you're both rushing out of here with coffee to go."

"Sometimes you need to slow down," Martinez replied, surprising Claire with the philosophical tone.

As they finished their coffee and prepared to return to the precinct, where a new case awaited their attention, Claire noticed Martinez seemed more relaxed than usual.

The burden of believing a false narrative had been lifted, and perhaps Martinez herself had begun to change as well. Only time would tell how that evolution would progress, but for now, it was enough that the truth had finally surfaced, offering the possibility of healing.

"Ready?" Martinez asked, laying money on the table for their coffee.

"Ready," Claire replied, falling into step beside her colleague, her friend, as they headed back to work.

Chapter Seven

Symmetry

Claire Morrison stared at the crime scene photos spread across her desk, the familiar knot of tension forming between her shoulder blades. Two victims, posed in mirror image positions, their bodies arranged with meticulous precision. One man, one woman, both in their early thirties, both found in abandoned warehouses on opposite sides of Baltimore, both killed on the same day exactly three days ago.

"Tell me I'm not seeing what I think I'm seeing," she said to Detective Sara Martinez, who stood beside her desk, eyes fixed on the same disturbing images.

"If you're seeing two killers working in coordinated opposition, then we're seeing the same thing," Martinez replied.

Claire popped a tic tac into her mouth. Three and a half years sober now. "The positioning is too precise to be coincidental. Look at the angle of the arms, the placement of the personal effects. Everything about the female victim is the exact mirror image of the male."

Martinez nodded. The scar beneath her right eye, a memento from her past life in intelligence that Claire had helped uncover months earlier, caught the fluorescent light. "The medical examiner's report confirms they died the same way, manual strangulation followed by incisions along the torso. But the cuts on Jane Doe run right to left, while John Doe's run left to right."

"Like looking in a mirror," Claire murmured. She reached for her notebook, jotting down observations. "And the timing of discovery, the first victim found yesterday at 8:47 AM in the Harbor East warehouse district, the second found this morning at 8:51 AM in the warehouse zone near Westport. But Dr. Patel confirms both died Sunday evening, with evidence suggesting the killings were coordinated."

"East and west," Martinez noted. "Another opposition."

Claire leaned back in her chair, feeling the pieces of the profile beginning to assemble in her mind. "We're not looking for a single unsub with a fascination for symmetry. We're looking at two killers working together, or perhaps against each other, with a shared obsession."

"Partners?" Martinez suggested.

"Or rivals," Claire countered. "Either way, this level of coordination suggests intimate knowledge of each other's methods. They know exactly what the other will do, or they're communicating their actions."

Chief Matthews appeared at Claire's desk. In his long tenure leading the homicide division, he'd developed an uncanny sense for when cases were about to spiral into the public eye.

"Please tell me we're not looking at what the Feds call a 'complementary killer' scenario," he said. "The press will have a field day."

"The evidence points that way," Claire admitted, gesturing to the photos. "Two killers, working in exact opposition but with coordinated purpose. The symbolism is deliberate: east and west, male and female, right and left." She hesitated before adding, "This level of ritualistic behavior suggests they'll strike again. Killers who invest this much symbolic meaning into their work rarely stop at one demonstration."

Matthews ran a hand across his face, the gesture betraying his concern. "I want a preliminary profile by end of the day. Martinez, assemble a task force. And for God's sake, keep this quiet until we have something concrete. Last thing we need is public panic about killer duos staging artistic murder scenes across my city."

After Matthews left, Martinez pulled up a chair. "What's our first move?"

"We need to understand the symbolism," Claire said, studying the photos again. "The mirror imagery, the east-west positioning, it's all communicating something. And we need the full autopsy results to confirm whether the wounds were inflicted by right-handed and left-handed individuals."

"Dr. Patel is prioritizing both cases. He should have preliminary results this afternoon." Martinez paused, her gaze lingering on Claire's expression. "There's something else, isn't there? Something about this case that's bothering you beyond the obvious."

Claire sometimes forgot how perceptive Martinez had become in their time working together. After the ordeal they'd shared during the previous case when Martinez had disappeared overseas and Claire had helped bring her home, they'd developed a deeper connection. The detective had a way of reading her that few others managed.

"This level of coordination suggests history," Claire explained. "Deep, personal history. These aren't random killers who found each other online or through some dark web connection. They know each other intimately, probably for years. And that kind of connection leaving no digital footprint? It's rare."

Martinez nodded. "I'll have the tech team look for any similar cases nationwide. If they've done this before, we'll find it."

As Martinez left to organize the investigation, Claire turned back to the photos, her mind already building pathways between the fragmented evidence. Two killers, working in mirrored precision. A deadly symmetry unfolding across the city. She reached for her phone and dialed Dr. Leland's number. Her weekly therapy session wasn't until tomorrow, but this case was already crawling under her skin in a way that demanded processing.

"Dr. Morrison," Leland answered, her warm voice a contrast to the cold reality of the crime scene photos. "This is unexpected."

"We've got a new case," Claire said simply. "Two killers working in mirrored opposition."

"Ah," Leland replied, understanding immediately. "And you're concerned about the psychological immersion this will require."

"It's not just that," Claire admitted. "There's something about the symmetry that feels... personal. Like I'm missing something."

"The human mind is naturally drawn to patterns and symmetry," Leland noted. "It's why we see faces in random objects, why we find balanced compositions aesthetically pleasing. These killers are exploiting that tendency, creating scenes that demand attention because they satisfy our innate desire for order."

"While creating profound disorder," Claire said, the irony not lost on her.

Back in her apartment that evening, Claire pinned the crime scene photos to her investigation board, mapping out the connections and oppositions with colored threads. Darwin, her orange tabby, watched from his perch atop the bookcase, eyes tracking her movements with curiosity.

"What do you think, Darwin? What are they trying to tell us?" she mused, not expecting an answer but finding comfort in the familiar ritual of thinking aloud to her companion. Darwin had been with her since her early recovery days, a living marker of her sobriety and a constant in her sometimes chaotic life.

The cat's tail twitched as if in response, his attention fixed not on her but on a particular photo, the female victim's left hand, positioned with fingers splayed in what might be interpreted as a gesture or might simply be the final arrangement by her killer.

Claire moved closer to examine it. The positioning didn't seem random; there was intention in the way the fingers were arranged. She pulled out her magnifying glass, studying the hand more carefully. There appeared to be some faint, unusual markings on the skin between the fingers, though she couldn't quite distinguish what they were in the photographs.

She made a note to check the original evidence documentation and request detailed photos of both victims' hands. If there were messages inscribed on the bodies, they might provide the key to understanding what these killers were communicating, and to whom.

Her phone buzzed with a text from Martinez: "ME report in. Both victims show matching defensive wounds, but mirror opposite patterns. Female victim's wounds indicate right-handed attacker, male victim's suggest left-handed. Different killers confirmed."

Claire texted back: "Need detailed photos of victims' hands. Possible markings between fingers."

The reply came almost immediately: "On it."

Her phone rang just as she was preparing for bed. Her father's name appeared on the screen.

"Dad?" she answered, concern edging her voice. Her relationship with her father had improved markedly over the past six months, evolving from strained formality to something more genuine, especially since they'd been trapped together during the Baltimore blizzard, but unscheduled late night calls were still unusual.

"Claire," Richard said. "I've just been informed about your new case. Chief Matthews contacted me."

Claire felt a flicker of irritation at Matthews going over her head, but it made sense. Richard Morrison was still one of the most respected forensic psychologists in the country. If anyone might have insight into dual killers working in symbolic opposition, it would be him.

"Two killers, working in mirrored opposition," Claire confirmed. "Have you encountered anything similar in your research?"

"Not directly, but there are historical precedents. The concept appears in several mythological traditions, opposing forces working in balance, neither able to exist without the other." Richard paused. "I'd like to consult on this case, if you're amenable. The psychological dynamics at play are... intriguing."

"Of course," Claire agreed, surprised but pleased at the offer. Working with her father presented its own challenges, but his insight would be invaluable. The blizzard case and their subsequent dinner discussions had shown her that they could now collaborate effectively, their approaches complementing rather than clashing. "I'll send you the files first thing tomorrow."

"Thank you. And Claire? Be careful with this one. Killers who operate on this level of symbolism often have elaborate endgames planned. Whatever this is, it's only beginning."

Morning brought new evidence. Claire arrived at the station to find Martinez already at her desk.

"You were right about the markings," Martinez said, handing Claire a folder. "Both victims had tiny symbols inked between their fingers. Different symbols, but the same placement."

Claire opened the folder to find high-resolution photos of the victims' hands. Between each finger of both victims were tiny markings, barely visible to the naked eye. On closer inspection, they weren't numbers as she'd initially thought, but symbols, geometric shapes on the female victim, and what appeared to be alchemical symbols on the male.

"Dr. Patel found traces of a special UV-reactive ink," Martinez continued. "The symbols would be nearly invisible under normal lighting. Someone wanted these found, but not by just anyone."

"They're leaving a message for someone who knows to look," Claire mused, studying the symbols. "Someone familiar with their methodology, their thinking."

"Another killer?"

"Possibly. Or law enforcement. They might be playing a game, leaving breadcrumbs for us to follow." Claire arranged the photos side by side. "Have we identified the victims yet?"

Martinez nodded, pulling out her notebook. "Jane Doe is Elizabeth Hoffman, 32, art history professor at Johns Hopkins. John Doe is Michael Richt, 34, architect with a firm downtown. No obvious connection between them, but we're still digging."

"An academic and an architect," Claire noted. "Both creative professions involving structure, pattern, and interpretation." She paused, a thought forming. "What if they weren't chosen randomly? What if they represent something specific to the killers?"

"Like what?"

"I'm not sure yet. But these professions, combined with the symbolic markings... the killers are communicating something specific about these victims. We need to look deeper into their backgrounds, their work, their possible connections."

They spent the morning assembling the rest of the task force, bringing in specialists from various departments and briefing them on the unusual nature of the case. Chief Matthews had arranged for a dedicated conference room, its walls soon covered with crime scene photos, maps showing the discovery locations, and timelines of both victims' last known movements.

Richard Morrison arrived mid-morning, his tall frame and silver hair commanding attention as he entered the room. Claire watched the subtle shifts in posture as officers recognized him, the author of the textbooks many of them had studied, the legendary profiler whose methodologies had revolutionized the field.

The task force briefing proceeded efficiently, with Martinez outlining what they knew about the victims and the circumstances of their deaths. When it came time for the psychological assessment, Matthews gestured for Claire to take the floor.

"We're dealing with two killers working in coordinated opposition," she began, indicating the crime scene photos. "The symmetrical positioning, the mirrored wounds, the east-west placement, all of it suggests a deeply intertwined relationship between the perpetrators. They know each other's methods intimately, suggesting a long-standing connection."

She moved to the board where she'd arranged photos of the symbols found on the victims' hands. "These markings were placed by the unsubs using ink that's clearly visible under UV light. They wanted these messages found, but not easily. The female victim, Elizabeth Hoffman, has geometric symbols, specifically, variations of the golden ratio and sacred geometry patterns. The male victim, Michael Richt, has alchemical symbols representing transformation and opposition."

"Both sets of symbols relate to harmony, balance, and the union of opposites," Richard added, stepping forward to stand beside Claire. "In many mythological and philosophical traditions, true power comes from the perfect balance of opposing forces, light and dark, male and female, creation and destruction."

"So these killings are what, some kind of ritual?" an officer asked from the back of the room.

"Possibly," Claire acknowledged. "Or a demonstration. A performance designed to communicate something about the relationship between the killers themselves."

"Based on the coordinated nature of the killings, we believe they're working on some kind of schedule," Martinez interjected. "But we haven't yet determined the timing of their next move."

"Dr. Morrison, both of you," Matthews said, "I want a comprehensive profile by tomorrow morning. We need to identify connections between the victims, any possible link to other cases nationally, and most importantly, any patterns that might help us predict when and where they'll strike next."

As the briefing concluded and officers dispersed to their assignments, Richard approached Claire, his expression thoughtful.

"The symbols are significant," he said quietly. "I have a colleague in the Philosophy Department at the university who specializes in alchemical symbolism. If you'd allow me to consult with her, discreetly, of course, she might provide insight into what these killers are trying to communicate."

"That would be helpful," Claire agreed. "I was also planning to speak with Elizabeth Hoffman's director in the Art History Department. If the killers selected her for her expertise, her work might tell us something about their motivations."

"A sound approach," Richard nodded. "Shall we coordinate our university visits? It might be more efficient."

The offer of collaboration surprised her. Her father usually preferred to work independently, his academic approach sometimes at odds with the more flexible requirements of active investigation. But his expertise in symbolic communication would be invaluable, and working together would allow them to cover more ground.

"I'd like that," she said simply.

Martinez joined them, files in hand. "We've got the complete background checks on both victims. Nothing immediately jumps out as connecting them, but there are some interesting coincidences. They both traveled to Geneva, Switzerland last year, though at different times. They both attended the same charity gala at the Baltimore Museum of Art six months ago. And they both made significant career changes approximately two years ago, Hoffman shifting her research focus from Renaissance art to sacred geometry, Richt moving from commercial architecture to focus on alchemical principles in architectural design."

"The same principles represented in the symbols on their bodies," Claire noted, the connections beginning to form. "These aren't random victims. They were chosen specifically for their work with these principles."

"Which suggests our killers are themselves connected to these fields," Richard concluded. "Academic or artistic communities where these concepts hold significance."

The investigation moved into high gear as the day progressed. Martinez coordinated the task force's efforts, while Claire and Richard visited Johns Hopkins University to speak with Elizabeth Hoffman's director and Richard's philosophy contact.

The Art History Department was housed near the center of campus, its corridors lined with reproduction masterpieces and student works. Dr. Julia Whittier, the department chair, met them in her office, her expression grave.

"Elizabeth's death has devastated our department," she said, gesturing for them to sit. "She was one of our most promising young faculty members, brilliant and innovative in her approach to art history."

"We understand she recently shifted her research focus," Claire prompted. "From Renaissance art to sacred geometry?"

Dr. Whittier nodded. "About two years ago, yes. She'd always had an interest in mathematical principles in art, but after returning from a sabbatical in Italy, she became almost obsessed with sacred geometry, the golden ratio, divine proportion, how these mathematical concepts appear across cultures and throughout history."

"Was this change unusual?" Richard asked, his tone neutral.

"For an academic, changing research focus isn't unheard of, but the suddenness was surprising. And the intensity..." Dr. Whittier hesitated. "Elizabeth began seeing patterns everywhere, connections between disparate art forms that others couldn't follow. She was brilliant, don't misunderstand me, but there was something almost... zealous about her approach."

"Did she mention any specific colleagues or collaborators who shared this interest?" Claire inquired.

"She corresponded with several researchers internationally. And locally, she mentioned consulting with an architect who was incorporating alchemical principles into his designs. He wanted her expertise on the historical and artistic context of alchemical symbolism." Dr. Whittier frowned, trying to recall. "Richt, I believe? Michael Richt. She said he was working on some fascinating projects involving alchemical concepts in architecture."

Claire and Richard exchanged glances. The connection between the victims was now explicit, they had known each other, collaborated professionally around the very principles represented in the symbols marked on their bodies.

"Did Dr. Hoffman ever express any concerns for her safety?" Claire asked. "Any unusual incidents, people showing too much interest in her work?"

"Not that she mentioned to me," Dr. Whittier replied. "Though she did become quite protective of her research in recent months. She was preparing a major paper on what she called 'The Symmetry Principle', the idea that certain mathematical ratios represent a perfect balance between opposing forces, and that this balance appears consistently across artistic traditions throughout history."

The phrase caught Claire's attention immediately. "The Symmetry Principle," she repeated. "Did she leave any of this research in her office or university files?"

After Dr. Whittier arranged for them to access Hoffman's office later that afternoon, Claire and Richard made their way across campus to the Philosophy Department. Richard had called ahead to arrange a meeting with his colleague.

Dr. Margaret Hammond was a small woman with intense eyes and a rapid speaking style. Her office was cluttered with books, artifacts, and scrolls covered in various symbolic languages.

"The progression represents transformation through opposition," Dr. Hammond explained, studying the symbol on Michael Richt's hand. "Specifically, the concept that perfect balance can only be achieved through the harmonious integration of opposing forces."

"Similar to the concept of sacred geometry that Elizabeth Hoffman was researching," Claire noted.

"Precisely! There's a philosophical tradition dating back centuries that connects these concepts, the idea that perfect symmetry, perfect balance between opposites, represents a kind of transcendence. In alchemical terms, it's the ultimate transformation, not just lead into gold, but the perfection of the self through the integration of opposing aspects of human nature."

"And these specific symbols," Richard prompted. "What do they represent in that context?"

"This sequence tells a story of transformation through partnership," Dr. Hammond explained. "Each symbol represents a stage in the process, separation, purification, union, transformation. But there's something unusual about the arrangement..." She frowned, studying the photos more carefully. "They're in reverse order from how they would traditionally be presented. It's as if the sequence is meant to be read backward, or in a mirror."

"Like the mirrored positioning of the bodies," Claire said, the connections crystallizing in her mind. "The killers aren't just demonstrating opposition; they're enacting a ritual of transformation through perfect symmetry."

An hour later, using the access Dr. Whittier had provided, Claire and Richard entered Elizabeth Hoffman's office in the Art History Department.

Elizabeth Hoffman's office reflected her academic focus, walls covered with prints showing geometric patterns in art throughout history, bookshelves filled with texts on sacred geometry, and a large whiteboard covered with equations and diagrams. But it was the bulletin board behind her desk that immediately caught Claire's attention.

In the center was a complex diagram labeled "The Symmetry Principle," surrounded by images connected with red thread, artwork, architectural designs, natural patterns, all seemingly illustrating the same mathematical concept. And among those connected images was a photograph of what appeared to be a modern building, its distinctive geometric design immediately recognizable.

"That's one of Michael Richt's buildings," Claire said, moving closer to examine the photo. "The Avalon."

She studied the diagram more carefully, taking in the entire board. "This isn't just conceptual connections. These are geographical ones." She traced the pattern with her finger, then pulled out her phone to compare it with a map of Baltimore. "Each of these points corresponds to a location in the city where these mathematical principles appear in architecture or public art."

Richard looked over her shoulder. "Including the warehouses where the bodies were found?"

"Yes," Claire confirmed, matching the locations. "East and west, exactly opposite each other on this pattern."

"They're killing according to a geometric pattern," Richard observed.

"Which means we can possibly predict where they'll strike next," Claire realized.

Richard, who had been examining Hoffman's desk, turned around. "Not just where, but when. Look at this." He indicated a calendar, certain dates marked with the same symbols they'd found on the victims' hands. "Three days ago is marked - the date of the first killings. And here, exactly eleven days from now - two weeks from the first pair. And here..." She pointed to the final date, marked with the complex combined symbol. "Six weeks out - this appears to be the culmination."

"They've compressed the timeline," Claire said, photographing the calendar. "And look at the symbols, they progress through a sequence, different for each date. I think we're looking at a ritual performed in stages, culminating on this final date." She pointed to the date, marked with a complex symbol combining elements of both the geometric and alchemical sets.

"The union of opposites," Richard murmured. "The final transformation."

Claire turned back to the bulletin board, studying the map more carefully. She counted the marked points. "Six locations total, arranged in a geometric pattern. And here..." She pointed to the center of the pattern, where all the threads converged. "The Baltimore Museum of Art. It's positioned as the focal point of the entire design."

Armed with this new understanding, they returned to the station to update the task force. The pattern identified from Hoffman's office allowed them to map six potential locations for the next killings, while analysis of the symbols suggested the next victims would be marked with the next sequence in the progression.

"These aren't random killings," Claire explained to the assembled officers. "They're an enactment of what Dr. Hoffman called 'The Symmetry Principle', a philosophical concept about transformation through the perfect balance of opposites. The killers are following a geometric pattern across the city, with each pair of killings representing a stage in this transformation process."

"And based on the markings and the calendar we found, we believe they're working on a compressed schedule," Martinez added, indicating a point on the map they'd constructed. "The next pair of killings is scheduled for eleven days from now - exactly two weeks from the first pair. The final stage will occur here: the Baltimore Museum of Art, specifically the contemporary wing where an exhibition on sacred geometry in modern art is currently being installed."

The gravity of that statement settled over the room. Eleven days to identify two killers working in perfect, deadly synchronization across the city.

"So we've got the locations and the timing," Matthews summarized. "But we still don't know who these killers are or how to identify them before they strike again."

"The selection of victims provides insight," Richard offered. "Both Hoffman and Richt were experts in these mathematical principles, both had recently intensified their focus on these concepts. The killers chose them not just as vessels for their message, but because they represented the very principles the killers are enacting."

"Which means the next victims are likely also connected to these concepts," Claire concluded. "We need to identify potential targets in Baltimore who work with sacred geometry, golden ratio principles, or alchemical symbolism. Anyone whose work involves the balance or union of opposites."

The task force divided into teams, each assigned to monitor one of the six locations identified for the next stage of killings. Meanwhile, Martinez coordinated with museum security to enhance protection around the contemporary wing in preparation for what they believed would be the final stage. Claire and Richard began the process of identifying potential victims who might be targeted in the immediate next phase of the killers' plan.

Claire found herself back at her apartment, her investigation board now covered with photos, maps, and connections traced in colored thread. Darwin watched from his perch on the bookcase, occasionally batting at the dangling threads as if helping with the investigation.

Her phone rang, Martinez, calling with an update. "We've identified two potential victims who fit the profile," she reported. "Dr. James Norman, mathematics professor specializing in sacred geometry. Sarah Delmar, sculptor whose work incorporates golden ratio principles."

"All working with principles of symmetry and balance," Claire noted. "Have they been notified?"

"We're placing them under protection without revealing the full details," Martinez confirmed. "But Morrison, there's something else. We ran the symbol patterns through the FBI database. There was a match, a series of unsolved murders in Prague five years ago. Three pairs of victims, killed in precisely the same mirrored pattern, with similar symbolic markings."

"Prague," Claire repeated, the significance registering immediately. "The historical center of alchemical study in Europe."

"Exactly. And here's the kicker, the final killing in that sequence took place at a museum exhibition dedicated to alchemical art. Two curators, positioned in perfect symmetry on opposite sides of the central exhibition hall."

"They've done this before," Claire realized.

"No, and there's more. Similar patterns appeared in Vienna three years ago, and in Florence two years ago. Always the same progression, always culminating at a location representing the union of the principles they're demonstrating."

"International killers, following a pattern across historically significant cities." Claire's mind raced with the implications. "Are there any suspects from those cases?"

"Nothing concrete, but there were witness reports from the Prague scene, a man and a woman seen leaving the museum separately, both described as having 'striking appearances.' The man with unusual white-blond hair, the woman with distinctive scarlet-colored hair."

As Martinez shared this critical information, Claire's phone buzzed with a text from her father: "Found records of academic couple matching our killers' MO. Dr. Jonathan and Dr. Eleanor Wakefield, specialists in symmetry principles. Coming over now with files and photos."

Her doorbell rang twenty minutes later. Through the peephole, she saw her father with a leather satchel.

She opened the door and Richard immediately stepped inside, spreading photographs on her kitchen table. "The Wakefields," he said. "Jonathan with platinum-blond hair, Eleanor with vibrant red hair - exact matches to your Prague witnesses."

"I think we have our killers," Claire told Martinez, who was still on the line. "My dad found records of an academic couple, Dr. Jonathan and Dr. Eleanor Wakefield, specialists in symmetry principles. Their appearances match our witnesses' descriptions exactly."

"The Wakefields," Martinez repeated, making note of the names. "I'll run them through every database we have. If they're in Baltimore, we'll find them."

After ending the call, Claire turned back to her father.

"There's more," Richard said, pulling out a yellowed folder. "I've been going through my old research files. Something about this case kept nagging at me, the symbolic opposition, the ritual element. I remembered a case study from nearly twenty years ago."

He handed the file folder to Claire. Inside were crime scene photos showing two victims positioned in mirror image arrangement, with symbolic markings like those they were currently investigating.

"Boston, 2005," Richard said as Claire examined the photos. "Two professors from different universities, both experts in esoteric mathematical principles. Killed in the same manner as our current victims, positioned in perfect opposition. The case was never solved."

"The same killers?" Claire asked, comparing the photos to those on her board.

"Possibly. The methodology is consistent, though less evolved than what we're seeing now. But there's something else." Richard pulled out another document, a conference program from 2004. "Both victims attended this symposium on 'Mathematical Principles in Philosophical Traditions.' Look at the keynote speakers."

Claire scanned the names, most unfamiliar academic figures, until she reached the final entry: "Dr. Jonathan and Dr. Eleanor Wakefield, University of Edinburgh, 'The Symmetry Principle: Transformation Through Perfect Opposition.'"

"The Symmetry Principle," she repeated, the connection immediate. "The same concept Elizabeth Hoffman was researching. The same title she gave her diagram."

"I've been trying to track the Wakefields," Richard continued. "They were rising academic stars in the early 2000s, husband and wife team bridging mathematics and philosophy. They published several papers on symmetrical principles in various traditions, then seemed to disappear from academic circles around 2007."

"Two years after the Boston killings," Claire noted.

"Precisely. And here's where it gets interesting, Dr. Eleanor Wakefield was known for her striking red hair, while Dr. Jonathan Wakefield had a genetic condition resulting in platinum-blond hair."

"The same descriptions as the suspects from Prague," Claire said, the pieces falling into place. "Have you been able to find any recent trace of them?"

"Nothing definitive," Richard admitted. "But there are references to visiting scholars matching their descriptions at universities in Vienna and Florence during the periods when the killings occurred in those cities."

Claire added this information to her board, connecting the locations, dates, and descriptions. "They're not just killers," she said slowly, understanding dawning. "They're enacting their own research, literally embodying the principles they studied academically."

"Taking their theory to its ultimate conclusion," Richard agreed. "If they believe in the transformative power of perfect symmetry through opposition, what could be more powerful than enacting that symmetry with human lives?"

"And with each cycle, they're progressing toward some ultimate transformation," Claire concluded. "The final stage, the union of opposites."

"Which leaves us ten days to identify and apprehend them before they claim their next victims," Richard said grimly.

The next morning brought a development that shifted the investigation into even higher gear. A security guard at Johns Hopkins reported an attempted break-in at Elizabeth Hoffman's office during the night. The perpetrator had escaped, but security cameras captured a glimpse of a woman with distinctive red hair.

"They're monitoring our investigation," Martinez reported as the task force assembled. "They know we've found Hoffman's research and are trying to recover or destroy evidence."

"Or they're collecting something they need for the next stage," Claire suggested. "Either way, they're aware of our presence and still proceeding with their plan. That suggests absolute confidence, or commitment to completing their ritual regardless of obstacles."

With the security footage confirming the suspected identity of at least one of the killers, the investigation gained momentum. Immigration records showed no official entry for anyone matching the Wakefields' descriptions, but hotel records revealed a British couple checking into the Four Seasons Baltimore three weeks earlier. Their description matched, though they were using the names James and Emily Richardson.

"We've got their current location," Matthews announced as the leads solidified. "Four Seasons, suite 1407. SWAT is preparing for entry, but we need to be careful, these killers have demonstrated precise planning and may have contingencies in place."

Claire studied the hotel's floor plan as the tactical team prepared. "Suite 1407 is on the east side of the building," she noted. "If they're maintaining their pattern of symmetrical opposition..."

"There should be a corresponding location on the west side," Martinez finished her thought. "Suite 1414 is directly opposite."

A quick check with hotel management confirmed that suite 1414 had been booked under a different name but paid for with the same credit card as 1407.

"They're maintaining their opposition even in their accommodations," Claire realized. "One east, one west, perfect symmetry across the hotel."

The tactical approach required coordinated entry to both suites simultaneously. Claire would accompany the team entering suite 1407, while Richard would observe the entry to 1414 from the command post established in the hotel's security office.

The coordinated entry went precisely as planned, both doors breached simultaneously, tactical teams sweeping each suite. But both rooms were empty, showing signs of recent occupation but no current inhabitants.

"They're gone," a tactical officer reported over the radio, holstering his weapon as the all-clear was given. "But they left in a hurry. Clothing still in the closets, toiletries in the bathroom."

Claire examined suite 1407, attention immediately drawn to the desk where papers and books were spread out in careful arrangement. Unlike the rest of the room, which showed signs of hasty departure, the desk had been deliberately organized, a map of Baltimore at its center, marked with the same pattern they'd identified from Elizabeth Hoffman's research, with two new locations circled in red.

"These locations weren't in the original pattern. They're adapting," Claire said, studying the map.

"Why leave this behind?" another officer asked. "They've been careful about evidence until now."

"Because it's not evidence, it's a message," Claire realized. "They want us to follow. They're incorporating us into their ritual."

In suite 1414, the tactical team reported a similar scene, hastily abandoned but with a deliberately arranged desk. Richard coordinated the evidence collection, ensuring that the arrangement was thoroughly documented before being disturbed.

"The books are different in each suite," he reported over the radio. "Suite 1407 has texts on alchemy and philosophical transformation. Suite 1414 has works on sacred geometry and mathematical principles. Divided by subject matter, just like the symbols on the victims."

When photographed and compared side by side, the desk arrangements in both suites formed a perfect mirror image, books arranged in corresponding patterns, papers aligned with identical precision, even the pens placed in mirrored positions.

"They're maintaining the symmetry even as they flee," Claire noted. "The ritual is more important than escape."

As the evidence was cataloged, Martinez received an alert from the officers monitoring the potential victims they'd identified. "Dr. James Norman, the mathematics professor, has gone missing. Last seen leaving his office at Johns Hopkins three hours ago. Never arrived at his scheduled protection detail."

"Check the sculptor, Sarah Delmar," Claire instructed immediately. "If they're maintaining their pattern..."

"Already on it," Martinez confirmed. "No response from her protection detail either."

The pattern was holding. Two victims, taken simultaneously from opposite sides of the city, their disappearances coordinated with perfect precision. But the locations marked on the Wakefields' map suggested they'd deviated from the original sequence identified from Hoffman's research.

"They know we've figured out the pattern, so they're changing it," Claire explained as the task force regrouped at the station. "But they're still maintaining the core principle, symmetrical opposition across the city, east and west."

"So much for having eleven days," Richard said grimly, referring to the calendar prediction.

Richard studied the new locations marked on the maps they'd recovered. "These sites are significant. This eastern location is the rebuilt Lazarus Foundry, a building historically used for metalwork and transformation of raw materials. And the western location is the old Botanical Laboratory, where plant specimens were studied and classified."

"Transformation through different means," Claire said, understanding the symbolism. "Industrial versus natural, technological versus biological."

"And architecturally, they mirror each other," Richard added. "The foundry features predominantly vertical design elements, while the laboratory is characterized by horizontal structures. Opposition in physical form as well as function."

The task force mobilized immediately, with teams dispatched to both locations. SWAT units prepared for simultaneous entry, while Claire headed to the Foundry on the east side of the city. Outside of the Laboratory, Martinez would coordinate the tactical operation, with

Richard providing consultation on the psychological aspects of the synchronized action.

The Lazarus Foundry loomed against the darkening sky, its industrial silhouette a reminder of Baltimore's manufacturing past. Now partially renovated into artist studios, the building retained its original facade and much of its internal structure, massive spaces with high ceilings, steel beams, and brick walls blackened by decades of smoke.

"Thermal imaging shows heat signatures on the third floor," the SWAT commander reported as they established a perimeter. "Two figures, one mobile, one stationary."

"Our victim and one of the killers," Claire surmised. "Any sign of explosives or traps?"

"Unknown, but we're proceeding with caution."

"Entry teams in position," came the confirmation through their earpieces. "Ready on both sites."

"Execute," Martinez ordered, her voice steady.

The operation unfolded with precision, simultaneous breaches at both locations, tactical teams flowing into the buildings. Claire followed the second team into the Lazarus Foundry, the sound of boots on metal stairs echoing.

The third floor had been converted into a single open studio, with massive windows along one wall and original foundry equipment preserved as industrial art pieces. In the center of the space, illuminated by spotlights, was an elaborate arrangement, a chair positioned on a painted circular design, its occupant bound but conscious.

Dr. James Norman looked up as the tactical team entered, his expression shifting from terror to relief. But it was the figure beside him that captured Claire's attention, a tall man with striking white-blond hair, dressed entirely in black, standing with his hands raised in surrender.

"Dr. Jonathan Wakefield," the man confirmed before anyone could speak. "I've been expecting you."

As the tactical team secured Wakefield and medical personnel attended to Norman, Claire observed the scene with growing unease. The surrender had been too easy, the timing too perfect. Wakefield showed no resistance, no surprise at their arrival.

"Where is your wife?" she asked directly, studying his reaction.

"Precisely where I am," Wakefield replied with a slight smile. "On the opposite side of the equation."

Claire's radio crackled with Martinez's voice: "We have the second victim secure. Sarah Delmar is unharmed. But Morrison, the female suspect surrendered without resistance. Says she was expecting us."

The symmetry was holding, two locations, two victims, two killers, all acting in perfect coordination despite being physically separated.

As Mr. Wakefield was escorted from the building, Claire examined the arrangement around Norman's chair. The circular design painted on the floor contained the same symbols they'd found on the previous victims, but arranged in a new pattern. And positioned precisely at compass points around the circle were small objects, artifacts representing different elements of transformation.

"Don't disturb the arrangement," she instructed the evidence technicians. "Document everything exactly as it is before moving anything. The positioning is significant."

Back at the station, the Wakefields were placed in separate interrogation rooms on opposite sides of the building, Jonathan in East Interview 1, Eleanor in West Interview 1. The symmetry of their opposition maintained even in custody.

"They requested it specifically," Matthews reported as the team prepared for the interviews. "Said they would only cooperate if kept in 'perfect balance.' Given what we're dealing with, I authorized it."

Claire reviewed the preliminary psychological assessments as they prepared their approach. "They're highly intelligent, obviously, with extensive academic backgrounds. But what's most significant is their absolute commitment to their philosophical system. This isn't just a belief for them, it's their reality."

"How do we approach individuals who've constructed such an elaborate justification for murder?" Richard asked, the question clearly rhetorical, a prompt for Claire to articulate her strategy rather than a request for guidance.

"We don't challenge the system directly," she replied. "That would only reinforce their opposition. Instead, we acknowledge the principles while separating them from the actions. And most importantly, we maintain absolute symmetry in our approach to both of them."

The strategy required perfect coordination, Claire would interview Eleanor Wakefield while Richard spoke with Jonathan, both interviews conducted simultaneously, with identical opening questions. Martinez would monitor both, ensuring the pattern was maintained.

Eleanor Wakefield sat composed in the west interrogation room, her striking red hair pulled back in a bun. Unlike the disheveled appearance typical of suspects after arrest, she looked immaculate, almost serene.

"Dr. Morrison," she greeted Claire as she entered. "I've been following your work. Your paper on symbolic communication in ritualized violence was particularly insightful."

Claire maintained a neutral expression, setting her notebook on the table with deliberate care. "Dr. Wakefield. I appreciate your cooperation thus far."

"Of course. The ritual requires it." Eleanor smiled slightly. "You've become part of the symmetry now, you and your father. The practitioner and the academic, application and theory. Perfect opposition within your own familial bond."

The observation, delivered with such casual certainty, sent a chill through Claire. The Wakefields hadn't just adapted their plan to accommodate the investigation, they had incorporated it as an element of their ritual.

"Let's talk about your work," Claire began, following the agreed-upon script. "The Symmetry Principle that you and your husband developed. When did it evolve from academic theory to application?"

"Its application was inevitable once we understood its transformative potential," Eleanor replied. "The principle exists in reality, we merely discovered it, documented it."

In the east interrogation room, Jonathan Wakefield was giving an same answer to Richard's identical question, the symmetry of their responses maintained across physical separation.

"Boston, 2005," Claire continued. "That was your first enactment of the principle, wasn't it?"

Eleanor's expression revealed nothing. "The beginning of our understanding, yes. But not the first. The principle has always existed, has always been enacted through perfect oppositions throughout history. We simply became conscious participants rather than unconscious vessels."

"And the subsequent enactments, Prague, Vienna, Florence, and now Baltimore, each represents a progression in this understanding?"

"Each city has its own symmetry," Eleanor explained, her tone scholarly rather than defensive. "Its own balance of opposing forces. Prague with its imperial grandeur and artistic rebellion. Vienna with its ancient mysticism and modern pragmatism. Florence with its sacred traditions and secular innovations. And Baltimore..." She smiled slightly. "Baltimore with its industrial past and technological future, its east-west division of wealth and poverty, development and decay. Perfect oppositions seeking resolution."

Claire maintained her professional demeanor despite the growing certainty that they were dealing with a level of delusion far more sophisticated and dangerous than initially assessed. "And the victims? How did they fit into this principle?"

"They were already part of it," Eleanor said simply. "Already studying the very patterns they embodied. We merely helped them complete their understanding through perfect transformation."

"By killing them."

"By elevating them," Eleanor corrected. "Death is merely the transition point between states of being. The perfect symmetry of existence and non-existence, the ultimate opposition from which all transformation emerges."

The interview continued, with Eleanor explaining their philosophy in academic terms, never showing remorse or doubt about the deaths they had caused. She described their mission as a scientific necessity, a demonstration of universal principles that transcended conventional morality.

Comparing notes afterward, Claire and Richard confirmed that both Wakefields had given nearly identical responses, often using the same phrasing despite having no way to communicate with each other during the interviews.

"They've internalized their opposition so completely that they function as mirror aspects of a single entity," Claire explained to the task force. "They're maintaining perfect symmetry even in custody, which suggests their ritual isn't complete."

"But we've apprehended them," Matthews pointed out. "The next killings have been prevented."

"I'm not convinced," Claire said, studying her notes. "Their surrender was too easy, too coordinated. And they seem too confident, as if custody was part of their plan all along."

"The museum," Martinez said suddenly. "The Baltimore Museum of Art, it was the final location in their original pattern. An exhibition on sacred geometry in modern art is being installed there."

"The union of opposites," Richard recalled. "The final stage of their ritual."

Claire's phone buzzed with a notification from the evidence team processing the Wakefields' hotel suites. The message contained photographs of additional materials found in the room safe, detailed floor plans of the Baltimore Museum of Art, with the contemporary wing highlighted and specific measurements noted along a perfect east-west axis through the main gallery.

"They've already planned the final stage," she realized. "And I don't think they need to be physically present to complete it."

The realization prompted an immediate reexamination of everything they'd collected from the Wakefields. Their belongings, the arrangements at the Lazarus Foundry and Botanical Laboratory, the symbols painted on the floor, all contained elements that had initially seemed decorative but now revealed themselves as components of a larger design.

"These aren't just symbolic arrangements," Claire explained as she assembled the evidence. "They're precisely calculated coordinates and timings. Look at the angles marked on these designs, they align perfectly with the east-west axis through the museum gallery. And these numbers hidden in the patterns? They're not just measurements; they're timestamps."

Claire studied the timestamps more carefully, her expression shifting. "Wait. These calculations don't match what we found on Hoffman's calendar. They've accelerated the timeline again." She pointed to the notations. "When we found Hoffman's research, the final stage was marked for six weeks out. But they've compressed it further. According to these coordinates and astronomical calculations, the final stage triggers tomorrow."

"They've set something in motion that will trigger at the museum, even without their presence," Martinez concluded.

"Exactly. And given their methodology and symbolism, it's likely something that will create the 'perfect union of opposites' they've been building toward, possibly an elaborate mechanism designed to trigger at a specific moment, when the sun's position creates particular light patterns in the gallery."

With less than twenty-four hours until the final stage, the task force mobilized to secure the museum and search for whatever mechanism the Wakefields might have installed. The contemporary wing was evacuated, exhibitions temporarily relocated, and specialists brought in to examine every inch of the space.

Meanwhile, Claire and Richard continued their interviews with the Wakefields, now focusing on what might be waiting at the museum. But both suspects maintained their academic detachment, discussing their philosophy in abstract terms while revealing nothing about specific plans.

"They're stalling," Claire realized after the third round of interviews yielded no new information. "Keeping us focused on them while something else unfolds."

"Or someone else," Richard suggested. "We've been assuming they're working alone because their philosophy emphasizes the duality of their partnership. But what if there are others involved? Disciples or assistants who understand the principles and can complete the ritual in their absence?"

This new possibility expanded the investigation, with Martinez coordinating background checks on everyone connected to the Wakefields, former students, academic colleagues, individuals who had attended their lectures or corresponded with them about their work.

As they processed the hotel evidence, Martinez's background check team identified a concerning lead: a former graduate student named Jacob Leighton who had studied under the Wakefields at Edinburgh before their disappearance from academic circles. Leighton had published several papers expanding on their theories and had recently arrived in Baltimore, ostensibly for a visiting position at Johns Hopkins.

"His area of focus is the application of transformative symmetry in architectural spaces," Martinez reported. "And he arrived in Baltimore exactly one day before the first killings."

Surveillance was immediately established on Leighton, who had taken a temporary apartment near the museum district. Within hours of being placed under watch, he made a visit to the Baltimore Museum of Art, touring the contemporary wing as part of a public group.

"He could have placed something during that visit," Claire suggested as they reviewed the surveillance footage. "Something small, designed to activate at a specific time tomorrow."

"Or he could be completely innocent, just an academic with similar interests to the Wakefields," Martinez countered. "We need more before we bring him in."

The decision was made to maintain surveillance while accelerating the search of the museum. Security teams worked through the night, scanning every surface, examining electrical systems, checking for any device or mechanism that might have been concealed within the exhibition space.

By morning, nothing had been found, no explosive device, no chemical agent, no technological trigger that might enact whatever 'union of opposites' the Wakefields had planned. But as the sun rose, casting its first light through the eastern windows of the contemporary gallery, Claire noticed something that had been overlooked.

The gallery itself was the mechanism.

"It's the architecture," she explained urgently as the task force assembled at the museum. "Look at the design of this wing, the eastern windows are positioned to capture the morning light at a specific angle. The western windows do the same with the afternoon sun. And the central space, it's designed around sacred geometry principles, with the golden ratio governing the proportions."

Richard examined the architectural plans they'd obtained. "The museum was renovated five years ago. And look who consulted on the design of the contemporary wing, Michael Richt, our second victim."

"The entire space is a massive demonstration of the Symmetry Principle," Claire realized. "At a specific moment today, likely noon, when the sun is directly overhead, the light patterns from both east and west will create a perfect union at the center of the gallery."

"So what happens at that moment?" Matthews asked, the practical concern of law enforcement cutting through the academic analysis.

"I don't know," Claire admitted. "But the Wakefields believe it will complete their ritual of transformation. Given their history, that likely involves death, either their own or others'."

As noon approached, the museum remained evacuated, with tactical teams positioned throughout the building and bomb disposal experts standing by. Claire and Martinez waited in the contemporary gallery, watching as the light patterns evolved with the sun's movement, creating shifting geometric designs across the floor.

"There," Claire said as the clock approached midday. "The patterns are converging toward the center."

The sunlight streaming through the windows began to form intricate intersecting patterns on the gallery floor, creating a complex geometric design that seemed to pulse with the subtle movements of light and shadow.

At precisely noon, the patterns aligned perfectly, forming a complete symbol at the center of the gallery, the same combined alchemical and geometric symbol they had identified as the final stage of the Wakefields' ritual.

And within moments of noon, in their separate cells on opposite sides of the detention facility, Jonathan and Eleanor Wakefield each ingested poison they had somehow concealed on their persons. The timing wasn't perfectly synchronized - Jonathan at 12:01, Eleanor at 11:59 - but close enough to suggest they had both been watching for the appointed hour.

By the time the alarm was raised and medical personnel reached them, both were beyond saving, their final act of symmetry complete, their physical opposition resolved through simultaneous transformation.

In the aftermath, as Claire and Martinez pieced together the full scope of the Wakefields' plan, Jacob Leighton was brought in for questioning. But the former student proved to be exactly what he claimed, an academic following similar research interests, with no knowledge of the Wakefields' criminal activities.

"They used him," Claire explained as they reviewed the evidence one final time. "Not as an accomplice, but as a symbol. His presence in Baltimore at this time, his interest in the same principles, it was another piece in their pattern, another to be balanced."

"They believed they were revealing a universal truth," Richard said as he and Claire finalized their report on the case. "That perfect transformation could only be achieved through the precise balance of opposing forces, culminating in their own simultaneous deaths as the ultimate demonstration of the principle."

"A philosophical system that justified murder as necessary demonstration," Claire added. "Academic theory perverted into ritualized violence."

"The most dangerous killers are often those who believe they're serving a higher purpose," Richard noted. "The Wakefields saw themselves not as murderers but as scientists conducting necessary experiments, revealing patterns they believed governed reality itself."

As they closed the case file, Claire reflected on the symmetry that had defined not just the Wakefields' crimes but the investigation itself: east and west, father and daughter, theory and application, all moving in coordinated opposition toward resolution. The pattern that had seemed so alien at the beginning now felt almost familiar, a reminder of how thin the line could be between understanding destructive patterns and being caught in their web.

After wrapping up the case, Claire found herself at Rusty's Diner. The worn vinyl booths and checkerboard floor had become a comforting refuge when cases weighed heavily on her mind.

"Well, if it isn't Dr. Morrison," called Betty. She moved with grace that came from decades of balancing coffee pots and plates. "Your usual booth is open, honey."

Claire settled into the corner booth with its view of the street, nodding gratefully as Betty appeared with coffee without being asked.

"You look like you've been wrestling with a tough one," Betty observed, filling the mug with the diner's famously strong brew. "Cream and sugar's already on the table."

"Thanks, Betty," Claire replied, adding a splash of cream to the steaming coffee. "And yes, just closed a case."

"The one that's been all over the news? Those killers arranging their victims like some kind of art project?" Betty's direct manner was part of why Claire appreciated this place, no pretense, just straightforward human connection.

"That's the one," Claire confirmed, taking a welcome sip of coffee.

Betty shook her head. "People get these ideas in their heads, think they've figured out some grand pattern to the universe, and use it to justify the most horrible things." She placed a menu on the table though they both knew Claire would order the same thing she always did. "You want your usual? Apple pie with vanilla ice cream?"

Claire smiled. "You know me too well."

"Been feeding you for what, three years now? Ever since you started showing up here at all hours when cases kept you up." Betty jotted down the order from memory. "Your father was in here yesterday, you know. Same booth, different order. Said he was consulting on a case with you."

"He mentioned he'd found this place," Claire said, surprised but pleased at the connection. "What did he order?"

"Reuben on rye, hold the thousand island, side salad instead of fries." Betty smirked. "You two are different sides of the same coin, I swear. Both so precise in your own ways."

As Betty moved away to put in her order, Claire considered the waitress's casual observation. Different sides of the same coin. Another form of symmetry, she and her father, approaching the world from different angles but connected by the same principles.

A week later, Claire sat across from Dr. Leland in their regular therapy session, the Wakefield case officially closed but still echoing in her thoughts.

"You're troubled by the resolution," Leland observed, her practiced eye noting Claire's restlessness.

"Not the resolution itself," Claire clarified. "More the… satisfaction of it. The Wakefields achieved exactly what they wanted, their perfect union through symmetrical death. Their ritual completed exactly as they planned, despite our intervention."

"Does that feel like failure?"

Claire considered the question. "Not failure, exactly. But there's something disturbing about killers who incorporate their own apprehension and death into their plan. It challenges our concept of justice."

"Because justice typically involves interrupting the killer's design rather than becoming part of it," Leland suggested.

"Exactly. They used us, used me and my father specifically, as elements in their pattern. Our opposition of approaches, our professional symmetry, became another demonstration of their principle." Claire paused, reaching for the words to articulate her discomfort. "It makes me question how much our response to them was our own choice versus playing a role they had anticipated."

"The eternal question of free will versus determinism," Leland smiled slightly. "A philosophical problem as old as human thought."

"The Wakefields would say our actions were predetermined by the patterns governing reality," Claire noted. "That we were simply enacting our assigned opposition within the greater symmetry."

"And what do you say?"

Claire thought about the investigation, about the choices made, the insights gained, the connections forged. "I say that meaning emerges from our response to patterns, not from the patterns themselves. The Wakefields mistook the map for the territory, the symbol for the reality."

"A common error among those who become obsessed with symbolic systems," Leland agreed. "They begin to see only what confirms their structure, missing the messy complexity that doesn't fit their design."

Later that evening, as she and Richard discussed the case over dinner, Claire found herself appreciating the subtle asymmetry of their conversation, the places where their perspectives diverged in productive ways, where disagreement led to deeper understanding rather than perfect opposition.

"The Wakefields would have seen us as perfect opposites," Richard noted as they finished their meal. "Academic versus practitioner, theoretical versus applied. But that's always been a false dichotomy, hasn't it?"

"All dichotomies simplify what they claim to explain," Claire agreed. "Human relationships are never just binary oppositions."

"Nor are human minds," Richard added, his expression thoughtful. "We contain multitudes, as Whitman would say. Our contradictions and complexities can't be reduced to simple symmetries."

Back in her apartment, she found Darwin in his usual spot atop the bookcase, watching the city lights. As she settled on the couch, Darwin abandoned his perch to curl up beside her, offering simple animal contentment.

As Darwin purred against her hand while she scratched behind his ears, Claire thought about the patterns that defined her life, the weekly therapy sessions, the case debriefs with Martinez, the evolving relationship with her father, the quiet evenings at home with Darwin.

None were perfectly symmetrical. None followed rigid geometric principles. Each contained variations, exceptions, and developments that couldn't be predicted by any philosophical system, no matter how elegant.

And in that wonderful asymmetry, that beautiful imperfection, lay the true pattern of living, not the rigid balance of perfect opposition, but the dynamic, ever-evolving dance of genuine human experience.

Outside, Baltimore continued its urban rhythms, patterns forming and dissolving in endless variety. And Claire Morrison, forensic psychologist, found herself exactly where she needed to be, not at the center of opposing forces, but happily, and humanly off-balance in the best possible way.

Chapter Eight

Anonymous Gift

D r. Claire Morrison was updating her case files when the call
came from Chief Matthews. She'd just finished documenting
the final psychological assessment from the Wakefield case.

"Morrison, I need you in my office," Matthews said. "We've got a
situation involving a cold case."

Claire had learned to recognize when Matthews' tone carried more
weight than usual. This was one of those moments. She saved her
work, grabbed her jacket, and reached instinctively for the packet of
tic tacs in her pocket. Nearly four years sober.

"On my way, sir," she replied.

Martinez was already in Matthews' office when Claire arrived, her
posture indicating this wasn't a routine briefing. After working together on multiple cases, Claire could read her partner's subtle tells as
easily as crime scene evidence.

"Dr. Morrison," Matthews began as she took a seat, "yesterday
the Baltimore County Police forwarded us a cold case file that's been
flagged for review. The Katherine Morrison missing persons case from
1998."

Claire gripped the arms of her chair. "What?"

"Your mother," Matthews confirmed, his expression neutral. "New evidence has surfaced that requires investigation. Given the obvious conflict of interest, I should assign this to another team, but the evidence specifically mentions your name."

He slid a manila folder across his desk. "No fingerprints were found. We've made copies for analysis, but here's the original evidence." Inside was an envelope addressed to "Dr. Claire Morrison, Baltimore Police Department" containing a small package with a flash drive and a note in block letters: "Your mother deserved better. The truth is in her data."

Claire examined the envelope first, seeing her name clearly written on the front, then turned her attention to the flash drive with trembling hands. A small label on the drive read K.M. Research Archives - 1998. The sight of her mother's initials sent a chill through her.

"The package was found at Baltimore County yesterday," Matthews explained. "No postmark, no delivery service markings, no sender information. Someone left it there. We've already examined the contents; it contains research files that apparently belonged to your mother, along with documentation suggesting her disappearance may not have been voluntary."

"Anonymous evidence about a case from over two decades ago," Martinez observed. "Someone wants this investigation reopened."

Claire clutched the drive tightly. Her mother, Dr. Katherine Morrison, had disappeared when she was nine, vanishing without a trace after episodes of apparent paranoia that had shaped her understanding of both her mother and herself.

That fear had driven her toward the bottle in her late twenties. During her doctoral program, the pressure of academia combined with her terror of developing the same "paranoia" that had taken her mother had sent Claire spiraling into alcohol-fueled nights that nearly destroyed her career before it began. The memories of that dark period still haunt her.

Martinez watched her partner's reaction with protective concern. Their professional relationship had evolved into something more than family, especially after the cases that had tested them both.

"What's on the drive?" Claire asked, her voice controlled despite the emotions churning beneath the surface.

Matthews turned his monitor toward them, showing the analysis results. "Research data, experiment notes, correspondence. And what appears to be evidence that your mother believed she was being monitored by pharmaceutical companies. I want both of you to review this material."

Claire and Martinez spent the next day in the conference room, reviewing the files. What they found challenged everything Claire had been told about her mother's disappearance.

The drive contained dozens of files, mostly research data, experiment notes, and correspondence spanning Katherine's final months at Johns Hopkins. Claire opened a document titled Final Conclusions - SECURE COPY.

"My God," she whispered as she scanned the contents. "Her research was on neurological reconfiguration in traumatized children. Non-pharmaceutical approaches to rewiring neural pathways affected by severe trauma."

"Is that significant?" Martinez asked, sliding her chair closer.

"It could be revolutionary," Claire replied, continuing to scan the detailed methodology. "Current research is just now validating many of these approaches. She was decades ahead of her time. Look at these preliminary results: significant improvement in trauma responses without any pharmaceutical intervention."

As they reviewed more files, Claire uncovered evidence that filled her with dread. Katherine's final weeks had been marked by observations of equipment malfunctions, missing research data, and strange encounters with individuals in restricted research areas.

"This doesn't read like paranoid delusions," Martinez observed. "These are clinical observations, meticulous record-keeping. She documented times, dates, and incidents."

Claire felt a chill as she read her mother's increasingly urgent notes. "My father always told me her paranoia was part of her mental breakdown. That she became convinced people were monitoring her, poisoning her. But these notes..." She paused, sorting through more files until she found one labeled External Threat Assessment.

The document contained Katherine Morrison's growing suspicions that pharmaceutical companies were monitoring her research, particularly one called Archon Pharmaceuticals. She had recorded power outages during critical experiments, stolen files from locked cabinets, and encounters with individuals who claimed to be conducting routine inspections.

"Look at this," Claire said, opening another file. "She kept a detailed log of physical symptoms she believed resulted from deliberate poisoning. Documented everything: times of onset, duration, severity."

Martinez studied the log, her expression growing more troubled with each entry. "These symptoms align with specific toxicological profiles. Anxiety induction, cognitive disruption, mild paranoia. If someone wanted to make your mother appear mentally unstable..."

"They'd target exactly those effects," Claire finished, the realization making her blood run cold.

"Then your mother's disappearance might not have been what it seemed," Martinez concluded, her voice taking on the quiet intensity Claire recognized from their most serious cases.

Claire sat back in her chair, mind racing through decades of assumptions that were suddenly crumbling. If her mother hadn't been paranoid at all, but perceptive... if Katherine Morrison had been the victim of corporate a conspiracy rather than mental illness... what did that mean for Claire? Her greatest fear, inheriting her mother's "illness," had driven her to self-destruct, to throw away years of her life chasing oblivion in a bottle.

"I need to talk to my father," she said finally. "And Dr. Theresa Morgan, who worked with my mother. She's still at JHU."

Martinez nodded, already organizing the files for further analysis. "I'll start running background checks on Archon Pharmaceuticals, see if there's anything in our databases." She hesitated, then added, "Claire, if someone is sending you this now, after all this time, there might be a reason beyond simply correcting the historical record."

"You think I might be in danger?" Claire asked, though she'd already considered the possibility.

"I think information that was worth making someone disappear for back in 1998 might still be sensitive today," Martinez replied, her expression carrying the careful concern that had become characteristic of their partnership. "We need to be careful. Document everything."

Claire called her father from her desk phone, her hands still unsteady. The weight of the revelations pressed against her chest, making each breath feel deliberate and measured.

"Dad, we need to talk."

"Claire," Richard's voice carried immediate concern, but there was something else underneath it that she couldn't quite identify. "What's happened? You sound distressed."

"New evidence has surfaced about Mom's disappearance. Research files, documentation that suggests she wasn't paranoid at all. That she was actually being monitored by pharmaceutical companies, possibly poisoned to induce symptoms of mental illness." Claire found herself speaking faster as the implications tumbled out. "Dad, there are detailed logs of surveillance, equipment failures, unauthorized people in her lab. This wasn't mental illness."

A long pause. When Richard spoke again, his voice carried a mixture of emotions Claire couldn't quite parse. "I'll come to the station immediately. Don't discuss this with anyone else until I arrive."

"Dad, did you know any of this was possible? Did you ever suspect..."

"We'll talk when I get there," Richard interrupted, with a firmness that suggested the conversation was over. "Fifty minutes. And Claire? Be very careful who you trust with this information. If corporate interests were involved in your mother's disappearance, they may still be watching."

After hanging up, she found herself studying the flash drive with new wariness. Someone had wanted her to have this information, but as Martinez had pointed out, the timing and method of delivery raised as many questions as the contents answered.

While they waited, Martinez continued background checks on Archon Pharmaceuticals, her fingers flying across the keyboard. The information that emerged painted a disturbing picture.

"This is bigger than we thought," Martinez said, looking up from her screen. "Archon Pharmaceuticals has grown into one of the largest pharmaceutical companies in the country, specializing in psychotropic medications. Their flagship products are primarily focused on childhood trauma and behavioral disorders."

"The exact market my mother's non-pharmaceutical approaches would have threatened," Claire realized, the pieces beginning to form a pattern.

"Look at this," Martinez continued, pulling up financial records. "Archon's market capitalization is over thirty billion dollars, with the majority of their revenue coming from pediatric psychiatric medications. If your mother's research had been validated and widely adopted..."

"It would have cost them billions in lost revenue," Claire finished. "That's motive."

Martinez printed the relevant documents, organizing them into a preliminary case file. "We need to be meticulous about this. If we're dealing with corporate conspiracy and researcher suppression, there might be other victims, other cases."

Richard Morrison arrived earlier than expected, his usually composed academic demeanor showing signs of strain. His hair was slightly disheveled, and his typically neat attire seemed hastily assembled. He embraced Claire with the warmth that had become natural between them since their reconciliation, but she noticed a tension in his shoulders.

"Show me everything," he said simply.

They moved to the larger conference room, spreading the files across the table in chronological order. Richard studied them with the logical approach Claire recognized from their shared work, but his reaction was stronger and more immediate than she'd expected.

"Katherine was right," he said quietly after reviewing several documents, his voice carrying a weight of regret Claire had never heard before. "She was being monitored, harassed, undermined. I should have taken her concerns more seriously."

"You knew about this?" Martinez asked, her tone sharpening.

"I knew she was concerned about corporate interference with her research," Richard replied, removing his glasses to clean them with movements that seemed more agitated than usual. "At the time, I thought... I hoped it was stress manifesting as paranoia. It was easier to believe she was developing mental illness than to accept she might be in genuine danger."

"Dad," Claire said, "we need you to tell us everything you remember about those final weeks. Every detail, no matter how insignificant it might seem."

For the next two hours, Richard recounted the circumstances of Katherine's disappearance. His academic training served them well as he recalled conversations, dates, behavioral changes, and the names of everyone who had contacted Katherine in her final days. But it was the level of detail that began to concern Martinez, whose detective instincts were finely tuned to inconsistencies.

"She became increasingly concerned about surveillance in those final weeks," Richard explained, his narrative flowing with unusual smoothness for events that had occurred decades earlier, "Convinced she was being poisoned, that her research was being monitored. She showed me evidence: hair samples, water samples from her office, food she believed had been tampered with."

Claire leaned forward. "You had them tested?"

"I arranged for private analysis through a laboratory. The results showed elevated levels of certain compounds, but within ranges that could be explained by environmental factors or occupational exposure." Richard paused, his expression growing troubled. "What I didn't tell you at the time was that I began investigating myself after receiving those results."

"What kind of investigation?" Martinez asked, making notes with particular attention to Richard's unusually specific knowledge of testing procedures.

"I hired a private security consultant to check Katherine's lab and office for surveillance equipment. He found sophisticated monitoring devices, not amateur academic espionage but professional-grade equipment. Military specification, he called it."

Claire felt a chill of vindication mixed with horror. "Who would have had that level of capability in 1998?"

"Corporate security firms, certainly. Intelligence agencies. The consultant had military background and said the equipment was similar to what he'd encountered in classified operations." Richard ran a hand through his hair; a gesture of distress Claire had never witnessed. "I confronted the head of Katherine's department with this evidence, demanded a formal investigation. Two days later, Katherine was gone."

"You believe she was taken," Claire said, not a question but a statement of growing understanding.

"I never found definitive proof," Richard replied. "Initially, the police opened a full investigation; treated it as a potential abduction given the surveillance equipment we'd discovered. But when they couldn't find evidence of foul play, and with Katherine's recent erratic behavior, they reclassified it as a voluntary disappearance and scaled back their efforts significantly."

Martinez leaned back in her chair, studying Richard with the analytical gaze she brought to witness interviews. "Dr. Morrison, your memory for specific details after all these years is quite remarkable. Even for someone personally involved in a traumatic event."

"Details burn themselves into memory during traumatic experiences," Richard replied. "The phenomenon is well-documented in psychological literature. During extreme stress, the mind often creates indelible memories of seemingly minor details."

"Of course," Martinez agreed, but she continued taking notes with particular attention to the technical aspects of Richard's knowledge. "Tell us about that initial investigation, before they reclassified the case. What did the police focus on?"

Richard's narrative of the official investigation was equally detailed, encompassing not just the emotional trauma of a husband losing his wife, but specific knowledge of evidence processing, crime scene procedures, and investigative techniques that seemed unusually comprehensive for a family member, even one with professional expertise in psychology.

Martinez made detailed notes, cross-referencing Richard's account with the original case files. "What was the detective's name?"

"James Harmon. He retired about ten years ago, moved to Florida, I believe." Richard's recall was immediate and precise. "He was thorough but ultimately concluded that Katherine had left voluntarily, probably suffering from a psychological breakdown."

"Why tell me she had a mental breakdown?" Claire asked, struggling to reconcile these new revelations with the narrative she'd grown up believing. Her voice rose with sudden anger. "Do you have any idea what that did to me? I spent years terrified I'd inherit her 'illness.' It nearly destroyed me."

Richard's face filled with profound regret. "Because I couldn't prove otherwise," he said simply. "And because a nine-year-old girl deserved closure I couldn't provide if I pursued dangerous truths. I made a choice, Claire; to be your father rather than Katherine's avenger." He hesitated, then added softly, "I never imagined that fear would drive you to drinking. By the time the damage my decision had caused, you were already deep in addiction. I failed you both."

The admission hung in the air between them, with decades of complicated history and missed opportunities for honesty. Claire felt her anger transform into something more complex: understanding mixed with lingering resentment and a new appreciation for the impossible choices her father had faced.

"We need to investigate this properly," Martinez decided. "Starting with current information about Archon Pharmaceuticals and any other researchers who might have faced similar circumstances."

Claire made arrangements to meet with Dr. Theresa Morgan at Johns Hopkins. Dr. Morgan's office was filled with the controlled chaos of active research: brain scans, monitoring equipment, and stacks of journals that reflected decades of dedication to understanding the human mind.

"I've been wondering when someone would finally ask about Katherine's work," Dr. Morgan said. "When you called about new evidence in your mother's case, I realized it was time to speak about what really happened in those final months."

Dr. Morgan had worked alongside Katherine in the late 1990s, focusing on approaches to childhood trauma. She was one of the few colleagues who had taken Katherine's concerns about surveillance seriously.

"Your mother's research was extraordinary," Dr. Morgan explained. "Her theories about non-pharmaceutical neurological interventions for childhood trauma were revolutionary. What she predicted about neural pathway modification has only recently been validated by modern imaging technology."

"Did you witness the harassment she documented?" Claire asked.

"I did. Research files corrupted on her computer, mysterious power outages during critical experiments, unknown substances found in her coffee." Dr. Morgan's expression grew troubled. "The pattern was too coordinated to be coincidental. Someone was deliberately sabotaging her work."

"Why didn't you speak up at the time?"

"I tried," Dr. Morgan replied."But without concrete proof, and with Katherine's behavior becoming increasingly erratic due to what she believed was deliberate poisoning, my concerns were dismissed as loyalty to a colleague who was suffering a psychological breakdown."

Dr. Morgan provided documentation she had secretly maintained throughout the intervening years: copies of Katherine's research, photographs of damaged equipment, and her own detailed observations of the harassment they had both witnessed.

"Katherine was brilliant. She was right about what was being done to her," Dr. Morgan concluded. "I've carried the guilt of not doing more to help her for all these years."

Their breakthrough came through an unexpected channel. Dr. Eleanor Fourier, a former Archon research director who had retired three years earlier, approached them through intermediaries after learning about their investigation through academic networks. News of the Katherine Morrison case had begun circulating quietly through research communities, reaching individuals who had long carried the weight of uncomfortable knowledge.

"I worked for Archon from 1990 up till 3 years ago." Fourier explained as she served coffee in her living room. "I retired as research director with knowledge that's been weighing on my conscience for years."

Fourier was exactly as Dr. Morgan had described: mid-fifties, professional, with the sharp eyes of a scientist and the careful manner of someone accustomed to measuring her words. Her decision to come forward represented significant personal risk, as her retirement benefits and non-disclosure agreements could be jeopardized by her revelations.

"Why come forward now?" Claire asked directly, studying Fourier's face for signs of deception or hidden agenda.

"Because Katherine Morrison's research is being validated by modern science, and Archon is once again moving to suppress it," Fourier replied. "And because I've spent over two decades carrying the knowledge of what was done to a brilliant scientist whose only crime was developing better ways to help traumatized children."

Fourier provided documentation that painted an alarming picture of corporate suppression spanning decades. "We called it 'competitive intelligence,' but it was corporate espionage involving surveillance, research theft, and when necessary, direct interference with researchers who threatened our market position."

"Katherine Morrison was a primary target?" Martinez prompted.

"Yes. Her non-pharmaceutical approaches showed preliminary results that outperformed our best medications, without the side effects that concerned parents and medical professionals. The financial implications were staggering."

"What exactly did Archon do to my mother?" Claire asked, her voice tight.

"Initially, standard surveillance and research theft. Monitoring her communications, copying her data, attempting to identify weaknesses in her procedures that could be exploited." Fourier's professional facade began to crack as she described escalating tactics. "When that proved insufficient, they escalated to direct interference: corrupting her computer files, and eventually introducing low-level toxins designed to induce symptoms that would make her appear mentally unstable."

Claire felt sick. "You're saying they deliberately poisoned her to make her appear paranoid?"

"Yes. Specific compounds known to induce anxiety, paranoia, and cognitive disorganization. Not enough to cause permanent damage, just enough to make her behavior increasingly erratic, to make her claims about being poisoned seem delusional." Fourier's voice carried genuine remorse. "The psychological manipulation was as important as the chemical intervention. Isolating her from colleagues, undermining her credibility, and making her question her own perceptions."

"And when that didn't work?" Martinez pressed.

"That's when they sent in their enforcer, Edward Browne, to make direct threats and pressure her to abandon her research entirely." Fourier pulled out a folder containing photocopied internal documents. "According to records I accessed before leaving the company, Katherine refused to back down. She told Browne she had secured samples proving the deliberate contamination, that she was taking them to the authorities."

"And then she disappeared," Claire said, the pieces of a horrifying puzzle falling into place.

"I believe Browne arranged for her removal," Fourier confirmed. "Though I wasn't privy to the specific details, I learned later that there were protocols for handling researchers who couldn't be discredited through conventional means."

Fourier provided them with names, locations, and documentation that revealed a network of corporate operatives who had targeted researchers across the country. The scope of the conspiracy involved not just Archon but multiple pharmaceutical companies who had collaborated to suppress research that threatened their collective interests.

"Is my mother still alive?" Claire asked, the question she'd been afraid to voice.

"I don't know with certainty," Fourier admitted. "But there were references in internal communications to long-term facilities where 'problematic individuals' could be housed until their cases were resolved."

The information Fourier provided connected Katherine's case to a broader federal investigation that had been ongoing for years. Agents Sarah Germain and Thomas Jackson from the FBI, arrived at the Baltimore PD with files from investigations spanning multiple states; part of a broader federal effort to combat corporate interference with medical research.

"Dr. Morrison," Agent Germain began, spreading photographs across the conference table, "your mother's case connects to a pattern we've been tracking. Researchers whose work threatened pharmaceutical profits, facing escalating harassment that culminated in career destruction or disappearance."

The photographs showed men and women of various ages. "Seven confirmed missing," Agent Jackson added grimly. "Including your mother. But we suspect the actual number is higher, as many cases were dismissed as voluntary disappearances or mental health crises."

The federal investigation provided resources that local law enforcement couldn't match. Within days, they had traced financial connections, communications networks, and travel patterns that revealed the scope of the conspiracy. Katherine's case became a crucial piece in a much larger puzzle of research suppression.

"Edward Browne is still alive," Agent Jackson reported during one of their daily briefings. "Retired in Arizona, but he's been maintaining contact with former colleagues. We've established surveillance, and he's made several calls to numbers we've connected to the old Archon network since our investigation became known."

"He knows we're closing in," Martinez observed.

"Which means he might be willing to cooperate to avoid prosecution," Agent Germain suggested. "We're prepared to offer limited immunity in exchange for information about your mother's fate."

The decision to confront Browne directly required thorough preparation. His cooperation could provide definitive answers about Katherine's disappearance, and it also represented their best chance of locating her if she was still alive.

"I want to be there when you question him," Claire told the federal agents. "I need to hear whatever he has to say directly."

The flight to Arizona gave Claire time to process the implications of their investigation. Martinez sat beside her, offering the steady presence that had become one of the most important relationships in Claire's life.

"You know this changes everything about your recovery, right?" Martinez said quietly as they reviewed their interview strategy.

"How so?" Claire asked, though she suspected what Martinez meant.

"You got sober believing you were fighting an inherited mental illness. But you were fighting the trauma of losing your mother under false circumstances. That's not genetic predisposition; that's a normal response to an abnormal situation."

Claire considered this perspective as she watched clouds drift past the airplane window. "I'm not sure it matters why I drank. What matters is that I stopped."

"It matters because it changes how you see yourself," Martinez replied. "And how you see your mother. She wasn't a cautionary tale about genetic vulnerability. She was a victim."

Edward Browne's retirement home was in a gated community outside Phoenix, all manicured lawns and artificial lakes designed to create an illusion of peaceful isolation. At seventy-three, he retained the polished appearance of a successful executive, but his hands shook slightly as the agents showed him their badges.

The interview room at the local FBI field office was designed to be intimidating: stark white walls, fluorescent lighting, and a metal table that reflected the harsh illumination. Browne sat across from them, his composure gradually eroding as the evidence was presented.

"Mr. Browne," Agent Germain began, "we're investigating the disappearance of Dr. Katherine Morrison in 1998. We understand you had extensive contact with her in the weeks before she vanished."

Browne's initial denials crumbled quickly when confronted with Fourier's documentation and the communication intercepts the FBI had obtained. Claire studied his face, noting the micro-expressions her training had taught her to recognize: the brief downward glance that suggested deception, the tightening around his eyes that indicated calculation of options.

"What happened to my mother?" Claire asked directly, her voice steady despite the emotions beneath the surface.

Browne looked at her for a long moment, perhaps seeing something of Katherine in her features. "Your mother wouldn't listen to reason," he said finally.

"What kind of reason?" Agent Germain pressed.

"The kind that pointed out her research threatened treatments that were helping thousands of children," Browne replied, his voice gaining strength as he fell back on justifications. "Non-pharmaceutical approaches might work in controlled settings, but real-world implementation required the reliability and standardization that only pharmaceutical solutions could provide."

Claire stared at him with barely controlled rage. "You're talking about my mother like she was a business problem to be solved."

Something in Browne's expression shifted, perhaps seeing the pain in her eyes. His shoulders sagged slightly, and when he spoke again, his voice had lost its defensive edge.

The confession, when it finally came, was devastating. Browne described a network that had operated for decades, designed to neutralize research threats through surveillance, sabotage, and when necessary, "permanent solutions."

"The contamination was supposed to be sufficient," Browne explained, his corporate euphemisms failing to disguise the horror of what he was describing. "Low-level chemical exposure to induce apparent paranoia, making her seem unstable. But Katherine was too intelligent, too analytic. She documented everything, prepared evidence that could have destroyed our entire operation."

"So you escalated to kidnapping," Claire said, her voice tight.

"The decision was made at levels above my authority," Browne said defensively. "I was told she would be relocated to a secure facility where her condition could be managed until the threat she represented was neutralized."

"Where?" Agent Jackson demanded.

Browne provided details about a private psychiatric facility outside Baltimore that had been used to house "problematic individuals" whose cases required long-term management. According to his testimony, Katherine had been transferred there in early 1999, where she was to be kept sedated and isolated under a false identity until Archon could determine how to handle her.

"Is she still alive?" Claire asked, the question that had haunted her for decades.

"I don't know," Browne replied, and for the first time, he seemed genuinely remorseful. "The facility burned down in mid 1999. There were casualties, but the records were destroyed in the fire. I was told your mother had died, but I never saw proof."

The investigation of the burned facility yielded both disturbing evidence and unexpected hope. Forensic teams found remains of medical equipment, restraint systems, and chemical storage areas that confirmed the facility had been used for illegal detention. But they also found a crucial witness.

Margaret Halley had worked as a nurse at the facility in the late 1990s. Now retired and living in a nursing home outside Baltimore, she agreed to speak with investigators after being granted immunity.

"We called it a treatment center," Halley explained, her hands shaking as she recounted memories. "But most of the patients weren't there voluntarily. They were researchers, whistleblowers, people who had information that certain corporations wanted suppressed."

"Do you remember Dr. Katherine Morrison?" Claire asked, hope and dread warring in her chest.

Halley's eyes sharpened with immediate recognition. "The neuroscientist. Beautiful woman, brilliant mind. She was brought in during the spring of 1999, following some kind of corporate dispute. I remember her clearly because she was so different from our usual patients."

Claire felt her heart racing. "What was her condition when she arrived?"

"Physically healthy but psychologically traumatized by whatever had been done to her before arrival. She kept insisting she was Dr. Katherine Morrison, that she had a daughter named Claire, that her research was being suppressed by pharmaceutical companies." Halley's voice grew stronger. "The administrators claimed it was all delusional, part of her diagnosed paranoid schizophrenia. But her knowledge was too specific, too detailed."

"You didn't believe the diagnosis," Martinez observed.

"No, I did not. She could describe neurological procedures, discuss research methodologies. She knew details about Johns Hopkins University, about specific faculty members and research programs. That's not how delusions present in patients with genuine psychiatric conditions."

"What happened to her?" Claire asked, dreading the answer but needing to know.

Ms. Halley was quiet for a moment, clearly struggling with memories that had tormented her conscience. "Two days before the fire, there was an emergency patient transfer. Several individuals were moved to another facility for 'specialized long-term care.' Katherine was one of them."

"Where?" Agent Germain demanded.

"I was never told the specific location, but I overheard one of the administrators mention a facility in western Maryland, somewhere remote where 'difficult cases' could be managed indefinitely with minimal oversight."

The search for the second facility consumed several weeks of intensive investigation. Using financial records, property transfers, and corporate shell companies, the FBI team identified three possible locations in western Maryland that had been associated with Archon Pharmaceuticals or its subsidiaries during the relevant time.

The breakthrough came when Agent Jackson discovered a pattern in the financial records; regular payments from an Archon subsidiary to Broomhaven Behavioral Health, a private facility specializing in long-term care for patients with severe mental health conditions. The payments had continued for over two decades, far exceeding what would be normal for any legitimate corporate health services.

The facility maintained strict privacy policies and limited outside oversight; making it ideal for housing individuals who needed to be kept isolated from public scrutiny.

Within 48 hours, Agent Germain had secured federal search warrants.

Claire felt a mixture of hope and terror as their caravan of federal agents and local police approached Broomhaven. After believing her mother was dead for so long, the possibility of finding her alive was almost overwhelming. Richard sat beside her in the back seat of Agent Germain's vehicle, his hands clasped tightly together, knuckles white with tension.

"I never stopped hoping," Richard said quietly as they turned into the facility's driveway. "Even when all logic suggested otherwise, some part of me always believed she might still be alive."

Claire reached over and took his hand. Despite everything they'd learned about the corporate conspiracy and deliberate deception, she could see the genuine terror in her father's eyes; the fear that they might find Katherine alive but too damaged to recognize them, or worse, that this final lead would prove to be another dead end.

"We'll get through this together," she said softly. "Whatever we find."

The facility itself was designed to project clinical expertise and discretion. The main building featured stone architecture and large windows overlooking manicured grounds, with a discreet sign identifying it as "Broomhaven Behavioral Health." Everything about the appearance was calculated to suggest legitimate medical care rather than illegal detention.

The facility administrator, Dr. Howard Jenkins, met them in a paneled office. His initial cooperation dissolved when Agent Germain presented their search warrant, his professional demeanor shifting to barely concealed panic.

"This is highly irregular," Jenkins protested as agents began examining patient records. "Our patients' privacy is protected by federal law. These individuals are here voluntarily or through proper legal guardianship arrangements."

"So is their right not to be held against their will," Agent Jackson replied curtly, directing the search of patient files.

They found their answer when they cross-referenced patient admission dates with the timing of Katherine's transfer from the burned facility. A female patient had been admitted in late March 1999, listed as "Katherine Miller," suffering from "severe paranoid schizophrenia with delusional features."

"Is she still here?" Claire asked, her voice barely steady as she stared at the admission record that might represent her mother.

Richard had gone completely still beside her, his composure cracking as the reality of the moment hit him. After decades of uncertainty, they might be minutes away from seeing Katherine alive.

Jenkins consulted his computer with obvious reluctance. "Yes, but I must caution you that the patient suffers from severe psychosis. She's been under our care for over twenty years, receiving appropriate treatment for her diagnoses."

"We'll need to see her medical records and speak with her attending physician," Agent Germain demanded, her authority cutting through Jenkins' protests.

The patient file Jenkins provided, painted a picture of deliberate psychological suppression. "Katherine Miller" had been admitted following a "psychiatric break" at her previous facility, with symptoms including "paranoid delusions about being a research scientist, claims of having a family, and persistent beliefs about pharmaceutical conspiracy." Her treatment had involved a combination of antipsychotic medications, mood stabilizers, and sedatives that would have been sufficient to keep anyone in a state of cognitive impairment.

Claire studied the photograph in the patient file, her heart breaking at the image of a woman who bore little resemblance to the vibrant researcher in her childhood memories. This woman looked fragile, withdrawn, her eyes holding the vacant quality that suggested a disconnect from reality.

Richard leaned over to see the photograph, and Claire heard his sharp intake of breath. "That's her," he whispered. "That's Katherine."

"Has she ever claimed to be someone other than Katherine Miller?" Claire asked the attending physician, Dr. Jasmine Fredericks.

Dr. Fredericks consulted her notes with obvious discomfort. "There have been periods when she's insisted her name is Dr. Katherine Morrison, that she has a daughter named Claire, that she was brought here as part of a conspiracy to suppress her research. Given her diagnoses, these statements were interpreted as persistent delusional constructs."

"They weren't delusions," Martinez said quietly. "They were the truth."

The walk to Katherine's room was endless. Claire and Richard moved together down the sterile corridor, both struggling with emotions. The woman they were about to meet had been isolated from reality for over twenty-five years; chemically suppressed and psychologically manipulated to the point where her grasp on truth might be permanently damaged.

Katherine Morrison, or the woman who had once been Katherine Morrison, sat in a chair by the window of her room, gazing out at the mountains beyond. Her once-dark hair was now completely gray, her thin frame draped in a simple blue sweater and slacks. When she turned at the sound of approaching footsteps, Claire saw the green eyes she had inherited.

Richard stopped in the doorway, his breath catching at the sight of his wife after all those years. She looked so different, so much older and more fragile, but he could see traces of the brilliant, vibrant woman he'd married in the careful way she studied their faces.

"Mom?" Claire said softly, stepping into the room with her heart pounding.

The woman studied her with careful assessment. "Do I know you?" she asked, her voice carrying the hesitant quality of someone unsure about the reality of her own perceptions.

"I'm Claire," she said, moving slowly toward her so as not to startle or threaten. "Your daughter."

Something flickered in Katherine's eyes then: recognition fighting against decades of chemical suppression and psychological conditioning. "Claire?" she repeated, the name seeming to unlock memories that had been buried beneath years of imposed doubt. "You were... small. A child."

"I was nine when you disappeared," Claire confirmed, kneeling beside her mother's chair and taking her hand gently. "I'm thirty-five now."

Katherine's gaze moved to Richard, still standing in the doorway as if afraid to come closer. For a long moment, they stared at each other across the lost decades of separation and forced forgetfulness.

"Richard," she said finally, her voice barely a whisper. "I kept trying to remember you. They said you weren't real, that I'd never been married, never had a family. But I could never forget your face completely."

Richard stepped into the room, tears streaming down his face as he approached his wife. "I'm here," he said simply. "We're both here. And we're taking you home."

Katherine's gaze moved to the other figures in the room: Martinez, the federal agents, the medical staff who had accompanied them. "Are you real?" she asked with uncertainty. "They told me for so long that my memories weren't real, that I never had a family, that I imagined being a scientist."

"We're real, Mom," Claire said, her voice thick with emotion she could no longer control. "And we've found you."

Over the following days, the reunion proved overwhelming for Katherine, whose mental state alternated between moments of startling lucidity and confusion induced by decades of medication. But in her clearer periods, she displayed flashes of the brilliant mind that had once revolutionized approaches to childhood trauma treatment.

"I never stopped trying to remember," Katherine told Claire during one of their moments together, her voice gaining strength as memories surfaced like fragments of a half-remembered dream. "Even when the drugs made everything blur together, I held onto certain images. Your science project about the butterfly metamorphosis. The way you organized your books by color. How you always asked three questions before bed."

Claire felt tears threatening as these intimate details emerged, proof that somewhere beneath the chemical suppression, her mother had carried their connection through decades of isolation. "I still organize my books by color," she whispered. "It drives Martinez crazy."

"Your favorite stuffed animal was a blue elephant," Katherine continued, her eyes brightening with the joy of confirmed memory. "You named him Professor Trunk because you said he looked wise. You used to tell him about your day before bed, like he was your confidant."

"I did," Claire confirmed, amazed that these small moments had survived attempts to erase Katherine's identity. "I talked to him about missing you. About wondering where you went."

Katherine's expression grew troubled, shadows of suppressed memories passing across her face like clouds blocking sunlight. "I tried to tell them about you, about my research, about what they were doing to me. But every time I insisted on the truth, they increased my medication. Said I was becoming agitated, that I needed 'adjustment' to accept reality."

Dr. Morgan worked tirelessly to develop a treatment plan for gradually reversing the effects of Katherine's long-term medication regimen. Dr. Morgan had been brought in as an independent psychiatric consultant to assess Katherine's condition. While she had worked with Katherine originally, she had no connection to Broomhaven or the conspiracy, making her evaluation crucial for understanding the extent of the psychological damage. Richard insisted on being present for every consultation, every decision about her care. The process was delicate, requiring careful monitoring as each drug dosage was slowly reduced to prevent dangerous withdrawal effects while allowing Katherine's natural neurological function to reassert itself.

"Over two decades of chemical restraint," Dr. Morgan explained to Richard and Claire during one of their consultations. "They used compounds specifically designed to suppress memory formation while maintaining basic cognitive function. It's essentially a form of chemical lobotomy, designed to leave the person functional enough to appear normal while destroying their ability to maintain coherent identity or resist authority." She paused, then continued, "Recovery will be a long process, and complete restoration may not be possible after so many years of interference, but I'm optimistic that we'll see significant improvement in her cognitive function, memory consolidation, and emotional stability. She's already shown remarkable resilience."

As the weeks passed and Katherine's medication was gradually reduced, moments of startling clarity began to emerge more frequently. During one of Richard's daily visits, she suddenly looked at him with complete recognition and said, "You told Claire I was mentally ill."

The accusation hung in the air between them, gentle but devastating. Richard had been dreading this conversation since Katherine's rescue, knowing that eventually she would remember enough to understand the narrative he'd constructed about her disappearance.

"I thought you were dead," Richard said quietly. "The police found no evidence of foul play. Your behavior in those final weeks had been so erratic and paranoid. It seemed more merciful to tell a nine-year-old that her mother was sick rather than..." He paused, struggling with the admission. "Rather than to tell her that her mother had simply abandoned us."

Katherine studied his face with the analytical gaze he remembered from their early years together. "But you suspected the truth, didn't you? You hired a security consultant. You found the surveillance equipment."

"I found evidence," Richard confirmed. "But not proof. Not enough to convince anyone that you'd been taken rather than having left voluntarily. And by the time I was ready to pursue it more aggressively, you'd been gone for months. The trail was cold."

"So you chose the comfortable lie," Katherine said, but her voice carried understanding rather than condemnation. "For Claire's sake."

"I thought I was protecting her," Richard replied. "I never imagined that fear would drive her to drinking. By the time the damage my decision had caused, she was already deep in addiction."

Katherine reached for his hand, her touch still trembling but warm. "We were all victims, Richard. You, me, and Claire. They didn't just take me away; they poisoned our entire family with lies."

Three months after Katherine's rescue, the three of them sat together in Dr. Leland's office for their first family therapy session. Claire had requested the session, wanting professional guidance as they navigated the complex process of rebuilding relationships that had been shattered by decades of separation and deception.

"This is an unprecedented situation," Dr. Leland acknowledged as they settled into the comfortable chairs arranged in a circle. "We're dealing with trauma on multiple levels: the original corporate conspiracy, the forced separation, the long-term chemical abuse, and the psychological impact of false narratives."

Katherine's cognitive function had improved dramatically as her system cleared of the suppressive medications, but she still struggled with memory gaps and occasional confusion. "I remember fragments," she explained to Dr. Leland. "Pieces of our life together, moments with Claire as a child. But decades of artificial interference has left... gaps."

"What's important," Dr. Leland said, "is that you're all here now, committed to rebuilding what was taken from you. The question is how to move forward in a way that honors both the past and the reality of who you've all become."

Claire found herself studying her parents during the sessions, noting the subtle ways they still connected despite the lost years. Richard's protective instincts toward Katherine, the way he adjusted his speaking pace when she seemed confused. Katherine's recognition of his mannerisms, the small smile that crossed her face when he used academic terminology out of habit.

But there were also signs of the time they'd lost. Katherine was sometimes startled by how much Claire had changed, struggling to reconcile the nine-year-old she remembered with the professional, accomplished woman sitting before her.

"I've been thinking about the investigation," Katherine said during one of these sessions, her voice gaining strength as her clarity improved. "About how the evidence surfaced when it did. Someone wanted this truth to come out now, after all this time."

It was Martinez who had been quietly pursuing that same question. Over the months following Katherine's rescue, she'd begun noticing patterns in Richard's behavior that didn't align with his story of a husband desperate to find his missing wife. His knowledge of investigative procedures was unusually detailed, his recall of specific evidence too precise, his familiarity with corporate espionage techniques too comprehensive.

During one of their case review sessions, Martinez shared her concerns with Claire with careful directness.

"Your father's knowledge of certain technical aspects of the original investigation is unusually precise," Martinez observed, her tone carrying professional neutrality that Claire recognized as barely concealed suspicion. "Even for someone personally involved in a traumatic event."

"He's always been detail-oriented," Claire replied, though she sensed something deeper in Martinez's observation. "His academic training emphasizes rigorous and methodical thinking."

"The level of specific information he recalls about evidence processing, crime scene protocols, even aspects that weren't typically shared with family members..." Martinez paused, choosing her words carefully. "It suggests more intimate knowledge of investigative procedures than would be normal for a civilian, even one with his professional background."

"What are you saying, Sara?"

"I'm not saying anything definitive," Martinez replied carefully. "But I've been cross-referencing some travel records, academic conferences, dates and locations. Your father was present in several cities where other researchers disappeared over the years. Researchers whose work challenged pharmaceutical interests, just like your mother's."

Claire felt the blood drain from her face. "Sara, what are you suggesting? You think my father is involved in... what, kidnapping and murder? That's insane."

"I'm not accusing him of anything," Martinez said quickly. "I'm just pointing out patterns that concern me. It could be coincidence."

Claire stared at her partner, feeling like the ground was shifting beneath her feet. "This is my father we're talking about. The man who raised me, who just got his wife back after losing her for decades."

The implications of Martinez's observations haunted Claire during her quiet moments, but she found herself reluctant to pursue them. Her family was finally healing, Katherine was recovering, and the corporate conspirators were facing prosecution. The last thing any of them needed was additional trauma based on what might be circumstantial evidence.

But Martinez's professional instincts wouldn't let the matter rest. Late at night in her apartment, she continued building her encrypted file of inconsistencies, mapping timelines and connections that painted an increasingly disturbing picture of Richard Morrison's potential involvement in events far beyond his wife's disappearance.

Nine months after Katherine's rescue, Claire sat with her mother in the garden behind the rehabilitation facility where Katherine was slowly relearning how to navigate the world. Katherine's progress had been remarkable but uneven, a series of breakthroughs and plateaus that required constant adaptation and patience from everyone involved in her care.

"You never stopped looking," Katherine said during one of her clearer periods, watching a butterfly navigate the flowering bushes with the focused attention of a scientist observing natural phenomena.

"I stopped for a long time," Claire admitted, the guilt of those lost years still painful. "I believed what they wanted us to believe."

Katherine's smile held both sadness and hard-won wisdom, though Claire could see the effort required to maintain complex thoughts and conversations. "But when the moment came, when the anonymous gift arrived, you recognized the truth it contained."

"Yes."

"That's all we can ask of ourselves," Katherine said, reaching for her daughter's hand with fingers that still trembled slightly. "To recognize truth when it presents itself, no matter how painful or beautiful it might be."

The butterfly rose on the afternoon breeze, its delicate wings catching the sunlight as it ascended over the garden wall. Katherine and Claire watched it disappear, two scientists reunited by forces neither could have anticipated; witnesses to transformation that defied every reasonable expectation.

"Claire," Katherine said suddenly, her voice becoming clearer and more focused than it had been in weeks. "I need to tell you something about your father."

"What is it, Mom?" Claire asked, leaning closer and sensing the importance of this rare moment of lucidity.

"The night I disappeared…" Katherine began, but her words were cut short by the appearance of Richard at the garden entrance.

"There you two are," he said warmly, approaching with the easy manner that had characterized their interactions since their reconciliation. "Dr. Morgan just called. She wants to review Katherine's latest test results with us."

The moment was lost. Katherine's expression shifted, the clarity fading from her eyes as she nodded and allowed Richard to help her up from the bench.

That same evening, Detective Sara Martinez sat at her desk across town. The Katherine Morrison case was officially closed. Corporate executives were facing prosecution, a family had been reunited, and justice was finally being served after more than two decades. It should have felt like a complete victory.

Yet something nagged at her, patterns in Richard's behavior and knowledge that suggested depths to this case they hadn't fully explored. She continued to build a file, documenting inconsistencies and coincidences that troubled her professional instincts. But with Katherine finally safe and Claire beginning to heal, Martinez found herself reluctant to pursue suspicions that might shatter their hard-won peace.

The truth would have to wait. Katherine needed time to heal, and Claire deserved a chance to reconnect with her mother. But Martinez would be watching, building her case quietly. When the time was right, she would act.

Some mysteries, Martinez reflected, required patience before they could be properly solved.

Chapter Nine

Fragments

The butterfly on the windowsill caught Katherine Morrison's attention, its wings slowly opening and closing in the spring sunlight. Her eyes tracked its movements, watching as it explored the edges of the window frame.

"Katherine?" Dr. Morgan's voice brought her back to the room. "Are you still with us?"

Claire Morrison watched her mother reorient, the momentary distraction giving way to recognition.

"Yes," Katherine replied, her voice gaining strength. "The butterfly reminded me of Claire's science project. The metamorphosis study." She turned to her daughter, a spark of clarity in her eyes. "You were nine. You kept the chrysalides in that homemade habitat with the cheesecloth top."

"That's right," Claire confirmed. The memory of that childhood project now carried new significance. At the time, it had simply been schoolwork. Now it represented one of the last normal moments before her mother had vanished from her life.

Dr. Theresa Morgan nodded encouragingly, making notes on her tablet. The weekly cognitive recovery sessions had become the backbone of Katherine's rehabilitation since her rescue six months earlier. After twenty-six years of being drugged in a private psychiatric facility, her mind was slowly rebuilding connections, recovering fragments of her past from beneath layers of chemical suppression.

And for six months, Detective Martinez had held her suspicions about Richard Morrison in careful check. Katherine's recovery had been the priority, and Claire needed time to rebuild her relationship with her mother without the devastating possibility that her father might be the real villain. But Katherine's increasing clarity and consistency in her memories, combined with new evidence that had surfaced through the ongoing Archon investigation, had finally pushed Martinez to the point where she could no longer remain silent.

"Today I'd like to try something different," Dr. Morgan explained. "We've been working primarily with positive memories, building a foundation of trust and familiarity. But to fully recover, Katherine, we need to address the more difficult memories as well."

Claire tensed slightly. They had avoided discussions of Katherine's abduction, focusing instead on rebuilding her sense of self through earlier, happier memories. "Are you sure she's ready?"

"I believe so," Dr. Morgan replied. "Katherine's cognitive functioning has improved significantly over the past month. The nightmares and flashbacks suggest her mind is already processing these memories, but in an unstructured way. Addressing them directly might help integrate them more effectively."

Katherine's hands smoothed the fabric of her slacks, a gesture Claire had come to recognize as self-regulation. "I want to try," she said firmly. "The fragments come anyway, especially at night. I'd rather face them while I'm awake."

Claire nodded, reaching for her mother's hand. Since they'd found Katherine at Broomhaven, their connection had deepened beyond what Claire could have imagined possible after years of separation. Each recovered memory, each moment of recognition, felt like another piece of her mother returning from the void that had claimed her.

"Very good," Dr. Morgan said. "I want to focus specifically on your last day at the university, Katherine. October 19, 1998. What can you recall about that day?"

Katherine closed her eyes, her breathing pattern changing as she accessed the fragmented memories. "My office... I was organizing research files. The backup drive was in my desk drawer." Her brow furrowed with concentration. "Someone knocked on my door. A man in a dark suit."

"Do you remember who it was?" Dr. Morgan prompted gently.

"Edward Browne," Katherine said, her voice hardening at the name. "He claimed to be interested in research partnerships, but I knew he was from Archon. He'd been monitoring my work for months."

Claire watched her mother carefully, noticing the subtle changes in her expression as she accessed memories that had been buried for decades. The investigation into Archon Pharmaceuticals had confirmed much of what Katherine had claimed about corporate surveillance of her research. Edward Browne had been identified as the company's "research protection specialist," a euphemism for the man who neutralized threats to their product lines.

"What happened during that meeting?" Dr. Morgan asked.

"He threatened me," Katherine continued, her eyes still closed. "Not directly, but the implication was clear. Said my research was 'fundamentally flawed' and publication would 'damage my reputation irreparably.' When I challenged him, he became more explicit. Said some researchers who pursued 'problematic directions' found themselves unable to continue their careers."

Claire had heard this part before, both from her mother's earlier recollections and from Browne's testimony. The former Archon executive had admitted to threatening Katherine that day, though he continued to deny direct involvement in her abduction.

"After he left," Katherine continued, "I was frightened but determined. I had secured samples proving someone had tampered with my research materials. Evidence of the low-level toxins they'd been exposing me to." Her breathing quickened slightly. "I called…"

She stopped abruptly, her eyes opening wide. Her gaze darted around the room as if reorienting herself.

"Katherine?" Dr. Morgan leaned forward. "What is it? Who did you call?"

"I called Richard," Katherine said, her voice suddenly uncertain. "I told him what happened with Browne, that I had evidence of tampering and poisoning. I said I was going to the authorities first thing the next morning."

Claire felt a cold sensation spreading through her chest. This detail hadn't appeared in any of Katherine's previous recollections. "What did Dad say?"

"He was concerned," Katherine replied slowly. "Said he'd meet me at home to discuss it. But then…" Her expression changed, confusion giving way to something darker. "That can't be right."

"What can't be right, Katherine?" Dr. Morgan prompted.

"When I went to my car in the parking garage, Richard was there." Katherine's voice had become almost mechanical, as if reciting something without fully understanding it. "But he couldn't have been. He said he'd meet me at home."

Claire and Dr. Morgan exchanged glances. Richard Morrison had maintained for twenty-six years that he'd been at home that evening, waiting for Katherine to return from work. He'd reported her missing the next morning when she never arrived.

"Is it possible you're confusing two different memories?" Dr. Morgan suggested gently. "Perhaps seeing Richard in the parking garage on a different day?"

Katherine's hands trembled slightly. "No. It was that night. I remember the file box in my arms, the weight of it. The evidence samples were hidden inside a false bottom I'd created." She pressed her fingers to her temples. "I saw Richard standing near my car. And there was someone with him."

"Who was with him, mom?" Claire asked.

"Edward Browne," Katherine whispered. "They were talking. When they saw me, they stopped. Richard looked... surprised. I guess he hadn't expected me to come to the garage so soon."

Claire felt her stomach tighten. The professional part of her mind recognized this as a significant inconsistency in her father's account. But everything else recoiled from the implications. "Mom, are you certain about this? Dad always said he was at home that night."

Katherine's gaze met Claire's, a sudden clarity sharpening her features. "He was there, Claire. Your father was there."

Before Claire could respond, Katherine winced, pressing her hands harder against her temples. "I can't... it's slipping away again. There's something about Richard's face when he saw me. Something important."

Dr. Morgan intervened as Katherine's distress increased. "That's enough for today. You've done excellent work, Katherine." She made a quick note on her tablet. "These memories are difficult, and it's normal for them to come in fragments, especially after such prolonged suppression."

Claire walked with her mother back to the car, troubled by this new discrepancy. Her dad had never mentioned being at the university that night. In fact, his alibi, that he'd been home waiting for Katherine, had been a cornerstone of the original investigation.

"Are you all right?" Claire asked as they drove home, watching her mother gaze out the window at the Baltimore cityscape.

"I remember more than I can say sometimes," Katherine replied softly. "The memories come and go, like tuning an old radio. Sometimes clear, sometimes just static." She turned to Claire. "But that memory of the parking garage is clear, Claire. Like it happened yesterday."

Claire nodded, unsure how to respond. Her father had been her constant support through all of this, helping Katherine readjust, coordinating with medical professionals, assisting with the ongoing investigation into Archon Pharmaceuticals. The idea that he might have lied about something so fundamental was difficult to accept.

"We'll figure it out," Claire assured her mother, reaching across to squeeze her hand. "The important thing is that you're recovering more memories. Each piece helps complete the picture."

Katherine nodded, but her expression remained troubled. "Some pieces don't seem to fit the picture I've been given."

When they arrived at her parents' house, Richard was waiting in the driveway. He'd taken a sabbatical from his university position to help with Katherine's recovery, converting his home office into a comfortable bedroom on the ground floor where Katherine could avoid stairs on her difficult days. Claire visited daily to help with her mother's care.

"How did the session go?" he asked, helping Katherine from the car.

"Progress," Claire answered before Katherine could speak. "Mom remembered more about the day she disappeared." She watched her father's face carefully for any reaction but saw only his usual composed interest.

"That's excellent," Richard said, guiding Katherine toward the house with a supportive hand under her elbow. "What specifically came back to you, Katherine?"

Claire noticed her mother's subtle withdrawal, the slight stiffening of her posture as Richard touched her. These physical cues of discomfort around her husband had been consistent since her return, though they had attributed them to the general trauma of her ordeal rather than anything specific to Richard.

"The butterfly," Katherine said vaguely, deflecting the question. "Claire's science project. The metamorphosis."

Richard smiled, accepting this apparent non-sequitur with the patience he'd shown throughout Katherine's recovery. "Wonderful. Those positive memories create anchors for your sense of self."

Later that evening, after Katherine had retired to her room, Claire found her father in his study, preparing testimony for the upcoming Archon trials. As the leading forensic psychologist in the field, Richard had been invaluable in building the case against the corporation, and now prosecutors were relying on his expert testimony about the psychological manipulation techniques employed against Katherine and the other targeted researchers.

"Dad," Claire began, choosing her words carefully. "Mom mentioned something unusual today. She said she remembered seeing you at the university parking garage the night she disappeared."

Richard looked up from his files. His expression remained composed but attentive. "That's interesting. Did she provide any context for this memory?"

"She said she called you after Browne left her office, that you said you'd meet her at home. But then she saw you in the parking garage with Browne."

Richard removed his reading glasses, placing them on the desk. "That's not accurate. I was home all evening. I was grading papers until about ten o'clock, then went to bed assuming she was working late, as she often did during intensive research periods."

Claire watched his face carefully. Something felt off about his response, though she couldn't pinpoint exactly what. "Could you have forgotten going to campus that night? It was twenty-six years ago."

"No, Claire. That night is permanently etched in my memory because it was the last time I saw your mother." His voice remained even, reasonable. "Your mother's memory is still fragmented, still rebuilding. False memories and confused timelines are common. Dr. Morgan warned us to expect inconsistencies."

Claire nodded slowly. His explanation was logical, aligned with everything they'd been told about Katherine's recovery process. Yet something in her mother's certainty had unsettled her.

"Of course," she said finally. "I just wanted to mention it."

Richard smiled, the familiar expression that had comforted her throughout childhood. "It's good that you did. Documenting these inconsistencies helps us understand her cognitive progress." He returned to his files, the conversation clearly concluded in his mind.

Claire returned to the kitchen, pouring herself a glass of water. Her gaze drifted to the window above the sink, the nighttime reflection showing her troubled expression. After years of training and experience in forensic psychology, she had developed an instinct for discrepancies, for the subtle indicators that something wasn't quite right. And something about her father's response had triggered that instinct. Not in what he'd said, but in how he'd said it. The complete absence of surprise or confusion at Katherine's clearly incorrect memory. Most people, when confronted with a false account that placed them at a scene they hadn't attended, would react with some degree of bewilderment or concern. Richard had simply categorized it as an expected symptom of Katherine's condition.

Claire's phone buzzed with a text from Detective Martinez: "Any chance you can meet tomorrow? Found something you should see."

Claire texted back 'yes', her unease growing. Martinez had mentioned continuing to review cold case files related to Katherine's disappearance, looking for any missed connections or overlooked evidence. Claire had assumed it was routine follow-up work, but Martinez's request to meet suggested something more significant.

That night, she dreamed of butterflies trapped in glass jars, their wings beating frantically against their transparent prisons as they slowly suffocated. She woke in a cold sweat, the image of her mother's face superimposed over the dying insects.

Darwin lifted his head from where he'd been sleeping at the foot of the bed, his orange fur catching the streetlight filtering through her window. He moved closer, settling against her side with a low, rumbling purr that gradually steadied her breathing.

The coffee at the precinct had always been terrible, but Claire welcomed its bitter familiarity as she sat across from Martinez in the detective's small office. The space reflected its occupant's nature: organized files, minimal personal items, everything serving a clear purpose.

"Thanks for coming," Martinez said. "I know you're balancing a lot right now."

"You said you found something?" Claire prompted, preferring to get directly to the point.

Martinez nodded, opening a folder on her desk. "I've been reviewing the original investigation into your mother's disappearance. There are some discrepancies I can't explain."

She laid out several photos. "These are from the initial search of your mother's office. Standard procedure, looking for any indication of where she might have gone."

Claire examined the photographs, seeing the familiar space where her mother had worked: bookshelves, filing cabinets, the large desk with its orderly arrangement of materials.

"Your father noted during the original investigation that nothing seemed out of place in the office, that everything was exactly as Katherine would have left it at the end of a normal workday." Martinez pulled out another photograph. "Except for these footprints found just inside the door."

The image showed distinctive boot prints on the carpet, partially overlapping.

"Standard-issue work boots, size 10 or 11," Claire noted. "The original investigators concluded they belonged to maintenance staff."

"That was the official determination, yes." Martinez's tone suggested skepticism. "But I found something interesting when I looked at the university security logs from that week. No maintenance personnel had been scheduled for that floor on the day Katherine disappeared. The only unscheduled maintenance call was three days earlier, for a leaking pipe in the bathroom down the hall."

Claire frowned, studying the footprint more carefully. "That's unusual, but not necessarily significant. Someone could have entered without being logged."

"True," Martinez agreed. "Which is why I had the forensics team enhance the original image. Look at the wear pattern on the right heel."

She placed an enlarged photograph on the desk. The enhanced image showed a distinctive diagonal groove across the heel of the boot print.

"That's a very specific wear pattern," Claire observed. She felt a growing unease about where this was leading.

"I had our forensic team analyze the wear pattern and identify the boot type. Then I found this family photograph showing your father wearing what appears to be the same style of work boots shortly before Katherine's disappearance." She placed the photograph on the desk. "While we can't compare actual wear patterns from a photo, it does establish that he owned this type of footwear at the relevant time."

Claire stared at the images, her training warring with personal loyalty. That could be coincidental, she told herself. Even specific wear patterns weren't unique to one person. "My father doesn't wear work boots."

"No," Martinez acknowledged. "But he apparently did twenty-six years ago." She hesitated, then added, "There's something else, Claire. I found records of a consulting relationship between your father and Archon Pharmaceuticals."

Claire's head snapped up. "What?"

"Two short-term contracts in the years before Katherine's disappearance. Nothing unusual for an academic consultant. But he never mentioned this connection during our investigation of Archon's role in Katherine's abduction."

The implications sent a chill through Claire. Either her father had forgotten about professional work with the company implicated in his wife's disappearance or he had deliberately concealed the connection.

"That doesn't necessarily mean he was involved," Claire said, her voice sounding defensive even to her own ears. But even as she spoke, she recognized how weak her argument sounded.

"No, it doesn't," Martinez agreed carefully. "But combined with other inconsistencies I've found, it raises questions worth investigating." She pulled out another document. "I confirmed the pattern we discussed earlier: your father's presence at conferences in the same cities where three other researchers disappeared over the past two decades. Researchers whose work, like Katherine's, threatened pharmaceutical interests."

Claire felt nauseated. The logical part of her mind recognized this as a disturbing pattern, but emotionally she recoiled from the implications. "Correlation doesn't prove causation. My father attends dozens of academic conferences every year."

"Of course," Martinez said gently. "And I wouldn't mention any of this if it were based on a single coincidence. But the pattern of discrepancies troubles me, especially after you told me about your mother's new memory of seeing him with Browne in the parking garage."

Claire took a deep breath, forcing herself to think like the professional she was rather than the daughter she would always be. "What specifically are you suggesting?"

"I'm not suggesting anything definitive yet," Martinez clarified. "I'm gathering information, following the evidence where it leads. But I believe we need to seriously consider the possibility that your father knows more about your mother's disappearance than he's admitted."

The words hung in the air between them. Claire felt as if the ground had shifted beneath her feet. Everything she thought she knew about her family, about her father, about her own life was suddenly open to question.

"I need to think about this," Claire said finally. "And I need to talk to my mother."

Martinez nodded. "Of course. But Claire, if even some of this is accurate, Katherine could still be in danger. Someone who orchestrated her disappearance once might not hesitate to do so again if she starts remembering too much."

That evening, Claire went to her parents' home, unable to shake what Martinez had shown her. She found her mom in her room, writing in the journal Dr. Morgan had suggested she keep. Since her rescue, Katherine had filled several notebooks with recovered memories, observations, and reflections.

"May I come in?" Claire asked, pausing at the doorway.

Katherine looked up with a smile, gesturing to the chair beside her bed. "Of course."

Claire sat, watching her mother finish writing a paragraph before closing the journal. "That was an intense session today."

"Yes," Katherine agreed. "But clarifying in some ways. The fragments are beginning to connect."

"Mom," Claire began carefully, "how certain are you about seeing Dad at the parking garage that night?"

Katherine's eyes met hers directly. "As certain as I am that you're sitting here now. It's one of my clearest memories of that day. The shock of seeing him there when he said he'd be at home." She hesitated, then added, "There's something I haven't told Dr. Morgan yet. Something I remembered last night."

"What is it?"

"After they injected me with something and I was losing consciousness, I heard your father say something to Browne. 'Not here. This wasn't the plan.' And Browne replied, 'Plans change. She was going to the authorities.'" Katherine's hands trembled slightly. "I've been afraid to trust this memory. Afraid of what it means if it's true."

"You were injected?" Claire asked, focusing on this crucial detail. "They drugged you?"

"Yes," Katherine confirmed. "I remember the sharp pain in my neck, then everything became foggy."

Claire felt a weight settling on her chest. Combined with what Martinez had shown her, this new detail painted an increasingly disturbing picture. "Why didn't you mention this today?"

"Because I needed to tell you first." Katherine reached for Claire's hand. "You deserve to hear it from me, not in a therapy session. And..." she hesitated, "I wasn't sure if it was safe to say in front of others. I don't know who might be reporting back to Richard."

"You think Dad is monitoring your therapy sessions?"

"I know how it sounds," Katherine said quietly. "But yes, I do. Dr. Morgan has been wonderful, but she consults with him regularly about my progress. And my medication still comes through him."

Claire frowned. "Your medication is prescribed by Dr. Patel, not Dad."

"Yes, but your dad organizes the doses, ensures I take them on schedule." Katherine leaned closer. "Claire, have you noticed how my clarity varies dramatically from day to day? Some mornings I wake sharp and focused, other days I can barely string thoughts together? That's not a natural pattern of recovery."

Claire had noticed this inconsistency but attributed it to the normal fluctuations expected during recovery from long-term drugging.

"Observe him during my evening medication routine," Katherine continued. "The way he makes sure I swallow each pill. I've been pretending to take them but hiding some under my tongue when I can. The days I'm clearest are when I've managed to avoid the full doses."

Claire's mind raced. She found herself automatically reaching for the explanation her father would offer; that Katherine was experiencing paranoid ideation as part of her recovery process. Yet her mother's account was detailed, specific, and consistent with the discrepancies Martinez had uncovered.

"I'll look into it," Claire promised, squeezing her mother's hand. "But please be careful. If what you're suggesting is true…"

"I know," Katherine said softly. "I've survived twenty-six years of this, Claire. I can be patient a little longer."

That evening, Claire observed her father preparing her medications with new attention. His movements were indeed precise, placing each pill in a small paper cup, watching carefully as Katherine took each one.

"All set?" he asked after Katherine had swallowed the last pill.

"Yes, thank you," Katherine replied.

After helping Katherine to bed, Richard returned to his study while Claire gathered her things. "I'm going to grab dinner with a colleague before heading back to my apartment," she told him.

Instead of going to meet anyone, Claire drove straight to her apartment. Katherine's warnings about Richard's surveillance echoed in her mind. Instead of going inside, however, she parked down the street and waited, testing a suspicion she hoped would prove unfounded. Twenty minutes later, she saw her father's car pull up to the building. Richard entered using a key she didn't know he possessed, remained inside for approximately fifteen minutes, then departed.

Claire waited until his car had disappeared around the corner before approaching her apartment. Inside, nothing seemed obviously disturbed, but her instincts told her someone had been there. Even Darwin seemed unsettled, staying close to her feet as she moved through the rooms. She conducted a systematic search, eventually discovering a small listening device attached under her kitchen table, professional-grade, not something an amateur would have access to.

Her phone buzzed with a text from Martinez: "Need to meet urgently. New information about the facility where Katherine was initially held."

Claire responded with a location, Rusty's Diner three blocks from her apartment, then checked her phone for surveillance software. Finding nothing obvious, she nevertheless left the device on her kitchen counter as she left, unwilling to risk being tracked.

Martinez was waiting at a corner booth, her expression grave. "We've identified the initial facility where Katherine was held before being transferred to Broomhaven. It was a private research institution called the Lamstead Center, ostensibly conducting studies on neurological disorders."

"Let me guess," Claire said, though her stomach was already dropping. "Funded by Archon Pharmaceuticals."

"Through several shell companies, yes. But here's what's interesting, one of the center's advisory board members was your father."

Claire felt the weight of the evidence crushing down on her. "The depth of his involvement just keeps getting worse."

"I've found records of six visits he made to the Lamstead Center during the period Katherine would have been there," Martinez said. "All logged under his academic credentials, officially consulting on research protocols."

"Six visits," Claire repeated, the implications sinking in.

Claire struggled to process the information against the backdrop of a lifetime of trust in her father. "I found a listening device in my apartment tonight. Professional grade. After watching my father enter using a key I never gave him."

Martinez's expression hardened. "We need to move your mother to a secure location immediately. If Richard realizes how much she's remembering, or that we're investigating him..."

"He wouldn't hurt her," Claire protested automatically, though she no longer believed it herself.

"Claire," Martinez said, "if what we're uncovering is accurate, he's been keeping her drugged and institutionalized for twenty-six years. That's not someone I'd trust with her safety now that she's remembering the truth."

The reality of the situation crashed over Claire with nauseating force. If even half of what they suspected was true, her father, the man who had shaped her understanding of psychology, of evidence, of truth itself, might be responsible for the decades-long imprisonment of her mother under the guise of mental illness.

"I need to see what's in her journal," Claire said suddenly. "She's been documenting her recovered memories for months. If there's a pattern in what she remembers on her clearer days versus her foggy ones..."

"We'll need to get it without alerting Richard," Martinez warned. "And we need a plan to ensure Katherine's safety."

That night, Claire went to her parents' home, finding Richard asleep upstairs. She crept to her mother's room on the ground floor, relieved to find Katherine awake and alert.

"Claire?" Katherine whispered, sitting up in bed. "What is it?"

"I need your journal," Claire explained quietly. "And we need to get you somewhere safe. Detective Martinez and I have uncovered information about Dad's potential involvement in what happened to you."

Katherine didn't seem surprised. "The journals are hidden. I've kept different ones. The ones Richard knows about contain only benign memories, nothing that would concern him. The real ones are inside a pillowcase I put at the bottom of the linen closet. It looks like spare bedding."

Claire's surprise must have shown on her face, because Katherine smiled slightly. "I've had to be careful about what Richard might find."

Retrieving the hidden journals proved simple enough. Claire found the linen closet and felt around the bottom shelf until her fingers found the pillowcase. Inside were several notebooks, carefully wrapped in plastic bags. She quickly secured them in her bag.

"I need to get these to Martinez and then I'll come back," Claire whispered. "We need to move you tomorrow. Can you be ready?"

"I'll be ready", Katherine replied, her voice steady despite the fear visible in her eyes.

Katherine had a medical appointment scheduled for the following morning, a routine follow-up with her neurologist that Richard had no reason to question. Claire used this opportunity. The plan was simple: Martinez would meet them at the hospital and escort both Katherine and Claire to a safe house, leaving Richard behind. Claire stayed overnight.

That night, Claire barely slept, the weight of what they were planning, of what she now suspected about her father, keeping her mind racing into the early hours. When she finally drifted off, she dreamed of her mother locked in a glass box, mouth open in a silent scream while Richard stood calmly observing, taking notes on a clipboard.

Morning brought a tense breakfast, with Richard reviewing his calendar; while Katherine sat quietly, her gaze distant in the way Claire now recognized as deliberate performance rather than actual fogginess.

"I can take Mom to her appointment," Claire offered casually. "You mentioned having that faculty meeting this morning."

"That's all right," Richard replied. "I've rescheduled. Your mother's health is the priority right now."

Claire felt her pulse quicken but maintained her composed expression. "You don't need to do that. It's just a routine follow-up, and I'm free all morning."

"I prefer to be involved in all medical consultations," Richard insisted, his tone pleasant but firm. "Given the complexity of your mother's condition, it's important to have consistent communication with her healthcare providers."

The control inherent in this statement struck Claire differently now than it would have a week earlier. What she had previously interpreted as devoted care now revealed itself as something more sinister, a determination to monitor and manage every aspect of Katherine's recovery.

"Of course," Claire conceded, texting Martinez under the table: "Change of plans. Father insisting on coming to appointment. Need alternative strategy."

Claire stared at her phone, waiting for a response that didn't come. Her pulse quickened as seconds stretched into a full minute. Richard continued reviewing his calendar, seemingly oblivious to her tension, while Katherine maintained her vacant expression.

Finally, the reply came: "Understood. Will be in waiting room with backup. Proceed as planned."

Claire released a breath she hadn't realized she was holding. The plan could still work, even with Richard's unexpected insistence on accompanying them.

The drive to the hospital passed in tense silence, Katherine in the back seat while Richard drove and Claire beside him, hyperaware of every subtle movement, every glance he cast in the rearview mirror at his wife.

In the hospital parking garage, Claire's phone buzzed with a call from the precinct. She answered, listening briefly before turning to Richard. "There's a situation with one of my cases. I need to make a quick call. You two go ahead, and I'll catch up."

Richard hesitated, clearly reluctant to proceed without her. "We can wait."

"No need," Claire insisted. "I'll be there in five minutes."

After a moment, Richard nodded, helping Katherine from the car. "We'll see you inside."

As soon as they were out of sight, Claire raced to the predetermined meeting point where Martinez waited with two plainclothes officers.

"They're heading to the neurology department," Claire reported breathlessly. "Third floor, east wing."

"We've coordinated with hospital security," Martinez assured her. "They'll create a diversion that will separate Richard from your mother. When that happens, we move."

The plan worked with surprising simplicity. A security alert in the hospital wing where Katherine's appointment was scheduled prompted staff to temporarily evacuate patients into the hallway. In the controlled chaos, Martinez and her officers intercepted Katherine and Claire, escorting them to a service elevator while Richard was directed to a different waiting area by hospital staff who had been briefed on the situation.

From the service elevator, Claire caught a final glimpse of her father becoming increasingly agitated, demanding information about where Katherine had been taken. His controlled facade cracked momentarily, revealing a flash of something cold and calculating that sent a chill through Claire's body. This was not the concerned husband searching for his vulnerable wife; this was someone who had lost control of an asset he had carefully managed for decades.

Martinez's phone buzzed with updates as they left the hospital. "My team has Richard under surveillance," she reported as they drove toward the safe house. "He's making phone calls, appears increasingly agitated. They'll keep an eye on him."

At the safe house later that afternoon, Claire found her mother looking more like herself; not dramatically different, but with a subtle clarity that came from being in a truly safe space for the first time in months.

"The combination of drugs Richard was giving me kept me disoriented most of the time," Katherine explained, sitting at a small kitchen table with Martinez and Claire. "Just functional enough to create the appearance of recovery, but the days I managed to avoid my full doses were when I could think clearly and access my memories."

"Mom," Claire began gently, "we need to understand exactly what you remember about Dad's involvement. I know this is difficult, but it's important."

Katherine nodded, her hands steady as she opened one of her journals. "I've been recording everything I could remember on my clearer days. At first, the memories were fragmented, difficult to trust. But as I reduced my medication, the patterns became consistent." She turned to a specific page. "October 18, 1998. Richard asked unusually detailed questions about my research backup locations. He claimed it was for security purposes, but now I remember his face when I mentioned the samples I'd hidden."

She flipped through more pages, showing Claire entries that documented a pattern of suspicious behaviors leading up to her disappearance. "Richard had been consulting for Archon for some years before I was abducted. I discovered the connection accidentally when I saw his name on a payment document left in our home printer. When I confronted him, he claimed it was a one-time consultation on general psychological effects of medication, nothing specific to my research."

Martinez leaned forward. "Did you know about his relationship with Edward Browne?"

"Not until that night in the parking garage," Katherine replied. "Seeing them together was shocking, not just because Richard had told me he'd be at home, but because they clearly knew each other well. The way they stood, the familiarity in their body language… it wasn't a first meeting."

Claire listened with growing unease as her mother detailed more recovered memories. Richard adjusting her medication at the facility where she was initially held, his face appearing periodically during her early captivity, always observed through drugged consciousness but unmistakable.

"The most damning memory was…," Katherine continued, turning to a more recent entry. "I was at the Lamstead Center for about six months. Richard visited regularly, always when I was heavily sedated, but one day the dose wasn't as effective. I heard him discussing my case with the doctor. 'Maintain the current protocol,' he said. 'If she shows any signs of breaking through, increase the haloperidol. We can't risk her remembering the correct sequence of events.'"

Claire felt physically ill. "This implies premeditation, not just opportunistic involvement after you were already taken."

"Yes," Katherine agreed, her voice steady despite the pain evident in her eyes. "In my clearest moments, I've come to believe that Richard orchestrated my disappearance from the beginning. Not as Archon's agent, but as their partner. They provided the resources, the facility, the medical cover, but Richard provided the expertise on how to break me psychologically, how to ensure I would never be believed if I tried to tell the truth."

Martinez had been taking notes throughout. "We've confirmed Richard's involvement with the Lamstead Center through their personnel records. He was listed as a 'special consultant on cognitive restructuring.' We've also identified financial transfers from Archon-linked accounts to offshore holdings we believe belong to him."

"But why?" Claire asked, the question that had been haunting her since these suspicions first emerged. "Why would he do this to you, to his own wife?"

Katherine's expression softened with sorrow. "That's the question that's tormented me for twenty-six years. I believe it started as professional opportunism. Archon offered him significant compensation and career advancement in exchange for helping neutralize the threat my research posed. But it evolved into something more complex."

She hesitated before continuing. "Richard has always been fascinated by the malleability of human psychology, how the mind can be shaped, memories altered or suppressed. In his academic work, he could only theorize and observe. With me, with the resources Archon provided, he could experiment directly."

"You think he saw you as a research subject?" Claire asked, horrified.

"I think he saw me as the perfect opportunity to test his theories on memory manipulation and cognitive control in real time, with a subject he knew intimately." Katherine's voice remained steady, though her hands trembled.

Martinez picked up a folder from beside her chair. "This aligns with what we've found in university archives. Your father's publication record shows a marked shift in focus after Katherine's disappearance. His earlier work centered on criminal psychology and witness reliability. But from 1999 onward, he published increasingly on memory manipulation, cognitive restructuring, and the psychology of belief formation."

"He built his academic reputation on what he learned from breaking my mind," Katherine said quietly. "And he's been maintaining that experiment for twenty-six years, adjusting variables, documenting responses."

Claire struggled to reconcile this monstrous portrait with the father she had known and respected throughout her life. "If this is true, and I believe you, Mom, then my entire understanding of him has been a carefully constructed facade."

"Not entirely," Katherine said gently. "The brilliant psychologist, the meticulous observer, the dedicated professional; those aspects are real. But they exist alongside something darker, something willing to sacrifice others for his own advancement and intellectual curiosity." She reached for Claire's hand. "I know how devastating this must be for you."

Claire squeezed her mother's hand, forcing herself to focus on the immediate concerns rather than the overwhelming personal implications. "We need to compile all this evidence formally. Martinez, what's our next step legally?"

"We're building a case," the Sara explained. "Financial records, witness statements from former Lamstead staff we've located, Katherine's testimony, and the journals Richard kept if we can locate them. The surveillance team is watching Richard's actions as we speak."

Martinez's phone rang, and she answered it with a quick "Go ahead." She listened intently, making notes. "Understood. Stay on him but maintain distance."

She hung up and turned to Claire and Katherine. "Richard went to his university office first. The team watched him removing files from a locked cabinet and shredding them; he appeared to be clearing out anything sensitive. Then he went to a storage facility on the outskirts of town, entered a unit for about twenty minutes, and left carrying a bag. His final stop was a bank where he accessed a safety deposit box briefly before leaving."

"He knows we're onto him," Claire said, the reality of the situation settling more firmly with each new discovery.

Katherine became alarmed. "You need to be careful. Richard is methodical, calculating. He's had twenty-six years to prepare for the possibility that someone might investigate too closely."

"What do you mean?" Claire asked. "Anything specific?"

"I don't know the specifics, but I overheard things over the years. Comments about 'insurance policies' against Archon if they ever tried to abandon him, references to evidence hidden where 'no one would think to look.' And he's not alone in this. There are others who've helped him, people in positions of authority who've facilitated his work."

Martinez's expression hardened. "We'll take every precaution. Judge Watkins has already signed search warrants for his office, storage unit, and safety deposit box. Teams are preparing to execute them within the hour."

As the detective left to coordinate the warrant executions, Claire sat with her mother in silence for several minutes, both women processing the enormity of what they were confronting.

"I never wanted you to know this side of him," Katherine finally said. "Even in my clearest moments at Broomhaven, when I recognized how deeply he was involved in what happened to me, I hoped to spare you this truth."

"I've spent my career analyzing the psychology of deception," Claire replied, her voice hollow. "I've profiled killers, abusers, manipulators of every variety. And I never saw what was right in front of me."

"Because he's exceptional at what he does," Katherine said gently. "And because he's your father. The people closest to us exist in our blind spots. We see what we need to see to maintain our understanding of the world." She squeezed Claire's hand. "And he was careful never to give you reason to doubt him. Your relationship with him was separate from what he did to me."

"Was it?" Claire wondered aloud. "Or was I just another experiment to him? Another subject to manipulate and observe?"

The question hung in the air, unanswerable but devastating in its implications.

Claire's phone rang with an update from Martinez. "Richard's gone. The surveillance team lost him at BWI Airport; he switched vehicles in the parking garage. We've issued alerts, but he had a head start."

Claire felt the words settle like lead in her stomach. "And the warrants?"

"We've executed the warrants, but Richard was one step ahead of us. His office had been cleared of anything potentially incriminating, same with the storage unit. The safety deposit box contained only family photographs and your mother's wedding ring."

"As I said, he knew we were onto him," Claire said, unsurprised. "He's had decades to prepare for this possibility."

"There's more," Martinez continued, her voice tense. "When we went to your parent's home with the warrant, we found something. In his study, Richard had laid out files; documents about Katherine's case, photos of the Lamstead Center, financial records linking him to Archon. Almost as if..."

"As if he wanted them to be found," Claire finished, a cold sensation spreading throughout her body. "It's too convenient. What else?"

"He left a letter addressed to you," Martinez said. "We've had it checked for contaminants; it's clean. I can bring it to you."

An hour later, Claire sat at the table in the safe house, her father's letter before her. The handwriting was as precise as everything else about him:

Claire,

By the time you read this, I'll be gone. Your surveillance today was skillful but not undetected. I've always recognized your exceptional observational abilities, a trait you inherited from me.

You're discovering fragments of a complex situation, pieces of a puzzle you cannot possibly understand from your limited perspective. Katherine's memories, while genuine to her, have been shaped by decades of chemical intervention and institutional living. What she believes is a patchwork of actual events, therapeutic suggestions, and confabulations.

I won't insult your intelligence by denying my involvement with Archon or the Lamstead Center. Those connections existed, though not in the form Katherine remembers or Martinez may have suggested to you. What began as legitimate psychiatric consultation evolved into something more complicated when your mother's mental state deteriorated rapidly in the late 1990s.

The paranoia you witnessed as a child was real, Claire. Katherine's brilliant mind began to fragment under pressure. When she became convinced that corporate interests were poisoning her, I sought help from colleagues with resources beyond traditional psychiatric care.

The Lamstead Center offered innovative treatment for researchers experiencing psychological breakdowns. My involvement there was as Katherine's husband, attempting to secure the best possible care for her condition.

What followed was a tragic series of miscalculations and institutional failures. By the time I realized the center's methods were exacerbating rather than alleviating Katherine's condition, she had been transferred to Broomhaven through administrative channels I couldn't reverse.

The evidence you're seeking about my culpability exists, but alongside it is documentation that provides critical context. Before you condemn me completely, I ask that you examine all the evidence.

I've secured this complete documentation where it cannot be destroyed or altered. If you wish to find it, return to where your mother's journey began, her original office at the university. The truth has always been hiding in plain sight.

Whatever you discover, remember that I have always been proud of you, Claire. Your mind, your resilience, your commitment to truth; these are qualities I've respected even when we disagreed. I expect no forgiveness, only understanding that reality is rarely as simple as victim and villain.

Your father, Richard

Claire read the letter twice, analyzing its psychological construction with professional detachment despite its personal nature. Even in fleeing, Richard was still making excuses, still trying to control her perception of events. The careful balance of admission and denial, the strategic undermining of Katherine's reliability, the emotional appeal to their relationship, and the tantalizing promise of 'complete' evidence were all classic manipulation techniques designed to create doubt and delay judgment. He couldn't simply disappear; he had to leave behind one final attempt to justify the unjustifiable.

Yet the reference to Katherine's office was specific, testable. If evidence existed there after all this time, it might clarify rather than obscure the truth.

"What does it say?" Katherine asked, having given Claire privacy to read the letter first.

Claire handed it to her mother. "He's gone. And he's left what he claims is exculpatory evidence at your old university office."

Katherine read quickly, her expression hardening. "This is consistent with his approach throughout my captivity; acknowledge enough reality to seem truthful while subtly distorting critical details."

Martinez, who had brought the letter, frowned. "We checked university records. Katherine's old office has been renovated multiple times in the past twenty-six years. It's currently part of the computer science department."

"That doesn't mean evidence couldn't still be hidden there," Claire pointed out. "If Richard concealed something within the structure itself rather than in the furnishings, it might have survived the renovations."

"It's almost certainly a trap," Martinez warned. "Or a distraction to buy him time to escape."

"Probably both," Claire agreed. "But I need to know what's there."

After extensive discussion and planning, they arranged for a search of Katherine's former office the following morning. Martinez coordinated with campus security and brought a forensics team specialized in finding hidden compartments and concealed evidence.

"We found something," Martinez said over the phone. "A hidden compartment behind where the old built-in bookshelves used to be. It contained a waterproof case with journals."

"Have you examined the contents?" Claire asked, standing up and beginning to pace.

"Preliminarily. The journals appear to be Richard's personal records from 1998 to present, documenting his involvement with both Archon and Katherine's case." Martinez's voice was tight with controlled anger. "Claire, these aren't exculpatory. They're detailed accounts of a deliberate plan to discredit and institutionalize Katherine."

Claire felt her throat constrict. "Why would he leave evidence that incriminates him?"

"That's what concerns me," Martinez replied. "It seems too deliberate, too complete. The final journal entry, dated yesterday, includes detailed observations of you. Your behavior patterns, your psychological responses to finding Katherine, even predictions about how you would react to discovering his involvement."

The revelation hit Claire like a physical blow. "I've been part of the experiment all along."

The journals, when Martinez delivered them to the safe house later that day, proved even more disturbing than anticipated. Richard's documentation revealed a man who had compartmentalized his life completely; a loving father in one context, calculating researcher in another, and a corporate conspirator in a third.

Most troubling were the entries from recent months, after Katherine's rescue. Richard had recorded his careful manipulation of her medication, adjusting dosages to ensure periods of clarity followed by confusion, creating a pattern designed to make her emerging memories seem unreliable.

"This final entry...," Claire noted, turning to the last written page. "He knew we were close to discovering the truth."

"He never intended to be caught," Claire realized. "These records were left deliberately, as the final documentation of his 'research.' He wanted us to find them once he was safely gone."

"The ultimate publication of his life's work," Katherine said bitterly. "With us as the documented subjects."

The investigation that followed confirmed their worst fears, but Richard Morrison had vanished without a trace. International law enforcement agencies joined the search, but he had planned his disappearance as meticulously as everything else.

Six months after Richard's disappearance, Claire sat with her mother on the porch of a new safe house. The evening was mild, fireflies beginning to appear in the gathering dusk.

"What happens now?" Claire asked, watching a particularly bright insect trace patterns in the darkening air.

"Healing," Katherine replied simply. "For both of us. Different wounds, same process."

Claire nodded, understanding the parallel journeys they faced. Katherine recovering from decades of captivity and chemical manipulation, Claire from the psychological devastation of discovering her father's true nature.

"I keep thinking about the butterflies," Claire said after a moment. "My science project when I was a kid. How we watched them transform, emerge. You said something that day that I've never forgotten: 'The caterpillar doesn't actually grow wings, Claire. It dissolves completely inside the chrysalis and rebuilds itself from its own liquid remains. Transformation isn't just change, it's dissolution and reconstruction.'"

Katherine smiled at the memory. "I always did have a flair for metaphors."

"But you were right," Claire insisted. "That's exactly what this feels like. Everything I thought I knew about him, about our family, about myself, it's all dissolved. And now I have to reconstruct a coherent understanding from the fragments that remain."

"We'll do it together," Katherine promised, reaching for her daughter's hand. "Fragment by fragment, memory by memory. The truth isn't always kind, but it's the only foundation worth building upon."

In the distance, thunder rumbled, a summer storm approaching. Claire thought about her father, wondering where he might be; perhaps still documenting his observations, still seeing their pain as data rather than human experience.

"He'll never stop watching us," she said quietly. "Even from a distance, we're still part of his study."

"Then let's show him something unexpected," Katherine suggested, her eyes reflecting the determination that had helped her survive years of captivity. "Let's rebuild ourselves into something his models and predictions never accounted for."

Claire squeezed her mother's hand, feeling the first raindrops touch her skin as the storm drew closer. "He documented our breakdown. He doesn't get to document our reconstruction."

As the rain began to fall, mother and daughter remained on the porch, watching the storm transform the landscape before them. Somewhere in the garden, protected from the rain, chrysalides hung from sheltered branches, their inhabitants neither what they had been nor what they would become, but something in-between, dissolution preceding reconstruction.

Claire watched the rain cleanse the air, washing away the dust of the day, and felt the first tenuous stirrings of whatever she might eventually become.

Chapter Ten

Blood Ties

Claire Morrison studied the crime scene photos spread across her desk, a familiar knot forming in her stomach. Four victims, all discovered in different cities over the past fifteen years. All appearing to have died from natural causes until someone looked closer. And someone finally had.

"Tell me again how you connected these," she said to Martinez.

"It started with the Westlake case in Boston," Martinez explained, her finger tapping the photo of a middle-aged woman slumped over her desk. "Medical examiner initially ruled it as a stroke, but when the family requested a second opinion, toxicology found trace amounts of a compound that mimics the effects of a cerebral hemorrhage."

Claire studied the image, trying to maintain professional detachment despite the growing suspicion she couldn't shake. "And the others?"

"Similar patterns. Apparent natural deaths that weren't natural. Different cities, different years, but the same compounds. And Claire," Martinez hesitated, the scar beneath her right eye becoming more pronounced as her expression tightened, "each victim was a researcher working on trauma-responsive neuroplasticity. Each one had published work that challenged pharmaceutical approaches to trauma treatment."

Claire's gaze shifted to the map Martinez had created, red pins marking the locations of each death. A pattern was emerging that she desperately wanted to deny but couldn't. The cities correlated with her father's academic speaking engagements over the past fifteen years. The timing aligned with gaps in his university schedule.

"There's something else," Martinez continued, sliding a folder across the desk. "I found connections between each victim and Archon Pharmaceuticals."

It had been six months since they'd discovered the truth about Katherine Morrison's disappearance twenty-six years earlier, six months since Claire had been forced to acknowledge that her father, Dr. Richard Morrison, a respected forensic psychologist, had orchestrated her mother's imprisonment at Broomhaven.

Six months since Richard had disappeared, leaving behind damning evidence of his crimes but escaping justice. International law enforcement had tracked him to Zürich, then Vienna, then lost his trail.

During those six months, while Katherine had been recovering and Claire had been processing the devastating revelations about her father, Martinez had been conducting her own investigation. Working with cold case files and international law enforcement databases, she had tracked the deaths of researchers whose work threatened pharmaceutical interests, looking for patterns that might connect to the Archon conspiracy.

"You think these deaths are connected to what happened to my mother," Claire said, a statement rather than a question.

"I've been working this angle since your father disappeared," Martinez replied. "The pattern started with Dr. Helen Northrop in Singapore. When I dug deeper into her death, I found similar cases going back over a decade. What we thought was an isolated conspiracy involving your mother appears to be part of something much bigger."

Claire felt the familiar urge for a drink, the automatic response to overwhelming stress that had dominated her life for years. Nearly five years sober and still the craving surfaced in moments of acute distress. She reached into her pocket instead, finding the smooth surface of her sobriety chip, running her thumb over its edges.

"I think your father didn't start with Katherine," Martinez continued. "I think she was unique because he kept her alive for observation. The others... I believe they were earlier experiments that weren't 'needed' anymore."

"I need to show these to my mother," Claire said finally. "She might find something we could be missing."

Martinez nodded. "Of course. I'll drive you."

Katherine Morrison was staying at a secluded cottage on the Chesapeake Bay, part of the federal protection program that had been established after her husband disappeared. The peaceful surroundings were helping her recovery.

Claire had been letting Darwin stay with her mother more frequently over the past months. He had taken to Katherine immediately during Claire's first visit with him, as if sensing her need for companionship. Katherine, who had never had pets as a child due to her father's allergies, found Darwin's presence enormously comforting.

They found Katherine in the garden when they arrived, Darwin perched contentedly on the stone bench beside her as she pruned roses. At sixty-four, Katherine's face showed the strain of her ordeal, but her eyes remained as piercing and intelligent as in the photographs Claire remembered from her childhood.

"Sara, Claire," Katherine greeted them, removing her gardening gloves while Darwin stretched and hopped down to wind around Claire's ankles. "This isn't a social call, is it?"

"We have some cases we'd like you to look at," Claire explained, embracing her mother briefly while scratching Darwin behind the ears. "Potential connections to Archon. And possibly to Dad."

Katherine's expression hardened slightly at the mention of her husband. "Let's go inside. Darwin, come along."

The kitchen table soon became covered with photographs and case files, Katherine examining each. Darwin had claimed his usual spot on the window seat, where he could observe both the room and the garden outside. She worked silently for nearly an hour, occasionally making notes or asking for clarification about specific details.

"These is Richard's work," she finally said, looking up at them. "I recognize his rationale. The compounds that mimic natural processes, the attention to the victims' specific research areas." She tapped the photo of a man found dead in his Chicago apartment. "Dr. Leonard Volkov. I knew him briefly before my... disappearance. His work on neurological regeneration post-trauma was revolutionary."

"You're certain it's Richard?" Martinez asked.

"As certain as I can be," Katherine confirmed. "During my more lucid periods at Broomhaven, I overheard staff referring to me as 'Subject 16.' I always wondered who were the previous fifteen." She gestured to the photographs. "I believe I'm looking at some of them now."

Claire watched her mother's face carefully as the implications settled. Over the past months, Katherine had recovered more memories of her imprisonment, and they had all painted an increasingly disturbing picture of Richard's involvement. But this suggestion that his crimes extended far beyond Katherine's case was a new level of horror.

"You think he's been doing this for years," Claire said. "Not just participating in your abduction, but also eliminating researchers."

"The pattern fits," Katherine said, her voice steady despite the pain evident in her eyes. "Richard has always been systematic, patient. If he was willing to imprison me for twenty-six years to suppress my research, why wouldn't he simply eliminate others whose work posed similar threats?"

"My God," Claire whispered, the implications settling over her. "Serial murder disguised as natural death. Clinical experimentation masked as psychiatric treatment. He was developing techniques for years, refining them."

"And I was his masterpiece," Katherine said. "The one subject he couldn't bring himself to eliminate completely but couldn't allow to remain free."

Darwin seemed to sense the tension in the room, jumping up on Katherine's lap and purring.

"Why?" Claire asked, the question that had haunted her since discovering her father's involvement in her mother's abduction. "Why would he do this? These researchers weren't threats to him personally."

"They were threats to something he valued more than personal relationships," Katherine replied, one hand absently stroking Darwin's fur while the other sorted through photos. "Knowledge as power. Control over human cognition. Richard always believed that understanding the mind's vulnerabilities gave him not just insight but control." She paused in her sorting. "Each of these researchers were developing methods to help trauma survivors rebuild neural pathways independently, without pharmaceutical intervention. Each one represented a challenge to the idea that human cognition could be externally controlled."

"And Archon provided the resources for his experiments," Martinez added, "believing they were simply suppressing competitive research."

"A mutually beneficial arrangement," Katherine agreed. "Archon eliminated threats to their product lines. Richard gained access to facilities, compounds, and subjects for his research."

Martinez spread out additional files she had brought. "Over the past six months, I've been working with Interpol to track suspicious deaths of researchers in this field. The pattern extends back nearly three decades, with researchers dying of apparent natural causes in cities where your father had speaking engagements or consulting work."

Claire stood and walked to the window, needing space to process these revelations. The man who had raised her, who had taught her to analyze patterns and understand human behavior, had potentially been murdering researchers after documenting their psychological deterioration.

"We need to find him," she said finally, turning back to face them. "He's been gone for six months, but these cases suggest a pattern going back at least thirty years. Whatever he's working on isn't finished."

"I've been thinking about that," Katherine said carefully, Darwin stretched across her lap like a furry barrier between her and the disturbing photographs. "Richard doesn't abandon experiments. He documents them meticulously through completion. The journals he left behind, the evidence of his crimes... that wasn't just carelessness or arrogance. It was deliberate."

"He wanted us to find those records," Martinez said.

"Everything Richard does serves a specific purpose in his experimental design," Katherine said. "Including his disappearance, and especially the evidence he left behind."

"Then what's the purpose?" Claire asked, her mind already racing through possibilities. "If he knew we'd discover his involvement, why leave a trail that implicates him in multiple murders?"

"Because his experiment isn't about the researchers he used and killed," Katherine said, meeting her daughter's gaze directly. "It's about you, Claire. It always has been."

The statement hung in the air between them, its implications expanding in Claire's mind like ripples from a stone dropped in still water. Her father's documentation had included observations of her psychological development since childhood, with particular attention to her reaction to her mother's disappearance, her subsequent fear of inheriting what she believed was her mother's mental illness, her descent into alcoholism, and her eventual recovery. And the paper he published about her without revealing it was her.

"The journals included detailed predictions about how you would respond to discovering his involvement in my abduction," Katherine continued gently. "He was studying your psychological resilience, your capacity to process betrayal from the person who shaped your understanding of the world."

Claire felt nauseated. "You're saying my entire life has been part of his research?"

"Not your entire life," Katherine clarified. "But your responses to key events he either created or anticipated. Your career choice, following his path into psychological profiling. Your alcoholism, triggered by fear of inheriting what you believed was my condition. Your recovery, demonstrating psychological resilience. And now, your investigation into his crimes."

Martinez, who had been silent during this exchange, spoke up. "If Katherine is right, then Richard didn't just flee to escape justice. He's continuing the experiment from afar, observing your reaction to these new revelations."

"Which means he might still be watching," Claire concluded. "And potentially manipulating what we discover about him."

"Almost certainly," Katherine agreed. "Richard never does anything without purpose. If we're finding evidence of his earlier victims now, it's because he wants us to."

As the evening approached, Claire reluctantly left the cottage, but Darwin remained with Katherine as had become their routine. The cat had grown particularly attached to Katherine, seeming to understand her need for companionship.

Back at her apartment that night, Claire found herself missing Darwin's presence as she paced the living room, her mind still processing the implications of the day's discoveries. Her father was not just complicit in her mother's abduction and imprisonment. He was potentially responsible for over a dozen murders spanning nearly thirty years. And Claire herself had been an unwitting subject in his psychological experiment.

Her phone rang, Martinez checking in as she had regularly since the revelations about Richard had first emerged.

"How are you holding up?" the she asked, the background noise suggesting she was at the precinct.

"Processing," Claire replied honestly. "It's one thing to discover your father helped imprison your mother. It's another to realize he's likely a serial killer who's also been studying your psychological responses since childhood."

"We'll find him, Claire," Martinez assured her. "International law enforcement has been updated with the new evidence. With the connections to the other victims, the net is tightening."

Claire wasn't so certain. Her father had evaded capture for six months already, and that was before they understood the full scope of his capabilities.

"There's something else," Martinez continued after a brief hesitation. "Another case has emerged that fits the pattern. Dr. Ricardo Gomes found dead in his Lisbon condo two weeks ago. Apparent heart failure, but the preliminary toxicology shows anomalies consistent with our other victims."

"Two weeks ago," Claire repeated, the timing significant. "He's still active."

"It appears so. Dr. Gomes was leading a research team developing methods built directly on your mother's earlier work."

"He's continuing the same pattern," Claire said. "Eliminating researchers who threaten pharmaceutical approaches to trauma treatment."

"But with a new urgency," Martinez pointed out. "The previous cases were spaced years apart. If Dr. Gomes' death is connected, it suggests he's accelerating his timeline."

After ending the call, Claire's mind was racing. Her father's academic career had taken him to universities worldwide, always with the same focus on memory formation, trauma response, and cognitive restructuring. His published work had established him as a leading authority on how the mind processes and adapts to extreme experiences.

What had once seemed like brilliant academic insight now revealed itself as something much darker. His research was conducted not just through ethical observation but through deliberate experimental manipulation of unwitting subjects.

A sudden inspiration struck her. If her father was continuing his pattern of eliminating researchers related to her mother's research, there would be logical next targets. She opened her laptop and began searching for current research in the field.

By morning, she had compiled a list of five researchers whose work directly built on the approaches pioneered by her mother and the other victims. All were developing methods that could potentially reduce or eliminate the need for pharmaceutical treatment of trauma, particularly in children.

She called Martinez. "I've identified potential targets based on the pattern of previous victims. We need to warn them, set up protection."

Within hours, an international alert had been issued, with law enforcement contacting each researcher on Claire's list. Four immediately accepted protection. But the fifth, Dr. Julia Flores at The University of Maryland, insisted on continuing her work without disruption, agreeing only to basic security measures that wouldn't interfere with her schedule.

"Flores is the most vulnerable," Claire told Martinez as they drove to the university. "Not just because she's refused full protection, but because her work most directly expands on my mother's original research. She's developed a protocol for neural recalibration after trauma that's showing remarkable results in clinical trials."

"And she's in Maryland, where Richard has the most extensive knowledge of the area," Martinez added grimly.

Dr. Flores was a formidable woman in her late fifties, with a steel-gray hair cut, and the direct gaze of someone unaccustomed to wasting time. Her office was meticulously organized, with research journals arranged in specific order on shelves that lined the walls.

"I understand your concerns," she told them after they explained the situation. "But I've been receiving threats since I published my preliminary findings three years ago. Corporate interests have tried to discredit my work, block my funding, even plant unfavorable reviews in academic journals. I won't be intimidated into hiding, now that we're finally seeing clinical validation."

"This isn't about intimidation, Dr. Flores," Claire explained carefully. "The killer we're tracking has successfully eliminated at least sixteen researchers in your field, making their deaths appear natural. Without full protection, you're at significant risk."

Flores studied Claire. "You're Katherine Morrison's daughter," she said, recognition dawning in her expression. "Your mother's work on neural pathway reconstruction was groundbreaking. It formed the foundation for much of what we're doing now."

"Yes," Claire confirmed, surprised by the connection. "You knew her?"

"Not personally, but every researcher in this field knows Katherine Morrison's contributions. When she disappeared, it set our understanding of non-pharmaceutical trauma treatment back by decades." Flores shook her head. "I always wondered what happened to her. There were rumors she had suffered some kind of breakdown, but her work showed such clarity, such precise understanding of neurological responses to trauma. It never made sense to me."

"Those rumors were deliberately planted," Claire said, deciding to trust Flores with at least part of the truth. "My mother was abducted and institutionalized to prevent her research from threatening pharmaceutical profits. The same parties responsible for her disappearance are likely targeting you now."

Flores's expression hardened. "I suspected corporate involvement in the obstacles we've faced, but this level of criminality..." She took a deep breath. "What exactly do you need from me?"

"Full protective custody until we apprehend the suspect," Martinez said firmly. "Limited contact with anyone outside the security team, restricted access to your lab and research, and potentially temporary relocation."

"Out of the question," Flores replied without hesitation. "We're in the final phase of a clinical trial that could help countless children recover from severe trauma without pharmaceutical dependence. I won't abandon that work, not even for my personal safety."

Claire recognized the determination in Flores's eyes, the same commitment to scientific truth at any cost that had characterized her mother's work. "Then we need to set a trap," she said, the plan forming even as she spoke. "Use your research as bait, but under controlled conditions where we can anticipate and prevent an attack."

"You want to use me as bait." Flores said, not a question but an observation.

"To catch my father," Claire confessed, the admission painful despite the months she'd had to adjust to the truth. "Dr. Richard Morrison. Former consultant to Archon Pharmaceuticals and the architect of my mother's abduction."

Flores's expression shifted from shock to determination. "I'll do it."

The plan came together over the next twenty-four hours. Dr. Flores would announce a breakthrough in her research, a refinement of her protocol that showed even more dramatic results than previous trials. She would schedule a presentation at the university, ostensibly to share these findings with colleagues, but actually to create an opportunity for Richard to approach under controlled conditions.

"He's methodical, not impulsive," Claire explained to the tactical team assembled in the precinct's conference room. Chief Matthews sat at the head of the table, reviewing the operational details. "He won't simply appear at the presentation. He'll conduct surveillance first, assess security measures, and identify vulnerabilities."

"Which gives us time to identify him before he makes his move," Martinez added. "We'll have undercover officers throughout the campus and surrounding areas, facial recognition running on all security cameras, and Dr. Flores will be wearing a tracking device."

"What makes you think he'll take the bait?" Chief Matthews asked, his usual gruff exterior masking genuine concern. He had known Richard Morrison for years, considered him a respected colleague until the revelations about Katherine.

"Because we're making Dr. Flores appear to represent the culmination of what my mother started," Claire replied. "The fabricated research breakthroughs we're having her announce will validate my mother's approach. She's not just another researcher; we're creating the illusion that she's the proof my mother was right all along."

"And your father can't allow that validation to stand," Matthews concluded.

"No, he can't," Claire confirmed.

The night before Flores's presentation, Claire found herself unable to sleep. She sat on her small balcony, watching the city lights shimmer across the harbor. The weight of tomorrow's operation pressed heavily on her mind, not just the tactical considerations but the personal implications of drawing her father into a trap.

Her phone buzzed with a text from an unknown number: *"Rigorous experimental design requires control groups. You've forgotten this fundamental principle, Claire."*

"Claire tried to catch her breath. The message could only be from her father. The clinical language, the reference to experimental design, it was unmistakably his perspective. She immediately called Martinez.

'I just got a text from him,' Claire said when Martinez answered.

I'm coming over,' Martinez replied, her voice sharp with urgency.

Twenty minutes later, Martinez stood in Claire's living room, reading the text.

"Can we trace it?" Claire asked, already knowing the answer.

Martinez shook her head. "Burner phone, almost certainly. But this confirms he's monitoring our investigation, possibly our communications."

"It also suggests he knows about the trap," Claire added. "The reference to control groups. He's saying we're missing something, that our approach is scientifically flawed."

"Or he's trying to make you doubt yourself," Martinez countered. "Psychological manipulation has been his method from the beginning."

Claire knew Martinez was right, that her father's message was designed to create exactly the uncertainty she was now feeling. Yet she couldn't shake the sense that they were missing something crucial, that Richard was already several steps ahead in a game they didn't fully understand.

The university auditorium filled gradually as doctors, researchers, and students gathered for Dr. Flores's presentation. Claire sat near the back, scanning the audience for any sign of her father while trying to remain inconspicuous. Martinez was positioned near the main entrance, coordinating with the security team, monitoring all access points.

Dr. Flores began her presentation on schedule, outlining her protocol for neural recalibration after childhood trauma. Halfway through, Claire's phone vibrated with a text from Martinez: "All entrances secure, no sign of him."

A sense of unease grew in Claire's mind. If her father had been monitoring her communications, as the earlier message suggested, he would know about the security measures, the facial recognition systems, and the undercover officers.

"Rigorous experimental design requires control groups."

The text message replayed in her mind, its meaning suddenly shifting. Control groups. Parallel experiments conducted simultaneously to isolate variables and confirm results. They weren't missing something in their operational planning; they were missing something in their understanding of her father's experimental design.

Dr. Flores wasn't the only target. She was just one variable in a larger experiment.

Claire stood abruptly, drawing glances from nearby attendees, and moved quickly to the exit. In the hallway, she called Martinez.

"We've been looking at this wrong," she said urgently. "Dr. Flores isn't the only target. He's running parallel experiments, multiple subjects simultaneously."

"The other researchers on your list," Martinez realized immediately. "They're all under protection…"

"Not all of them," Claire interrupted. "My mother. She's the foundation of his research. If he's truly conducting a comprehensive final phase, he would include her."

"But your mother has protection too," Martinez reminded her. "Federal marshals at the cottage, security systems…"

"But he knows how we think, how we operate," Claire said, already moving toward the building exit. "He's been watching our investigation, maybe even our security arrangements. Richard doesn't use brute force, he uses knowledge. What if he's found a vulnerability we didn't anticipate?"

A new terror gripped Claire. Darwin was with Katherine at the cottage. If something had happened to her mother, her beloved cat could be in danger too.

The drive to the Chesapeake Bay cottage took forty-five agonizing minutes, every second amplifying Claire's fear. She tried calling her mother repeatedly, each unanswered ring increasing her certainty that something was terribly wrong. When Katherine didn't answer, she tried calling the federal marshals assigned to protect her; no response from any of them either. Martinez had dispatched local officers to the cottage while coordinating with the team still at the university, ensuring Dr. Flores remained secure.

When Claire finally reached the cottage, two police cruisers were already in the driveway, officers examining the exterior of the building. Detective Johnson, who had worked with Claire on several cases, met her as she hurried up the path.

"No sign of forced entry," he reported. "But no response from inside either. The federal marshals who were supposed to be on duty are missing. We're preparing to breach."

"Where are the marshals?" Claire demanded.

"That's the concerning part," Johnson replied. "The shift change happened three hours ago, but the replacement team never checked in. No sign of the previous team either."

The tactical team breached the cottage, searching each room. Claire followed behind them, heart pounding as they confirmed what she already feared: Katherine was gone. And Darwin was missing. But the cottage showed no signs of struggle.

"Wait," one of the officers called from the back bedroom. "Found something under the bed."

Claire rushed to the room to find the officer gently coaxing Darwin out from beneath the bed. The cat emerged slowly, his fur disheveled and his eyes wide with stress, but appearing unharmed.

"Darwin," Claire breathed, gathering him into her arms. He clung to her, purring frantically as if trying to communicate his distress. "What happened, buddy? Where's Katherine?"

"Dr. Morrison!" one of the officers called from another room. "You need to see this!"

Still holding Darwin, Claire made her way to Katherine's study. The officer was standing beside her mother's desk, pointing to a sheet of paper.

Claire approached and saw a note written in her father's handwriting:

"The final phase requires the original subject. Comprehensive experimental design demands symmetry in closure. You know where this began, Claire. That's where it must end."

"Where this began," Claire repeated, her mind immediately making the connection while Darwin trembled in her arms. "At JHU. In the original lab, where Mom's research was conducted before she disappeared."

"But that was demolished years ago," Martinez reminded her, having arrived shortly after Claire. "The building was torn down to make way for the new science center."

"Not the building," Claire clarified. "The lab equipment, the research materials. They would have been relocated. My mother's original lab setup, where would it have gone?"

A call to JHU archives confirmed what Claire had begun to suspect. Katherine Morrison's laboratory equipment and research materials had later been placed in storage after her disappearance, to a university warehouse facility on the outskirts of the city. According to the records, no one had accessed those materials in nearly twenty years until six months ago, when a request had been filed by the Psychology Department to review the historical archives.

"He's recreating the original scene," Claire told Martinez as they raced toward the warehouse facility. She secured Darwin in his carrier in the back seat. "Bringing my mother back to where her research began, where her abduction was first conceived. It's perfect symmetry in his experimental design, returning to the starting point to document the final phase."

The warehouse was a massive structure of corrugated metal and concrete, housing decades of academic materials deemed worth preserving but not actively used. A security guard at the entrance confirmed that someone had indeed accessed the facility earlier that day, a professor with proper credentials reviewing historical materials for a departmental project.

"I need to go in alone," Claire said as they prepared to enter, tactical teams taking position around the building. Darwin meowed anxiously from his carrier, as if sensing the danger ahead.

"Absolutely not," Martinez responded immediately. "Your father is dangerous, Claire. He's already killed multiple people, abducted your mother twice..."

"And he's expecting a tactical response," Claire interrupted. "He's prepared for armed officers. What he's not prepared for is my understanding the true nature of his experiment." She met Martinez's concerned gaze directly. "This was never about eliminating researchers or suppressing my mother's work. That was just the cover for his actual study, the impact of extreme betrayal and manipulation on specifically selected psychological profiles, particularly mine."

"All the more reason not to face him alone," Martinez insisted.

"It's the only way to end this," Claire replied. "He designed this entire scenario, from my mother's abduction twenty-six years ago to the evidence he left behind after fleeing. Every element has been calculated to test my psychological responses, my resilience, and my capacity to recognize patterns. If we approach this as a standard tactical operation, we're still playing by his rules, still subjects in his experiment."

After intense discussion, they reached a compromise. Claire would enter first, wearing a wire and tracking device. Tactical teams would maintain positions outside but would not enter unless the situation became clearly dangerous. Martinez would coordinate from a mobile command post, ready to initiate if necessary.

The warehouse interior was dimly lit, rows of tall shelving units creating a labyrinth of academic history. Claire moved carefully through the space, following signs pointing toward the storage section for the Department of Neuropsychology. The familiar scent of old paper and dust reminded her of countless hours spent in university archives during her doctoral studies, a time when she had still believed in her father's integrity.

She found them in a cleared area at the back of the warehouse, where laboratory equipment had been assembled to recreate Katherine Morrison's original research space. Beakers, microscopes, and specialized neuro-imaging devices were arranged as they would have been twenty-six years earlier, based on photographs Claire recognized from department archives.

Katherine sat in a chair in the center of the recreated lab, apparently unrestrained but unnaturally still. Her eyes tracked Claire's approach, but she made no attempt to speak or move.

And there, standing beside a vintage computer terminal that had been part of Katherine's original setup, was Richard Morrison. At seventy-two, he remained an imposing figure, tall and straight-backed, with the same piercing green eyes Claire saw in her own reflection. His silver hair was cut differently than when she had last seen him, and he had grown a short beard.

"Right on schedule," Richard said, his voice measured and precise. "I calculated forty-seven minutes from your realization at the presentation to your arrival here, accounting for traffic patterns and coordination with law enforcement. You're three minutes early, which suggests heightened adrenal response affecting your driving speed."

"Where I'm concerned, you've always had a blind spot in your calculations," Claire replied, her voice steadier than she felt. "You analyze the data points but miss the human element."

Richard smiled slightly, an expression of what appeared to be genuine pride. "Not a blind spot, Claire. A controlled variable." He gestured to Katherine. "Your mother is unharmed, merely sedated with a mild paralytic."

Claire took a step forward, maintaining eye contact with her father while assessing Katherine's condition. Her mother's breathing appeared normal, though her unnatural stillness confirmed Richard's claim.

"What exactly is the purpose of all this?" Claire asked, gesturing to the recreated laboratory. "Years of deception, multiple murders disguised as natural deaths, elaborate psychological manipulation. What possible research value could justify such extremes?"

"The most comprehensive longitudinal study of psychological resilience ever conducted," Richard replied. He pulled out a small notebook and made a brief notation. "Conventional research is constrained by ethical limitations, institutional review boards, the artificial nature of laboratory conditions. My work transcends these limitations."

"Your 'work' has destroyed lives," Claire said, struggling to maintain her professional demeanor as anger threatened to overwhelm her. "The researchers you killed, the families left behind, the years you stole from my mother, from both of us."

"The advancement of knowledge always carries a cost," Richard replied calmly, making another note in his book. "Every breakthrough requires sacrifice."

As Richard continued documenting her responses, Claire noticed something about the laboratory recreation that struck her as odd. Certain elements were as they would have been in Katherine's original lab, clearly based on departmental photographs and records. But other items seemed out of place, modern equipment partially disguised to appear vintage.

This wasn't just a recreation of the past, she realized. It was a functional research space, recently used.

"You've been continuing Mom's original research," she said, interrupting Richard's documentation. "Not just recreating her lab but actually advancing her work on non-pharmaceutical approaches to neurological trauma."

Richard's expression shifted almost imperceptibly, a flicker of surprise quickly masked by his usual controlled demeanor. "Very observant, Claire. Yes, Katherine's research has continued throughout her captivity."

"So while publicly supporting pharmaceutical approaches through your relationship with Archon, you were privately validating the non-pharmaceutical methods you were helping to suppress," Claire said. "Why?"

"Because knowledge is neutral; its application has consequences," Richard explained, his voice taking on the familiar cadence of his academic lectures. "Katherine's methods work. They're more effective than pharmaceutical interventions. But they require individualized treatment, specialized practitioners, lengthy therapeutic processes. They can't be packaged, mass-produced, or distributed globally."

"So you suppressed more effective treatments to protect corporate interests?" Claire's disgust was evident.

"I preserved more efficient treatment distribution," Richard corrected, making another note. "Archon's medications reach millions of trauma survivors worldwide. Yes, they're less effective than Katherine's methods, but they're accessible, scalable, and profitable."

"That wasn't your decision to make," Claire said, taking another step forward. "You appointed yourself arbiter of who deserves optimal treatment and who should receive 'suboptimal' care."

As they spoke, Claire had been carefully assessing the situation, noting potential exits, the precise location of the tactical team outside, and the gradual return of mobility to her mother's extremities as the paralytic began to wear off. She needed to keep Richard talking while maneuvering into a position that would allow for intervention.

"And where does your current research fit into this arrangement?" she asked, gesturing to the laboratory equipment.

"Synthesis," Richard replied, his expression brightening with what appeared to be genuine academic enthusiasm. "The integration of Katherine's neurological approach with pharmaceutical delivery systems. Targeted compounds that facilitate neural recalibration without the lengthy therapeutic process her original methods required."

"And the final phase of this synthesis requires returning to the original research environment," Claire said, understanding dawning.

"Precisely," Richard confirmed. "Symmetry. The experiment begins and ends in the same location, with the primary subject, but with years of accumulated data informing the conclusion."

"And my role in this symmetry?" Claire asked.

"Secondary subject becomes primary observer," Richard said, his clinical detachment momentarily giving way to what appeared to be genuine paternal pride. "Your psychological development has been perhaps the most fascinating aspect of this entire study, Claire."

The casual reference to her role as a research subject triggered a sharp pain. She reached reflexively for the sobriety chip in her pocket, fingers finding the familiar ridges.

"Nearly five years sober," she said, her voice steady despite the emotion roiling beneath the surface. "Despite discovering that my family was built on lies."

Something flickered in Richard's eyes, not remorse, precisely, but perhaps recognition of a variable his calculations hadn't fully accounted for. "Your recovery exceeded all statistical probability," he acknowledged. "Based on environmental stressors and trauma history, your likelihood of maintaining long-term sobriety was less than twenty percent."

"I'm not a data point," Claire said, anger sharpening her voice. "I'm your daughter. Mom isn't Subject 16; she's your wife. The researchers you killed weren't experimental subjects; they were people with families."

As Claire spoke, she noticed Katherine's fingers beginning to move slightly, the paralytic wearing off. She needed to keep him focused on her, engaged, while her mother gradually regained mobility.

"You misunderstand the nature of my work," Richard replied, his tone remaining measured despite Claire's evident anger. "I don't lack emotional connection; I simply compartmentalize it appropriately."

"Love doesn't abduct and imprison," Claire countered. "Love doesn't experiment on the mind of someone who trusted you."

Richard smiled thinly. "A convenient statement. But consider this: every significant advance in understanding human psychology has come from research that would be considered unethical by contemporary standards."

"Those researchers didn't kill their subjects," Claire pointed out. "And their experiments were eventually subject to ethical review and regulation precisely because such methods aren't justified by scientific curiosity."

As they continued this philosophical exchange, Claire was maneuvering gradually toward Katherine, using the conversation to mask her movement. She could see her mother's awareness returning as the paralytic's effects diminished.

Claire was now positioned where she could see both her father and the main entrance to their section of the warehouse, the tactical team visible through gaps in the shelving units. Katherine's right hand had begun to move more purposefully, though she maintained the appearance of paralysis.

"Your documentation methods," Claire said, drawing Richard's attention back to his research protocols. "I've seen the journals you left behind, the clinical observations of Mom's degradation, of my psychological development. But there must be more comprehensive records for a longitudinal study spanning decades."

It was a calculated risk, hoping Richard's academic pride would override his caution.

"Secured off-site," Richard replied. "Multiple redundant storage methods, encrypted, and compartmentalized. The complete dataset represents the most comprehensive documentation of psychological adaptation under extreme conditions ever compiled."

"You still believe your research will be published?" Claire asked, with genuine disbelief.

"History is replete with initially rejected discoveries, but later embraced when their value became apparent," Richard said calmly.

As Richard continued elaborating on his justifications, Claire saw her opportunity. Katherine had regained sufficient movement to potentially stand, though she maintained the appearance of paralysis. The tactical team was in position, awaiting the signal Claire had established with Martinez.

"You've planned for every contingency, haven't you?" Claire said, deliberately shifting to a tone of reluctant admiration. "The security protocols, the offshore data storage, the calculated risk of returning to Baltimore. Your experimental design accounts for all variables except one."

"And what variable is that?" Richard asked, his expression showing genuine curiosity.

"The human capacity for choice outside predicted parameters," Claire replied, making eye contact with her mother.

But Richard interrupted, his voice taking on a newly clinical tone. "Interesting that you would highlight choice as the unpredictable variable, given your own highly predictable responses throughout your development. Your alcoholism, for instance, onset at age twenty-seven, precisely when statistical models would predict."

Claire felt a cold wave wash through her body. "Stop."

"Your consumption patterns followed the classic progression," Richard continued, as if delivering an academic lecture. "Initial social drinking transitioning to solitary vodka consumption, hidden bottles, morning tremors by age twenty-eight."

"I said stop." Claire's hands had begun to tremble.

Richard's eyes brightened with clinical interest. "Ah, and now the defensive anger response, another predictable pattern."

"I am not a data point," Claire said, her voice dangerously quiet. "I am your daughter."

"You're both," Richard replied smoothly. "Just as I am your father and a researcher."

Claire became aware of a roaring in her ears, blood pounding in her temples as her father continued to clinically dissect the most painful periods of her life.

"Your recovery narrative is particularly interesting from a research perspective," Richard continued. "The psychological mechanisms you employed to maintain sobriety despite extreme stressors demonstrate remarkable resilience."

Claire's hand moved almost unconsciously toward her weapon, a motion Richard tracked with immediate interest.

"And now we observe the potential for violence emerging from the attachment injury," he noted, his voice remaining perfectly calm. "This is precisely the kind of authentic psychological response that cannot be ethically induced in conventional research settings."

Martinez had been monitoring through Claire's concealed microphone, recognizing the escalating psychological manipulation. Through her earpiece, she heard Richard's clinical dissection of Claire's most vulnerable moments and made a tactical decision.

"Shut up," Claire whispered, her hand now resting on her holster. "Just shut up."

"The subject is now exhibiting classic signs of autonomic nervous system activation," Richard continued, taking out his notebook and jotting observations. "Pupil dilation, peripheral flush response, and increased respiratory rate."

Claire drew her weapon, her hand shaking visibly as she pointed it at her father. "Stop talking. Stop treating me like a laboratory animal."

Richard showed no fear, only continued analytical interest. "Subject has now progressed to a physical threat display, though physiological indicators suggest extreme ambivalence about potential violence."

Katherine, still partially affected by the paralytic, called out weakly. "Claire, don't. He's manipulating you."

"Of course I am," Richard acknowledged calmly. "That's the fundamental methodology of the study."

"You structured my alcoholism?" Claire asked, her voice breaking. "My recovery? The discovery of mom's imprisonment? This was all some sick experiment to you?"

"Not 'some sick experiment,'" Richard corrected. "The most comprehensive study of psychological resilience ever conducted under authentic conditions of extreme stress."

Claire's finger tensed on the trigger, her weapon aimed at her father's chest. The tactical detachment she'd relied on throughout her career had crumbled entirely, leaving raw pain and rage in its place. "You destroyed lives. You killed people. You imprisoned your own wife for twenty-six years. All for research data?"

"For knowledge that could not be obtained through any other methods," Richard replied. "The insights gained from this study will transform our understanding of ....."

The gunshot echoed through the warehouse, cutting off Richard's clinical justification mid-sentence. Claire flinched, momentarily disoriented until she realized the shot had come not from her weapon but from behind her. Martinez stood in the entrance to the storage area, her service weapon still raised.

Richard staggered backward, a look of surprise crossing his face as he looked down at the spreading crimson stain on his chest. He opened his mouth as if to make one final observation, but instead collapsed onto the concrete floor.

Claire stood frozen, her own weapon still raised, as Martinez approached quickly, kneeling beside Richard's motionless form. The detective checked for a pulse, then looked up at Claire with grim certainty.

"He's gone," Martinez said quietly.

The tactical team flooded into the area seconds later, their coordinated efficiency temporarily disrupted by the unexpected scene before them. As medical personnel confirmed what Martinez had already determined, Claire holstered her weapon with shaking hands and moved to her mother's side.

"What happened?" one of the tactical officers asked, as he surveyed the scene.

Martinez straightened, her expression composed but her eyes holding Claire's for a moment of silent communication. "He made a threatening movement toward the hostage. I perceived imminent danger and responded accordingly."

The warehouse became a flurry of activity, evidence technicians documenting the scene, medical preparing to remove Richard's body, officers securing the perimeter and beginning preliminary statements. Through it all, Claire sat beside her mother, both women watching the aftermath with expressions that combined shock, grief, and something more complex that defied simple categorization.

When they were briefly alone during a lull in the investigation, Katherine grasped Claire's hand tightly. "Are you all right?"

"I don't know," Claire answered honestly. "I was about to shoot him. If Martinez hadn't fired when she did..."

"He was manipulating you." Katherine said, her voice stronger as the paralytic's effects continued to fade. "Pushing you. He wanted to document your breaking point as the culmination of his so-called decades-long study."

Martinez rejoined them after giving her initial statement. "I'll need statements from both of you, but that can wait until we've moved to a more appropriate location."

"Martinez," Claire began, struggling to find words adequate to the situation, "what you did..."

"What I did was respond to a dangerous suspect who had already killed multiple people and was escalating an already volatile situation," Martinez interrupted firmly. "Richard Morrison made a sudden movement that I interpreted as a threat to the safety of civilians present. I responded as any officer would under the circumstances."

Claire understood what Martinez was doing, establishing the official narrative, protecting both Claire's professional reputation and her own actions. The reality of what had happened, Martinez recognizing Claire's psychological breaking point, and intervening with lethal force to prevent her from crossing a line she could never return from, would remain unspoken between them.

"Of course," Claire agreed quietly. "That's exactly what happened."

"I saw it too," Katherine added, as she met Martinez's eyes. "He made a threatening movement. Detective Martinez had no choice but to respond as she did."

The three women held this moment of shared understanding between them, a silent acknowledgment of the truth beneath the necessary official account.

As they were finally cleared to leave the warehouse hours later, Claire paused for one last look at the spot where her father had conducted his final act. The memory of his clinical voice detailing her alcoholism, her recovery, and her most painful struggles as mere data points in his research would haunt her for years to come. But that voice was silent now, the experiment concluded not with the documentation of her breaking point but with his own unexpected variable, Martinez's intervention cutting short the grand experiment at its climax.

"It's over," Martinez said quietly, standing beside her.

But Claire knew better. The psychological aftermath was just beginning; processing not just her father's betrayal but the complex grief of losing him forever, and the knowledge that the man who had shaped her understanding of forensic psychology had been a serial killer.

"Not over," she replied. "Just entering a different phase."

In the vehicle, Darwin meowed anxiously from his carrier until Claire opened it and took him into her arms. The cat seemed to understand that Katherine was safe, purring as he settled between them in the back seat. His presence provided comfort to both women.

In the weeks that followed, the case expanded as international law enforcement agencies reopened investigations into deaths previously ruled natural. Richard Morrison's meticulous records, eventually located through digital forensics experts tracking his encrypted communications, provided damning evidence connecting him to sixteen murders spanning nearly three decades.

The academic community reacted with collective horror as the full scope of his crimes became apparent. Universities removed his textbooks from required reading lists, journals retracted papers based on his potentially tainted research, and the entire field of forensic psychology faced a time of profound reckoning about the ethical foundations of its methodologies.

The internal investigation into Richard Morrison's death concluded with Martinez's actions deemed justified. Only Claire, Katherine, and Martinez knew the truth; that the detective had intervened to prevent Claire from crossing a line from which she might never have recovered.

Four months after the warehouse confrontation, Claire sat with her mother and Sara at Rusty's Diner. Darwin accompanied them in his travel carrier beside the table.

"How are you sleeping?" Martinez asked, adding cream to her coffee. "Last time we talked, you mentioned the nightmares were getting worse."

"They're better," Claire replied honestly, picking at her slice of apple pie while Darwin dozed contentedly in his carrier. "Still there, but less frequent." The emotions surrounding her father's death remained difficult to articulate, grief intertwined with relief, and loss complicated by the recognition of necessary endings. "The prosecution has requested access to all his research records for their cases against Archon executives."

"That's something, at least," Martinez said. "Accountability extending beyond Richard to the system that enabled him."

Betty, who had been serving Claire since her earliest days at the Baltimore PD, approached with a coffee pot. "Refills, ladies?" she offered, topping off their cups without waiting for confirmation. Her gaze lingered on Claire with motherly concern. "You doing okay, honey? Been reading about that case in the papers. Can't imagine what you're going through."

"I'm okay, Betty," Claire assured her with a small smile. "Taking it one day at a time."

"That's all any of us can do," Betty agreed with the wisdom acquired through decades of listening to customers' troubles. "One day at a time, and make sure you eat something besides pie. You're too thin." She glanced at the cat carrier. "And who's this little guy?"

"Darwin," Claire replied, opening the carrier so Darwin could poke his head out. "He's been through a lot with us lately."

Betty's expression softened as she looked at the orange cat. "Well, aren't you a handsome fellow. I'll bet you've been taking good care of these ladies." She moved away to attend to other customers, leaving the three women to their conversation.

"She's been mothering me since my first week on the job," Claire explained to Katherine. "Practically forced soup on me during my early recovery when I could barely eat."

"I like her," Katherine said, watching Betty interact with other regulars. "She sees people, not just customers. That kind of genuine human connection is what Richard never truly understood, what his research could never quantify."

Martinez nodded in agreement. "Speaking of connections, the department psych evaluation cleared you for full duty whenever you're ready to return. Matthews wants you back asap."

Claire had taken temporary leave, needing time to process the emotional impact of the case and spend time with her mother. The validation from Matthews was unexpected but welcome.

"I'm not sure I'm ready yet," she admitted. "There's still so much to work through."

"Take all the time you need," Martinez assured her.

Katherine reached across the table to squeeze Claire's hand. "You've been sober for five years despite discovering your family was built on lies. That speaks to a resilience that comes from something deeper than mere psychological conditioning."

Claire felt the familiar weight of her sobriety chip in her pocket, the tangible reminder of her daily commitment to facing reality without chemical buffers. Five years now, including some of the most psychologically challenging experiences imaginable.

"There are still days when I want a drink," she admitted quietly. "When the weight of everything that's happened feels too heavy to carry with full consciousness."

"But you don't drink," Martinez said, not a question but a statement of observed fact.

"No, I don't," Claire confirmed. "Because addiction would make me exactly what my father always viewed me as, a predictable set of psychological responses rather than a person capable of choices outside statistical probability."

The conversation shifted to more immediate concerns, Katherine's continued recovery, the restoration of her professional reputation as her original research was being validated, and the support group they had connected her with for survivors of long-term trauma. Throughout the discussion, Claire found herself observing the interaction with both personal engagement and professional awareness; noting the genuine emotional connection and the absence of calculation or manipulation.

Darwin, sensing the calmer atmosphere, had settled back to sleep in his carrier, his gentle purring a comforting background to their conversation.

As they prepared to leave, Betty stopped by their table one last time. "Almost forgot, there's a message for you, Dr. Morrison. A young man dropped it off earlier, said you'd be in today." She handed Claire a sealed envelope with her name printed in neat block letters.

Claire tensed immediately, the neutral delivery method triggering memories of the anonymous package that had first revealed her mother's true situation. She opened it carefully, finding a single note card inside with a brief message:

"Dr. Morrison, I'm a former student of your father's, currently researching ethical applications of trauma-responsive therapy based on your mother's pioneering work. I believe there's a way to salvage the valuable insights from decades of research while acknowledging the unethical methods used to obtain them. When you're ready to discuss this possibility, I can be reached at the enclosed number. Respectfully, Dr. Julian Hayes."

Claire shared the note with Katherine and Martinez, all three women considering its implications.

"It's beginning already," Katherine said quietly. "The debate about whether knowledge gained through unethical means should be used despite its origins."

Claire stared at the letter for a long moment, then stood and walked to the diner's trash bin. "Maybe that's what my father never anticipated," she said, dropping the envelope inside. "That I would choose not to engage with his legacy at all. Some patterns are meant to be broken completely."

Katherine and Martinez exchanged a look but said nothing as Claire returned to the table.

"There are other ways to help people," Claire said firmly. "Ways that don't require me to sort through the wreckage of my father's crimes. I'm done living in the shadow of his work."

As they stepped out of Rusty's into the crisp autumn air, Martinez headed toward her car with a wave. "See you both soon," she called over her shoulder.

Claire carried Darwin's carrier while Katherine walked beside her, both finding comfort in each other's presence. Claire felt something shift within her, not resolution or closure, but choice. The weight of her father's death remained, the complicated grief for both the relationship she had believed they shared, and the one that had existed beneath the surface. But she had chosen to step away from his legacy entirely, to forge her own path without the burden of his research.

Back at her apartment, Claire released Darwin from his carrier and watched him settle onto his favorite perch. Katherine had gotten her own place just a few blocks away. When she was ready, she would return to work, not as Richard Morrison's daughter, but simply as Dr. Claire Morrison, forensic psychologist. The choice was hers alone.

Afterword

Claire Morrison's journey through these cases transcends individual investigations. It maps the territory between survival and healing, between understanding evil and becoming consumed by it. Through mathematical killers, mirror-obsessed predators, and those who weaponize trust itself, Claire shows that choosing to remain human in the face of inhumanity is perhaps the most profound act of resistance.

Her sobriety becomes more than personal recovery. It represents the daily decision to see clearly, to choose difficult truths over comfortable lies, to maintain connection even when detachment would be easier. In a profession that demands she enter the minds of those who reduce people to patterns, Claire's greatest strength is her refusal to lose sight of individual humanity.

Detective Martinez's partnership with Claire reminds us that the most effective responses to evil are rarely solitary. In the moment when Claire stands ready to kill her own father, Martinez pulls the trigger first. It is an act of profound friendship: choosing to carry the weight of that death, to cross that irreversible line, so that Claire will not have to live with having done so. Their bond proves that sometimes love means bearing what another person cannot bear, even when the cost is carried forever.

The final revelation about Claire's father forces the ultimate test: Can someone maintain their moral center when everything they believed about love, family, and trust proves to be manipulation? Claire's answer suggests that our deepest wounds can become our greatest wisdom.

These stories don't promise easy answers or complete healing. Recovery, justice, and truth are ongoing processes, not destinations. But they offer something more valuable: evidence that we possess the capacity for choice, even in circumstances designed to eliminate choice entirely.

Claire Morrison continues her work, case by case, choice by choice, proving daily that patterns can be broken. Recovery and relapse, brilliance and monstrosity often exist side by side, but so do compassion and resilience.

For anyone who has faced their own darkness, questioned their own patterns, or wondered whether change is possible, Claire's story offers this: The most powerful force in human psychology isn't conditioning, manipulation or trauma. It's the quiet, stubborn insistence on remaining human, no matter what.

~J.S. Warner

About the author

J.S. Warner has published children's books and short stories in multiple genres. After spending 28 years as a high school math teacher and working as a corrections nurse, he now serves as an elementary school nurse. Warner is a comic book collector and travel enthusiast who lives at the Jersey Shore with his wife of over forty years. This is his first novel.

***

Visit him at jswarnerauthor.com